Ghost Stories

Ghost Stories

Cathay Books

This volume first published in
Great Britain in 1982 by
Octopus Books Limited
59 Grosvenor Street
London W1

This edition published 1984 by
Cathay Books Limited
59 Grosvenor Street
London W1

Arrangement and illustrations © 1982 Hennerwood
Publications Limited
Illustrated by Ian McCaig

ISBN 0 86178 297 6

Printed and Bound in Great Britain
by Collins, Glasgow

Contents

The Music of Erich Zann

H. P. LOVECRAFT

I have examined maps of the city with the greatest care, yet have never again found the Rue d'Auseil. These maps have not been modern maps alone, for I know that names change. I have on the contrary, delved deeply into all the antiquities of the place, and have personally explored every region, of whatever name, which could possible answer to the street I knew as the Rue d'Auseil. But despite all I have done, it remains a humiliating fact that I cannot find the house, the street, or even the locality, where, during the last months of my impoverished life as a student of metaphysics at the university, I heard the music of Erich Zann.

That my memory is broken, I do not wonder; for my health, physical and mental, was gravely disturbed throughout the period of my residence in the Rue d'Auseil, and I recall that I took none of my few acquaintances there. But that I cannot find the place again is both singular and perplexing; for it was within a half-hour's walk of the university and was distinguished by peculiarities which could hardly be forgotten by anyone who had been there. I have never met a person who has seen the Rue d'Auseil.

9

The Rue d'Auseil lay across a dark river bordered by precipitous brick blear-windowed warehouses and spanned by a ponderous bridge of dark stone. It was always shadowy along that river, as if the smoke of neighbouring factories shut out the sun perpetually. The river was also odorous with evil stenches which I have never smelled elsewhere, and which may some day help me find it, since I should recognize them at once. Beyond the bridge were narrow cobbled streets with rails; and then came the ascent, at first gradual, but incredibly steep as the Rue d'Auseil was reached.

I have never seen another street as narrow and steep as the Rue d'Auseil. It was almost a cliff, closed to all vehicles, consisting in several places of flights of steps, and ending at the top in a lofty ivied wall. Its paving was irregular, sometimes stone slabs, sometimes cobblestones, and sometimes bare earth with struggling greenish-grey vegetation. The houses were tall, peaked-roofed, incredibly old, and crazily leaning backward, forward and sidewise. Occasionally an opposite pair, both leaning forward, almost met across the street like an arch; and certainly they kept most of the light from the ground below. There were a few overhead bridges from house to house across the street.

The inhabitants of that street impressed me peculiarly. At first I though it was because they were all very old. I do not know how I came to live on such a street, but I was not myself when I moved there. I have been living in many poor places, always evicted for want of money; until at last I came upon that tottering house in the Rue d'Auseil kept by the paralytic Blandot. It was the third house from the top of the street, and by far the tallest of them all.

My room was on the fifth storey; the only inhabited room there, since the house was almost empty. On the night I arrived I heard strange music from the peaked garret overhead, and the next day asked old Blandot about it. He told me it was an old German viol-player, a strange dumb man who signed his name as Erich Zann, and who played evenings in a cheap theatre orchestra; adding that Zann's desire to play in the night after his return from the theatre was the reason he had chosen this lofty and isolated garret room, whose single gable window was the only point on the street from which one could look over the terminating wall at the declivity and panorama beyond.

Thereafter I heard Zann every night, and although he kept me awake, I was haunted by the weirdness of his music. Knowing little of the art myself, I was yet certain that none of his harmonies had any relation to music I had heard before; and concluded that he was a composer of highly original genius. The longer I listened, the more I was fascinated, until after a week I resolved to make the old man's acquaintance.

One night as he was returning from his work, I intercepted Zann in the hallway and told him that I would like to know him and be with him when he played. He was a small, lean, bent person, with shabby clothes, blue eyes, grotesque, satyr-like face, and nearly bald head; and at my first words seemed both angered and frightened. My obvious friendliness, however, finally melted him; and he grudgingly motioned to me to follow him up the dark, creaking and rickety attic stairs. His room, one of only two in the steeply pitched garret, was on the west side, towards the high wall that formed the upper end of the street. Its size was very great, and seemed the greater because of its extraordinary barrenness and neglect. Of furniture there was only a narrow iron bedstead, a dingy washstand, a small table, a large bookcase, an iron music-rack, and three old-fashioned chairs. Sheets of music were piled in disorder about the floor. The walls were of bare boards, and had probably never known plaster; whilst the abundance of dust and cobwebs made the place seem more deserted than inhabited. Evidently Erich Zann's world of beauty lay in some far cosmos of the imagination.

Motioning me to sit down, the dumb man closed the door, turned the large wooden bolt, and lighted a candle to augment the one he had brought with him. He now removed his viol from its moth-eaten covering, and, taking it, seated himself in the least uncomfortable of the chairs. He did not employ the music-rack, but, offering no choice and playing from memory, enchanted me for over an hour with strains I had never heard before; strains which must have been of his own devising. To describe their exact nature is impossible for one unversed in music. They were a kind of fugue, with recurrent passages of the most captivating quality, but to me were notable for the absence of any of the weird notes I had overheard from my room below on other occasions.

Those haunting notes I had remembered, and had often hummed and whistled inaccurately to myself, so when the player at length laid down his bow I asked him if he would render some of them. As I began my request the wrinkled satyr-like face lost the bored placidity it had possessed during the playing, and seemed to show the same curious mixture of anger and fright which I had noticed when first I accosted the old man. For a moment I was inclined to use persuasion, regarding rather lightly the whims of senility; and even tried to awaken my hosts's weirder mood by whistling a few of the strains to which I had listened the night before. But I did not pursue this course for more than a moment; for when the dumb musician recognized the whistled air his face grew suddenly distorted with an expression wholly beyond analysis, and his long, cold bony right hand reached out to stop my mouth and silence the crude imitation. As he did this he further demonstrated his eccentricity by casting a startled glance towards the lone curtained window, as if fearful of some intruder – a glance doubly absurd, since the garret stood high and inaccessible above all the adjacent roofs, this window being the only point of the steep street, as the concierge had told me, from which one could see over the wall at the summit.

The old man's glance brought Blandot's remark to mind, and with a certain capriciousness I felt a wish to look out over the wide and dizzying panorama of moonlit roofs and city lights beyond the hilltop, which of all the dwellers in the Rue d'Auseil only this crabbed musician could see. I moved towards the window and would have drawn aside the nondescript curtains, when with a frightened rage even greater than before, the dumb lodger was upon me again; this time motioning with his head toward the door as he nervously strove to drag me thither with both hands. Now thoroughly disgusted with my host, I ordered him to release me, and told him I would go at once. His clutch relaxed, and as he saw my disgust and offence, his own anger seemed to subside. He tightened his relaxing grip, but this time in a friendly manner, forcing me into a chair; then, with an appearance of wistfulness, crossed to the littered table, where he wrote many words with a pencil, in the laboured French of a foreigner.

The note which he finally handed me was an appeal for tolerance and forgiveness. Zann said that he was old, lonely, and afflicted with strange fears and nervous disorders connected with his music and with other things. He had enjoyed my listening to his music, and wished I would come again and not mind his eccentricities. But he could not play to another his weird harmonies, and could not bear hearing them from another; nor could he bear having anything in his room touched by another. He had not known until our hallway conversation that I could overhear his playing in my room, and now asked me if I would arrange with Blandot to take a lower room where I could not hear him in the night. He would, he wrote, defray the difference in rent.

As I sat deciphering the execrable French, I felt more lenient toward the old man. He was a victim of physical and nervous suffering, as was I; and my metaphysical studies had taught me kindness. In the silence there came a slight sound from the window – the shutter must have rattled in the night wind, and for some reason I started almost as violently as did Erich Zann. So when I had finished reading, I shook my host by the hand, and departed as a friend.

The next day Blandot gave me a more expensive room on the third floor, between the apartments of an aged money-lender and the room of a respectable upholsterer. There was no one on the fourth floor.

It was not long before I found that Zann's eagerness for my

company was not as great as it had seemed while he was persuading me to move down from the fifth storey. He did not ask me to call on him, and when I did call he appeared uneasy and played listlessly. This was always at night – in the day he slept and would admit no one. My liking for him did not grow, though the attic room and the weird music seemed to hold an odd fascination for me. I had a curious desire to look out of that window, over the wall and down the unseen slope at the glittering roofs and spires which must lie outspread there. Once I went up to the garret during theatre hours, when Zann was away, but the door was locked.

What I did succeed in doing was to overhear the nocturnal playing of the dumb old man. At first I would tip-toe to my old fifth floor, then I grew bold enought to climb the last creaking staircase to the peaked garret. There in the narrow hall, outside the bolted door with the covered keyhole, I often heard sounds which filled me with an indefinable dread – the dread of vague wonder and brooding mystery. It was not that the sounds were hideous, for they were not; but that they held vibrations suggesting nothing on this globe of earth, and that at certain intervals they assumed a symphonic quality which I could hardly conceive as produced by one player. Certainly, Erich Zann was a genius of wild power. As the weeks passed, the playing grew wilder, whilst the old musician acquired an increasing haggardness and furtiveness pitiful to behold. He now refused to admit me at any time, and shunned me whenever we met on the stairs.

Then one night as I listened at the door, I heard the shrieking viol swell into a chaotic babel of sound; a pandemonium which would have led me to doubt my own shaking sanity had there not come from behind that barred portal a piteous proof that the horror was real – the awful, inarticulate cry which only a mute can utter, and which rises only in moments of the most terrible fear or anguish. I knocked repeatedly at the door, but received no response. Afterwards I waited in the black hallway, shivering with cold and fear, till I heard the poor musician's effort to rise from the floor by the aid of a chair. Believing him just conscious after a fainting fit, I renewed my rapping, at the same time calling out my name reassuringly. I heard Zann stumble to the window and close both shutter and sash, then stumble to the door, which he falteringly unfastened to admit me. This time his delight at having me present was real; for his distorted face gleamed with relief while he clutched at my coat as a child clutches at its mother's skirts.

Shaking pathetically, the old man forced me into a chair whilst he sank into another, beside which his viol and bow lay carelessly on the floor. He sat for some time inactive, nodding oddly, but having a paradoxical suggestion of intense and frightened listening. Subsequently he seemed to be satisfied, and crossing to a chair by the table wrote a brief note, handed it to me, and returned to the table, where he began to write rapidly and incessantly. The note implored me in the name of mercy, and for the sake of my own curiosity, to wait where I was while he prepared a full account in German of all the marvels and terrors which beset him. I waited, and the dumb man's pencil flew.

It was perhaps an hour later, while I still waited and while the old musician's feverishly written sheets still continued to pile up, that I saw Zann start as from the hint of a horrible shock. Unmistakably he was looking at the curtained window and listening shudderingly. Then I half fancied I heard a sound myself; though it was not a horrible sound, but rather an exquisitely low and infinitely distant musical note, suggesting a player in one of the neighbouring houses, or in some abode beyond the lofty wall over which I had never been able to look. Upon Zann the effect was terrible, for, dropping his pencil, suddenly he rose, seized his viol, and commenced to rend the night with the wildest playing I had ever heard from his bow save when listening at the barred door.

It would be useless to describe the playing of Erich Zann on that dreadful night. It was more horrible than anything I had ever overheard, because I could now see the expression of his

This time the motive was stark fear

16

face, and could realize that this time the motive was stark fear. He was trying to make a noise; to ward something off or drown something out – what, I could not imagine, awesome though I felt it must be. The playing grew fantastic, delirious, and hysterical, yet kept to the last the qualities of supreme genius which I knew this strange old man possessed. I recognized the air – it was a wild Hungarian dance popular in the theatres, and I reflected for a moment that this was the first time I had ever heard Zann play the work of another composer.

Louder and louder, wilder and wilder, mounted the shrieking and whining of that desperate viol. The player was dripping with an uncanny perspiration and twisted like a monkey, always looking frantically at the curtained window. In his frenzied strains I could almost see shadowy satyrs and bacchanals dancing and whirling insanely through seething abysses of clouds and smoke and lightning. And then I thought I heard a shriller, steadier note that was not from the viol; a calm, deliberate, purposeful, mocking note from far away in the West.

At this juncture the shutter began to rattle in a howling night wind which had sprung up outside as if in answer to the mad playing within. Zann's screaming viol now outdid itself emitting sounds I had never thought a viol could emit. The shutter rattled more loudly, unfastened, and commenced slamming against the window. Then the glass broke shiveringly under the persistent impacts, and the chill wind rushed in, making the candles sputter and rustling the sheets of paper on the table where Zann had begun to write out his horrible secret. I looked at Zann, and saw that he was past conscious observation. His blue eyes were bulging, glassy and sightless, and the frantic playing had become a blind, mechanical unrecognizable orgy that no pen could even suggest.

A sudden gust, stronger than the others, caught up the manuscript and bore it towards the window. I followed the flying sheets in desperation, but they were gone before I reached the demolished panes. Then I remembered my old wish to gaze from the window, the only window in the Rue d'Auseil from which one might see the slope beyond the wall, and the city outspread beneath. It was very dark, but the city's lights always burned, and I expected to see them there amidst the raid and wind. Yet when I looked from that highest of all gable windows, looked while the candles sputtered and the insane viol howled with the night wind, I saw no city spread below, and no friendly lights gleamed from remembered streets, but only the blackness of space, illimitable; unimagined space alive with motion and music, and having no semblance of anything on earth. And as I stood there looking in terror, the wind blew out both the candles in that ancient peaked garret, leaving me in savage and impenetrable darkness with chaos and pandemonium before me, and the demon madness of that night-baying viol behind me.

I staggered back in the dark, without the means of striking light, crashing against the table, overturning a chair, and finally groping my way to the place where the blackness screamed with shocking music. To save myself and Erich Zann I could at least try, whatever the powers opposed to me. Once I thought some chill thing brushed me, and I screamed, but my scream could not be heard above that hideous viol. Suddenly out of the blackness the madly sawing bow struck me, and I knew I was close to the player. I felt ahead, touched the back of Zann's chair, and then found and shook his shoulder in an effort to bring him to his senses.

He did not respond, and still the viol shrieked on without slackening. I moved my hand to his head, whose mechanical nodding I was able to stop, and shouted in his ear that we must both flee from the unknown things of the night. But he neither answered me nor abated the frenzy of his unutterable music, while all through the garret strange currents of wind seemed to dance in the darkness and babel. When my hand touched his ear I shuddered, though I knew not why – knew not why till I felt the still face; the ice-cold, stiffened, unbreathing face whose glassy eyes bulged uselessly into the void. And then, by some miracle, finding the door and the large wooden bolt, I plunged wildly away from that glassy-eyed thing in the dark, and from the ghoulish howling of that accursed viol whose fury increased even as I plunged.

Leaping, floating, flying down those endless stairs through the dark house; racing mindlessly out into the narrow, steep, and ancient street of steps and tottering houses; clattering down steps and over cobbles to the lower streets and the putrid canyon-walled river; panting across the great dark bridge to the broader, healthier streets and boulevards we know; all these are terrible impressions that linger with me. And I recall that there was no wind, and that the moon was out, and that all the lights of the city twinkled.

Despite my most careful searches and investigations, I have never since been able to find the Rue d'Auseil. But I am not wholly sorry; either for this or for the loss in undreamable abysses of the closely written sheets which alone could have explained the music of Erich Zann.

The Ghost in the Bride's Chamber

CHARLES DICKENS

The house was a genuine old house of a very quaint description, teeming with old carvings, and beams, and panels, and having an excellent old staircase, with a gallery or upper staircase, cut off from it by a curious fence-work of old oak, or of the old Honduras Mahogany wood. It was, and is, and will be, for many a long year to come, a remarkably picturesque house; and a certain grave mystery lurking in the depth of the old mahogany panels, as if they were so many deep pools of dark water – such, indeed, as they have been much among when they were trees – gave it a very mysterious character after nightfall.

When Mr Goodchild and Mr Idle had first alighted at the door, and stepped into the sombre handsome old hall, they had been received by half-a-dozen noiseless old men in black, all dressed exactly alike, who glided up the stairs with the obliging landlord and waiter – but without appearing to get into their way, or to mind whether they did or no – and who had filed off to the right and left on the old staircase, as the guests entered their sitting-room. It was then broad, bright day. But, Mr Goodchild had said, when their door was shut, 'Who on earth are those old men?' And afterwards, both on going out and coming in, he had noticed that there were no old men to be seen.

Neither, had the old men, or any one of the old men, reappeared since. The two friends had passed a night in the house, but had seen nothing more of the old men. Mr Goodchild, in rambling about it, had looked along passages, and glanced in at doorways, but had encountered no old men; neither did it appear that any old men were, by any member of the establishment, missed or expected.

Another odd circumstance impressed itself on their attention. It was, that the door of their sitting-room was never left untouched for a quarter of an hour. It was opened with hesitation, opened with confidence, opened a little way, opened a good way, – always clapped-to again without a word of explanation. They were reading, they were writing, they were eating, they were drinking, they were talking, they were dozing; the door was always opened at an unexpected moment, and they looked towards it, and it was clapped-to again, and nobody was to be seen. When this had happened fifty times or so, Mr Goodchild had said to his companion, jestingly: 'I begin to think, Tom, there was something wrong with those six old men.'

Night had come again, and they had been writing for two or three hours: writing, in short, a portion of the lazy notes from which these lazy sheets are taken. They had left off writing, and glasses were on the table between them. The house was closed and quiet. Around the head of Thomas Idle, as he lay upon his sofa, hovered light wreaths of fragrant smoke. The temples of Francis Goodchild, as he leaned back in his chair, with his two hands clasped behind his head, and his legs crossed, were similarly decorated.

They had been discussing several idle subjects of speculation, not omitting the strange old men, and were still so occupied, when Mr Goodchild abruptly changed his attitude to wind up his watch. They were just becoming drowsy enough to be stopped in their talk by any such slight check. Thomas Idle, who was speaking at the moment, paused and said, 'How goes it?'

'One.' said Goodchild.

As if he had ordered One old man, and the order were

promptly executed (truly, all orders were so, in that excellent hotel), the door opened, and One old man stood there.

He did not come in, but stood with the door in his hand.

'One of the six, Tom, at last!' said Mr Goodchild, in a surprised whisper. – 'Sir, your pleasure?'

'Sir, *your* pleasure?' said the One old man.

'I didn't ring.'

'The bell did,' said the One old man.

He said *Bell*, in a deep strong way, that would have expressed the church Bell.

'I had the pleasure, I believe, of seeing you, yesterday?' said Goodchild.

'I cannot undertake to say for certain,' was the grim reply of the One old man.

'I think you saw me? Did you not?'

'Saw *you*?' said the old man. 'O yes, I saw *you*. But, I see many who never see me.'

A chilled, slow, earthy, fixed old man, A cadaverous old man of measured speech. An old man who seemed as unable to wink, as if his eyelids had been nailed to his forehead. An old man whose eyes – two spots of fire – had no more motion than if they had been connected with the back of his skull by screws driven through it, and rivetted and bolted outside, among his grey hairs.

The night had turned so cold, to Mr Goodchild's sensations, that he shivered. He remarked lightly, and half apologetically, 'I think somebody is walking over my grave.'

'No,' said the weird old man, 'there is no one there.'

Mr Goodchild looked at Idle, but Idle lay with his head enwreathed in smoke.

'No one there?' said Goodchild.

'There is no one at your grave, I assure you,' said the old man.

He had come in and shut the door, and he now sat down. He did not bend himself to sit, as other people do, but seemed to sink bolt upright, as if in water, until the chair stopped him.

'My friend, Mr Idle,' said Goodchild, extremely anxious to

introduce a third person into the conversation.

'I am,' said the old man, without looking at him, 'at Mr Idle's service.'

'If you are an old inhabitant of this place,' Francis Goodchild resumed:

'Yes.'

'Perhaps you can decide a point my friend and I were in doubt upon, this morning. They hang condemned criminals at the Castle, I believe?'

'*I* believe so,' said the old man.

'Are their faces turned towards that noble prospect?'

'Your face is turned,' replied the old man, 'to the Castle wall. When you are tied up, you see its stones expanding and contracting violently, and a similar expansion and contraction seem to take place in your own head and breast. Then, there is a rush of fire and an earthquake, and the Castle springs into the air, and you tumble down a precipice.'

His cravat seemed to trouble him. He put his hand to his throat, and moved his neck from side to side. He was an old man of a swollen character of face, and his nose was immovably hitched up on one side, as if by a little hook inserted in that nostril. Mr Goodchild felt exceedingly uncomfortable, and began to think the night was hot, and not cold.

'A strong description, Sir,' he observed.

'A strong sensation,' the old man rejoined.

Again, Mr Goodchild looked to Mr Thomas Idle; but Thomas lay on his back with his face attentively turned towards the One old man, and made no sign. At this time Mr Goodchild believed that he saw threads of fire stretch from the old man's eyes to his own, and there attach themselves. (Mr Goodchild writes the present account of his experience, and, with the utmost solemnity, protests that he had the strongest sensation upon him of being forced to look at the old man along those two fiery films, from that moment.)

'I must tell it to you,' said the old man, with a ghastly and a stony stare.

'What?' asked Francis Goodchild.

'You know where it took place. Yonder!'

Whether he pointed to the room above, or to the room below, or to any room in that old house, or to a room in some other old house in that old town, Mr Goodchild was not, nor is, nor ever can be, sure. He was confused by the circumstances that the right forefinger of the One old man seemed to dip itself in one of the threads of fire, light itself, and make a fiery start in the air, as it pointed somewhere. Having pointed somewhere, it went out.

'You know she was a Bride,' said the old man.

'I know they still send up Bride-cake,' Mr Goodchild faltered. 'This is a very oppressive air.'

'She was a Bride,' said the old man. 'She was a fair, flaxen-haired, large-eyed girl, who had no character, no purpose. A weak, credulous, incapable, helpless nothing. Not like her mother. No, no. It was her father whose character she reflected.

'Her mother had taken care to secure everything to herself, for her own life, when the father of this girl (a child at that time) died – of sheer helplessness; no other disorder – and then He renewed the acquaintance that had once subsisted between the mother and Him. He had been put aside for the flaxen-haired, large-eyed man (or non-entity) with Money. He could overlook that for Money. He wanted compensation in Money.

'So, he returned to the side of that woman the mother, made love to her again, danced attendance on her, and submitted himself to her whims. She wreaked upon him every whim she had, or could invent. He bore it. And the more he bore, the more he wanted compensation in Money, and the more he was resolved to have it.

'But lo! Before he got it, she cheated him. In one of her imperious states, she froze, and never thawed again. She put her hands to her head one night, uttered a cry, stiffened, lay in that attitude certain hours, and died. Again he had got no compensation from her in Money, yet. Blight and Murrain on her! Not a penny.

'He had hated her throughout that second pursuit, and had

longed for retaliation on her. He now counterfeited her signature to an instrument, leaving all she had to leave, to her daughter – ten years old then – to whom the property passed absolutely, and appointed himself the daughter's Guardian. When He slid it under the pillow of the bed on which she lay, He bent down in the deaf ear of Death, and whispered: 'Mistress Pride, I have determined a long time that, dead or alive, you must make me compensation in Money.'

'So, now there were only two left. Which two were, He, and the fair flaxen-haired, large-eyed foolish daughter, who afterwards became the Bride.

'He put her to school. In a secret, dark, oppressive, ancient house, he put her to school with a watchful and unscrupulous woman. "My worthy lady," he said, "here is a mind to be formed; will you help me to form it?" She accepted the trust. For which she, too, wanted compensation in Money, and had it.

'The girl was formed in the fear of him, and in the conviction, that there was no escape from him. She was taught, from the first, to regard him as her future husband – the man who must marry her – but destiny that overshadowed her – the appointed certainty that could never be evaded. The poor fool was soft white wax in their hands, and took the impression that they put upon her. It hardened with time. It became a part of herself. Inseparable from herself, and only to be torn away from her, by tearing life away from her.

'Eleven years she had lived in the dark house and its gloomy gardens. He was jealous of the very light and air getting to her, and they kept her close. He stopped the wide chimneys, shaded the little windows, left the strong-stemmed ivy to wander where it would over the house-front, the moss to accumulate on the untrimmed fruit-trees and red-walled garden, the weeds to over-run its green and yellow walks. He surrounded her with images of sorrow and desolation. He caused her to be filled with fears of the place and of the stories that were told of it, and then on pretext of correcting them, to be left in it in solitude, or made to shrink about in the dark. When her mind was most depressed

25

and fullest of terrors, then, he would come out of one of the hiding-places from which he overlooked her, and present himself as her sole recourse.

'Thus, by being from her childhood the one embodiment her life presented to her of power to coerce and power to relieve, power to bind and power to loose, the ascendency over her weakness was secured. She was twenty-one years and twenty-one days old, when he brought her home to the gloomy house, his half-witted, frightened, and submissive Bride of three weeks.

'He had dismissed the governess by that time – what he had left to do, he could best do alone – and they came back, upon a rainy night, to the scene of her long preparation. She turned to him upon the threshold, as the rain was dripping from the porch, and said:

'"O Sir, it is the Death-watch ticking for me!"

'"Well!" he answered. "And if it were?"

'"O Sir!" she returned to him, "look kindly on me, and be merciful to me! I beg your pardon. I will do anything you wish, if you will only forgive me!"

'That had become the poor fool's constant song: "I beg your pardon," and "Forgive me!"

'She was not worth hating; he felt nothing but contempt for her. But, she had long been in the way, and he had long been weary, and the work was near its end, and had to be worked out.

'"You fool," he said. "Go up the stairs!"

'She obeyed very quickly, murmuring, "I will do anything you wish!" When he came into the Bride's Chamber, having been a little retarded by the heavy fastening of the great door (for they were alone in the house, and he had arranged that the people who attended on them should come and go in the day), he found her withdrawn to the further corner, and there standing pressed against the panelling as if she would have shrunk through it: her flaxen hair all wild about her face, and her large eyes staring at him in vague terror.

'"What are you afraid of? Come and sit down by me."

26

' "I will do anything you wish. I beg your pardon, Sir. Forgive me!" Her monotonous tune as usual.

' "Ellen, here is a writing that you must write out tomorrow, in your own hand. You may as well be seen by others, busily engaged upon it. When you have written it all fairly, and corrected all mistakes, call in any two people there may be about the house, and sign your name to it before them. Then, put it in your bosom to keep it safe, and when I sit here again to-morrow night, give it to me."

' "I will do it all, with the greatest care. I will do anything you wish."

' "Don't shake and tremble, then."

' "I will try my utmost not to do it – if you will only forgive me!"

'Next day, she sat down at her desk, and did as she had been told. He often passed in and out of the room, to observe her, and always saw her slowly and laboriously writing; repeating to herself the worlds she copied, in appearance quite mechanically, and without caring or endeavouring to comprehend them, so that she did her task. He saw her follow the directions she had received, in all particulars; and at night, when they were alone again in the same Bride's Chamber, and he drew his chair to the hearth, she timidly approached him from her distant seat, took the paper from her bosom, and gave it into his hand.

'It secured all her possessions to him, in the event of her death. He put her before him, face to face, that he might look at her steadily; and he asked her, in so many plain words, neither fewer nor more, did she know that?

'There were spots of ink upon the bosom of her white dress, and they made her face look whiter and her eyes look larger as she nodded her head. There were spots of ink upon her hand with which she stood before him, nervously plaiting and folding her white skirts.

'She shrunk, and uttered a low, suppressed cry.

' "I am not going to kill you. I will not endanger my life for yours. Die!"

'He sat before her in the gloomy Bride's Chamber, day after day, night after night, looking the word at her when he did not utter it. As often as her large unmeaning eyes were raised from the hands in which she rocked her head, to the stern figure, sitting with crossed arms and knitted forehead, in the chair, they read in it, "Die!" When she dropped asleep in exhaustion, she was called back to shuddering consciousness, by the whisper, "Die!" When she fell upon her old entreaty to be pardoned, she was answered, "Die!" When she had out-watched and out-suffered the long night, and the rising sun flamed into the sombre room, she heard it hailed with, "Another day and not dead? – Die!"

'Shut up in the deserted mansion, aloof from all mankind, and engaged alone in such a struggle without any respite, it came to this – that either he must die, or she. he knew it very well, and concentrated his strength against her feebleness. Hours upon hours he held her by the arm when her arm was black where he held it, and bade her Die!

'It was done, upon a windy morning, before sunrise. He computed the time to be half-past four; but, his forgotten watch had run down, and he could not be sure. She had broken away from him in the night, with loud and sudden cries – the first of that kind to which she had given vent – and he had had to put his hands over her mouth. Since then, she had been quiet in the corner of the panelling where she had sunk down; and he had left her, and had gone back with his folded arms and his knitted forehead to his chair.

'Paler in the pale light, more colourless than ever in the leaden dawn, he saw her coming, trailing herself along the floor towards him – a white wreck of hair, and dress, and wild eyes, pushing itself on by an irresolute and bending hand.

' "O, forgive me! I will do anything. O, Sir, pray tell me I may live!"

' "Die!"

' "Are you so resolved? Is there no hope for me?"

' "Die!"

The Ghost in the Bride's Chamber

'Her large eyes strained themselves with wonder and fear; wonder and fear changed to reproach; reproach to blank nothing. It was done. He was not at first so sure it was done, but that the morning sun was hanging jewels in her hair – he saw the diamond, emerald, and ruby, glittering among it in little points, as he stood looking down at her – when he lifted her and laid her on her bed.

'She was soon laid in the ground. And now they were all gone, and he had compensated himself well.

'He had a mind to travel. Not that he meant to waste his Money, for he was a pinching man and liked his Money dearly (like nothing else, indeed), but, that he had grown tired of the desolate house and wished to turn his back upon it and have done with it. But, the house was worth Money, and Money must not be thrown away. He determined to sell it before he went. That it might look the less wretched and bring a better price, he hired some labourers to work in the overgrown garden; to cut out the dead wood, trim the ivy that dropped in heavy masses over the windows and gables, and clear the walks in which the weeds were growing mid-leg high.

'He worked, himself, along with them. He worked later than they did, and, one evening at dusk, was left working alone, with his bill-hook in his hand. One autumn evening, when the Bride was five weeks dead.

' "It grows too dark to work longer," he said to himself, "I must give over for the night."

'He detested the house, and was loath to enter it. He looked at the dark porch waiting for him like a tomb, and felt that it was an accursed house. Near to the porch, and near to where he stood, was a tree whose branches waved before the old bay-window of the Bride's Chamber, where it had been done. The tree swung suddenly, and made him start. it swung again, although the night was still. Looking up into it, he saw a figure among the branches.

'It was the figure of a young man. The face looked down, as he looked up; the branches cracked and swayed; the figure rapidly

29

descended, and slid upon its feet before him. A slender youth of about her age, with long light brown hair.

'"What thief are you?" he said, seizing the youth by the collar.

'The young man, in shaking himself free, swung him a blow with his arm across the face and throat. They closed, but the young man got from him and stepped back, crying, with great eagerness and horror, "Don't touch me! I would as lieve be touched by the Devil!"

'He stood still, with his bill-hook in his hand, looking at the young man. For, the young man's look was the counterpart of her last look, and he had not expected ever to see that again.

'"I am no thief. Even if I were, I would not have a coin of your wealth, if it would buy me the Indies. You murderer!"

'"What!"

'"I climbed it," said the young man, pointing up into the tree, "for the first time, nigh four years ago. I climbed it, to look at her. I saw her. I spoke to her. I have climbed it, many a time, to watch and listen for her. I was a boy, hidden among its leaves, when from that bay-window she gave me this!"

'He showed a tress of flaxen hair, tied with a mourning ribbon.

'"Her life," said the young man, "was a life of mourning. She gave me this, as a token of it, and a sign that she was dead to every one but you. If I had been older, if I had seen her sooner, I might have saved her from you. But, she was fast in the web when I first climbed the tree, and what could I do then to break it!"

'In saying these words, he burst into a fit of sobbing and crying: weakly at first, then passionately.

'"Murderer! I climbed the tree on the night when you brought her back. I heard her, from the tree, speak of the Death-watch at the door. I was three times in the tree while you were shut up with her, slowly killing her. I saw her, from the tree, lie dead upon her bed. I have watched you, from the tree, for proofs and traces of your guilt. The manner of it, is a mystery to me yet, but I will pursue you until you have rendered up your life to the hangman. You shall never, until then, be rid of me. I loved her! I can know no relenting towards you. Murderer, I loved her!"

'The youth was bareheaded, his hat having fluttered away in his descent from the tree. He moved towards the gate. He had to pass – Him – to get to it. There was breadth for two old-fashioned carriages abreast; and the youth's abhorrence, openly expressed in every feature of his face and limb in his body, and very hard to bear, had verge enough to keep itself at a distance in. He (by which I mean the other) had not stirred hand or feet, since he had stood still to look at the boy. He faced round, now, to follow him with his eyes. As the back of the bare light-brown head was turned to him, he saw a red curve stretch from his hand to it. He knew, before he threw the billhook, where it had alighted – I say, had alighted, and not, would alight; for, to his clear perception the thing was done before he did it. It cleft the head, and it remained there, and the boy lay on his face.

'He buried the body in the night, at the foot of the tree. As soon as it was light in the morning, he worked at turning up all the ground near the tree, and hacking and hewing at the neighbouring bushes and undergrowth. When the labourers came, there was nothing suspicious, and nothing suspected.

'But, he had, in a moment, defeated all his precautions, and destroyed the triumph of the scheme he had so long concerted, and so successfully worked out. He had got rid of the Bride, and had acquired her fortune without endangering his life; but now, for a death by which he had gained nothing, he had evermore to live with a rope around his neck.

'Beyond this, he was chained to the house of gloom and horror, which he could not endure. Being afraid to sell it or to quit it, lest discovery should be made, he was forced to live in it. He hired two old people, man and wife, for his servants; and dwelt in it, and dreaded it. His great difficulty, for a long time, was the garden. Whether he should keep it trim, whether he should suffer it to fall into its former state of neglect, what would be the least likely way of attracting attention to it?

31

'He took the middle course of gardening, himself, in his evening leisure, and of then calling the old serving-man to help him; but, of never letting him work there alone. And he made himself an arbour over against the tree, where he could sit and see that it was safe.

'As the seasons changed, and the tree changed, his mind perceived dangers that were always changing. In the leafy time, he perceived that the upper boughs were growing into the form of the young man – that they made the shape of him exactly, sitting in a forked branch swinging in the wind. In the time of the falling leaves, he perceived that they came down from the tree, forming tell-tale letters on the path, or that they had a tendency to heap themselves into a churchyard mound above the grave. In the winter, when the tree was bare, he perceived that the boughs swung at him the ghost of the blow the young man had given, and that they threatened him openly. In the spring, when sap was mounting in the trunk, he asked himself, were the dried-up particles of blood mounting with it: to make out more obviously this year than last, the leaf-screened figure of the young man, swinging in the wind?

'However, he turned his Money over and over, and still over. He was in the dark trade, the gold-dust trade, and most secret trades that yielded great returns. In ten years, he had turned his Money over, so many times, that the traders and shippers who had dealings with him, absolutely did not lie – for once – when they declared that he had increased his fortune, Twelve Hundred Per Cent.

'He possessed his riches one hundred years ago, when people could be lost easily. He had heard who the youth was, from hearing of the search that was made after him; but, it died away, and the youth was forgotten.

'The annual round of changes in the tree had been repeated ten times since the night of the burial at its foot, when there was a great thunder-storm over this place. It broke at midnight, and raged until morning. The first intelligence he heard from his old serving-man that morning was, that the tree had been struck by lightning.

'It had been riven down the stem, in a very surprising manner, and the stem lay in two blighted shafts: one resting against the house, and one against a portion of the old red garden-wall in which its fall had made a gap. The fissure went down the tree to a little above the earth, and there stopped. There was great curiosity to see the tree, and, with most of his former fears revived, he sat in his arbour – grown quite an old man – watching the people who came to see it.

'They quickly began to come, in such dangerous numbers, that he closed his garden-gate and refused to admit any more. But, there were certain men of science who travelled from a distance to examine the tree, and, in an evil hour, he let them in – Blight and Murrain on them, let them in!

'They wanted to dig up the ruin by the roots, and closely examine it, and the earth about it. Never, while he lived! They offered money for it. They! Men of science, whom he could have bought by the gross, with a scratch of his pen! He showed them the garden-gate again, and locked and barred it.

'But they were bent on doing what they wanted to do, and they bribed the old serving-man – a thankless wretch who regularly complained when he received his wages, of being underpaid – and they stole into the garden by night with their lanters, picks, and shovels, and fell to at the tree. He was lying in a turret-room on the other side of the house (the Bride's Chamber had been unoccupied ever since), but he soon dreamed of picks and shovels, and got up.

'He came to an upper window on that side, whence he could see their lanterns, and them, and the loose earth in a heap which he had himself disturbed and put back, when it was last turned to the air. It was found. They had that minute lighted on it. They were all bending over it. One of them said, "The skull is fractured;" and another, "See here the bones;" said another, "See here the clothes;" and then the first struck in again, and said, "A rusty bill-hook!"

'He became sensible, next day, that he was already put under a strict watch, and that he could go nowhere without being followed. Before a week was out, he was taken and laid in hold.

The circumstances were gradually pieced together against him, with a desperate malignity, and an appalling ingenuity. But, see the justice of men, and how it was extended to him! He was further accused of having poisoned that girl in the Bride's Chamber. He, who had carefully and expressly avoided imperilling a hair of his head for her, and who had seen her die of her own incapacity!

'There was doubt for which of the two murders he should be first tried; but, the real one was chosen, and he was found Guilty, and cast for Death. Bloodthirsty wretches! They would have made him Guilty of anything, so set they were upon having his life.

'His money could do nothing to save him, and he was hanged. *I* am He, and I was hanged at Lancaster Castle with my face to the wall, a hundred years ago!'

At this terrific announcement, Mr Goodchild tried to rise and cry out. But, the two fiery lines extending from the old man's eyes to his own, kept him down, and he could not utter a sound. His sense of hearing, however, was acute, and he could hear the clock strike Two. No sooner had he heard the clock strike Two, than he saw before him Two old men!

Two.

The eyes of each, connected with his eyes by two films of fire: exactly like the other: each, addressing him at precisely one and the same instant: each, gnashing the same teeth in the same head, with the same twitched nostril above them, and the same suffused expression around it. Two old men. Differing in nothing, equally distinct to the sight, the copy no fainter than the original, the second as real as the first.

'At what time,' said the Two old men, 'did you arrive at the door below?'

'At Six.'

'And there were Six old men upon the stairs!'

Mr Goodchild having wiped the perspiration from his brow, or tried to do it, the Two old men proceeded in one voice, and in the singular number:

34

The Ghost in the Bride's Chamber

'I had been anatomised, but had not yet had my skeleton put together and re-hung on an iron hook, when it began to be whispered that the Bride's Chamber was haunted. It *was* haunted, and I was there.

'*We* were there. She and I was there. I, in the chair upon the hearth; she, a white wreck again, trailing itself towards me on the floor. But, I was the speaker no more, and the one word that she said to me from midnight until dawn was, 'Live!'

'The youth was there, likewise. In the tree outside the window. Coming and going in the moonlight, as the tree bent and gave. He has, ever since, been there, peeping in at me in my torment; revealing to me by snatches, in the pale light and slatey shadows where he comes and goes, bareheaded – a bill-hook, standing edgewise in his hair.

'In the Bride's Chamber, every night from midnight until dawn – one month in the year excepted, as I am going to tell you – he hides in the tree, and she comes towards me on the floor; always approaching; never coming nearer; always visible as if by moonlight, whether the moon shines or no; always saying, from midnight until dawn, her one word, 'Live!'

'But, in the month wherein I was forced out of this life – this present month of thirty days – the Bride's Chamber is empty and quiet. Not so my old dungeon. Not so the rooms where I was restless and afraid, ten years. Both are fitfully haunted then. At One in the morning, I am what you saw me when the clock struck that hour – One old man. At Two in the morning, I am Two old men. At Three, I am Three. By Twelve at noon, I am Twelve old men. One for every hundred per cent. of old gain. Every one of the Twelve, with Twelve times my old power of suffering and agony. From that hour until Twelve at night, I, Twelve old men in anguish and fearful foreboding, wait for the coming of the executioner. At Twelve at night, I, Twelve old men turned off, swing invisible outside Lancaster Castle, with Twelve faces to the wall!

'When the Bride's Chamber was first haunted, it was known to me that this punishment would never cease, until I could make its nature, and my story, known to two living men

35

together. I waited for the coming of two living men together into the Bride's Chamber, years upon years. It was infused into my knowledge (of the means I am ignorant) that if two living men, with their eyes open, could be in the Bride's Chamber at One in the morning, they would see me sitting in my chair.

'At length, the whispers that the room was spiritually troubled, brought two men to try the adventure. I was scarcely struck upon the hearth at midnight (I come there as if the Lightning blasted me into being), when I heard them ascending the stairs. Next, I saw them enter. One of them was a bold, gay, active man, in the prime of life, some five and forty years of age; the other, a dozen years younger. They brought provisions with them in a basket, and bottles. A young woman accompanied them, with wood and coals for the lighting of the fire. When he has lighted it, the bold, gay, active man accompanied her along the gallery outside the room, to see her safely down the staircase, and came back laughing.

'He locked the door, examined the chamber, put out the contents of the basket on the table before the fire – little recking of me, in my appointed station on the hearth, close to him – and filled the glasses, and ate and drank. His companion did the same, and was as cheerful and confident as he: though he was the leader. When they had supped, they laid pistols on the table, turned to the fire, and began to smoke their pipes of foreign make.

'They had travelled together, and had been much together, and had an abundance of subjects in common. In the midst of their talking and laughing, the younger man made a reference to the leader's being always ready for any adventure; that one, or any other. He replied in these words:

' "Not quite so, Dick; if I am afraid of nothing else, I am afraid of myself."

'His companion seemed to grow a little dull, asked him, in what sense? How?

' "Why, thus," he returned. "Here is a Ghost to be disproved. Well! I cannot answer for what my fancy might do if I were alone here, or what tricks my senses might play with me if they had me to themselves. But, in company with another man, and especially with you, Dick, I would consent to outface all the Ghosts that were ever told of in the universe.''

' ''I had not the vanity to suppose that I was of so much importance to-night,'' said the other.

' ''Of so much,'' rejoined the leader, more seriously than he had spoken yet, ''that I would, for the reason I have given, on no account have undertaken to pass the night here alone.''

'It was within a few minutes of One. The head of the younger man had dropped when he made his last remark, and it drooped lower now.

' ''Keep awake, Dick!'' said the leader, gaily. ''The small hours are the worst.''

'He tried, but his head drooped again.

' ''Dick!'' urged the leader. ''Keep awake!''

' ''I can't,'' he indistinctly muttered. ''I don't know what strange influence is stealing over me. I can't.''

'His companion looked a him with a sudden horror, and I, in my different way, felt a new horror also: it was on the stroke of One, and I felt that the second watcher was yielding to me, and that the curse was upon me that I must send him to sleep.

' ''Get up and walk, Dick!'' cried the leader. ''Try!''

'It was in vain to go behind the slumberer's chair and shake him. One o'clock sounded, and I was present to the elder man, and he stood transfixed before me.

'To him alone, I was obliged to relate my story, without hope of benefit. To him alone, I was an awful phantom making a quite useless confession. I foresee it will ever be the same. The two living men together will never come to release me. When I appear, the senses of one of the two will be locked in sleep; he will neither see nor hear me; my·communication will ever be made to a solitary listener, and will ever be unserviceable. Woe! Woe! Woe!'

As the Two old men, with these words, wrung their hands, it shot into Mr Goodchild's mind that he was in the terrible situation of being virtually alone with the spectre, and that Mr Idle's immovability was explained by his having been charmed asleep at One o'clock. In the terror of this sudden discovery which produced an indescribable dread, he struggled so hard to get free from the four fiery threads, that he snapped them, after he had pulled them out to a great width. Being then out of bonds, he caught up Mr Idle from the sofa and rushed downstairs with him.

A School Story

M. R. JAMES

Two men in a smoking-room were talking of their private-school days. 'At *our* school,' said A., 'we had a ghost's foot-mark on the staircase. What was it like? Oh, very unconvincing. Just the shape of a shoe, with a square toe, if I remember right. The staircase was a stone one. I never heard any story about the thing. That seems odd, when you come to think of it. Why didn't somebody invent one, I wonder?'

'You never can tell with little boys. They have a mythology of their own. There's a subject for you, by the way – "The Folklore of Private Schools".'

'Yes; the crop is rather scanty, though. I imagine, if you were to investigate the cycle of ghost stories, for instance, which the boys at private schools tell each other, they would all turn out to be highly-compressed versions of stories out of books.'

'Nowadays the *Strand* and *Pearson's*, and so on, would be extensively drawn upon.'

'No doubt: they weren't born or thought of in *my* time. Let's see. I wonder if I can remember the staple ones that I was told. First, there was the house with a room in which a series of people insisted on passing a night; and each of them in the morning was found kneeling in a corner, and had just time to say, "I've seen it," and died.'

'Wasn't that the house in Berkeley Square?'

'I dare say it was. Then there was the man who heard a noise in the passage at night, opened his door, and saw someone crawling towards him on all fours with his eye hanging out on his cheek. There was besides, let me think – Yes! the room where a man was found dead in bed with a horseshoe mark on his forehead, and the floor under the bed was covered with marks of horseshoes also; I don't know why. Also there was the lady who, on locking her bedroom door in a strange house, heard a thin voice among the bed-curtains say, "Now we're shut in for the night." None of those had any explanations or sequel. I wonder if they go on still, those stories.'

'Oh, likely enough – with additions from the magazines, as I said. You never heard, did you, of a real ghost at a private school? I though not; nobody has that ever I came across.'

'From the way in which you said that, I gather that *you* have.'

'I really don't know; but this is what was in my mind. It happened at my private school thirty-odd years ago, and I haven't any explanation of it.

'The school I mean was near London. It was established in a large and fairly old house – a great white building with very fine grounds about it; there were large cedars in the garden, as there are in so many of the older gardens in the Thames valley, and ancient elms in the three or four fields which we used for our games. I think probably it was quite an attractive place, but boys seldom allow that their schools possess any tolerable features.

'I came to the school in a September, soon after the year 1870; and among the boys who arrived on the same day was one whom I took to: a Highland boy, whom I will call McLeod. I needn't spend time in describing him: the main thing is that I got to know him very well. He was not an exceptional boy in any way – not particularly good at books or games – but he suited me.

'The school was a large one: there must have been from 120 to 130 boys there as a rule, and so a considerable staff of masters was required, and there were rather frequent changes among them.

A School Story

'One term – perhaps it was my third or fourth – a new master made his appearance. His name was Sampson. He was a tallish, stoutish, pale, black-bearded man. I think we liked him: he had travelled a good deal, and had stories which amused us on our school walks, so that there was some competition among us to get within earshot of him. I remember too – dear me, I have hardly thought of it since then – that he had a charm on his watch-chain that attracted my attention one day, and he let me examine it. It was, I now suppose, a gold Byzantine coin; there was an effigy of some absurd emperor on one side; the other side had been worn practically smooth, and he had had cut on it – rather barbarously – his own initials, G.W.S., and a date, 24 July 1865. Yes, I can see it now: he told me he had picked it up in Constantinople: it was about the size of a florin, perhaps rather smaller.

'Well, the first odd thing that happened was this. Sampson was doing Latin grammar with us. One of his favourite methods – perhaps it is rather a good one – was to make us construct sentences out of our own heads to illustrate the rules he was trying to make us learn. Of course that is a thing which gives a silly boy a chance of being impertinent: there are lots of school stories in which that happens – or anyhow there might be. But Sampson was too good a disciplinarian for us to think of trying that one with him. Now, on this occasion he was telling us how to express *remembering* in Latin: and he ordered us each to make a sentence bringing in the verb *memini*, "I remember." Well, most of us made up some ordinary sentence such as "I remember my father," or "He remembers his book," or something equally uninteresting: and I dare say a good many put down *memino librum meum*, and so forth: but the boy I mentioned – McLeod – was evidently thinking of something more elaborate than that. The rest of us wanted to have our sentences passed, and get on to something else, so some kicked him under the desk, and I, who was next to him, poked him and whispered to him to look sharp. But he didn't seem to attend. I looked at his paper and saw he had put down nothing at all. So I

41

jogged him again harder than before and upbraided him sharply for keeping us all waiting. That did have some effect. He started and seemed to wake up, and then very quickly he scribbled about a couple of lines on his paper, and showed it up with the rest. As it was the last, or nearly the last, to come in, and as Sampson had a good deal to say to the boys who had written *meminiscimus patri meo* and the rest of it, it turned out that the clock struck twelve before he had got to McLeod, and McLeod had to wait afterwards to have his sentence corrected. There was nothing much going on outside when I got out, so I waited for him to come. He came very slowly when he did arrive, and I guessed there had been some sort of trouble. "Well," I said, "what did you get?" "Oh, I don't know," said McLeod, "nothing much: but I think Sampson's rather sick with me." "Why, did you show him up some rot?" "No fear," he said. "It was all right as far as I could see: it was like this. *Memento* – that's right enough for remember, and it takes a genitive ⊥ *memento putei inter quatuor taxos.*" "What silly rot!" I said. "What made you shove that down? What does it mean?" "That's the funny part," said McLeod. "I'm not quite sure what it does mean. All I know is, it just came into my head and I corked it down. I know what I *think* it means, because just before I wrote it down I had a sort of picture of it in my head: I believe it means 'Remember the well among the four' – what are those dark sort of trees that have red berries on them?" "Mountain ashes, I s'pose you mean." "I never heard of them," said McLeod; "no, *I'll* tell you – yews." "Well, and what did Sampson say?" "Why, he was jolly odd about it. When he read it he got up and went to the mantelpiece and stopped quite a long time without saying anything, with his back to me. And then he said, without turning round, and rather quiet, 'What do you suppose that means?' I told him what I thought; only I couldn't remember the name of the silly tree: and then he wanted to know why I put it down, and I had to say something or other. And after that he left off talking about it, and asked me how long I'd been here, and where my people lived, and things like that: and then I came away: but he wasn't looking a bit well."

A School Story

'I don't remember any more that was said by either of us about this. Next day McLeod took to his bed with a chill or something of the kind, and it was a week or more before he was in school again. And as much as a month went by without anything happening that was noticeable. Whether or not Mr Sampson was really startled, as McLeod had thought, he didn't show it. I am pretty sure, of course, now, that there was something very curious in his past history, but I'm not going to pretend that we boys were sharp enough to guess any such thing.

'There was one other incident of the same kind as the last which I told you. Several times since that day we had had to make up examples in school to illustrate different rules, but there had never been any row except when we did them wrong. At last there came a day when we were going through those dismal things which people call Conditional Sentences, and we were told to make a conditional sentence, expressing a future consequence. We did it, right or wrong, and showed up our bits of paper, and Sampson began looking through them. All at once he got up, made some sort of noise in his throat, and rushed out by a door that was just by his desk. We sat there for a minute or two, and then – I suppose it was incorrect – but we went up, I and one or two others, to look at the papers on his desk. Of course I thought someone must have put down some nonsense or other, and Sampson had gone off to report him. All the same, I noticed that he hadn't taken any of the papers with him when he ran out. Well, the top paper on the desk was written in red ink – which no one used – and it wasn't in anyone's hand who was in the class. They all looked at it – McLeod and all – and took their dying oaths that it wasn't theirs. Then I thought of counting the bits of paper. And of this I made quite certain: that there were seventeen bits of paper on the desk, and sixteen boys in the form. Well, I bagged the extra paper, and kept it, and I believe I have it now. And now you will want to know what was written on it. It was simple enough, and harmless enough, I should have said.

' "*Si tu non veneris ad me, ego veniam ad te*," which means, I suppose, "If you don't come to me, I'll come to you." '

'Could you show me the paper?' interrupted the listener.

'Yes, I could: but there's another odd thing about it. That same afternoon I took it out of my locker – I know for certain it was the same bit, for I made a finger-mark on it – and no single trace of writing of any kind was there on it. I kept it, as I said, and since that time I have tried various experiments to see whether sympathetic ink had been used, but absolutely without result.

'So much for that. After about half an hour Sampson looked in again: said he felt very unwell, and told us we might go. He came rather gingerly to his desk, and gave just one look at the uppermost paper: and I suppose he thought he must have been dreaming: anyhow, he asked no questions.

'That day was a half-holiday, and next day Sampson was in school again, much as usual. That night the third and last incident in my story happened.

'We – McLeod and I – slept in a dormitory at right angles to the main building. Sampson slept in the main building on the first floor. There was a very bright full moon. At an hour which I can't tell exactly, but some time between one and two, I was woken up by somebody shaking me. It was McLeod; and a nice state of mind he seemed to be in. "Come," he said – "come! there's a burglar getting through Sampson's window." As soon as I could speak, I said, "Well, why not call out and wake everybody up?" "No, no," he said, "I'm not sure who it is: don't make a row: come and look." Naturally I came and looked, and naturally there was no one there. I was cross enough, and should have called McLeod plenty of names: only – I couldn't tell why – it seemed to me that there *was* something wrong – something that made me very glad I wasn't alone to face it. We were still at the window looking out, and as soon as I could, I asked him what he had heard or seen. "I didn't *hear* anything at all," he said, "but about five minutes before I woke you, I found myself looking out of this window here, and there was a man sitting or kneeling on Sampson's window-sill, and looking in, and I thought he was beckoning." "What sort of man?" McLeod wriggled. "I don't know," he said, "but I can tell you one thing

44

– he was beastly thin: and he looked as if he was wet all over: and," he said, looking round and whispering as if he hardly liked to hear himself, "I'm not at all sure that he was alive."

'We went on talking in whispers some time longer, and eventually crept back to bed. No one else in the room woke or stirred the whole time. I believe we did sleep a bit afterwards, but we were very cheap next day.

'And next day Mr Sampson was gone: not to be found: and I believe no trace of him has ever come to light since. In thinking it over, one of the oddest things about it all has seemed to me to be the fact that neither McLeod nor I ever mentioned what we had seen to any third person whatever. Of course no questions were asked on the subject, and if they had been, I am inclined to believe that we could not have made any answer: we seemed unable to speak about it.

'That is my story,' said the narrator. 'The only approach to a ghost story connected with a school that I know, but still, I think, an approach to such a thing.'

The sequel to this may perhaps be reckoned highly conventional; but a sequel there is, and so it must be produced. There had been more than one listener to the story, and, in the latter part of that same year, or of the next, one such listener was staying at a country house in Ireland.

One evening his host was turning over a drawer full of odds and ends in the smoking-room. Suddenly he put his hand upon a little box. 'Now,' he said, 'you know about old things; tell me what that is.' My friend opened the little box, and found in it a thin gold chain with an object attached to it. He glanced at the object and then took off his spectacles to examine it more narrowly. 'What's the history of this?' he asked. 'Odd enough,' was the answer. 'You know the yew thicket in the shrubbery: well, a year or two back we were cleaning out the old well that used to be in the clearing here, and what do you suppose we found?'

'Is it possible that you found a body?' said the visitor, with an odd feeling of nervousness.

'We did that: but what's more, in every sense of the word, we found two.'

'Good Heavens! Two? Was there anything to show how they got there? Was this thing found with them?'

'It was. Amongst the rags of the clothes that were on one of the bodies. A bad business, whatever the story of it may have been. One body had the arms tight round the other. They must have been there thirty years or more – long enough before we came to this place. You may judge we filled the well up fast enough. Do you make anything of what's cut on that gold coin you have there?'

'I think I can,' said my friend, holding it to the light (but he read it without much difficulty); 'it seems to be G. W. S., 24 July 1865.'

The Canterville Ghost

A Hylo-Idealistic Romance

OSCAR WILDE

When Mr Hiram B. Otis, the American minister, bought Canterville Chase, every one told him he was doing a very foolish thing, as there was no doubt at all that the place was haunted. Indeed, Lord Canterville himself, who was a man of the most punctilious honour, had felt it his duty to mention the fact to Mr Otis, when they came to discuss terms.

'We have not cared to live in the place ourselves,' said Lord Canterville, 'since my grand-aunt, the Dowager Duchess of Bolton, was frightened into a fit, from which she never really recovered, by two skeleton hands being placed on her shoulders as she was dressing for dinner, and I feel bound to tell you, Mr Otis, that the ghost has been seen by several living members of my family, as well as by the rector of the parish, the Rev. Augustus Dampier, who is a fellow of King's College, Cambridge. After the unfortunate accident to the Duchess, none of our younger servants would stay with us, and Lady Canterville often got very little sleep at night, in consequence of the mysterious noises that came from the corridor and the library.'

'My lord,' answered the Minister, 'I will take the furniture

47

and the ghost at a valuation. I come from a modern country, where we have everything that money can buy; and with all our spry young fellows painting the Old World red, and carrying off your best actresses and prima-donnas, I reckon that if there were such a thing as a ghost in Europe, we'd have it at home in a very short time in one of our public museums, or on the road as a show.'

'I fear that the ghost exists,' said Lord Canterville, smiling, 'though it may have resisted the overtures of your enterprising impresarios. It has been well known for three centuries, since 1584 in fact, and always makes its appearance before the death of any member of our family.

'Well, so does the family doctor for that matter, Lord Canterville. But there is no such thing, sir, as a ghost, and I guess the laws of nature are not going to be suspended for the British aristocracy.'

'You are certainly very natural in America,' answered Lord Canterville, who did not quite understand Mr Otis's last observation, 'and if you don't mind a ghost in the house, it is all right. Only you must remember I warned you.'

A few weeks after this, the purchase was completed, and at the close of the season the Minister and his family went down to Canterville Chase. Mrs Otis, who, as Miss Lucretia R. Tappan, of West 53rd Street, had been a celebrated New York belle, was now a very handsome middle-aged woman, with fine eyes, and a superb profile. Many American ladies on leaving their native land adopt an appearance of chronic ill-health, under the impression that it is a form of European refinement, but Mrs Otis had never fallen into this error. She had a magnificent constitution, and a really wonderful amount of animal spirits. Indeed, in many respects, she was quite English, and was an excellent example of the fact that we have really everything in common with America nowadays, except, of course, language. Her eldest son, christened Washington by his parents in a moment of patriotism, which he never ceased to regret, was a fair-haired, rather good-looking young man, who had qualified himself for American diplomacy by leading the German at the Newport Casino for three successive seasons, and even in London was well known as an excellent dancer. Gardenias and the peerage were his only weaknesses. Otherwise he was extremely sensible. Miss Virginia E. Otis was a little girl of fifteen, lithe and lovely as a fawn, and with a fine freedom in her large blue eyes. She was a wonderful amazon, and had once raced old Lord Bilton on her pony twice round the park, winning by a length and a half, just in front of Achilles statue, to the huge delight of the young Duke of Cheshire, who proposed to her on the spot, and was sent back to Eton that very night by his guardians, in floods of tears. After Virginia came the twins, who were usually called 'The Stars and Stripes' as they were always getting swished. They were delightful boys, and with the exception of the worthy Minister the only true republicans of the family.

As Canterville Chase is seven miles from Ascot, the nearest railway station, Mr Otis had telegraphed for a waggonette to meet them, and they started on their drive in high spirits. It was a lovely July evening, and the air was delicate with the scent of the pinewoods. Now and then they heard a wood pigeon brooding over its own sweet voice, or saw, deep in the rustling fern, the burnished breast of the pheasant. Little squirrels peered at them from the beech-trees as they went by, and the rabbits scudded away through the brushwood and over the mossy knolls, with their white tails in the air. As they entered the avenue of Canterville Chase, however, the sky became suddenly overcast with clouds, a curious stillness seemed to hold the atmosphere, a great flight of rooks passed silently over their heads, and, before they reached the house, some big drops of rain had fallen.

Standing on the steps to receive them was an old woman, neatly dressed in black silk, with a white cap and apron. This was Mrs Umney, the housekeeper, whom Mrs Otis, at Lady Canterville's earnest request, had consented to keep on in her former position. She made them each a low curtsey as they alighted, and said in a quaint, old-fashioned manner, 'I bid you welcome to Canterville Chase.' Following her, they passed through the fine Tudor hall into the library, a long, low room, panelled in black oak, at the end of which was a large stained-glass window. Here they found tea laid out for them, and, after taking off their wraps, they sat down and began to look around, while Mrs Umney waited on them.

Suddenly Mrs Otis caught sight of a dull red stain on the floor just by the fireplace and, quite unconscious of what it really signified, said to Mrs Umney, 'I am afraid something has been spilt there.'

'Yes, madam,' replied the old housekeeper in a low voice, 'blood has been spilt on that spot.'

'How horrid,' cried Mrs Otis; 'I don't at all care for blood-stains in a sitting room. It must be removed at once.'

The old woman smiled, and answered in the same low, mysterious voice, 'It is the blood of Lady Eleanore de Canterville, who was murdered on that very spot by her own husband, Sir Simon de Canterville, in 1575. Sir Simon survived her nine years, and disappeared suddenly under very mysterious circumstances. His body has never been discovered, but his guilty spirit still haunts the Chase. The blood-stain has been much admired by tourists and others, and cannot be removed.'

'That is all nonsense,' cried Washington Otis; 'Pinkerton's Champion Stain Remover and Paragon Detergent will clean it up in no time,' and before the terrified housekeeper could interfere he had fallen upon his knees, and was rapidly scouring the floor with a small stick of what looked like a black cosmetic. In a few moments no trace of the blood-stain could be seen.

'I knew Pinkerton would do it,' he exlaimed triumphantly, as he looked round at his admiring family; but no sooner had he said these words than a terrible flash of lightning lit up the sombre room, a fearful peal of thunder made them all start to their feet, and Mrs Umney fainted.

'What a monstrous climate!' said the American Minister calmly, as he lit a long cheroot. 'I guess the old country is so overpopulated that they have not enough decent weather for everybody. I have always been of opinion that emigration is the only thing for England.'

'My dear Hiram,' cried Mrs Otis, 'what can we do with a woman who faints?'

'Charge it to her like breakages,' answered the Minister, 'she won't faint after that;' and in a few moments Mrs Umney certainly came to. There was no doubt, however, that she was extremely upset, and she sternly warned Mr Otis to beware of some trouble coming to the house.

'I have seen things with my own eyes, sir,' she said, 'that would make any Christian's hair stand on end, and many and many a night I have not closed my eyes in sleep for the awful things that are done here.' Mr Otis, however, and his wife warmly assured the honest soul that they were not afraid of ghosts, and, after invoking the blessings of Providence on her new master and mistress, and making arrangements for an increase of salary, the old housekeeper tottered off to her own room.

The storm raged fiercely all that night, but nothing of particular note occurred. The next morning, however, when they came down to breakfast, they found the terrible stain of blood once again on the floor. 'I don't think it can be the fault of the Paragon Detergent,' said Washington, 'for I have tried it with everything. It must be the ghost.' He accordingly rubbed out the stain a second time, but the second morning it appeared again. The third morning also it was there, though the library had been locked up at night by Mr Otis himself, and the key carried upstairs. The whole family were now quite interested; Mr Otis began to suspect that he had been too dogmatic in his denial of the existence of ghosts, Mrs Otis expressed her intention of joining the Psychical Society, and Washington prepared a long letter to Messrs. Myers and Podmore on the subject of the Permanence of Sanguineous Stains when connected with crime. That night all doubts about the objective existence of phantasmata were removed for ever.

The day had been warm and sunny; and, in the cool of the evening, the whole family went out for a drive. They did not return home till nine o'clock, when they had a light supper. The conversation in no way turned upon ghosts, so there were not even those primary conditions of receptive expectation which so often precede the presentation of psychical phenomena. The subjects discussed, as I have since learned from Mr Otis, were merely such as form the ordinary conversation of cultured Americans of the better class, such as the immense superiority of Miss Fanny Davenport over Sarah Bernhardt as an actress; the difficulty of obtaining green corn, buckwheat cakes, and hominy, even in the best English houses; the importance of Boston in the development of the world-soul; the advantages of the baggage check system in railway travelling; and the sweetness of the New York accent as compared to the London drawl. No mention at all was made of the supernatural, nor was Sir Simon de Canterville alluded to in any way. At eleven o'clock the family retired and by half-past all the lights were out. Some time after, Mr Otis was awakened by a curious noise in the corridor, outside the room. It sounded like the clank of metal, and seemed to be coming nearer every moment. He got up at once, struck a match, and looked at the time. It was exactly one o'clock. He was quite calm, and felt his pulse, which was not at all feverish. The strange noise still continued, and with it he heard distinctly the sound of footsteps. He put on his slippers, took a small oblong phial out of his dressing-case, and opened the door. Right in front of him he saw, in the wan moonlight, an old man of terrible aspect. His eyes were as red as burning coals; long grey hair fell over his shoulders in matted coils; his garments, which were of antique cut, were soiled and ragged, and from his wrists and ankles hung heavy manacles and rusty gyves.

'My dear sir,' said Mr Otis, 'I really must insist on your oiling those chains, and have brought you for that purpose a small bottle of the Tammany Rising Sun Lubricator. It is said to be completely efficacious upon one application, and there are

The ghost started up with a wild shriek of rage

several testimonials to that effect on the wrapper from some of our most eminent native divines. I shall leave it here for you by the bedroom candles, and will be happy to supply you with more should you require it.' With these words the United States Minister laid the bottle down on a marble table, and, closing the door, retired to rest.

For a moment the Canterville ghost stood quite motionless in natural indignation; then, dashing the bottle violently upon the polished floor, he fled down the corridor, uttering hollow groans, and emitting a ghastly green light. Just, however, as he reached the top of the great oak staircase, a door was flung open, two little white-robed figures appeared, and a large pillow whizzed past his head! There was evidently no time to be lost, so, hastily adopting the Fourth Dimension of Space as a means of escape, he vanished through the wainscoting, and the house became quite quiet.

On reaching a small secret chamber in the left wing, he leaned up against a moonbeam to recover his breath, and began to try and realise his position. Never, in a brilliant and uninterrupted career of three hundred years, had he been so grossly insulted. He thought of the Dowager Duchess, whom he had frightened into a fit as she stood before the glass in her lace and diamonds; of the four housemaids, who had gone off into hysterics when he merely grinned at them through the curtains of one of the spare bedrooms; of the rector of the parish, whose candle he had blown out as he was coming late one night from the library, and who had been under the care of Sir William Gull ever since, a perfect martyr to nervous disorders; and of old Madame de Tremouillac, who, having wakened up one morning early and seen a skeleton seated in an arm-chair by the fire reading her diary had been confined to her bed for six weeks with an attack of brain fever, and, on her recovery, had become reconciled to the Church, and had broken off her connection with that notorious sceptic Monsieur de Voltaire. He remembered the terrible night when the wicked Lord Canterville was found choking in his dressing-room, with the knave of diamonds half-way down his

throat, and confessed, just before he died, that he had cheated
Charles James Fox out of £50,000 at Crockford's by means of
that very card, and swore that the ghost had made him swallow
it. All his great achievements came back to him again, from the
butler who had shot himself in the pantry because he had seen a
green hand tapping at the window pane, to the beautiful Lady
Stutfield, who was always obliged to wear a black velvet band
round her throat to hide the mark of five fingers burnt upon her
white skin, and who drowned herself at last in the carp-pond at
the end of the King's Walk. With the enthusiastic egotism of the
true artist he went over his most celebrated performances, and
smiled bitterly to himself as he recalled to mind his last
appearance as 'Red Ruben, or the Strangled Babe,' his *début* as
'Gaunt Gibeon, the Blood-sucker of Bexley Moor,' and the
furore he had excited one lonely June evening by merely playing
ninepins with his own bones upon the lawn-tennis ground. And
after all this, some wretched modern Americans were to come
and offer him the Rising Sun Lubricator, and throw pillows at
his head! It was quite unbearable. Besides, no ghosts in history
had ever been treated in this manner. Accordingly, he determined to have vengeance, and remained till daylight in an
attitude of deep thought.

  The next morning when the Otis family met at breakfast, they
discussed the ghost at some length. The United States Minister
was naturally a little annoyed to find that his present had not
been accepted. 'I have no wish,' he said, 'to do the ghost any
personal injury, and I must say that considering the length of
time he has been in the house, I don't think it is at all polite to
throw pillows at him' – a very just remark, at which, I am sorry
to say, the twins burst into shouts of laughter. 'Upon the other
hand,' he continued, 'if he really declines to use the Rising Sun
Lubricator, we shall have to take he chains from him. It would
be quite impossible to sleep, with such a noise going on outside
the bedrooms.'
  For the rest of the week, however, they were undisturbed, the

only thing that excited any attention being the continual renewal of the blood-stain on the library floor. This certainly was very strange, as the door was always locked at night by Mr Otis, and the windows kept closely barred. The chameleon-like colour, also, of the stain excited a good deal of comment. Some mornings it was a dull (almost Indian) red, then it would be vermilion, then a rich purple, and once when they came down for family prayers, according to the simple rites of the Free American Reformed Episcopalian Church, they found it a bright emerald-green. These kaleidoscopic changes naturally amused the party very much, and bets on the subject were freely made every evening. The only person who did not enter into the joke was little Virginia, who, for some unexplained reason, was always a good deal distressed at the sight of the blood-stain, and very nearly cried the morning it was emerald-green.

The second appearance of the ghost was on Sunday night. Shortly after they had gone to bed they were suddenly alarmed by a fearful crash in the hall. Rushing downstairs, they found that a large suit of old armour had become detached from its stand, and had fallen on the stone floor, while, seated in a high-backed chair, was the Canterville Ghost, rubbing his knees with an expression of acute agony on his face. The twins, having brought their peashooters with them, at once discharged two pellets on him, with that accuracy of aim which can only be attained by long and careful practice on a writing-master while the United States Minister covered him with his revolver, and called upon him in accordance with Californian etiquette, to hold up his hands! The ghost started up with a wild shriek of rage, and swept through them like a mist, extinguishing Washington Otis's candle as he passed, and so leaving them all in total darkness. On reaching the top of the staircase he recovered himself, and determined to give his celebrated peal of demoniac laughter. This he had on more than one occasion found extremely useful. It was said to have turned Lord Raker's wig grey in a single night, and had certainly made three of Lady Canterville's French governesses give warning before their month was up. He accordingly laughed his most horrible laugh, till the old vaulted roof rang and rang again, but hardly had the fearful echo died away when the door opened, and Mrs Otis came out in a light blue dressing-gown. 'I am afraid you are far from well,' she said, 'and have brought you a bottle of Dr. Dobell's tincture. If it is indigestion, you will find it a most excellent remedy.' The ghost glared at her in fury, and began at once to make preparations for turning himself into a large black dog, an accomplishment for which he was justly renowned, and to which the family doctor always attributed the permanent idiocy of Lord Canterville's uncle, the Hon. Thomas Horton. The sound of approaching footsteps, however, made him hesitate in his fell purpose, so he contented himself with becoming faintly phosphorescent, and vanished with a deep church-yard groan, just as the twins had come up to him.

On reaching his room he entirely broke down, and became a prey to the most violent agitation. The vulgarity of the twins, and the gross materialism of Mrs Otis, were naturally extremely annoying, but what really distressed him most was, that he had been unable to wear the suit of mail. He had hoped that even modern Americans would be thrilled by the sight of a Spectre In Armour, if for no more sensible reason, at least out of respect for their national poet Longfellow, over whose graceful and attractive poetry he himself had whiled away many a weary hour when the Cantervilles were up in town. Besides, it was his own suit. He had worn it with success at the Kenilworth tournament, and had been highly complimented on it by no less a person than the Virgin Queen herself. Yet when he had put it on, he had been completely overpowered by the weight of the huge breastplate and steel casque, and had fallen heavily on the stone pavement, barking both his knees severely, and bruising the knuckles of his right hand.

For some days after this he was extremely ill, and hardly stirred out of his room at all, except to keep the blood-stain in proper repair. However, by taking great care of himself, he recovered, and resolved to make a third attempt to frighten the

United States Minister and his family. He selected Friday, the 17th of August, for his appearance, and spent most of the day in looking over his wardrobe, ultimately deciding in favour of a large slouched hat with a red feather, a winding-sheet frilled at the wrists and neck, and a rusty dagger. Towards evening a violent storm of rain came on, and the wind was so high that all the windows and doors in the old house shook and rattled. In fact, it was just such weather as he loved. His plan of action was this. He was to make his way quietly to Washington Otis's room, gibber at him from the foot of the bed, and stab himself three times in the throat to the sound of slow music. He bore Washington a special grudge, being quite aware that it was he who was in the habit of removing the famous Canterville blood-stain, by means of Pinkerton's Paragon Detergent. Having reduced the reckless and foolhardy youth to a condition of abject terror, he was then to proceed to the room occupied by the United States Minister and his wife, and there to place a clammy hand on Mrs Otis's forehead, while he hissed into her trembling husband's ear the awful secrets of the charnel-house. With regard to little Virginia, he had not quite made up his mind. She had never insulted him in any way, and was pretty and gentle. A few hollow groans from the wardrobe he thought, would be more than sufficient, or, if that failed to wake her, he might grabble at the counterpane with palsy-twitching fingers. As for the twins, he was quite determined to teach them a lesson. The first thing to be done was, of course, to sit upon their chests, so as to produce the stifling sensation of nightmare. Then, as their beds were quite close to each other, to stand between them in the form of a green, icy-cold corpse, till they became paralysed with fear, and finally, to throw off the winding-sheet, and crawl round the room, with white bleached bones and one rolling eyeball, in the character of 'Dumb Daniel, or the Suicide's Skeleton,' a *rôle* in which he had on more than one occasion produced a great effect, and which he considered quite equal to his famous part of 'Martin the Maniac, or the Masked Mystery.'

At half-past ten he heard the family going to bed. For some

time he was disturbed by wild shrieks of laughter from the twins, who, with the light-hearted gaiety of schoolboys, were evidently amusing themselves before they retired to rest, but at a quarter-past eleven all was still, and, as midnight sounded, he sallied forth. The owl beat against the window panes, the raven croaked from the old yew-tree, and the wind wandered moaning round the house like a lost soul; but the Otis family slept unconscious of their doom, and high above the rain and storm he could hear the steady snoring of the Minister for the United States. He stepped stealthily out of the wainscoting, with an evil smile on his cruel, wrinkled mouth, and the moon hid her face in a cloud as he stole past the great oriel window, where his own arms and those of his murdered wife were blazoned in azure and gold. On and on he glided, like an evil shadow, the very darkness seeming to loathe him as he passed. Once he thought he heard something call, and stopped; but it was only the baying of a dog from the Red Farm, and he went on, muttering strange sixteenth-century curses, and ever and anon brandishing the rusty dagger in the midnight air. Finally he reached the corner of the passage that led to luckless Washington's room. For a moment he paused there, the wind blowing his long grey locks about his head, and twisting into grotesque and fantastic folds the nameless horror of the dead man's shroud. Then the clock struck the quarter, and he felt the time was come. He chuckled to himself, and turned the corner; but no sooner had he done so, than, with a piteous wail of terror, he fell back, and hid his blanched face in his long, bony hands. Right in front of him was standing a horrible spectre, motionless as a carven image, and monstrous as a madman's dream! Its head was bald and burnished; its face round, and fat, and white; and hideous laughter seemed to have writhed its features into an eternal grin. From the eyes streamed rays of scarlet light, the mouth was a wide well of fire, and a hideous garment, like his own, swathed with its silent snows the Titan form. On its breast was a placard with strange writing in antique characters, some scroll of shame it seemed, some record of wild sins, some awful calendar of crime, and, with its right hand, it bore aloft a falchion of gleaming steel.

Never having seen a ghost before, he naturally was terribly frightened, and, after a second hasty glance at the awful phantom, he fled back to his room, tripping up in his long winding-sheet as he sped down the corridor, and finally dropping the rusty dagger into the Minister's jack-boots, where it was found in the morning by the butler. Once in the privacy of his own apartment, he flung himself down on a small pallet-bed and hid his face under the clothes. After a time, however, the brave old Canterville spirit asserted itself, and he determined to go and speak to the other ghost as soon as it was daylight. Accordingly, just as the dawn was touching the hills with silver, he returned towards the spot where he had first laid eyes on the grisly phantom, feeling that, after all, two ghosts were better than one, and that, by the aid of his new friend, he might safely grapple with the twins. On reaching the spot, however, a terrible sight met his gaze. Something had evidently happened to the spectre, for the light had entirely faded from its hollow eyes, the gleaming falchion had fallen from its hand, and it was leaning up against the wall in a strained and uncomfortable attitude. He rushed forward and seized it in his arms, when, to his horror, the head slipped off and rolled on the floor, the body assumed a recumbent posture, and he found himself clasping a white dimity bed-curtain, with a sweeping-brush, a kitchen cleaver, and a hollow turnip lying at his feet! Unable to understand this curious transformation, he clutched the placard with feverish haste, and there, in the grey morning light, he read these fearful words:—

YE OTIS GHOSTE

Ye Onlie True and Originale Spook.
Beware of Ye Imitationes.
All others are Counterfeite.

The whole thing flashed across him. He had been tricked, foiled, and outwitted! The old Canterville look came into his eyes; he ground his toothless gums together; and, raising his withered hands high above his head, swore, according to the picturesque phraseology of the antique school, that when Chanticleer had sounded twice his merry horn, deeds of blood would be wrought, and Murder walk abroad with silent feet.

Hardly had he finished this awful oath when, from the red-tiled roof of a distant homestead, a cock crew. He laughed a long, low, bitter laugh, and waited. Hour after hour he waited, but the cock, for some strange reason, did not crow again. Finally, at half-past seven, the arrival of the housemaids made him give up his fearful vigil, and he stalked back to his room, thinking of his vain hope and baffled purpose. There he consulted several books of ancient chivalry, of which he was exceedingly fond, and found that, on every occasion on which his oath had been used, Chanticleer had always crowed a second time. 'Perdition seize the naughty fowl,' he muttered, 'I have seen the day when, with my stout spear, I would have run him through the gorge, and made him crow for me an 'twere in death!' He then retired to a comfortable lead coffin, and stayed there till evening.

The next day the ghost was very weak and tired. The terrible excitement of the last four weeks was beginning to have its effect. His nerves were completely shattered, and he started at the slightest noise. For five days he kept his room, and at last made up his mind to give up the point of the blood-stain on the library floor. If the Otis family did not want it, they clearly did not deserve it. They were evidently people on a low, material plane of existence, and quite incapable of appreciating the symbolic value of sensuous phenomena. The question of phantasmic apparitions, and the development of astral bodies, was of course quite a different matter, and really not under his control. It was his solemn duty to appear in the corridor once a week, and to gibber from the large oriel window on the first and third Wednesday in every month, and he did not see how he could honourably escape from his obligations. It is quite true that his life had been very evil, but, upon the other hand, he was most conscientious in all things connected with the supernatural. For the next three Saturdays, accordingly, he traversed the corridor as usual between midnight and three o'clock, taking every possible precaution against being either heard or seen. He removed his boots, trod as light as possible on the old worm-eaten boards, wore a large black velvet cloak, and was careful to use the Rising Sun Lubricator for oiling his chains. I am bound to acknowledge that it was with a good deal of difficulty that he brought himself to adopt this last mode of protection. However, one night, while the family were at dinner, he slipped into Mr Otis's bedroom and carried off the bottle. He felt a little humiliated at first, but afterwards was sensible enough to see that there was a great deal to be said for the invention, and, to a certain degree, it served his purpose. Still, in spite of everything, he was not left unmolested. Strings were continually being stretched across the corridor, over which he tripped in the dark, and on one occasion, while dressed for the part of 'Black Isaac, or the Huntsman of Hogley Woods,' he met with a severe fall, through treading on a butter-slide, which the twins had constructed from the entrance of the Tapestry Chamber to the top of the oak staircase. This last insult so enraged him, that he resolved to make one final effort to assert his dignity and social position, and determined to visit the insolent young Etonians the next night in his celebrated character of 'Reckless Rupert, or the Headless Earl.'

He had not appeared in this disguise for more than seventy years; in fact, not since he had so frightened pretty Lady Barbara Modish by means of it, that she suddenly broke off her engagement with the present Lord Canterville's grandfather, and ran away to Gretna Green with handsome Jack Castleton, declaring that nothing in the world would induce her to marry into a family that allowed such a horrible phantom to walk up and down the terrace at twilight. Poor Jack was afterwards shot in a duel by Lord Canterville on Wandsworth Common, and

Lady Barbara died of a broken heart at Tunbridge Wells before the year was out, so, in every way, it had been a great success. It was, however, an extremely difficult 'make-up,' if I may use such a theatrical expression in connection with one of the greatest mysteries of the supernatural, or, to employ a more scientific term, the higher-natural world, and it took him fully three hours to make his preparations. At last everything was ready, and he was very pleased with his appearance. The big leather riding-boots that went with the dress were just a little too large for him, and he could only find one of the two horse-pistols, but, on the whole, he was quite satisfied, and at a quarter-past one he glided out of the wainscoting and crept down the corridor. On reaching the room occupied by the twins, which I should mention was called the Blue Bed Chamber, on account of the colour of its hangings, he found the door just ajar. Wishing to make an effective entrance, he flung it wide open, when a heavy jug of water fell right down on him, wetting him to the skin, and just missing his left shoulder by a couple of inches. At the same moment he heard stifled shrieks of laughter proceeding from the four-post bed. The shock to his nervous system was so great that he fled back to his room as hard as he could go, and the next day he was laid up with a severe cold. The only thing that at all consoled him in the whole affair was the fact that he had not brought his head with him, for, had he done so, the consequences might have been very serious.

He now gave up all hope of ever frightening this rude American family, and contented himself, as a rule, with creeping about the passages in list slippers, with a thick red muffler round his throat for fear of draughts, and a small arquebuse, in case he should be attacked by the twins. The final blow he received occurred on the 19th of September. He had gone downstairs to the great entrance-hall, and was amusing himself by making satirical remarks on the large Saroni photographs of the United States Minister and his wife, which had now taken the place of the Canterville family pictures. He was simply but neatly clad in a long shroud, spotted with churchyard mould, had tied up his jaw with a strip of yellow linen, and carried a small lantern and a sexton's spade. In fact, he was dressed for the character of 'Jonas the Graveless, or the Corpse-Snatcher of Chertsey Barn,' one of his most remarkable impersonations, and one which the Canter-villes had every reason to remember, as it was the real origin of their quarrel with their neighbour, Lord Rufford. It was about a quarter past two o'clock in the morning, and, as far as he could ascertain, no one was stirring. As he was strolling towards the library, however, to see if there were any traces left of the blood-stain, suddenly there leaped out on him from a dark corner two figures, who waved their arms wildly above their heads, and shrieked out 'BOO!' in his ear.

Seized with panic, which, under the cirumstances, was only natural, he rushed for the staircase, but found Washington Otis waiting for him there with a big garden-syringe; and being thus hemmed in by his enemies on every side, and driven almost to bay, he vanished into the great iron stove, which, fortunately for him, was not lit, and he had to make his way home through the flues and chimneys, arriving at his own room in a terrible state of dirt, disorder, and despair.

After this he was not seen again on any nocturnal expedition. The twins lay in wait for him on several occasions, and strewed the passages with nutshells every night to the great annoyance of their parents and the servants, but it was of no avail. It was quite evident that his feelings were so wounded that he would not appear. Mr Otis consequently resumed his great work on the history of the Democratic Party, on which he had been engaged for some years; Mrs Otis organised a wonderful clambake, which amazed the whole county; the boys took to lacrosse, euchre, poker, and other Americal national games; and Virginia rode about the lanes on her pony, accompanied by the young Duke of Cheshire, who had come to spend the last week of his holidays at Canterville Chase. It was generally assumed that the ghost had gone away, and, in fact, Mr Otis wrote a letter to that effect to Lord Canterville, who, in reply, expressed his great pleasure at the news, and sent his best congratulations to the Minister's worthy wife.

The Otises, however, were deceived, for the ghost was still in the house, and though now almost an invalid, was by no means ready to let matters rest, particularly as he heard that among the guests was the young Duke of Cheshire, whose grand-uncle, Lord Francis Stilton, had once bet a hundred guineas with Colonel Carbury that he would play dice with the Canterville ghost, and was found the next morning lying on the floor of the card-room in such a helpless paralytic state, that though he lived on to a great age, he was never able to say anything again but 'Double Sixes.' The story was well known at the time, though, of course, out of respect to the feelings of the two noble families, every attempt was made to hush it up; and a full account of all the circumstances connected with it will be found in the third volume of Lord Tattle's *Recollections of the Prince Regent and his Friends.* The ghost, then, was naturally very anxious to show that he had not lost his influence over the Stiltons, with whom indeed, he was distantly connected, his own first cousin having been married *en secondes noces* to the Sieur de Bulkeley, from whom, as every one knows, the Dukes of Cheshire are lineally descended. Accordingly, he made arrangements for appearing to Virginia's little lover in his celebrated impersonation of 'The Vampire Monk, or, the Bloodless Benedictine,' a performance so horrible that when old Lady Startup saw it, which she did on one fatal New Year's Eve, in the year 1764, she went off into the most piercing shrieks, which culminated in violent apoplexy, and died in three days, after disinheriting the Cantervilles, who were her nearest relations, and leaving all her money to her London apothecary. At the last moment, however, his terror of the twins prevented his leaving his room, and the little Duke slept in peace under the great feathered canopy in the Royal Bedchamber, and dreamed of Virginia.

A few days after this, Virginia and her curly-haired cavalier went out riding on Brockley meadows, where she tore her habit so badly in getting through a hedge, that, on her return home, she made up her mind to go up by the back staircase so as not to be seen. As she was running past the Tapestry Chamber, the door of which happened to be opened, she fancied she saw some one inside, and thinking it was her mother's maid, who sometimes used to bring her work there, looked in to ask her to mend her habit. To her immense surprise, however, it was the Canterville Ghost himself! He was sitting by the window, watching the ruined gold of the yellow trees fly throught the air, and the red leaves dancing madly down the long avenue. His head was leaning on his hand, and his whole attitude was one of extreme depression. Indeed, so forlorn, and so much out of repair did he look, that little Virginia, whose first idea had been to run away and lock herself in her room, was filled with pity, and determined to try and comfort him. So light was her footfall, and so deep his melancholy, that he was not aware of her presence till she spoke to him.

'I am so sorry for you,' she said, 'but my brothers are going back to Eton to-morrow, and then, if you behave yourself, no one will annoy you.'

'It is absurd asking me to behave myself,' he answered, looking round in astonishment at the pretty little girl who had ventured to address him, 'quite absurd. I must rattle my chains, and groan through keyholes, and walk about at night, if that is what you mean. It is my only reason for existing.'

'It is no reason at all for existing, and you know you have been very wicked. Mrs Umney told us, the first day we arrived here, that you had killed your wife.'

'Well, I quite admit it,' said the Ghost petulantly, 'but it was a purely family matter, and concerned no one else.'

'It is very wrong to kill any one,' said Virginia, who at times had a sweet Puritan gravity, caught from some old New England ancestor.

'Oh, I hate the cheap severity of abstract ethics! My wife was very plain, never had my ruffs properly starched, and knew nothing about cookery. Why, there was a buck I had shot in Hogley Woods, a magnificent pricket, and do you know how she had it sent up to table? However, it is no matter now, for it is all over, and I don't think it was very nice of her brothers to starve me to death, though I did kill her.'

'Starve you to death? Oh, Mr Ghost, I mean Sir Simon, are you hungry? I have a sandwich in my case. Would you like it?'

'No, thank you, I never eat anything now; but it is very kind of you, all the same, and you are much nicer than the rest of your horrid, rude, vulgar, dishonest family.'

'Stop!' cried Virginia, stamping her foot, 'it is you who are rude, and horrid, and vulgar; and as for dishonesty, you know you stole the paints out of my box to try and furbish up that ridiculous blood-stain in the library. First you took all my reds, including the vermilion, and I couldn't do any more sunsets, then you took the emerald-green and the chrome-yellow, and finally I had nothing left but indigo and Chinese white, and could only do moonlight scenes, which are always depressing to look at, and not at all easy to paint. I never told on you, though I was very much annoyed, and it was most ridiculous, the whole thing; for who ever heard of emerald-green blood?'

'Well, really,' said the Ghost, rather meekly, 'what was I to do? It is a very difficult thing to get real blood nowadays, and, as your brother began it all with his Paragon Detergent, I certainly saw no reason why I should not have your paints. As for colour, that is always a matter of taste: the Cantervilles have blue blood, for instance, the very bluest in England; but I know you Americans don't care for things of this kind.'

'You know nothing about it, and the best thing you can do is to emigrate and improve your mind. My father will be only too happy to give you a free passage, and though there is a heavy duty on spirits of every kind, there will be no difficulty about the Custom House, as the officers are all Democrats. Once in New York, you are sure to be a great success. I know lots of people there who would give a hundred thousand dollars to have a grandfather, and much more than that to have a family ghost.'

'I don't think I should like America.'

'I suppose because we have no ruins and no curiosities,' said Virginia satirically.

'No ruins! no curiosities!' answered the Ghost; 'you have your navy and your manners.'

'Good evening; I will go and ask papa to get the twins an extra week's holiday.'

'Please don't go, Miss Virginia,' he cried; 'I am so lonely and so unhappy, and I really don't know what to do. I want to go and sleep and I cannot.'

'That's quite absurd! You have merely to go to bed and blow out the candle. It is very difficult sometimes to keep awake, especially at church, but there is no difficulty at all about sleeping. Why, even babies know how to do that, and they are not very clever.'

'I have not slept for three hundred years,' he said sadly, and Virginia's beautiful blue eyes opened in wonder; 'for three hundred years I have not slept, and I am so tired.'

'Poor, poor Ghost,' she murmured; 'have you no place where you can sleep?'

'Far away beyond the pine-woods,' he answered, in a low dreamy voice, 'there is a little garden. There the grass grows long and deep, there are the great white stars of the hemlock flower, there the nightingale sings all night long. All night long he sings, and the cold, crystal moon looks down, and the yew-tree spreads out its giant arms over the sleepers.'

Virginia's eyes grew dim with tears, and she hid her face in her hands.

'You mean the Garden of Death,' she whispered.

'Yes, Death. Death must be so beautiful. To lie in the soft brown earth, with the grasses waving about one's head, and listen to silence. To have no yesterday, and no to-morrow. To forget time, to forgive life, to be at peace. You can help me. You can open for me the portals of Death's house, for Love is always with you, and Love is stronger than Death is.'

Virginia trembled, a cold shudder ran through her, and for a few moments there was silence. She felt as if she was in a terrible dream.

Then the Ghost spoke again, and his voice sounded like the sighing of the wind.

'Have you ever read the old prophecy on the library window?'

'Oh, often,' cried the little girl, looking up; 'I know it quite well. It is painted in curious black letters, and it is difficult to read. There are only six lines:

> When a golden girl can win
> Prayer from out the lips of sin,
> When the barren almond bears,
> And a little child gives away its tears,
> Then shall all the house be still
> And peace come to Canterville.

But I don't know what they mean.'

'They mean,' he said sadly, 'that you must weep for me for my sins, because I have no tears, and pray with me for my soul, because I have no faith, and then, if you have always been sweet, and good, and gentle, the Angel of Death will have mercy on me. You will see fearful shapes in darkness, and wicked voices will whisper in your ear, but they will not harm you, for against the purity of a little child the powers of Hell cannot prevail.'

Virginia made no answer, and the Ghost wrung his hands in wild despair as he looked down at her bowed golden head. Suddenly she stood up, very pale, and with a strange light in her eyes. 'I am not afraid,' she said firmly, 'and I will ask the Angel to have mercy on you.'

He rose from his seat with a faint cry of joy, and taking her hand bent over it with old-fashioned grace and kissed it. His fingers were as cold as ice, and his lips burned like fire, but Virginia did not falter, as he led her across the dusky room. On the faded green tapestry were broidered little huntsmen. They blew their tasselled horns and with their tiny hands waved to her to go back. 'Go back! little Virginia,' they cried, 'go back!' but the Ghost clutched her hand more tightly, and she shut her eyes against them. Horrible animals with lizard tails, and goggle eyes, blinked at her from the carven chimney-piece, and murmured 'Beware! little Virginia, beware! we may never see you again,' but the Ghost glided on more swiftly, and Virginia did not listen. When they reached the end of the room he stopped, and muttered some words she could not understand. She opened her eyes, and saw the wall slowly fading away like a mist, and a great black cavern in front of her. A bitter cold wind swept round them, and she felt something pulling at her dress. 'Quick, quick,' cried the Ghost, 'or it will be too late,' and, in a moment the wainscoting had closed behind them, and the Tapestry Chamber was empty.

About ten minutes later, the bell rang for tea, and, as Virginia did not come down, Mrs Otis sent up one of the footmen to tell her. After a little time he returned and said that he could not find Miss Virginia anywhere. As she was in the habit of going out to the garden every evening to get flowers for the dinner-table, Mrs Otis was not at all alarmed at first, but when six o'clock struck, and Virginia did not appear, she became really agitated, and sent the boys out to look for her, while she herself and Mr Otis searched every room in the house. At half-past six the boys came back and said that they could find no trace of their sister anywhere. They were all now in the greatest state of excitement, and did not know what to do, when Mr Otis suddenly remembered that, some few days before, he had given a band of gypsies permission to camp in the park. He accordingly at once set off for Blackfell Hollow, where he knew they were, accompanied by his eldest son and two of the farm-servants. The little Duke of Cheshire, who was perfectly frantic with anxiety, begged hard to be allowed to go too, but Mr Otis would not allow him, as he was afraid there might be a scuffle. On arriving at the spot, however, he found that the gypsies had gone, and it was evident that their departure had been rather sudden, as the fire was still burning, and some plates were lying on the grass. Having sent off Washington and the two men to scour the district, he ran home, and despatched telegrams to all the police inspectors in the county, telling them to look out for a little girl who had been kidnapped by tramps or gypsies. He then ordered his horse to be brought round, and, after insisting on his wife and the three boys sitting down to dinner, rode off down the Ascot Road with a groom. He had hardly, however, gone a couple of miles when he heard somebody galloping after him, and, looking round, saw the little Duke coming up on his pony, with his face very flushed and no hat. 'I'm awfully sorry, Mr Otis,' gasped out the boy, 'but I can't eat any dinner as long as Virginia is lost. Please, don't be angry with me; if you had let us be engaged last year, there would never have been all this trouble. You won't send me back, will you? I can't go! I won't go!'

The Minister could not help smiling at the handsome young scapegrace, and was a good deal touched at his devotion to Virginia, so leaning down from his horse, he patted him kindly on the shoulders, and said, 'Well, Cecil, if you won't go back I suppose you must come with me, but I must get you a hat at Ascot.'

'Oh, bother my hat! I want Virginia!' cried the little Duke, laughing, and they galloped on to the railway station. There Mr Otis inquired of the station-master if any one answering the description of Virginia had been seen on the platform, but could get no news of her. The station-master, however, wired up and down the line, and assured him that a strict watch would be kept for her, and, after having bought a hat for the little Duke from a linen-draper, who was just putting up his shutters, Mr Otis rode off to Bexley, a village about four miles away, which he was told was a well-known haunt of the gypsies, as there was a large common next to it. Here they roused up the rural policeman, but could get no information from him, and, after riding all over the common, they turned their horses' heads homewards, and reached the Chase about eleven o'clock, dead-tired and almost heartbroken. They found Washington and the twins waiting for them at the gate-house with lanterns, as the avenue was very dark. Not the slightest trace of Virginia had been discovered. The gypsies had been caught at Broxley meadows, but she was not with them, and they had explained their sudden departure by saying that they had mistaken the date of Chorton Fair, and had gone off in a hurry for fear they might be late. Indeed, they had been quite distressed at hearing of Virginia's disappearance, as they were very grateful of Mr Otis for having allowed them to camp in his park, and four of their number had stayed behind to help in the search. The carp-pond had been dragged, and the whole Chase thoroughly gone over, but without any result. It was evident that, for that night at any rate, Virginia was lost to them; and it was in a state of deepest depression that Mr Otis and the boys walked up to the house, the groom following behind with the two horses and the pony. In the hall they found a group of frightened servants and lying on a sofa in the library was poor Mrs Otis, almost out of her mind with terror and anxiety, and having her forehead bathed with eau-de-Cologne by the old housekeeper. Mr Otis at once insisted on her having something to eat, and ordered up supper for the whole party. It was a melancholy meal, as hardly any one spoke, and even the twins were awestruck and subdued, as they were very fond of their sister. When they had finished, Mr Otis, in spite of the entreaties of the little Duke, ordered them all to bed, saying that nothing more could be done that night, and that he would telegraph in the morning to Scotland Yard for some detectives to be sent down immediately. Just as they were passing out of the dining-room, midnight began to boom from the clock tower, and when the last stroke sounded they heard a crash and a sudden shrill cry; a dreadful peal of thunder shook the house, a strain of unearthly music floated through the air, a panel at the top of the staircase flew back with a loud noise, and out on the landing looking very pale and white, with a little casket in her hand, stepped Virginia. In a moment they had all rushed to her. Mrs Otis clasped her passionately in her arms, the Duke smothered her with violent kisses, and the twins executed a wild war-dance round the group.

'Good heavens! child, where have you been?' said Mr Otis, rather angrily, thinking that she had been playing some foolish trick on them. 'Cecil and I have been riding all over the country looking for you, and your mother has been frightened to death. You must never play these practical jokes any more.'

'Except on the Ghost! except on the Ghost!' shrieked the twins, as they capered about.

'My own darling, thank God you are found; you must never leave my side again,' murmured Mrs Otis, as she kissed the trembling child, and smoothed the tangled gold of her hair.

'Papa,' said Virginia quietly, 'I have been with the Ghost. He is dead, and you must come and see him. He had been very wicked, but he was really sorry for all that he had done, and he gave me this box of beautiful jewels before he died.'

The whole family gazed at her in mute astonishment, but she was quite grave and serious; and, turning round, she led them through the opening in the wainscoting down a narrow secret corridor, Washington following with a lighted candle, which he had caught up from the table. Finally, they came to a great oak door, studded with rusty nails. When Virginia touched it, it swung back on its heavy hinges, and they found themselves in a little low room, with a vaulted ceiling, and one tiny grated window. Imbedded in the wall was a huge iron ring, and chained to it was a gaunt skeleton, that was stretched out at full length on the stone floor, and seemed to be trying to grasp with its long fleshless fingers an old-fashioned trencher and ewer, that were placed just out of its reach. The jug had evidently been once filled with water, as it was covered inside with green mould. There was nothing on the trencher but a pile of dust. Virginia knelt down beside the skeleton, and, folding her little hands together, began to pray silently, while the rest of the party looked on in wonder at the terrible tragedy whose secret was now disclosed to them.

'Hallo!' suddenly exclaimed one of the twins, who had been looking out of the window to try and discover in what wing of the house the room was situated. 'Hallo! the old withered almond-tree has blossomed. I can see the flowers quite plainly in the moonlight.'

'God has forgiven him,' said Virginia gravely, as she rose to her feet, and a beautiful light seemed to illumine her face.

'What an angel you are!' cried the young Duke, and he put his arm round her neck and kissed her.

Four days after these curious incidents a funeral started from Canterville Chase at about eleven o'clock at night. The hearse was drawn by eight black horses, each of which carried on its head a great tuft of nodding ostrich-plumes, and the leaden coffin was covered by a rich purple pall, on which was embroidered in gold the Canterville coat-of-arms. By the side of the hearse and the coaches walked the servants with lighted torches, and the whole procession was wonderfully impressive. Lord Canterville was the chief mourner, having come up specially from Wales to attend the funeral, and sat in the first carriage along with little Virginia. Then came the United States Minister and his wife, then Washington and the three boys, and in the last carriage was Mrs Umney. It was generally felt that, as she had been frightened by the ghost for more than fifty years of her life, she had a right to see the last of him. A deep grave had been dug in the corner of the churchyard, just under the old yew-tree, and the service was read in the most impressive manner by the Rev. Augustus Dampier. When the ceremony was over the servants according to an old custom observed in the Canterville family, extinguished their torches, and, as the coffin was being lowered into the grave, Virginia stepped forward and laid on it a large cross made of white and pink almond-blossoms. As she did so, the moon came out from behind the cloud, and flooded with its silent silver the little churchyard, and from a distant copse a nightingale began to sing. She thought of the ghost's description of the Garden of Death, her eyes became dim with tears, and she hardly spoke a word during the drive home.

The next morning, before Lord Canterville went up to town, Mr Otis had an interview with him on the subject of the jewels the ghost had given to Virginia. They were perfectly magnificent, especially a certain ruby necklace with old Venetian setting, which was really a superb specimen of sixteenth-century work, and their value was so great that Mr Otis felt considerable scruples about allowing his daughter to accept them.

'My Lord,' he said, 'I know that in this country mortmain is held to apply to trinkets as well as to land, and it is quite clear to me that these jewels are, or should be, heirlooms in your family. I must beg you, accordingly, to take them to London with you, and to regard them simply as a portion of your property which has been restored to you under certain strange conditions. As for my daughter, she is merely a child, and has as yet, I am glad to say, but little interest in such appurtenances of idle luxury. I am also informed by Mrs Otis, who, I may say, is no mean authority upon Art – having had the privilege of spending several winters in Boston when she was a girl – that these gems are of great monetary worth, and if offered for sale would fetch a tall price. Under these circumstances, Lord Canterville, I feel sure that you will recognise how impossible it would be for me to allow them to remain in the possession of any member of my family; and, indeed, all such vain gauds and toys, however suitable or necessary to the dignity of the British aristocracy, would be completely out of place among those who have been brought up on the severe, and I believe immortal, principles of republican simplicity. Perhaps I should mention that Virginia is very anxious that you should allow her to retain the box as a memento of your unfortunate but misguided ancestor. As it is extremely old, and consequently a good deal out of repair, you may perhaps think fit to comply with her request. For my own part, I confess I am a good deal surprised to find a child of mine expressing sympathy with mediaevalism in any form, and can only account for it by the fact that Virginia was born in one of your London suburbs shortly after Mrs Otis had returned from a trip to Athens.'

Lord Canterville listened very gravely to the worthy Minister's speech, pulling his grey moustache now and then to hide an involuntary smile, and when Mr Otis had ended, he shook him cordially by the hand, and said, 'My dear sir, your charming little daughter rendered my unlucky ancestor, Sir

Simon, a very important service, and I and my family are very much indebted to her for her marvellous courage and pluck. The jewels are clearly hers, and, egad, I believe that if I were heartless enough to take them from her, the wicked old fellow would be out of his grave in a fortnight, leading me the devil of a life. As for their being heirlooms, nothing is an heirloom that is not so mentioned in a will or legal document, and the existence of the jewels had been quite unknown. I assure you I have no more claim on them than your butler, and when Miss Virginia grows up I daresay she will be pleased to have pretty things to wear. Besides, you forget, Mr Otis, that you took the furniture and the ghost at a valuation, and anything that belonged to the ghost passed at once into your possession, as, whatever activity Sir Simon may have shown in the corridor at night, in point of law he was really dead, and you acquired his property by purchase.'

Mr Otis was a good deal distressed at Lord Canterville's refusal, and begged him to reconsider his decision, but the good-natured peer was quite firm, and finally induced the Minister to allow his daughter to retain the present the ghost had given her, and when, in the spring of 1890, the young Duchess of Cheshire was presented at the Queen's first drawing-room on the occasion of her marriage, her jewels were the universal theme of admiration. For Virginia received the coronet, which is the reward of all good little American girls, and was married to her boy-lover as soon as he came of age. They were both so charming, and they loved each other so much, that every one was delighted at the match, except the old Marchioness of Dumbleton, who had tried to catch the Duke for one of her seven unmarried daughters, and had given no less than three expensive dinner-parties for that purpose, and, strange to say, Mr Otis himself. Mr Otis was extremely fond of the young Duke personally, but, theoretically, he objected to titles, and, to use his own words, 'was not without apprehension lest, amid the enervating influences of a pleasure-loving aristocracy, the true principles of republican simplicity should be forgotten.' His objections, however, were completely overruled, and I believe that when he walked up the aisle of St George's, Hanover Square, with his daughter leaning on his arm, there was not a prouder man in the whole length and breadth of England.

The Duke and Duchess, after the honeymoon was over, went down to Canterville Chase, and on the day after their arrival they walked over in the afternoon to the lonely churchyard by the pine-woods. There had been a great deal of difficulty at first about the inscription on Sir Simon's tombstone, but finally it had been decided to engrave on it simply the initials of the old gentleman's name, and the verse from the library window. The Duchess had brought with her some lovely roses, which she strewed upon the grave, and after they had stood by it for some time they strolled into the ruined chancel of the old abbey. There the Duchess sat down on a fallen pillar, while her husband lay at her feet smoking a cigarette and looking up at her beautiful eyes. Suddenly he threw his cigarette away, took hold of her hand, and said to her, 'Virginia, a wife should have no secrets from her husband.'

'Dear Cecil! I have no secrets from you.'

'Yes, you have,' he answered, smiling, 'you have never told me what happened to you when you were locked up with the ghost.'

'I have never told any one, Cecil,' said Virginia gravely.

'I know that, but you might tell me.'

'Please don't ask me, Cecil, I cannot tell you. Poor Sir Simon! I owe him a great deal. Yes, don't laugh, Cecil, I really do. He made me see what Life is, and what Death signifies, and why Love is stronger than both.'

The Duke rose and kissed his wife lovingly.

'You can have your secret as long as I have your heart,' he murmured.

'You have always had that, Cecil.'

'And you will tell our children some day, won't you?'

Virginia blushed.

The Tell-Tale Heart

EDGAR ALLAN POE

True! – nervous – very, very dreadfully nervous I had been and am; but why *will* you say that I am mad? The disease had sharpened my senses – not destroyed – not dulled them. Above all was the sense of hearing acute. I heard all things in the heaven and in the earth. I heard many things in hell. How, then, am I mad? Hearken! and observe how healthily – how calmly I can tell you the whole story.

It is impossible to say how first the idea entered my brain; but once conceived, it haunted me day and night. Object there was none. Passion there was none. I loved the old man. He had never wronged me. He had never given me insult. For his gold I had no desire. I think it was his eye! yes, it was this! One of his eyes resembled that of a vulture – a pale blue eye, with a film over it. Whenever it fell upon me, my blood ran cold; and so by degrees – very gradually – I made up my mind to take the life of the old man, and thus rid myself of the eye for ever.

Now this is the point. You fancy me mad. Madmen know nothing. But you should have seen *me*. You should have seen how wisely I proceeded – with what caution – with what foresight – with what dissimulation I went to work! I was never kinder to the old man than during the whole week before I killed him. And every night, about midnight, I turned the latch of his door and opened it – oh, so gently! And then, when I had made an opening sufficient for my head, I put in a dark lantern, all closed, closed, so that no light shone out, and then I thrust in my head. Oh, you would have laughed to see how cunningly I thrust it in! I moved it slowly – very, very slowly, so that I might not disturb the old man's sleep. It took me an hour to place my whole head within the opening so far that I could see him as he lay upon his bed. Ha! – would a madman have been so wise as this? And then, when my head was well in the room, I undid the lantern, cautiously – oh, so cautiously – cautiously (for the hinges creaked) I undid it just so much that a single thin ray fell upon the vulture eye. And this I did for seven long nights – every night just at midnight – but I found the eye always closed; and so it was impossible to do the work; for it was not the old man who vexed me, but his Evil Eye. And every morning, when the day broke, I went boldly into the chamber, and spoke courageously to him, calling him by name in a hearty tone, and inquiring how he had passed the night. So you see he would have been a very profound old man, indeed, to suspect that every night, just at twelve, I looked in upon him while he slept.

Upon the eighth night I was more than usually cautious in opening the door. A watch's minute hand moves more quickly than did mine. Never before that night had I *felt* the extent of my own powers – of my sagacity. I could scarcely contain my feelings of triumph. To think that there I was, opening the door, little by little, and he not even to dream of my secret deeds or thoughts. I fairly chuckled at the idea; and perhaps he heard me – for he moved on the bed suddenly, as if startled. Now you may think that I drew back – but no. His room was as black as pitch with the thick darkness (for the shutters were close-fastened, through fear of robbers), and so I knew that he could not see the opening of the door, and I kept pushing it on steadily, steadily.

I had my head in, and was about to open the lantern, when my thumb slipped upon the tin fastening, and the old man sprang up in the bed, crying out, 'Who's there?'

I kept quite still and said nothing. For a whole hour I did not move a muscle, and in the meantime I did not hear him lie down. He was still sitting up in the bed, listening – just as I have done, night after night, hearkening to the death-watches in the wall.

Presently I heard a groan, and I knew it was the groan of mortal terror. It was not a groan of pain or of grief – oh, no! – it was the low stifled sound that arises from the bottom of the soul when overcharged with awe. I knew the sound well. Many a night, just at midnight, when all the world slept, it has welled up from my own bosom, deepening, with its dreadful echo, the terrors that distracted me. I say I knew it well. I knew what the old man felt, and pitied him, although I chuckled at heart. I knew that he had been lying awake ever since the first slight noise, when he had turned in the bed. His fears had been ever since growing upon him. He had been trying to fancy them causeless, but could not. He had been saying to himself, 'It is nothing but the wind in the chimney – it is only a mouse crossing the floor,' or 'It is merely a cricket which has made a single chirp.' Yes, he had been trying to comfort himself with these sup-positions; but he had found all in vain. *All in vain*; because Death, in approaching him, had stalked with his black shadow before him, and enveloped the victim. And it was the mournful influence of the unperceived shadow that caused him to feel – although he neither saw nor heard – to *feel* the presence of my head within the room.

When I had waited a long time, very patiently, without hearing him lie down, I resolved to open a little – a very, very little crevice in the lantern. So I opened it – you cannot imagine how stealthily, stealthily – until, at length, a single dim ray, like the thread of the spider, shot from out the crevice and fell upon the vulture eye.

It was open – wide, wide open – and I grew furious as I gazed upon it. I saw it with perfect distinctness – all a dull blue, with a hideous veil over it that chilled the very marrow in my bones; but I could see nothing else of the old man's face or person, for I had directed the ray, as if by instinct, precisely upon the damned spot.

The Tell-Tale Heart

And now have I not told you that what you mistake for madness is but over-acuteness of the senses? – now, I say, there came to my ears a low, dull, quick sound, such as a watch makes when enveloped in cotton. I knew *that* sound well, too. It was the beating of the old man's heart. It increased my fury, as the beating of a drum stimulates the soldier into courage.

But even yet I refrained and kept still. I scarcely breathed. I held the lantern motionless. I tried how steadily I could maintain the ray upon the eye. Meantime the hellish tattoo of the heart increased. It grew quicker, and louder and louder every instant. The old man's terror *must* have been extreme! It grew louder, I say, louder every moment! – do you mark me well? I have told you that I am nervous: so I am. And now, at the dead hour of the night, amid the dreadful silence of that old house, so strange a noise as this excited me to uncontrollable terror. Yet, for some minutes longer, I refrained and stood still. But the beating grew louder, louder! I thought the heart must burst. And now a new anxiety seized me – the sound would be heard by a neighbour! The old man's hour had come! With a loud yell I threw open the lantern and leaped into the room. He shrieked once – once only. In an instant I dragged him to the floor, and pulled the heavy bed over him. I then smiled gaily, to find the deed so far done. But, for many minutes, the heart beat on with a muffled sound. This, however, did not vex me; it would not be heard through the wall. At length it ceased. The old man was dead. I removed the bed and examined the corpse. Yes, he was stone, stone dead. I placed my hand upon the heart and held it there many minutes. There was no pulsation. He was stone dead. His eye would trouble me no more.

If still you think me mad, you will think so no longer when I describe the wise precautions I took for the concealment of the body. The night waned, and I worked hastily, but in silence. First of all I dismembered the corpse. I cut off the head and the arms and the legs.

I then took up three planks from the flooring of the chamber and deposited all between the scantlings. I then replaced the boards so cleverly, so cunningly, that no human eye – not even *his* – could have detected anything wrong. There was nothing to wash out – no stain of any kind – no blood-spot whatever. I had been too wary for that. A tub had caught all – ha! ha!

When I had made an end of these labours, it was four o'clock – still dark as midnight. As the bell sounded the hour, there came a knocking at the street door. I went down to open it with a light heart – for what had I *now* to fear? There entered three men, who introduced themselves, with perfect suavity, as officers of the police. A shriek had been heard by a neighbour during the night; suspicion of foul play had been aroused; information had been lodged at the police office, and they (the officers) had been deputed to search the premises.

I smiled – for *what* had I to fear? I bade the gentlemen welcome. The shriek, I said, was my own in a dream. The old man, I mentioned, was absent in the country. I took my visitors all over the house. I bade them search – search *well*. I led them, at length, to *his* chamber. I showed them his treasures, secure, undisturbed. In the enthusiasm of my confidence, I brought chairs into the room, and desired them *here* to rest from their fatigues, while I myself, in the wild audacity of my perfect triumph, placed my own seat upon the very spot beneath which reposed the corpse of the victim.

The officers were satisfied. My manner had convinced them. I was singularly at ease. They sat, and while I answered cheerily, they chatted of familiar things. But, ere long, I felt myself getting pale and wished them gone. My head ached, and I fancied a ringing in my ears; but still they sat and still they chatted. The ringing became more distinct – it continued and became more distinct. I talked more freely to get rid of the feeling; but it continued and gained definitiveness – until, at length, I found that the noise was *not* within my ears.

No doubt I now grew very pale; but I talked more fluently, and with a heightened voice. Yet the sound increased – and what could I do? It was *a low, dull, quick sound – much such a sound as a watch makes when enveloped in cotton.* I gasped for breath – and yet the officers heard it not. I talked more quickly – more

82

vehemently; but the noise steadily increased. I arose and argued about trifles, in a high key and with violent gesticulations; but the noise steadily increased. Why *would* they not be gone? I paced the floor to and fro with heavy strides, as if excited to fury by the observations of the men – but the noise steadily increased. O God! what *could* I do? I foamed – I raved – I swore! I swung the chair upon which I had been sitting, and grated it upon the boards, but the noise arose over all continually increased. It grew louder – louder – *louder!* And still the men chatted pleasantly, and smiled. Was it possible they heard not? Almighty God! – no, no! They heard! – they suspected! – they *knew!* – they were making a mockery of my horror! – this I thought, and this I think. But anything was better than this agony! Anything was more tolerable than this derision! I could bear those hypocritical smiles no longer! I felt that I must scream or die! – and now – again! hark! louder! louder! louder! *louder!*—

'Villains!' I shrieked, 'dissemble no more! I admit the deed! – tear up the planks! – here, here! – it is the beating of his hideous heart!'

The Cat Room

R. CHETWYND-HAYES

When the Goodridge family moved into Balaclava Cottage, Sabrina lost no time in exploring the empty rooms, leaving her parents to supervise the furniture removal men, who kept enquiring: 'Where do you want this, ma'am?' and 'Where shall we put the whatnot, ma'am?'

The 'cottage' had six rooms upstairs and six down, a fact that caused Mrs Goodridge grave concern, for she had shaken her head several times and expressed doubt that she could keep such a barn of a place clean.

'My great-uncle managed all right,' Mr Goodridge pointed out, 'and he only had a charlady in three times a week.'

'Yes, and a fine old mess it was, too,' Mrs Goodridge said. 'Still, he left the place to you, and we mustn't look a gift horse in the mouth. Vanman, that sofa goes in the front parlour.'

Sabrina ran up the stairs and began opening doors, peering into bedrooms and trying to decide which one she would like for herself. The large master bedroom would obviously be used by her parents and was, in fact, already fitted with an almost new Axminster carpet, of which her mother was vastly proud. But a much smaller room, situated at the back of the house, had two deep cupboards, a fascinating little iron fireplace and faded wallpaper with a most unusual pattern. It had a yellow background and rows of black cats' heads that ran diagonally across the paper, creating the impression that they had sprung out of the ceiling and were sliding down behind the wainscoting.

Sabrina had never seen wallpaper that had looked even remotely like this and decided that this room must be hers.

'What!' Mr Goodridge was trying to move a sideboard that refused to go against the dining-room wall. 'Those cat-heads will drive you crazy.'

'No, they won't. Daddy, all my life I've wanted a room with cat-heads on the wallpaper. Never – never have I wanted anything so much.'

'Well . . . you'd better ask your mother.'

Mrs Goodridge was watching the removal men with a critical eye as they carried a sofa into the sitting-room and did not view the idea with any great enthusiasm.

'But I wanted you to have the room next to ours. Frankly, that awful wallpaper gives me the shivers. I want your father to strip it off and paint the walls with a nice pink emulsion.'

'But all of my life I've wanted . . .'

'Don't be so silly.'

'*Please*. I'll clean all of the windows once a week if you'll let me have that room.'

Mrs Goodridge flinched when one of the men bumped an armchair against a door-frame.

'Oh, very well. I suppose I'll get no peace until you have your way. But don't blame me if you have horrid dreams.'

Once the 'cat room' – which was Sabrina's own name for her new retreat – was furnished, it did look rather cosy. Her brass bedstead, complete with bright yellow spread, stood against the wall facing the window; bookcases seemed to smile benignly at the wardrobe, which nestled snugly beside the old fireplace recess, and the pretty frills of her dressing-table brightened a dark corner. When the pink-shaded bedside lamp was switched on, all the cat-heads on the walls appeared to grin with unstinted appreciation.

'Not bad,' Mrs Goodridge nodded her reluctant approval. 'But I'm still not happy about that wallpaper. The old man must have been mad.'

Mr Goodridge grinned and switched on the overhead light.

'Eccentric, maybe. But he was a clever commercial artist. Probably designed that wallpaper himself.'

'Pity he couldn't have found a more useful way of spending his time,' Mrs Goodridge observed caustically. 'Sabrina, wash your hands. Dinner will soon be ready.'

It was two weeks before Balaclava Cottage acquired that 'lived in' atmosphere which is an absolute necessity before a house can be called a home. During that period extra furniture had to be purchased, fitted carpet laid in the hall and curtains made for most of the windows. Sabrina helped her father cut the grass, pull weeds from the sadly neglected garden and paint the front door a lovely emerald-green.

Then the nights began to draw in and the moon grew until it looked like a large ripe orange.

Sabrina woke up suddenly. One moment she was in a deep, dreamless sleep – the next wide awake, every sense alert, trying to determine what it was that had disturbed her. She raised her head and looked across the room. A full moon had transformed the window curtains into a silver screen, made the darkness retreat into corners, created slabs of shadow that lay before the bookcase and wardrobe, and turned the dressing-table mirror into a vast gleaming eye. A night breeze crept in through the partly open window and stirred the curtains, making it seem as if all the cat-heads on the wallpaper were opening and closing their mouths, as though sending out silent cries.

Then Sabrina heard the sound.

A low growl. She felt an icy wave of fear creep up from her feet and create chilly butterflies in her stomach, as she sat up and fumbled for the bedside lamp switch. Light exploded and shattered the silver gloom, sent out a pink-tinted radiance that formed a rough circle round the bed and was reflected in the wardrobe mirror.

The growl was repeated, only now it came from the region of the dressing-table. Sabrina strained her eyes, anxious to discover what caused this alarming noise, but at the same time terrified of what she might see. Suddenly she became aware of two little spots of yellow light that came round from behind the dressing-table and advanced into the room. Sabrina's hand flew to her mouth and she choked back a scream as an extremely large cat emerged into the circle of pink light. She had never seen such a cat before: long black fur that stood on end, ears laid back flat on either side of the round head, an open mouth that revealed long, pointed teeth, and eyes that glittered like polished amber discs. A long tail lashed from side to side.

The cat crept slowly forward, crouched low so that its stomach brushed the carpet. It stopped on reaching a position to the left of Sabrina's bed and looked up at her with hate-filled eyes. The growl rose to a terrifying howl. Sabrina, more frightened than at any time in her life, said the first words that came into her head.

'Nice puss . . . mice . . . milk. . . .'

The sound of her voice seemed partially to reassure the cat, for the pointed ears made an attempt to become upright, the tail ceased its angry lashing and the eyes blinked. Then, as though ashamed of a momentary weakness, the black cat turned, went back on to its hindquarters and jumped towards the mantelpiece.

It disappeared in mid-air.

After a few moments spent in trying to come to terms with this alarming phenomenon, Sabrina remembered her voice again – and screamed.

'That awful wallpaper!' Mrs Goodridge exclaimed for the seventh time. 'I knew it would give her nightmares, but no one

paid any attention to me. It doesn't take an ounce of com-
monsense to know that rows of cats' heads will do something to a
child's mind.'

'But, Mummy,' Sabrina insisted,' it wasn't a dream. The
black cat was really there. And it did disappear.'

Mr Goodridge of course did his best to be practical and line
up a number of indisputable facts in a neat row.

'Now,' he said heartily, 'let's put on our thinking caps. First,
we haven't got a cat. Secondly, all the doors were locked, and the
windows – was your window open, Sabrina?'

'Only a tiny bit,' said Sabrina. 'I don't think a kitten could
have got in, let alone such a monster cat. It was huge!'

'Thirdly, then,' went on Mr Goodridge, 'even if a cat did
manage somehow to get in, it couldn't possibly have disappeared in mid-air. Therefore you must have had a nasty dream.
I remember once dreaming about a donkey. .'

'But it could have been a ghost-cat,' Sabrina pointed out. 'A
very unhappy ghost-cat.'

Mrs Goodridge sat down and gave the impression she would
faint, if given the least encouragement.

'Did you hear, Clarence? The poor child's deranged! A ghost-
cat! She thinks the place is haunted!'

'A fertile imagination, my dear,' said Mr Goodridge comfort-
ingly. 'Takes after my side of the family, I shouldn't wonder.
Now, I propose that Sabrina spends the rest of the night in one
of the spare rooms and we all try to get some sleep. Tomorrow
we can decide what's to be done.'

'It wasn't a dream and it wasn't imagination!' Sabrina
announced angrily, exasperated – not for the first time – by the
gross stupidity that is so often displayed by even the nicest of
adults. 'I saw a ghost-cat, and I believe there's a reason why it's
haunting that room.'

Next morning, Mrs Coggins arrived. She was tall and thin
and wore a faded overall and plimsolls. She nodded her head in
Mrs Goodridge's direction.

'I used to come and oblige for the old gentleman, madam, and

I wondered if I could come and oblige you.'

Mrs Goodridge patted her forehead with a lace handkerchief. 'Oblige? I don't understand.'

'Do for him, madam. Do the housework, like. Me charges are quite moderate, and if you asks me to have a 'ot dinner, I won't say no.'

'It might be a good idea,' Mr Goodridge suggested, 'as this house is much larger than our old one. And if this good lady could char . . .'

'Oblige,' Mrs Coggins corrected.

'Yes, quite . . . oblige for a few hours a week, it would make things easier for you.'

Mrs Goodridge waved her handkerchief as a gesture depicting temporary helplessness.

'I'm certainly fit for nothing after last night. Let her remain by all means. Can she cook?'

Mrs Coggin frowned and drew herself upright.

'The name is Coggins, madam, and I can cook. Nothing fancy, but good wholesome fare such as the old gentleman found to his liking. If you feel poorly, just go upstairs and lie down and leave everything to me. I prefers not to have any interference.'

'I'm not at all certain . . .' Mrs Goodridge began, but her husband took her firmly by one arm and propelled her towards the stairs.

'Don't worry, dear. I'm sure Mrs Coggins will manage nicely, and Sabrina can make herself useful with the washing-up and so forth.'

With some reluctance, Mrs Goodridge allowed herself to be led upstairs, and Sabrina, who suddenly realised that she now had a source of information regarding her great-great-uncle – and even, possibly, the ghost-cat as well – carried a pile of plates into the kitchen, then grabbed a wiping-up towel.

'You show willing, I'lll say that for you,' Mrs Coggins remarked, rolling up her sleeves. 'Which is more than can be said for most kids these days. Mind you don't break any of your mother's china.'

For a while Sabrina busied herself with wiping plates and piling them on to the dresser. Then she asked:

'Did you work for my great-great-uncle for long?'

Mrs Coggins nodded. 'Yus, I obliged the old gentleman for nigh on ten years.'

'Was . . . was he a strange man?'

'I don't know about strange. He kept himself to himself, which I didn't hold against him.'

'Did he ever have a cat?'

'Not that I'm aware of. Of course there was that room that he'd never let me into, and I suppose he could have kept a cat in there. Certainly I once caught a glimpse of that outlandish wallpaper, and that must mean he liked 'em. Still – what's the harm? Lots of people like cats.'

'I do agree,' Sabrina hastened to reassure the old woman. 'I like them myself.'

Mrs Coggin placed a kettle on the gas stove.

'Mind you, there's them that say things went on in this house, that weren't right or proper for a honest Christain, but I never saw anything out of the way.'

Sabrina curbed a wave of excitement and waited until all of the china had been placed in the dresser before she spoke again.

'What sort of things – these things that went on?'

Mrs Coggins poured boiling water into a brown earthenware pot, then emptied it into the sink.

'Remember – always heat the pot. What sort of things? None that need concern you. Warlock, indeed!'

'What's a warlock?' Sabrina asked.

'A man witch. Stuff and nonsense! Now, let's have a nice cup of tea and don't you go asking me any more questions. I've got work to do.

Sabrina decided that no more information could be obtained from the old woman and presently made her way to the small room that Mr Goodridge had commandeered as a study. She removed a large dictionary from the bookcase and turned the pages over until she found the word *Warlock*.

The Cat Room

'A wizard, sorcerer, magician,' she read aloud. 'A man in league with, or under the influence of, evil spirits; male follower of the black art. A familiar in the shape of a black cat was said to relay orders from the devil to the warlock or witch.'

Sabrina closed the dictionary and leaned back in her father's swivel chair. The prospect that her bedroom was haunted by a ghost-cat that acted as messenger boy for the Devil was an exceedingly frightening one, but – when considered in broad daylight – rather exciting. However, if her great-great-uncle had been a warlock, she was certain the black cat had performed his satanic duties with great reluctance and now wanted to be set free, so he could go to wherever cats go when they die. She didn't know how she knew this – it was just something she felt sure about. After some rather fearful deliberation, Sabrina came to a heart-thumping decision. She was going to have a shot at laying the ghost-cat.

At two o'clock next morning – an hour when it was reasonable to suppose her parents were fast asleep – Sabrina crept over the dark landing, opened the door of the haunted room, then, after switching on the ceiling lamp, closed the door carefully behind her. The room still looked cosy and unhaunted as anyone could wish for, and the girl began to wonder if her terrifying experience, had, after all, been nothing more than an exceptionally vivid dream. Then she remembered the upright fur, the glaring eyes, and knew she had been fully awake, and no amount of self-deception could alter the fact. But how did one set about laying a ghost-cat?

Sabrina sat on her bed and gave the matter full consideration. Surely the first question that demanded an answer was – what made the cat appear? There was certainly no sign of it at present, which suggested that either the conditions were not favourable, or the apparition only appeared at a certain time. Sabrina tried to remember everything that had happened prior to hearing that terrifying growl. She had woken up and found the room bathed in moonlight, then she had switched on the bedside lamp. But . . . but the window had been slightly open, and the breeze was

91

The immense eyes became pools of yellow fire

disturbing the curtains . . . and all the cat-heads on the wallpaper seemed to be opening and closing their mouths. Sabrina gulped and tried very hard not to be frightened.

The wallpaper . . . the wallpaper was the key! No wonder she had though it to be so enthralling. Moonlight . . . waving curtains . . . dancing shadows . . . all doing something horrible to the wallpaper.

'Gosh!' Sabrina whispered, astonished at a thought that had just come to her. 'Maybe there never was a real cat at all! Perhaps it's a sort of extension of my great-great-uncle.'

She sat for some time looking at the wallpaper, and now it did appear to be very sinister indeed. Every cat-head seemed to have acquired yellow, glaring eyes, each open mouth gave the impression that it might produce a growl at any moment, and all appeared to be three-dimensional – straining to get off the wallpaper. Sabrina spoke again, deriving some small comfort from the sound of her own voice.

'I don't really want to – I'll be scared silly – but I must know.'

She got up and switched off the overhead lamp, then walked over to the window and opened it a fraction. The moon – as though waiting for such a signal – obligingly slid from behind a cloud and bathed the room in silver light. Sabrina slowly turned round and took up a position against the left hand wall. The curtains stirred and cast flimsy shadows over the wallpaper. Instantly, the cat-heads opened their mouths, while their eyes glittered like flickering stars on a frosty night.

Then, from behind the dressing-table came a distinct low growl, and the black cat crept into view, looking even larger and more ferocious than Sabrina remembered. It came forward with stomach brushing the carpet, ears laid back, fur standing on end, and stopped a few feet from the trembling girl.

The head went back, the immense eyes became pools of yellow fire, and the humped shoulders quivered as though the creature was about to leap. Suddenly the door opened, and Mr Goodridge, attired in a flower-patterned dressing-gown, entered. He said: 'I thought as much . . .' then stopped, his eyes

93

bulging when the ghost-cat spun round with one swift movement and faced the intruder. Sabrina did her best to speak calmly.

'Daddy, please turn the light on – quickly.'

'What . . . what in the name of sanity is it?'

'The ghost-cat. Please turn on the light, then I think it will jump towards the mantelpiece and disappear.'

Mr Goodridge took what seemed to be a long time fumbling for the light switch, but finally the lamp sprang into life, smothering the moonlight under a soft pink glow. Immediately the black cat turned and raced around the bed with incredible speed. When it reached the hearth-rug, it went back on it haunches, leapt towards the mantel-shelf and vanished in mid air.

'Thank God your mother's not awake. But I couldn't sleep, and I heard you creeping across the landing. A ghost-cat! Great heavens!'

Sabrina, whose courage had now revived, closed the window, then said: 'I think it's not only the wallpaper, but something behind the chimney breast. I mean, why else should the ghost-cat jump towards it and disappear?'

Mr Goodridge gave the fireplace an apprehensive glance.

'Don't ask me. I never reckoned on anything like this when I took the house over. What your mother will say when she finds out there really is a ghost-cat doesn't bear thinking about. Want to move, I shouldn't wonder.'

'If,' Sabrina said slyly, 'we were to clear the matter up tonight, she need never know. Let's examine that fireplace and see what we can find out.'

Her father looked anxiously around the room.

'I suppose there's no chance of that thing coming back? I don't think I could face it again.'

Sabrina crossed her fingers and gave what she hoped was the correct reply.

'No, of course not. One appearance a night is all it has – has strength for. Now, let's look at the fireplace.'

It was she who bent down and put her head into the opening and peered up the chimney. One thing was certain, a fire could never be lit in the grate, for the chimney had been bricked up, and, if the newness of the brickwork was anything to go by, quite recently, too.

She straightened up and ran an exploring hand over the chimney-breast. The surface was smooth, but when she tapped the wall there was a hollow sound in an area about one foot square, just above the shelf.

'I knew I was right,' she informed a still very distrubed Mr Goodridge. 'There's a small cupboard built into the chimney space. If you were to get a hammer and chisel, we could have it open in no time.'

'Perhaps tomorrow morning,' her father suggested.

'When mummy will want to know what you are doing?'

'I won't be a moment. My tool kit is in one of the spare rooms.'

While she was waiting, Sabrina tore away a strip of the wallpaper.

A shudder seemed to run round the entire room, and she jumped back. Zig-zag cracks appeared on all four walls, and the cat-heads began to fade. Presently, they took on the appearance of grey splodges. From behind the chimney-breast, Sabrina heard the distinct sound of a long-drawn-out sigh.

Mr Goodridge returned, carrying a large tool bag. He stopped just inside the door and looked around in amazement.

'What's happened to that awful wallpaper?'

Sabrina gave what she thought was a feasible answer.

'I tore some and sort of wounded the room. Well – that's the only way I can describe it. Look – there's a plain wooden panel here. All you've got to do is prise it out – then we'll see.'

The panel surrendered after Mr Goodridge had given it a few quiet taps with his hammer and chisel; it came away with a sharp, cracking sound – and revealed a dark recess. Mr Goodridge – after some hesitation – slid his right hand into the recess and brought out a small object: a grotesque image of the ghost-cat, complete with black fur and glittering eyes that seemed to be alive with hate and fear. He examined it with lively interest.

'It's quite heavy. I'd say bear skin over plaster. Let's see what else there is.'

He reached into the opening again and this time produced a roll of parchment, which he carried over to the dressing-table and laid out flat. Sabrina looked over her father's shoulder and read the following script, which had been written with a broad-nibbed pen and red ink. At least, she hoped it was red ink.

Extract from
'Unnatural Enmities and Their Retainment'
by
Conrad Von Holstein

Make ye an image in the likeness of Ye Black Cat of Set *and place it in a confined space. Then prepare a room with the same likeness depicted on all walls from floor to ceiling, each likeness to be not less than one hand's breadth from the next, all the while chanting the incantations prepared by the immortal Macradotus. Thus shall ye – when the time be right – be given power such as few men enjoy, and whatsoever worldly goods ye desire shall be yours. But be warned. Should death creep upon ye unawares, and the image be not destroyed, then shall ye walk the night hours on four feet, until that thing is done which ye left undone.*

Mr Goodridge took one long look at the open recess, the cracked wallpaper that was now beginning to peel from the walls, and finally at the cat image that lay on the bed. He sighed and said:

'Well, I guess I'll do that which was left undone. This cat thing and the piece of paper are going into the boiler – right now. And let's hope that's the end of the ghost-cat.'

It was. And before long the 'cat room' became the 'pink room', when Mr Goodridge gave the walls several coats of rose-coloured emulsion.

'Very nice, Clarence,' said Mrs Goodridge. 'And much more suitable than cats, Sabrina, don't you think?'

The Monk's Story

CATHERINE CROWE

One evening on which a merry Christmas party was assembled in an hospitable country mansion in the north of England, one of the company, a young man named Charles Lisle, called the host aside, as they were standing in the drawing-room before dinner, and whispered, 'I say, Graham, I wish you'd put me into a room that has either a bolt or a key.'

'They have all keys, or should have,' returned Mr Graham.

'The key of my room is lost,' returned the other. 'I asked the housemaid. It is always the first thing I look to when I enter a strange bed-chamber. I can't sleep unless the door is locked.'

'How very odd! I never locked my door in my life,' said Mr Graham. 'I say, Letitia,' continued he, addressing his wife, 'here's Charlie Lisle can't sleep unless his door's locked, and the room, you've put him into has no key.'

At this announcement all the ladies looked with surprise at Charlie Lisle, and all the gentlemen laughed; and 'how odd!' and 'what a strange fancy!' was echoed among them.

'I daresay you think it very odd, and indeed it must appear rather a lady-like particularity,' responded Lisle, who was a fine active young man, and did not look as if he were much troubled with superfluous fears; 'but a circumstance that occurred to me when I was on the continent last summer has given me a nervous

97

horror of sleeping in a room with an unlocked door, and I have never been able to overcome it. This is perhaps owing to my having been ill at the time, and I can scarcely say I have recovered from the effects of that illness yet.'

Naturally, everybody wanted to hear what this adventure was – the programme being certainly exciting – and so one of the visitors offered to exchange rooms with Charlie Lisle, provided he would tell them his story; which accordingly, when assembled round the fire in the evening, he began in the following words:-

'You must know, then, that last year, when I was wandering over the continent partly in search of the picturesque, and partly to remedy the effects of too much study, or rather too hasty study – for I believe a man may study as much as he pleases, if he will only take it easy, as the Irish say – I was surprised one evening by a violent storm of hail, and it became so suddenly dark, that I could scarcely see my horse's head. I had twelve miles to go to the town at which I intended to pass the night, and I knew that there was no desirable shelter nearer, unless I chose to throw myself on the hospitality of the monastery of Pierre Châtel, which lay embosomed amongst the hills a little to the east of the road I was travelling. There is something romantic and interesting in a residence at a convent, but of that I need not now say anything. After a short mental debate, I resolved to present myself at the convent gate, and ask them to give me a night's shelter. So I turned off the road, and rang the heavy bell, which was answered by a burly, rosy-cheeked lay brother, and he forthwith conducted me to the Prior, who was called the Père Jolivet. He received me very kindly, and we chatted away for some time on politics and affairs of the world; and when the brothers were summoned to the refectory, I begged leave to join them, and share their simple repast, instead of eating the solitary supper prepared for me.

'There were two tables in the hall, and I was seated next the Prior, in a situation that gave me a pretty good view of the whole company; and as I cast my eyes round to take a survey of the various countenances, they were suddenly arrested by one that struck me as about the most remarkable I had ever beheld. From the height of its owner as he sat, I judged he must be a very tall man, and the high round shoulders gave an idea of great physical strength; though at the same time the whole mass seemed composed of bone, for there was very little muscle to cover it. The colour of his great coarse face was of an unnatural whiteness, and the rigid immobility of his features favoured the idea that the man was more dead than alive. There was altogether something so remarkable in his looks, that I could with difficulty turn my eyes from him. My fixed gaze, I imagine, roused some emotions within him, for he returned my scrutiny with a determined and terrific glare. If I forced myself to turn away my head for a moment, round it would come again, and there were his two great mysterious eyes upon me; and that stiff jaw, slowly and mechanically moving from side to side, as he ate his supper, like something acted on by a pendulum. It was really dreadful; we seemed both bewitched to stare at each other; and I longed for the signal to rise, that I might be released from the strange fascination. This came at length; and though I had promised myself to make some inquiries of the Prior concerning the owner of the eyes, yet not finding myself alone with him during the evening, I forbore, and in due time retired to my chamber, intending to proceed on my journey the following day. But when the morning came, I found myself very unwell, and the hospitable Prior recommended me not to leave my bed; and finally, I was obliged to remain there not only that day, but many days; in short, it was nearly a month before I was well enough to quit the convent.

'In the meantime, however, I had learnt the story of Brother Lazarus, for so I found the object of my curiosity was called; and had thereby acquired some idea of the kind of influence he had exercised over me. The window of the little room I occupied looked into the burying-place of the monastery; and on the day I first left my bed, I perceived a monk below digging a grave. He was stooping forward, with his spade in his hand, and with his back towards me; and as my room was a good way from the ground, and the brothers were all habited alike, I could not distinguish which of them it was.

' "You have a death amongst you?" said I to the Prior when he visited me.

' "No," returned he; "we have even no serious sickness at present."

' "I see one of the brothers below, digging a grave," I replied.

' "Oh!" said he, looking out, "that is Brother Lazarus – he is digging his own grave."

' "What an extraordinary fancy!" said I. "But perhaps it's a penance?"

' "Not a penance imposed by me," replied the Prior, "but by himself. Brother Lazarus is a very strange person. Perhaps you may have observed him at the refectory – he sat nearly opposite you at the other table?"

' "Bless me! is that he? Oh, yes, I observed him indeed. Who could help observing him? He has the most extraordinary countenance I ever beheld."

' "Brother Lazarus is a somnambulist," returned the Prior; "a natural somnambulist; and is altogether, as I said before, a very extraordinary character."

' "What!" said I, my curiosity being a good deal awakened, "does he walk in his sleep? I never saw a somnambulist before, and should like to hear some particulars about him, if you have no objection to tell them me."

' "They are not desirable inmates, I assure you," answered the Prior. "I could tell you some very odd adventures connected with this disease of Brother Lazarus."

' "I should be very much obliged to you, if you would," said I, with no little eagerness.

' "Somnambulists are sometimes subject to strange hallucinations," he replied; "their dream is to them as real as our actual daily life is to us, and they not unfrequently act out the scenes of the drama with a terrible determination. I will just give you one instance of the danger that may accrue from a delusion of this nature. At the last monastery I inhabited, before I became Prior of Pierre Châtel, we had a monk who was known to be a somnambulist. He was a man of a sombre character and gloomy temperament; but it was rather supposed that his melancholy proceeded from physical causes, than from any particular source of mental uneasiness. His nightly wanderings were very irregular: sometimes they were frequent, sometimes there were long intermissions. Occasionally he would leave his cell, and after being absent from it several hours, would return of his own accord, still fast asleep, and lay himself in his bed: at other times he would wander so far away, that we had to send in search of him; and sometimes he would be met by the messengers on his way back, either awake or asleep, as it might happen.

' "This strange malady had caused us some anxiety, and we had not neglected to seek the best advice we could obtain with respect to its treatment; and at length the remedies applied seemed to have taken effect; the paroxysms became more rare, and the desease so far subsided, that it ceased to be a subject of observation amongst us. Several months had elapsed since I had heard anything of the nocturnal excursions of Brother Dominique, when one night that I had some business of importance in hand, instead of going to bed when the rest of the brotherhood retired to their cells, I seated myself at my desk, for the purpose of reading and answering certain letters concerning the affair in question. I had been some time thus occupied, and had just finished my work, and had already locked my desk preparatory to going to bed, when I heard the closing of a distant door, and immediately afterwards a foot in the long gallery that separated my room from the cells of the brotherhood. What could be the matter? Somebody must be ill, and was coming to seek assistance; and I was confirmed in this persuasion when I perceived that the foot was approaching my door, the key of which I had not turned. In a moment more it opened, and Fra Dominique entered, asleep. His eyes were wide open, but there was evidently no speculation in them; they were fixed and glassy, like the eyes of a corpse. He had nothing on but the tunic which he was in the habit of wearing at night, and in his hand he held a large knife. At this strange apparition I stood transfixed. From the cautious manner in which he had opened the door, and the stealthy pace with which he advance into the room, I could not doubt that he was bent upon mischief; but aware of the dangerous effects that frequently result from the too sudden awakening of a sleep-walker, I thought it better to watch in silence the acting out of this fearful drama, than venture to disturb him. With all the precautions he would have used not to arouse me had he been awake, he moved towards the bed, and in so doing he had occasion to pass quite close to where I stood, and as the light of the lamps fell upon his face, I saw that his brows were knit, and his features contracted into an expression of resolute malignity. When he reached the bed, he bent over it, felt with his hand in the place where I should have been, and then, apparently satisfied, he lifted up his arm, and struck successively three heavy blows – so heavy, that, having pierced the bed-clothes, the blade of the knife entered far into the mattress, or rather into the mat that served me for one. Suddenly, however, whilst his arm was raised for another blow, he started, and turning round, hastened towards the window, which he opened, and had it been large enough, I think would have thrown himself out. But finding the aperture too small, he changed his direction. Again he passed close to me, and I felt myself shrink back as he almost touched me with his tunic. The two lamps that stood on my table made no impression on his eyes; he opened and closed the door as before; and I heard him proceed rapidly along the gallery, and retire to his own cell. It would be vain to attempt to describe the amazement with which I had witnessed this terrible scene. I had been, as it were, the spectator of my own murder, and I was overcome by the horrors of this visionary assassination. Grateful to Providence for the danger I had escaped, I yet could not brace my nerves to look at it with calmness, and I passed the remainder of the night in a state of painful agitation. On the following morning, as soon as breakfast was over, I summoned Fra Dominique to my room. As he entered, I saw his eye glance at the bed, which was now, however, covered by other linen, so that there were no traces visible of his nocturnal visit. His countenance was sad, but expressed no confusion, till I inquired what had been the subject of his dreams the preceding night. Then he started, and changed colour.

'"Reverend father," said he, "why do you ask me this?"'

'"Never mind," said I; "I have my reasons."'

'"I do not like to repeat my dream," returned he; "it was too frightful; and I fear that it must have been Satan himself that inspired it."'

'"Nevertheless let me hear it."'

'"Well, reverend father, if you will have it so, what I dreamt was this – but that you may the better comprehend my dream, I must give you a short sketch of the circumstances in which it originated."'

'"Do so," said I; "and that we may not be interrupted, I'll lock the door." So having turned the key, and bade him seat himself on a stool opposite me, I prepared to listen to the story of his life.

'"I was a child," said he, "of eight years old when the event occurred in which my unhappy malady originated. My father had died, leaving my mother in tolerable circumstances and with two children, myself and a sister of marriageable years. This sister, as I have since understood, had become attached to an Italian stranger of very questionable character who had appeared in the town we inhabited, under the character of an itinerant artist. My father had discovered the connection, and had forbidden him the house; but when he died, the stranger's influence prevailed over my mother's authority, and one morning Adèle was missing. As the Italian disappeared at the same time, no doubt was entertained that they had gone off together, and a few weeks confirmed these apprehensions. They came back, declaring themselves married, and petitioning my mother's forgiveness and assistance. She granted them both; but finding her so easy to deal with, Ripa, the Italian, began to make such frequent demands upon her purse, and indulged in such violence when his drafts were not responded to, that she found it necessary to forbid him the house. I believe he had some talent, but he was idle and dissipated, and the habit of living upon us had so far augmented these vices, that he could no longer bring himself to work. The consequence was, that he soon fell into distress, and, finding my mother, whose resolution was sustained by her brother, inexorable, he had recourse to more desperate means of supplying his necessities. Many evil reports were circulated about him, and, at length, so much suspicion was excited, that, to my mother's great relief, they quitted the place, and several months elapsed without any tidings of their proceedings reaching her.

' "For my part, with the usual volatility of childhood, I had totally ceased to think either of Ripa or of my sister, of whom I had formerly been exceedingly fond, and I was wholly occupied with the prospect of going to school, a prospect which, as I had no companions of my own age at home, delighted me. My mother, on the contrary, suffered considerably from the idea of the impending separation; and the last night I was to sleep under her roof, she took me to lie in her bed.

' "I cannot part with you tonight, my child!' said she, as she kissed me, and led me to her chamber. 'You don't know what parting is yet, Dominique. You think only of the playfellows you are going to; you know not what you are about to lose!'

' "Little I dreamt of all I was going to lose, – nor she either.

' "I suppose I fell asleep directly, for I have no recollection of my mother's coming to bed, nor of anything else, till I was awakened by the pressure of a heavy hand on my breast, and, by the faint light of a lantern which stood on the table, I discovered my brother-in-law, Ripa, the Italian, hanging over me. But it was not at me he was looking, but at my mother, who, fast asleep, was lying on the other side of the bed. An instinctive terror kept me silent and motionless; and presently, having ascertained the position in which his victim was lying, he raised a large knife he held in his hand, and struck it repeatedly into her breast. At the third blow, my horror and anguish overcame my fears, and I uttered a cry which seems first to have revealed to him my presence; or perhaps he did not know it was me, but was only startled by the sudden noise, for, as his purpose was undoubtedly robbery, I do not see why he should not have despatched so insignificant an obstacle, and fulfilled his intentions. However this may be, he took fright and fled, first to the window, – for he seemed to have lost all presence of mind, – but finding no egress there, he turned and retreated by the door.

' "I was afraid he would return, and, almost dead with terror and grief, I lay still the rest of the night, without courage to rise, or to call the servant who slept in the kitchen. When she entered the room in the morning, she found my mother dead, and myself bathed in her blood. Ripa was pursued and taken, my testimony was fatal to him, and my poor sister died of a broken heart a few months after he had expiated his crime on the scaffold.

' "A long and fearful malady was the consequence to me of this dreadful event, and I have ever since been subject to these dreams!"

' "What dreams?" I asked.

' "Such as I had last night," he answered; "wherein I feel myself constrained to act over again the frightful scene I witnessed."

' "And pray," I inquired, "do you select any particular person as your victim in those dreams?"

' "Always."

' "And what does this selection depend upon? Is it enmity?"

' "No," returned Dominique; "it is a peculiar influence that I cannot explain. Perhaps," added he, after some hesitation, "you may have observed my eyes frequently fixed on you of late?" I remembered that I had observed this; and he then told me that whoever he looked at in that manner was the person he dreamt of.

' 'Such,' said Charlie Lisle, 'was the Prior's account of this strange personage. I confess, when I had heard his explanation,

I began to feel particularly queer, for I was already satisfied that Fra Dominique and Brother Lazarus were one and the same person; and I perceived that I was in considerable danger of being the selected victim of his next dream; and so I told Père Jolivet.

' "Never fear," said he; "we lock him up every night, and have done so since my adventure. Added to which, he is now very unwell; he was taken with a fit yesterday, and we have been obliged to bleed him."

' "But he is digging there below," said I.

' "Yes," replied the Prior; "he has a notion he is going to die, and entreated permission to prepare his grave. It is, however, a mere fancy I daresay. He had the same notion during the indisposition that succeeded the dream I have just related. I forgot to tell you, however, though you seem to have penetrated the secret, that this Fra Dominique changed his name to Lazarus when he accompanied me here, which he was allowed to do at his own urgent entreaty; why, I cannot tell, but ever after that conversation, he seemed to have imbibed a strong attachment to me; perhaps because I exhibited none of the distrust or aversion towards him which some persons might have been apt to entertain under the same circumstances."

'A week after this I was informed that Brother Lazarus was dead,' continued Lisle; 'and I confess I did not much regret his decease. I thought a man subject to such dangerous dreams was better out of the world than in it; more especially as by all account he had no enjoyment in life. On the day I quitted the monastery, I saw from my window one of the brothers completing the already partly-made grave, and learnt that he was to be buried that evening; and as I descended the stairs, I passed some monks who were carrying his coffin to his cell. "Rest his soul!" said I, as I buckled on my spurs; and having heartily thanked the good prior for his hospitality, I mounted my horse and rode away.'

Here Charlie Lisle rang the bell and asked for a glass of water.

'Is that all?' inquired Lady Araminta.

The Monk's Story

'Not quite,' said Charlie; 'the sequel is to come. My visit to the monastery of Pierre Châtel had occurred in the month of June. During the ensuing months I travelled over a considerable part of the south of France; and at length I crossed the Pyrenees, intending to proceed as far as Madrid, and winter there. Amongst the lions I had been recommended to visit was a monastery of Franciscans in the neighbourhood of Burgos, and I turned somewhat out of my road for the purpose of inspecting some curious manuscripts which the monks were reputed to possess. It was in the month of October, and a bright moonlight night, when I rang the bell, and requested to see the Padre Pachorra, to whom I had letters of introduction. I found him a dark, grave, sombre-looking man, not very unlike my old friend Brother Lazarus; and although he received me civilly enough, there was something in his demeanour that affected my spirits. The whole air of the convent, too, was melancholy; convents, like other establishments, taking their tone very much from the character of their superiors.

'As the monks had already supped when I arrived, I was served with some refreshment in the parlour; and the whole internal arrangements here being exceedingly strict, I immediately afterwards retired to my chamber, firmly resolved to take my departure the next day. I am not in the habit of going to bed early, and when I do, I never can sleep. By the time my usual sleeping hour is arrived, I have generally got so restless and nervous from lying awake, that slumber is banished altogether. Consequently, whenever I am under circumstances that oblige me to retire early to my room, I make a practice of reading till I find my eyelids heavy. But the dormitory assigned me in this Franciscan convent was so chilly, and the lamp gave so little light, that either remaining out of bed or reading in it was out of the question; so I yielded to necessity, and stretched myself on Padre Pachorra's hard couch; and a very hard one it was, I assure you. I was very cold too. There were not coverings enough on the bed to keep in my animal heat; and although I spread my own clothes over me also, still I lay shivering in a very uncomfortable manner, and, I am afraid, uttering sundry harsh remarks on the Padre's niggardly hospitality.

'In this agreeable occupation, as you may suppose, the flight of time was somewhat of the slowest. I do not know how many hours I had been there, but I had begun to think it never would be morning, when I heard something stirring in the gallery outside my door. The silence of a convent at night is the silence of the grave. Too far removed from the busy world without for external sounds to penetrate the thick walls, whilst within no slamming door, nor wandering foot, nor sacrilegious voice breaks in upon the stillness, the slightest noise strikes upon the ear with a fearful distinctness. I had no shutters to my window, so that I was aware it was still pitch-dark without, though, within, the feeble light of my lamp enabled me to see a little about me. I knew that the inmates of monasteries not only rise before daylight, but also that they perform midnight masses, and so forth; but then I had always observed that on these occasions they were summoned by a bell. Now, there was no bell; on the contrary, all was still as death, except the cautious foot which seemed to be approaching my room. "What on earth can it be?" thought I, sitting up in bed with an indescribable feeling of apprehension. At that moment a hand was laid upon the latch of my door. I cannot tell why, but instinctively I jumped out of bed – the door opened, and in walked what appeared to me to be Brother Lazarus, exactly as the Prior of Pierre Châtel had described him to me on the occasion of his nocturnal visit to his chamber. His eyes were open, but glazed, as of one dead; his face was of a ghastly paleness; he had nothing on but the grey tunic in which he slept; and in his hand he held a knife, such a one as was used by the monks to cut their large loaves with.

'You may conceive my amazement,' continued Charlie Lisle, whilst amongst his auditors every eye was firmly riveted. 'I rubbed my eyes, and asked myself if I were dreaming. Too surely I was awake – I had never even slumbered for an instant. Was I mad? I did not think I was; but certainly that was no proof to the contrary; and I almost began to doubt that Brother Lazarus was dead and buried on the other side of the Pyrenees. The Prior of Pierre Châtel had told me he was dead, and I had heard several others of the brotherhood alluding to his decease. I had seen his grave made ready, and I had passed his coffin as I descended to the hall; yet here he was in Spain, again rehearsing the frightful scene that Jolivet had described to me! Whilst all this was fleeting through my mind, I was standing *en chemise* betwixt the bed and the wall, on which side I had happened to leap out. In the meantime the apparition advanced with bare feet, and with the greatest caution, towards the other side of the bed; and as there were of course no curtains, I had a full view of his diabolical features, which appeared contracted with rage and malignity. As Jolivet has described to me, he first felt the bed, as if to ascertain if I were there; and I confess I was frightened out of my senses lest he should discover that I was not, and possibly detect me where I was. What could I have done, unarmed, and in my shirt, against this preternatural-looking monster? And to wake him – provided always it was really Brother Lazarus, and not his double, a point about which I felt exceedingly uncertain – I had learnt from Jolivet was extremely perilous. However, he did not discover that the bed was empty – his dream no doubt supplying a visionary victim for the occasion – and raising his arm, he plunged the knife into the mattress with a fierce determination that convinced me I should have had very little chance of surviving the blow had I been where he imagined me. Again and again he struck, I looking on with a horror that words could but feebly paint; and then he suddenly started, the uplifted arm was arrested – the pursuer was at hand: he first rushed to the window, and opened it, but being only a small lattice, there was no egress there, so he turned to the door, making his escape that way; and I could hear his foot distinctly flying along the gallery till he reached his own cell. By this time I was perfectly satisfied that it was no spirit I had seen, but the veritable Brother Lazarus, or Dominique, or whatever his name was – for he might have half a dozen *aliases* for aught I knew –

though how he had contrived to come to life again, if he were dead, or by what means, or for what purpose, he could have persuaded the monks of Pierre Châtel of his decease, if the fact were not so, I could not conceive. There was no fastening to my door, and the first question that occurred to me was, whether this diabolical dream of his was ever repeated twice in one night. I had often heard that the magic number of *three* is apt to prevail on these occasions; and if so, he might come back again. I confess I was horridly afraid that he would. In the meantime I found myself shivering with cold, and was, perforce, obliged to creep into the bed, where indeed I was not much warmer. Sleep was of course out of the question. I lay listening anxiously, expecting either the stealthy foot of Brother Lazarus, or the glad sound of the matin bell, that would summon the monks from their cells, and wondering which I should hear first. Fortunately for my nerves it was the latter; and with alacrity I jumped out of bed, dressed myself, and descended to the chapel.

'When I reached it, the monks were on their knees, and their cowls being over their heads, I could not, as I ran my eye over them, distinguish my friend the somnambulist; but when they rose to their feet, his tall gaunt figure and high shoulders were easily discernible, and I had identified him before I saw his face. As they passed out of the chapel, I drew near and saluted him, observing that I believed I had the pleasure of seeing him before at Pierre Châtel; but he only shook his head, as if in token of denial; and as I could obtain no other answer to my further attempts at conversation, I left him, and proceeded to pay my respects to the prior. Of course I felt it my duty to mention my adventure of the previous night, for Brother Lazarus might on some occasion chance to act out his dream more effectually than he had had the opportunity of doing with me and Père Jolivet.

'"I am extremely sorry indeed," said Padre Pachorra, when he had heard my story; "they must have omitted to lock him into his cell last night. I must speak about it, for the consequences might have been very serious."

'"Very serious to me certainly," said I. "But how is it I see this man here alive? When I quitted Pierre Châtel I was told he was dead, and I saw the preparations for his burial."

' "They believed him dead," returned the prior; "but he was only in a trance; and after he was screwed down in his coffin, just as they were about to lower it into the grave, they felt something was moving within. They opened it, and Fra Dominique was found alive. It appeared, from his own account, that he had been suffering extremely from his dreadful dream, on occasion of the visit of some young stranger – an Englishman, I think."

' "Myself, I have no doubt," said I.

' "Probably," returned the prior, "and this was either the cause, or the consequence of his illness, for it is difficult to decide which."

' "But how came he here?" I inquired.

' "It was in this monastery he commenced his vocation," answered the padre. "He was only at Pierre Châtel by indulgence, and after this accident they did not wish to retain him."

' "I do not wonder at that, I am sure," said I. "But why did he deny having been there? When I spoke of it to him just now, he only shook his head."

' "He did not mean to deny it, I daresay," said the prior; "but he never speaks. Fra Dominique has taken a vow of eternal silence." '

Here Charles Lisle brought his story to a conclusion. 'How extremely shocking' exclaimed Lady Araminta; whilst the whole company agreed that he had made out an excellent excuse for wishing to sleep with his door locked, and that he had very satisfactorily entitled himself to the promised exchange.

Laura

SAKI

'You aren't really dying, are you?' asked Amanda.

'I have the doctor's permission to live till Tuesday,' said Laura.

'But today is Saturday; this is serious!' gasped Amanda.

'I don't know about it being serious; it is certainly Saturday,' said Laura.

'Death is always serious,' said Amanda.

'I never said I was going to die. I am presumably going to leave off being Laura, but I shall go on being something. An animal of some kind, I suppose. You see, when one hasn't been very good in the life one has just lived, one reincarnates in some lower organism. I've been cruel and mean and vindictive and all that sort of thing when circumstances seemed to warrant it.'

'Circumstances never warrant that sort of thing,' said Amanda.

'If you don't mind my saying so,' observed Laura, 'Egbert is a circumstance that would warrant any amount of that sort of thing. You're married to him – that's different; you've sworn to love, honour and endure him: I haven't'

'I don't see what's wrong with Egbert,' protested Amanda.

'Oh, I dare say the wrongness has been on my part,' admitted

Laura dispassionately; 'he has merely been the extenuating circumstance. He made a thin, peevish kind of fuss for instance, when I took the collie puppies from the farm out for a run the other day.'

'They chased his young broods of speckled Sussex and drove two sitting hens off their nest, besides running all over the flower beds. You know how devoted he is to his poultry and garden.'

'Anyway, he needn't have gone on about it for the entire evening and then have said, "Let's say no more about it," just when I was beginning to enjoy the discussion. That's where one of my petty vindictive revenges came in,' added Laura with an unrepentant chuckle; 'I turned the entire family of speckled Sussex into his seedling shed the day after the puppy episode.'

'How could you?' exclaimed Amanda.

'It came quite easy,' said Laura; 'two of the hens pretended to be laying at the same time, but I was firm.'

'And we thought it was an accident.'

'You see,' resumed Laura, 'I really *have* some grounds for supposing that my next incarnation will be in a lower organism. I shall be an animal of some kind. On the other hand, I haven't been a bad sort in my way, so I think I may count on being a nice animal, something elegant and lively, with a love of fun. An otter, perhaps.'

'I can't imagine you as an otter,' said Amanda.

'Well, I don't suppose you can imagine me as an angel, if it comes to that,' said Laura.

Amanda was silent. She couldn't.

'Personally I think an otter life would be rather enjoyable,' continued Laura; 'salmon to eat all year round, and the satisfaction of being able to fetch the trout in their own homes without having to wait for hours till they condescend to rise to the fly you've been dangling before them; and an elegant svelte figure—'

'Think of the otter hounds,' interposed Amanda; 'how dreadful to be hunted and harried and finally worried to death!'

'Rather fun with half the neighbourhood looking on, and

anyhow not worse than this Saturday-to-Tuesday business of dying by inches; and then I should go on into something else. If I had been a moderately good otter I suppose I should get back into human shape of some sort; probably something primitive – a little brown, unclothed Nubian boy, I should think.'

'I wish you would be serious,' sighed Amanda; 'you really ought to be if you're only going to live till Tuesday.'

As a matter of fact Laura died on Monday.

'So dreadfully upsetting,' Amanda complained to her uncle-in-law, Sir Lulworth Quayne. 'I've asked quite a lot of people down for golf and fishing, and the rhododendrons are just looking their best.'

'Laura always was inconsiderate,' said Sir Lulworth; 'she was born during Goodwood week, with an Ambassador staying in the house who hated babies.'

'She had the maddest kind of ideas,' said Amanda; 'do you know if there was any insanity in her family?'

'Insanity? No, I never heard of any. Her father lives in West Kensington, but I believe he's sane on all other subjects.'

'She had an idea that she was going to be reincarnated as an otter,' said Amanda.

'One meets with those ideas of reincarnation so frequently, even in the West,' said Sir Lulworth, 'that one can hardly set them down as being mad. And Laura was such an unaccountable person in this life that I should not like to lay down definite rules as to what she might be doing in an after state.'

'You think she really might have passed into some animal form?' asked Amanda. She was one of those who shape their opinions rather readily from the standpoint of those around them.

Just then Egbert entered the breakfast-room, wearing an air of bereavement that Laura's demise would have been insufficient, in itself, to account for.

'Four of my speckled Sussex have been killed,' he exlaimed; 'the very four that were to go to the show on Friday. One of them was dragged away and eaten right in the middle of that new carnation bed that I've been to such trouble and expense over. My best flower bed and my best fowls singled out for destruction; it almost seems as if the brute that did the deed had special knowledge how to be as devastating as possible in a short space of time.'

'Was it a fox, do you think? asked Amanda.

'Sounds more like a polecat,' said Sir Lulworth.

'No,' said Egbert, 'there were marks of webbed feet all over the place, and we followed the tracks down to the stream at the bottom of the garden; evidently an otter.'

Amanda looked quickly and furtively across at Sir Lulworth.

Egbert was too agitated to eat any breakfast, and went out to superintend the strengthening of the poultry yard defences.

'I think she might at least have waited till the funeral was over,' said Amanda in a scandalized voice.

'It's her own funeral, you know,' said Sir Lulworth; 'it's a nice point in etiquette how far one ought to show respect to one's own mortal remains.'

Disregard for mortuary convention was carried to further lengths next day; during the absence of the family at the funeral ceremony the remaining survivors of the speckled Sussex were massacred. The marauder's line of retreat seemed to have embraced most of the flower beds on the lawn, but the strawberry beds in the lower garden had also suffered.

'I shall get the otter hounds to come here at the earliest possible moment,' said Egbert savagely.

'On no account! You can't dream of such a thing!' exclaimed Amanda. 'I mean, it wouldn't do, so soon after a funeral in the house.'

'It's a case of necessity,' said Egbert; 'once an otter takes to that sort of thing it won't stop.' 'Perhaps it will go elsewhere now that there are no more fowls left,' suggested Amanda.

'One would think you wanted to shield this beast,' said Egbert.

'There's been so little water in the stream lately,' objected Amanda; 'it seems hardly sporting to hunt an animal when it has so little chance of taking refuge anywhere.'

'Good gracious!' fumed Egbert, 'I'm not thinking about sport. I want to have the animal killed as soon as possible.'

Even Amanda's opposition weakened when, during church time on the following Sunday, the otter made its way into the house, raided half a salmon from the larder and worried it into scaly fragments on the Persian rug in Egbert's studio.

'We shall have it hiding under our beds and biting pieces out of our feet before long,' said Egbert, and from what Amanda knew of this particular otter she felt that the possibility was not a remote one.

On the evening preceeding the day fixed for the hunt Amanda spent a solitary hour walking by the banks of the stream, making what she imagined to be hound noises. It was charitably supposed by those who overheard her performance, that she was practising for farmyard imitations at the forthcoming village entertainment.

It was her friend and neighbour, Aurora Burret, who brought her news of the day's sport.

'Pity you weren't out; we had a quite good day. We found it at once, in the pool just below your garden.'

'Did you – kill' asked Amanda.

'Rather. A fine she-otter. Your husband got rather badly bitten in trying to "tail it". Poor beast, I felt quite sorry for it, it had such a human look in its eyes when it was killed. You'll call me silly, but do you know who the look reminded me of? My dear woman, what is the matter?'

When Amanda had recovered to a certain extent from her attack of nervous prostration Egbert took her to the Nile Valley to recuperate. Change of scene speedily brought about the desired recovery of health and mental balance. The escapades of an adventurous otter in search of variation of diet were viewed in their proper light. Amanda's normally placid temperament reasserted itself. Even a hurricane of shouted curses, coming from her husband's dressing-room, in her husband voice, but hardly in his usual vocabulary, failed to disturb her serenity as she made a leisurely toilet one evening in a Cairo hotel.

'What is the matter? What has happened?' she asked in amused curiosity.

'The little beast has thrown all my clean shirts into the bath! Wait till I catch you, you little—'

'What little beast?' asked Amanda, suppressing a desire to laugh; Egbert's language was so hopelessly inadequate to express his outraged feelings.

'A little beast of a naked brown Nubian boy,' spluttered Egbert.

And now Amanda is seriously ill.

Smoke Ghost

FRITZ LEIBER

Miss Millick wondered just what had happened to Mr Wran. He kept making the strangest remarks when she took dictation. Just this morning he had quickly turned around and asked, 'Have you ever seen a ghost, Miss Millick?' And she had tittered nervously and replied, 'When I was a girl there was a thing in white that used to come out of the closet in the attic bedroom when I slept there, and moan. Of course it was just my imagination. I was frightened of lots of things.' And he had said, 'I don't mean that kind of ghost. I mean a ghost from the world today, with the soot of the factories on its face and the pounding of machinery in its soul. The kind that would haunt coal yards and slip around at night through deserted office buildings like this one. A real ghost. Not something out of books.' And she hadn't known what to say.

He'd never been like this before. Of course he might be joking, but it didn't sound that way. Vaguely Miss Millick wondered whether he mightn't be seeking some sort of sympathy from her. Of course, Mr Wran was married and had a little child, but that didn't prevent her from having daydreams. The daydreams were not very exciting, still they helped fill up her mind. But now he was asking her another of those unprecedented questions.

'Have you ever thought what a ghost of our times would look like, Miss Millick? Just picture it. A smoky composite face with the hungry anxiety of the unemployed, the neurotic restlessness of the person without purpose, the jerky tension of the high-pressure metropolitan worker, the uneasy resentment of the striker, the callous opportunism of the scab, the aggressive whine of the panhandler, the inhibited terror of the bombed civilian, and a thousand other twisted emotional patterns. Each one overlying and yet blending with the other, like a pile of semitransparent masks?'

Miss Millick gave a little self-conscious shiver and said, 'That would be terrible. What an awful thing to think of.'

She peered furtively across the desk. She remembered having heard that there had been something impressively abonormal about Mr Wran's childhood, but she couldn't recall what it was. If only she could do something – laugh at his mood or ask him what was really wrong. She shifted the extra pencils in her left hand and mechanically traced over some of the shorthand curlicues in her notebook.

'Yet, that's just what such a ghost or vitalized projection would look like, Miss Millick,' he continued, smiling in a tight way. 'It would grow out of the real world. It would reflect the tangled, sordid, vicious things. All the loose ends. And it would be very grimy. I don't think it would seem white or wispy, or favour graveyards. It wouldn't moan. But it would mutter unintelligibly, and twitch at your sleeve. Like a sick, surly ape. What would such a thing want from a person, Miss Millick? Sacrifice? Worship? Or just fear? What could you do to stop it from troubling you?'

Miss Millick giggled nervously. There was an expression beyond her powers of definition in Mr Wran's ordinary, flat-cheeked, thirtyish face, silhouetted against the dusty window. He turned away and stared out into the grey downtown atmosphere that rolled in from the railroad yards and the mills. When he spoke again his voice sounded far away.

'Of course, being immaterial, it couldn't hurt you physically – at first. You'd have to be peculiarly sensitive to see it, or be aware of it at all. But it would begin to influence your actions. Make you do this. Stop you from doing that. Although only a projection, it would gradually get its hooks into the world of things as they are. Might even get control of suitably vacuous minds. Then it could hurt whomever it wanted.'

Miss Millick squirmed and read back her shorthand, like the books said you should do when there was a pause. She became aware of the failing light and wished Mr Wran would ask her to turn on the overhead. She felt scratchy, as if soot were sifting down on to her skin.

'It's a rotten world, Miss Millick,' said Mr Wran, talking at the window. 'Fit for another morbid growth of superstition. It's time the ghosts, or whatever you call them, took over and began a ride of fear. They'd be no worse than men.'

'But' – Miss Millick's diaphragm jerked, making her titter inanely – 'of course, there aren't any such things as ghosts.'

Mr Wran turned around.

'Of course there aren't, Miss Millick,' he said in a loud, patronizing voice, as if she had been doing the talking rather than he. 'Science and common sense and psychiatry all go to prove it.'

She hung her head and might even have blushed if she hadn't felt so all at sea. Her leg muscles twitched, making her stand up, although she hadn't intended to. She aimlessly rubbed her hand along the edge of the desk.

'Why, Mr Wran, look what I got off your desk,' she said, showing him a heavy smudge. There was a note of clumsily playful reproof in her voice. 'No wonder the copy I bring you always gets so black. Somebody ought to talk to those scrub-women. They're skimping on your room.'

She wished he would make some normal joking reply. But instead he drew back and his face hardened.

'Well, to get back,' he rapped out harshly, and began to dictate.

When she was gone, he jumped up, dabbed his finger experimentally at the smudged part of the desk, frowned worriedly at the almost inky smears. He jerked open a drawer, snatched out a rag, hastily swabbed off the desk, crumpled the rag into a ball and tossed it back. There were three or four other rags in the drawer, each impregnated with soot.

Then he went over to the window and peered out anxiously through the dusk, his eyes searching the panorama of roofs, fixing on each chimney and water tank.

'It's a neurosis. Must be. Compulsions. Hallucinations,' he muttered to himself in a tired, distraught voice that would have made Miss Millick gasp. 'It's that damned mental abnormality cropping up in a new form. Can't be any other explanation. But it's so damned real. Even the soot. Good thing I'm seeing the psychiatrist. I don't think I could force myself to get on the elevated tonight.' His voice trailed off, he rubbed his eyes, and his memory automatically started to grind.

It had all begun on the elevated. There was a particular little sea of roofs he had grown into the habit of glancing at just as the packed car carrying him homeward lurched around a turn. A dingy, melancholy little world of tar-paper, tarred gravel and smoky brick. Rusty tin chimneys with odd conical hats suggested abandoned listening posts. There was a washed-out advertisement of some ancient patent medicine on the nearest wall. Superficially it was like ten thousand other drab city roofs. But he always saw it around dusk, either in the smoky half-light, or tinged with red by the flat rays of a dirty sunset, or covered by ghostly wind-blown white sheets of rain-splash, or patched with blackish snow; and it seemed unusually bleak and suggestive; almost beautifully ugly though in no sense picturesque; dreary, but meaningful. Unconsciously it came to symbolize for Catesby Wran certain disagreeable aspects of the frustrated, frightened century in which he lived, the jangled century of hate and heavy industry and total wars. The quick daily glance into the half darkness became an integral part of his life. Oddly, he never saw it in the morning, for it was then his habit to sit on the other side of the car, his head buried in the paper.

One evening towards winter he noticed what seemed to be a

shapeless black sack lying on the third roof from the tracks. He did not think about it. It merely registered as an addition to the well-known scene and his memory stored away the impression for further reference. Next evening, however, he decided he had been mistaken in one detail. Its colour and texture, and the grimy stains around it, suggested that it was filled with coal dust, which was hardly reasonable. Then, too, the following evening it seemed to have been blown against a rusty ventilator by the wind – which could hardly have happened if it were at all heavy. Perhaps it was filled with leaves. Catesby was surprised to find himself anticipating his next daily glance with a minor note of apprehension. There was something unwholesome in the posture of the thing that stuck in his mind – a bulge in the sacking that suggested a misshaped head peering around the ventilator. And his apprehension was justified, for that evening the thing was on the nearest roof, though on the farther side, looking as if it had just flopped down over the low brick parapet.

Next evening the sack was gone. Catesby was annoyed at the momentary feeling of relief that went through him, because the whole matter seemed too unimportant to warrant feelings of any sort. What difference did it make if his imagination had played tricks on him, and he'd fancied that the object was slowly crawling and hitching itself closer across the roofs? That was the way any normal imagination worked. He deliberately chose to disregard the fact that there were reasons for thinking his imagination was by no means a normal one. As he walked home from the elevated, however, he found himself wondering whether the sack was really gone. He seemed to recall a vague, smudgy trail leading across the gravel to the nearer side of the roof, which was masked by a parapet. For an instant an unpleasant picture formed in his mind – that of an inky, humped creature crouched behind the parapet, waiting.

The next time he felt the familiar grating lurch of the car, he caught himself trying not to look out. That angered him. He turned his head quickly. When he turned it back, his compact face was definitely pale. There had been only time for a fleeting rearward glance at the escaping roof. Had he actually seen in silhouette the upper part of a head of some sort peering over the parapet? Nonsense, he told himself. And even if he had seen something, there were a thousand explanations which did not involve the supernatural or even true hallucination. Tomorrow he would take a good look and clear up the whole matter. If necessary, he would visit the roof personally, though he hardly knew where to find it and disliked in any case the idea of pampering a silly fear.

He did not relish the walk home from the elevated that evening, and visions of the thing disturbed his dreams, and were in and out of his mind all next day at the office. It was then that he first began to relieve his nerves by making jokingly serious remarks about the supernatural to Miss Millick, who seemed properly mystified. It was on the same day, too, that he became aware of a growing antipathy to grime and soot. Everything he touched seemed gritty, and he found himself mopping and wiping at his desk like an old lady with a morbid fear of germs. He reasoned that there was no real change in his office, and that he'd just now become sensitive to the dirt that had always been there, but there was no denying an increasing nervousness. Long before the car reached the curve, he was straining his eyes through the murky twilight, determined to take in every detail.

Afterwards he realized he must have given a muffled cry of some sort, for the man beside him looked at him curiously, and the woman ahead gave him an unfavourable stare. Conscious of his own pallor and uncontrollable trembling, he stared back at them hungrily, trying to regain the feeling of security he had completely lost. They were the usual reassuringly wooden-faced people everyone rides home with on the elevated. But suppose he had pointed out to one of them what he had seen – that sodden, distorted face of sacking and coal dust, that boneless paw which waved back and forth, unmistakably in his direction, as if reminding him of a future appointment – he involuntarily shut his eyes tight. His thoughts were racing ahead to tomorrow evening. He pictured this same windowed oblong

123

of light and packed humanity surging around the curve – then an opaque monstrous form leaping out from the roof in a parabolic swoop – an unmentionable face pressed close against the window, smearing it with wet coal dust – huge paws fumbling sloppily at the glass—

Somehow he managed to turn off his wife's anxious inquiries. Next morning he reached a decision and made an appointment for that evening with a psychiatrist a friend had told him about. It cost him a considerable effort, for Catesby had a well-grounded distaste for anything dealing with psychological abnormality. Visiting a psychiastrist meant raking up an episode in his past which he had never fully described even to his wife. Once he had made the decision, however, he felt considerably relieved. The psychiatrist, he told himself, would clear everything up. He could almost fancy him saying, 'Merely a bad case of nerves. However, you must consult the oculist whose name I'm writing down for you, and you must take two of these pills in water every four hours,' and so on. It was almost comforting, and made the coming revelation he would have to make seem less painful.

But as the smoky dusk rolled in, his nervousness had returned and he had let his joking mystification of Miss Millick run away with him until he had realized he wasn't frightening anyone but himself.

He would have to keep his imagination under better control, he told himself, as he continued to peer out restlessly at the massive, murky shapes of the downtown office buildings. Why, he had spent the whole afternoon building up a kind of neo-medieval cosmology of superstition. It wouldn't do. He realized then that he had been standing at the window much longer than he'd thought, for the glass panel in the door was dark and there was no noise coming from the outer office. Miss Millick and the rest must have gone home.

It was then he made the discovery that there would have been no special reason for dreading the swing around the curve that night. It was, as it happened, a horrible discovery. For, on the shadowed roof across the street and four storeys below, he saw the thing huddle and roll across the gravel and, after one upward look of recognition, merge into the blackness beneath the water tank.

As he hurriedly collected his things and made for the elevator, fighting the panicky impulse to run, he began to think of hallucination and mild psychosis as very desirable conditions. For better or for worse, he pinned all his hopes on the psychiatrist.

'So you find yourself growing nervous and . . . er . . . jumpy, as you put it,' said Dr Trevethick, smiling with dignified geniality. 'Do you notice any more definite physical symptoms? Pain? Headache? Indigestion?'

Catesby shook his head and wet his lips, 'I'm especially nervous while riding in the elevated,' he murmured swiftly.

'I see. We'll discuss that more fully. But I'd like you first to tell me about something you mentioned earlier. You said there was something about your childhood that might predispose you to nervous ailments. As you know, the early years are critical ones in the development of an individual's behaviour pattern.'

Catesby studied the yellow reflections of frosted gloves in the dark surface of the desk. The palm of his left hand aimlessly rubbed the thick nap of the armchair. After a while he raised his head and looked straight into the doctor's small brown eyes.

'From perhaps my third to my ninth year,' he began, choosing the words with care, 'I was what you might call a sensory prodigy.'

The doctor's expression did not change. 'Yes?' he inquired politely.

'What I mean is that I was supposed to be able to see through walls, read letters through envelopes and books through their covers, fence and play ping-pong blind-folded, find things that were buried, read thoughts.' The words tumbled out.

'And could you?' The doctor's voice was toneless.

'I don't know. I don't suppose so,' answered Catesby, long-lost emotions flooding back into his voice. 'It's all confused now.

125

I thought I could, but then they were always encouraging me.
My mother . . . was . . . well . . . interested in psychic phenomena. I was . . . exhibited. I seem to remember seeing things
other people couldn't. As if most opaque objects were transparent. But I was very young. I didn't have any scientific criteria
for judgement.'

He was reliving it now. The darkened rooms. The earnest
assemblages of gawking, prying adults. Himself alone on a little
platform, lost in a straight-backed wooden chair. The black silk
handkerchief over his eyes. His mother's coaxing, insistent
questions. The whispers. The gasps. His own hate of the whole
business, mixed with hunger for the adulation of adults. Then
the scientists from the university, the experiments, the big test.
The reality of those memories engulfed him and momentarily
made his forget the reason why he was disclosing them to a
stranger.

'Do I understand that your mother tried to make use of you as
a medium for communicating with the . . . er . . . other world?'

Catesby nodded eagerly.

'She tried to, but she couldn't. When it came to getting in
touch with the dead, I was a complete failure. All I could do – or
thought I could do – was see real, existing three-dimensional
objects beyond the vision of normal people. Objects anyone
could have seen except for distance, obstruction, or darkness. It
was always a disappointment to Mother.'

He could hear her sweetish, patient voice saying, 'Try again,
dear, just this once. Katie was your aunt. She loved you. Try to
hear what she's saying.' And he had answered, 'I can see a
woman in a blue dress standing on the other side of Dick's
house.' And she had replied, 'Yes, I know, dear. But that's not
Katie. Katie's a spirit. Try again. Just this once, dear.' The
doctor's voice gently jarred him back into the softly gleaming
office.

'You mentioned scientific criteria for judgement, Mr Wran.
As far as you know, did anyone ever try to apply them to you?'

Catesby's nod was emphatic.

'They did. When I was eight, two young psychologists from the university got interested in me. I guess they did it for a joke at first, and I remember being very determined to show them I amounted to something. Even now I seem to recall how the note of polite superiority and amused sarcasm drained out of their voices. I suppose they decided at first that it was very clever trickery, but somehow they persuaded Mother to let them try me out under controlled conditions. There were lots of tests that seemed very businesslike after Mother's slipshod little exhibitions. They found I was clairvoyant – or so they thought. I got worked up and on edge. They were going to demonstrate my supernormal sensory powers to the university psychology faculty. For the first time I began to worry about whether I'd come through. Perhaps they kept me going at too hard a pace, I don't know. At any rate, when the test came, I couldn't do a thing. Everything became opaque. I got desperate and made things up out of my imagination. I lied. In the end I failed utterly, and I believe the two young psychologists got into a lot of hot water as a result.'

He could hear the brusque, bearded man saying, 'You've been taken in by a child, Flaxman, a mere child. I'm greatly disturbed. You've put yourself on the same plane as common charlatans. Gentlement, I ask you to banish from your minds this whole sorry episode. It must never be referred to.' He winced at the recollection of his feeling of guilt. But at the same time he was beginning to feel exhilarated and almost light-hearted. Unburdening his long-repressed memories had altered his whole viewpoint. The episodes on the elevated began to take on what seemed their proper proportions as merely the bizarre workings of overwrought nerves and an overly suggestible mind. The doctor, he anticipated confidently, would disentangle the obscure subconscious causes, whatever they might be. And the whole business would be finished off quickly, just as his childhood experience – which was beginning to seem a little ridiculous now – had been finished off.

'From that day on,' he continued, 'I never exhibited a trace of my supposed powers. My mother was frantic and tried to sue the university. I had something like a nervous breakdown. Then the divorce was granted, and my father got custody of me. He did his best to make me forget it. We went on long outdoor vacations and did a lot of athletics, associated with normal matter-of-fact people. I went to business college eventually, I'm in advertising now. But,' Catesby paused, 'now that I'm having nervous symptoms, I've wondered if there mightn't be a connection. It's not a question of whether I was really clairvoyant or not. Very likely my mother taught me a lot of unconscious deceptions, good enough to fool even young psychology instructors. But don't you think it may have some important bearing on my present condition?'

For several moments the doctor regarded him with a professional frown. Then he said quietly, 'And is there some . . . er . . . more specific connection between your experiences then and now? Do you by any chance find that you are once again beginning to . . . er . . . see things?'

Catesby swallowed. He had felt an increasing eagerness to unburden himself of his fears, but it was not easy to make a beginning, and the doctor's shrewd question rattled him. He forced himself to concentrate. The thing he thought he had seen on the roof loomed up before his inner eye with unexpected vividness. Yet it did not frighten him. He groped for words.

Then he saw the doctor was not looking at him but over his shoulder. Colour was draining out of the doctor's face and his eyes did not seem so small. Then the doctor sprang to his feet, walked past Catesby, threw up the window and peered into the darkness.

As Catesby rose, the doctor slammed down the window and said in a voice whose smoothness was marred by a slight, persistent gasping, 'I hope I haven't alarmed you. I saw the face of . . . er . . . a Negro prowler on the fire escape. I must have frightened him, for he seems to have gotten out of sight in a hurry. Don't give it another thought. Doctors are frequently bothered by *voyeurs* . . . er . . . Peeping Toms.'

'A Negro?' asked Catesby, moistening his lips.

The doctor laughed nervously. 'I imagine so, though my first odd impression was that it was a white man in blackface. You see, the colour didn't seem to have any brown in it. It was dead-black.'

Catesby moved towards the window. There were smudges on the glass. 'It's quite all right, Mr Wran.' The doctor's voice had acquired a sharp note of impatience, as if he were trying hard to reassume his professional authority. 'Let's continue our conversation. I was asking you if you were' – he made a face – 'seeing things.'

Catesby's whirling thoughts slowed down and locked into place. 'No, I'm not seeing anything that other people don't see, too. And I think I'd better go now. I've been keeping you too long.' He disregarded the doctor's half-hearted gesture of denial. 'I'll phone you about the physical examination. In a way you've already taken a big load off my mind.' He smiled woodenly. 'Good night, Dr Trevethick.'

Catesby Wran's mental state was a peculiar one. His eyes searched every angular shadow, he glanced sideways down each chasm-like alley and barren basement passageway, and kept stealing looks at the irregular line of the roofs, yet he was hardly conscious of where he was going. He pushed away the thoughts that came into his mind, and kept moving. He became aware of a slight sense of security as he turned into a lighted street where there were people and high buildings and blinking signs. After a while he found himself in the dim lobby of the structure that housed his office. Then he realized why he couldn't go home, why he daren't go home – after what had happened at the office of Dr Trevethick.

'Hello, Mr Wran,' said the night elevator man, a burly figure in overalls, sliding open the grille-work door to the old-fashioned cage. 'I didn't know you were working nights now, too.'

Catesby stepped in automatically. 'Sudden rush of orders,' he murmured inanely. 'Some stuff that has to be gotten out.'

The cage creaked to a stop at the top floor. 'Be working very late, Mr Wran?'

He nodded vaguely, watched the car slide out of sight, found his keys, swiftly crossed the outer office, and entered his own. His hand went out to the light switch, but then the thought occurred to him that the two lighted windows, standing out against the dark bulk of the building, would indicate his wherabouts and serve as a goal towards which something could crawl and climb. He moved his chair so that the back was against the wall and sat down in the semi-darkness. He did not remove his overcoat.

For a long time he sat there motionless, listening to his own breathing and the faraway sounds from the streets below; the thin metallic surge of the crosstown streetcar, the farther one of the elevated, faint lonely cries and honking, indistinct rumblings. Words he had spoken to Miss Millick in nervous jest came back to him with the bitter taste of truth. He found himself unable to reason critically or connectedly, but by their own volition thoughts rose up into his mind and gyrated slowly and rearranged themselves with the inevitable movement of planets.

Gradually his mental picture of the world was transformed. No longer a world of material atoms and empty space, but a world in which the bodiless existed and moved according to its own obscure laws or unpredictable impulses. The new picture illuminated with dreadful clarity certain general facts which had always bewildered and troubled him and from which he had tried to hide; the inevitability of hate and war, the diabolically timed mischances which wreck the best of human intentions, the walls of wilful misunderstanding that divide one man from another, the eternal vitality of cruelty and ignorance and greed. They seemed appropriate now, necessary parts of the picture. And superstition only a kind of wisdom.

Then his thoughts returned to himself and the question he had asked Miss Millick, 'What would such a thing want from a person? Sacrifices? Worship? Or just fear? What could you do to stop it from troubling you?' It had become a practical question.

With an explosive jangle, the phone began to ring. 'Cate, I've been trying everywhere to get you,' said his wife. 'I never thought you'd be at the office. What are you doing? I've been worried.'

He said something about work.

'You'll be home right away?' came the faint anxious question. 'I'm a little frightened. Ronny just had a scare. It woke him up. He kept pointing to the window saying, "Black man, black man." Of course it's something he dreamed. But I'm frightened. You will be home? What's that, dear? Can't you hear me?'

'I will. Right away,' he said. Then he was out of the office, buzzing the night bell and peering down the shaft.

He saw it peering up the shaft at him from the deep shadows three floors below, the sacking face pressed against the iron grille-work. It started up the stair at a shockingly swift, shambling gait, vanishing temporarily from sight as it swung into the second corridor below.

Catesby clawed at the door to the office, realized he had not locked it, pushed it in, slammed and locked it behind him, retreated to the other side of the room, cowered between the filing cases and the wall. His teeth were clicking. He heard the grown of the rising cage. A silhouette darkened the frosted glass of the door, blotting out part of the grotesque reverse of the company name. After a little the door opened.

The big-globed overhead light flared on and, standing inside the door, her hand on the switch, was Miss Millick.

'Why, Mr Wran,' she stammered vacuously. 'I didn't know you were here. I'd just come in to do some extra typing after the movie. I didn't . . . but the lights weren't on. What were you—'

He stared at her. He wanted to shout in relief, grab hold of her, talk rapidly. He realized he was grinning hysterically.

'Why, Mr Wran, what's happened to you?' she asked embarrassedly, ending with a stupid titter. 'Are you feeling sick? Isn't there something I can do for you?'

131

It couldn't hurt you physically – at first . . .

He shook his head jerkily and managed to say, 'No, I'm just leaving. I was doing some extra work myself.'

'But you *look* sick,' she insisted, and walked over towards him. He inconsequently realized she must have stepped in mud, for her high-heeled shoes left neat black prints.

'Yes, I'm sure you must be sick. You're so terribly pale.' She sounded like an enthusiastic, incompetent nurse. Her face brightened with a sudden inspiration. 'I've got something in my bag, that'll fix you up right away,' she said. 'It's for indigestion.'

She fumbled at her stuffed oblong purse. He noticed that she was absent-mindedly holding it shut with one hand while she tried to open it with the other. Then, under his very eyes, he saw her bend back the thick prongs of metal locking the purse as if they were tinfoil, or as if her fingers had become a pair of steel pliers.

Instantly his memory recited the words he had spoken to Miss Millick that afternoon. 'It couldn't hurt you physically – at first . . . gradually get its hooks into the world . . . might even get control of suitably vacuous minds. Then it could hurt whom- ever it wanted.' A sickish, cold feeling grew inside him. He began to edge towards the door.

But Miss Millick hurried ahead of him.

'You don't have to wait, Fred,' she called. 'Mr Wran's decided to stay a while longer.'

The door of the cage shut with a mechanical rattle. The cage creaked. Then she turned around in the door.

'Why, Mr Wran,' she gurgled reproachfully. 'I just couldn't thing of letting you go home now. I'm sure you're terribly unwell. Why, you might collapse in the street. You've just got to stay here until you feel different.'

The creaking died away. He stood in the centre of the office, motionless. His eyes traced the coal-black course of Miss Millick's footprints to where she stood blocking the door. Then a sound that was almost a scream was wrenched out of him, for it seemed to him that the blackness was creeping up her legs under the thin stockings.

'Why, Mr Wran,' she said, 'You're acting as if you were crazy. You must lie down for a while. Here, I'll help you off with your coat.'

The nauseously idiotic and rasping note was the same; only it had been intensified. As she came towards him he turned and ran through the storeroom, clattered a key desperately at the lock of the second door to the corridor.

'Why, Mr Wran,' he heard her call, 'are you having some kind of a fit? You must let me help you.'

The door came open and he plunged out into the corridor and up the stairs immediately ahead. It was only when he reached the top that he realized the heavy steel door in front of him led to the roof. He jerked up the catch.

'Why, Mr Wran, you mustn't run away. I'm coming after you.'

Then he was out on the gritty gravel of the roof. The night sky was clouded and murky, with a faint pinkish glow from the neon signs. From the distant mills rose a ghostly spurt of flame. He ran to the edge. The street lights glared dizzily upwards. Two men were tiny round blobs of hat and shoulders. He swung around.

The thing was in the doorway. The voice was no longer solicitous but moronically playful, each sentence ending in a titter.

'Why, Mr Wran, why have you come up here? We're all alone. Just think, I might push you off.'

The thing came slowly towards him. He moved backwards until his heel touched the low parapet. Without knowing why, or what he was going to do, he dropped to his knees. He dared not look at the face as it came nearer, a focus for the worst in the world, a gathering point for poisons from everywhere. Then the lucidity of terror took possession of his mind, and words formed on his lips.

'I will obey you. You are my god,' he said. 'You have supreme power over man and his animals and his machines. You rule this city and all others. I recognize that.'

Again the titter, closer. 'Why, Mr Wran, you never talked like this before. Do you mean it?'

'The world is yours to do with as you will, save or tear to pieces,' he answered fawningly, the words automatically fitting themselves together in vaguely liturgical patterns. 'I recognize that. I will praise, I will sacrifice. In smoke and soot I will worship you for ever.'

The voice did not answer. He looked up. There was only Miss Millick, deathly pale and swaying drunkenly. Her eyes were closed. He caught her as she wobbled towards him. His knees gave way under the added weight and they sank down together on the edge of the roof.

After a while she began to twitch. Small noises came from her throat and her eyelids edged open.

'Come on, we'll go downstairs,' he murmured jerkily, trying to draw her up. 'You're feeling bad.'

'I'm terribly dizzy,' she whispered. 'I must have fainted, I didn't eat enough. And then I'm so nervous lately, about the war and everything, I guess. Why, we're on the roof! Did you bring me up here to get some air? Or did I come up without knowing it? I'm awfully foolish. I used to walk in my sleep, my mother said.'

As he helped her down the stairs, she turned and looked at him. 'Why, Mr Wran,' she said, faintly, 'you've got a big black smudge on your forehead. Here, let me get it off for you.' Weakly she rubbed at it with her handkerchief. She started to sway again and he steadied her.

'No, I'll be all right,' she said. 'Only I feel cold. What happened, Mr Wran? Did I have some sort of fainting spell?'

He told her it was something like that.

Later, riding home in the empty elevated car, he wondered how long he would be safe from the thing. It was a purely practical problem. He had no way of knowing, but instinct told him he had satisfied the brute for some time. Would it want more when it came again? Time enough to answer that question when it arose. It might be hard, he realized, to keep out of an insane asylum. With Helen and Ronny to protect, as well as himself, he would have to be careful and tight-lipped. He began to speculate as to how many other men and women had seen the thing or things like it.

The elevated slowed and lurched in a familiar fashion. He looked at the roofs near the curve. They seemed very ordinary, as if what made them impressive had gone away for a while.

The Phantom Ship

CAPTAIN MARRYAT

The ship was ready to sail for Europe; and Philip Vanderdecken went on board – hardly caring whither he went. To return to Terneuse was not his object; he could not bear the idea of revisiting the scene of so much happiness and so much misery. Amine's form was engraven on his heart, and he looked forward with impatience to the time when he should be summoned to join her in the land of spirits.

He had awakened as from a dream, after so many years of aberration of intellect. He was no longer the sincere Catholic that he had been; for he never thought of religion without his Amine's cruel fate being brought to his recollection. Still he clung on to the relic – he believed in that – and that only. It was his god – his creed – his everything – the passport for himself and for his father into the next world – the means whereby he should join his Amine – and for hours would he remain holding in his hand that object so valued – gazing upon it – recalling every important event in his life, from the death of his poor mother, and his first sight of Amine; to the last dreadful scene. It was to him a journal of his existence, and on it were fixed all his hopes for the future.

'When! oh, when is it to be accomplished!' was the constant subject of his reveries. 'Blessed, indeed, will be the day when I leave this world of hate, and seek that other in which "the weary are at rest".'

The vessel on board of which Philip was embarked as a passenger was the *Nostra Señora da Monte*, a brig of three hundred tons, bound for Lisbon. The Captain was an old Portuguese, full of superstition, and fond of arrack – a fondness rather unusual with the people of his nation. They sailed from Goa, and Philip was standing abaft, and sadly contemplating the spire of the Cathedral, in which he had last parted with his wife, when his elbow was touched, and he turned round.

'Fellow-passenger again!' said a well-known voice – it was that of the pilot Schriften.

There was no alteration in the man's appearance; he showed no marks of declining years; his one eye glared as keenly as ever.

Philip started, not only at the sight of the man, but at the reminiscences which his unexpected appearance brought to his mind. It was but for a second, and he was again calm and pensive.

'You here again, Schriften?' observed Philip. 'I trust your appearance forebodes the accomplishment of my task.'

'Perhaps it does,' replied the pilot; 'we both are weary.'

Philip made no reply; he did not even ask Schriften in what manner he had escaped from the fort; he was indifferent about it; for he felt that the man had a charmed life.

'Many are the vessels that have been wrecked, Philip Vander-decken, and many the souls summoned to their account by meeting with your father's ship, while you have been so long shut up,' observed the pilot.

'May our next meeting with him be more fortunate – may it be the last!' replied Philip.

'No, no! rather may he fulfil his doom, and sail till the day of judgement,' replied the pilot with emphasis.

'Vile caitiff! I have a foreboding that you will not have your detestable wish. Away! – leave me! or you shall find that although this head is blanched by misery, this arm has still some power.'

Schriften scowled as he walked away; he appeared to have some fear of Philip, although it was not equal to his hate. He now resumed his former attempts of stirring up the ship's company against Philip, declaring that he was a Jonas, who would occasion the loss of the ship, and that he was connected with *The Flying Dutchman*. Philip very soon observed that he was avoided; and he resorted to counter-statements, equally injurious to Schriften, whom he declared to be a demon. The appearance of Schriften was so much against him, while that of Philip, on the contrary, was so prepossessing, that the people on board hardly knew what to think. They were divided; some were on the side of Philip – some on that of Schriften; the captain and many others looking with equal horror upon both, and longing for the time when they could be sent out of the vessel.

The captain, as we have before observed, was very superstitious, and very fond of his bottle. In the morning he would be sober and pray; in the afternoon he would be drunk, and swear at the very saints whose protection he had invoked but a few hours before.

'May Holy Saint Antonio preserve us, and keep us from temptation,' said he, on the morning after a conversation with the passengers about the Phantom Ship. 'All the saints protect us from harm,' continued he, taking off his hat reverentially, and crossing himself. 'Let me but rid myself of these two dangerous men without accident, and I will offer up a hundred wax candles, of three ounces each, to the shrine of the Virgin, upon my safe anchoring off the tower of Belem.' In the evening he changed his language.

'Now, if that Maldetto Saint Antonio don't help us, may he feel the coals of hell yet; damn him and his pigs too; if he has the courage to do his duty, all will be well; but he is a cowardly wretch, he cares for nobody, and will not help those who call upon him in trouble. Carambo! that for you,' exclaimed the captain, looking at the small shrine of the saint at the bittacle, and snapping his fingers at the image – 'that for you, you useless wretch, who never help us in our trouble. The Pope must canonize some better saints for us, for all we have now are worn out. They could do something formerly, but now I would not give two ounces of gold for the whole calendar; as for you, you lazy old scoundrel,' continued the captain, shaking his fist at poor Saint Antonio.

The ship had now gained off the southern coast of Africa, and was about one hundred miles from the Lagullas coast; the morning was beautiful, a slight ripple only turned over the waves, the breeze was light and steady, and the vessel was standing on a wind, at the rate of about four miles an hour.

'Blessed be the holy saints,' said the captain, who had just gained the deck; 'another little slant in our favour, and we shall lay our course. Again I say, blessed be the holy saints, and particularly our worthy patron Saint Antonio, who has taken under his peculiar protection the *Nostra Señora da Monte*. We have a prospect of fine weather; come, signors, let us down to breakfast, and after breakfast we will enjoy our cigarros upon the deck.'

But the scene was soon changed; a bank of clouds rose up from the eastward, with a rapidity that, to the seamen's eyes, was unnatural, and it soon covered the whole firmament; the sun was obscured, and all was one deep and unnatural gloom; the wind subsided, and the ocean was hushed. It was not exactly dark, but the heavens were covered with one red haze, which gave an appearance as if the world was in a state of conflagration.

In the cabin the increased darkness was first observed by Philip, who went on deck; he was followed by the captain and passengers, who were in a state of amazement. It was unnatural and incomprehensible. 'Now, holy Virgin, protect us – what can this be?' exclaimed the captain in a fright. 'Holy Saint Antonio, protect us – but this is awful.'

'There! there!' shouted the sailors, pointing to the beam of the vessel. Every eye looked over the gunnel to witness what had occasioned such exclamations. Philip, Schriften, and the captain were side by side. On the beam of the ship, not more than two cables' length distant, they beheld, slowly rising out of the water, the tapering masthead and spars of another vessel. She rose, and rose gradually; her top-masts and top-sail yards, with the sails set, next made their appearance; higher and higher she rose up from the element. Her lower masts and rigging, and, lastly, her hull showed itself above the surface. Still she rose up till her ports, with her guns, and at last the whole of her floatage was above water, and there she remained close to them, with her main-yard squared, and hove-to.

'Holy Virgin!' exclaimed the captain, breathless; 'I have know ships to *go down*, but never to *come up* before. Now will I give one thousand candles, of ten ounces each; to the shrine of the Virgin to save us in this trouble. One thousand wax candles! Hear me, blessed lady; ten ounces each. Gentlemen,' cried the captain to the passengers, who stood aghast, 'why don't you promise? Promise, I say; promise, at all events.'

'The Phantom Ship – *The Flying Dutchman*,' shrieked Schriften; 'I told you so, Philip Vanderdecken; there is your father. He! he!'

Philip's eyes had remained fixed on the vessel; he perceived that they were lowering down a boat from her quarter. 'It is possible,' thought he, 'I shall now be permitted!' and Philip put his hand into his bosom and grasped the relic.

The gloom now increased, so that the strange vessel's hull could but just be discovered through the murky atmosphere. The seamen and passengers threw themselves down on their knees, and invoked their saints. The captain ran down for a candle, to light before the image of Saint Antonio, which he took out of its shrine, and kissed with much apparent affection and devotion, and then replaced.

Shortly afterwards the splash of oars was heard alongside, and a voice calling out, 'I say, my good people, give us a rope from forward.'

No one answered, or complied with the request. Schriften only went up to the captain, and told him that if they offered to send letters they must not be received or the vessel would be doomed, and all would perish.

A man now made his appearance from over the gunnel, at the gangway. 'You might as well have let me had a side rope, my hearties,' said he, as he stepped on deck; 'where is the captain?'

'Here,' replied the captain, trembling from head to foot. The man who accosted him appeared a weather-beaten seaman, dressed in a fur cap and canvas petticoats; he held some letters in his hand.

'What do you want?' at last screamed the captain.

'Yes – what do you want?' continued Schriften. 'He! he!'

'What, you here, pilot?' observed the man; 'well – I thought you had gone to Davy's locker, long enough ago.'

'He! he!' replied Schriften, turning away.

'Why the fact is, captain, we have had very foul weather, and we wish to send letters home; I do believe that we shall never get round this Cape.'

'I can't take them,' cried the captain.

'Can't take them! well, it's very odd – but every ship refuses to take our letters; it's very unkind – seamen should have a feeling for brother seamen, especially in distress. God knows, we wish to see our wives and families again; and it would be a matter of comfort to them, if they only could hear from us.'

'I cannot take your letters – the saints preserve us,' replied the captain.

'We have been a long while out,' said the seaman, shaking his head.

'How long?' inquired the captain, not knowing what to say.

'We can't tell; our almanack was blown overboard, and we have lost our reckoning. We never have our latitude exact now, for we cannot tell the sun's declination for the right day.'

'Let *me see* your letters,' said Philip, advancing, and taking them out of the seaman's hands.

'They must not be touched,' screamed Schriften.

'Out, monster!' replied Philip, 'who dares interfere with me?'

'Doomed – doomed – doomed!' shrieked Schriften, running and down the deck, and then breaking into a wild fit of laughter.

'Touch not the letters,' said the captain, trembling as if in an ague fit.

Philip made no reply, but held his hand out for the letters.

'Here is one from our second mate, to his wife at Amsterdam, who live on Waser Quay.'

'Waser Quay has long been gone, my good friend; there is now a large dock for ships where it once was,' replied Philip.

'Impossible!' replied the man; 'here is another from the boastwain to his father, who lives in the old market-place.'

'The old market-place has long been pulled down, and there now stands a church upon the spot.'

'Impossible!' replied the seaman; 'here is another from myself to my sweetheart, Vrow Ketser – with money to buy her a new brooch.'

Philip shook his head – 'I remember seeing an old lady of that name buried some thirty years ago.'

'Impossible! I left her young and blooming. Here's one for the house of Slutz & Co., to whom the ship belongs.'

'There is no such house now', replied Philip; 'but I have heard that many years ago there was a firm of that name.'

'Impossible! you must be laughing at me. Here is a letter from our captain to his son . . .'

'Give it me,' cried Philip, seizing the letter. He was about to break the seal when Schriften snatched it out of his hand, and threw it over the lee gunnel.

'That's a scurvy trick for an old shipmate,' observed the seaman. Schriften made no reply, but catching up the other letters which Philip had laid down on the capstan, he hurled them after the first.

The strange seaman shed tears, and walked again to the side. 'It is very hard – very unkind,' observed he, as he descended; 'the time may come when you may wish that your family should know your situation.' So saying, he disappeared – in a few seconds was heard the sound of the oars, retreating from the ship.

'Holy Saint Antonio!' exclaimed the captain, 'I am lost in wonder and fright. Steward, bring me up the arrack.'

The steward ran down for the bottle; being as much alarmed as his captain, he helped himself before he brought it up to his commander. 'Now,' said the captain, after keeping his mouth for two minutes to the bottle, and draining it to the bottom, 'what is to be done next?'

'I'll tell you,' said Schriften, going up to him. 'That man there has a charm hung round his neck; take it from him and throw it overboard, and your ship will be saved; if not, it will be lost, with every soul on board.'

'Yes, yes, it's all right, depend upon it,' cried the sailors.

'Fools,' replied Philip, 'do you believe that wretch? Did you not hear the man who came on board recognize him, and call him shipmate? He is the party whose presence on board will prove so unfortunate.'

'Yes, yes,' cried the sailors, 'it's all right, the man did call him shipmate.'

'I tell you it's all wrong,' cried Schriften; 'that is the man, let him give up the charm.'

'Yes, yes; let him give up the charm,' cried the sailors, and they rushed upon Philip.

Philip started back to where the captain stood. 'Madmen, know ye what ye are about? It is the holy cross that I wear round my neck. Throw it overboard if you dare, and your souls are lost for ever': and Philip took the relic from his bosom and showed it to the captain.

'No, no, men,' exclaimed the captain, who was now more settled in his nerves; 'that won't do – the saints protect us.'

The seamen, however, became clamorous; one portion were for throwing Schriften overboard, the other for throwing Philip; at last, the point was decided by the captain, who directed the small skiff, hanging astern, to be lowered down, and ordered both Philip and Schriften to get into it. The seamen approved of this arrangement, as it satisfied both parties. Philip made no objection; Schriften screamed and fought, but he was tossed into the boat. There he remained trembling in the stern sheets, while Philip, who had seized the sculls, pulled away from the vessel in the direction of the Phantom Ship.

In a few minutes the vessel which Philip and Schriften had

left was no longer to be discerned through the thick haze; the Phantom Ship was still in sight, but at a much greater distance from them than she was before. Philip pulled hard towards her, but although hove-to, she appeared to increase her distance from the boat. For a short time he paused on his oars to regain his breath, when Schriften rose up and took his seat in the stern sheets of the boat. 'You may pull and pull, Philip Vanderdecken,' observed Schriften; 'but you will not gain that ship – no, no, that cannot be – we may have a long cruise together, but you will be as far from your object at the end of it as you are now at the commencement. Why don't you throw me overboard again? You would be all the lighter – He! he!'

'I threw you overboard in a state of frenzy,' replied Philip, 'when you attempted to force from me my relic.'

'And have I not endeavoured to make others take it from you this very day? – Have I not – He! he!'

'You have,' rejoined Philip; 'but I am now convinced, that you are as unhappy as myself, and that in what you are doing, you are only following your destiny, as I am mine. Why and wherefore I cannot tell, but we are both engaged in the same mystery; – if the success of my endeavours depends upon guarding the relic, the success of yours depends upon your obtaining it, and defeating my purpose by so doing. In this matter we are both agents, and you have been, as far as my mission is concerned, my most active enemy. But, Schriften, I have not fogotten, and never will, that you kindly *did advise* my poor Amine; that you prophesied to her what would be her fate, if she did not listen to your counsel; that you were no enemy of hers, although you have been, and are still mine. Although my enemy, for her sake *I forgive you*, and will not attempt to harm you.'

'You do then *forgive your enemy*, Philip Vanderdecken; you have now made me your friend, and your wishes are about to be accomplished. You would know who I am. Listen: – when your father, defying the Almighty's will, in his rage took my life, he was vouchsafed a chance of his doom being cancelled, through the merits of his son. I had also my appeal which was for *vengeance*; it was granted that I should remain on earth, and thwart your will. That as long as we were enemies, you should not suceed; but that when you had conformed to the highest attribute of Christianity, proved on the holy cross, that of *forgiving your enemy*, your task should be fulfilled. Philip Vanderdecken, you have forgiven your enemy, and both our destinies are now accomplished.'

As Schriften spoke, Philip's eyes were fixed upon him. He extended his hand to Philip – it was taken; and as it was pressed, the form of the pilot wasted as it were into the air, and Philip found himself alone.

'Father of Mercy, I thank Thee.' said Philip, 'that my task is done, and that I again may meet my Amine.'

Philip then pulled towards the Phantom Ship, and found that she no longer appeared to leave him; on the contrary, every minute he was nearer and nearer, and at last he threw in his oars, climbed up her sides, and gained her deck.

The crew of the vessel crowded round him.

'Your captain,' said Philip; 'I must speak with your captain.'

'Who shall I say, sir?' demanded one, who appeared to be the first mate.

'Who?' replied Philip. 'Tell him his son would speak to him, his son Philip Vanderdecken.'

Shouts of laughter from the crew followed this answer of Philip's; and the mate, as soon as they ceased, observed with a smile:

'You forget, sir, perhaps you would say his father.'

'Tell him his son, if you please,' replied Philip; 'take no note of grey hairs.'

'Well, sir, here he is coming forward,' replied the mate, stepping aside, and pointing to the captain.

'What is all this?' inquired the captain.

'Are you Philip Vanderdecken, the captain of this vessel?'

'I am, sir,' replied the other.

'You appear not to know me! But how can you? You saw me

but when I was only three years old; yet may you remember a letter which you gave to your wife.'

'Ha!' replied the captain; 'and who then are you?'

'Time has stopped with you, but with those who live in the world he stops not! and for those who pass a life of misery, he hurries on still faster. In me, behold your son, Philip Vanderdecken, who has obeyed your wishes; and after a life of such peril and misery as few have passed, has at last fulfilled his vow, and now offer to his father this precious relic that he required to kiss.'

Philip drew out the relic, and held it towards his father. As if a flash of lightning had passed through his mind, the captain of the vessel started back, clasped his hands, fell on his knees, and wept.

'My son, my son!' exclaimed he, rising, and throwing himself into Philip's arms, 'my eyes are opened – the Almighty knows how long they have been obscured.' Embracing each other, they walked aft, away from the men, who were still crowded at the gangway.

'My son, my noble son, before the charm is broken – before we resolve, as we must, into the elements, oh! let me kneel in thanksgiving and contrition: my son, my noble son, receive a father's thanks,' exclaimed Vanderdecken. Then with tears of joy and penitence he humbly addressed himself to that Being whom he once so awfully defied.

The elder Vanderdecken knelt down: Philip did the same; still embracing each other with one arm, while they raised on high the other, and prayed.

For the last time the relic was taken from the bosom of Philip and handed to his father – and his father raised his eyes to heaven and kissed it. And as he kissed it, the long tapering upper spars of the Phantom vessel, the yards and sails that were set, fell into dust, fluttered in the air and sank upon the wave. Then mainmast, foremast bowsprit, everything above the deck, crumbled into atoms and disappeared.

Again he raised the relic to his lips and the work of destruction continued, the heavy iron guns sank through the decks and disappeared; the crew of the vessel (who were looking on) crumbled down into skeletons, and dust, and fragments of ragged garments; and there were none left on board the vessel in the semblance of life but the father and the son.

Once more did he put the sacred emblem to his lips, and the beams and timber separated, the decks of the vessel slowly sank, and the remnants of the hull floated upon the water; and as father and son – the one young and vigorous, the other old and decrepit – still kneeling, still embracing, with their hands raised to heaven, sank slowly under the deep blue wave, the lurid sky was for a moment illuminated by a lightning cross.

Then did the clouds which obscured the heavens roll away swift as thought – the sun again burst out in all his splendour – the rippling waves appeared to dance with joy. The screaming seagull again whirled in the air, and the scared albatross once more slumbered on the wing. The porpoise tumbled and tossed in his sportive play, the albicore and dolphin leaped from the sparkling sea. All nature smiled as if it rejoiced that the charm was dissolved for ever, and that the Phantom Ship was no more.

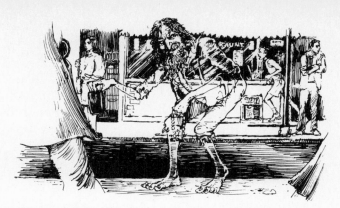

An Adelaide Ghost

LEON GARFIELD

I saw him in Rundle Street, where rainbow stores and signs, opals and ice-cream, and faces of such brazen health that they put the sun to shame passed me by in a shaking tapestry of heat. He was picking pockets.

An old, old man in a frayed blue coat to which three brass buttons clung like gleaming orphans in a shipwreck; a weird old man in tattered white knee-breeches below which poked skinny shanks and great naked feet, richly spotted with filth. He was wisping about among the crowds, grinning roguishly and dipping his mittened fingers where he would.

From his outlandish costume I took him to be a disused actor, who, having fallen on bad times, was busily making the most of them; and I waited, with a mixture of pity and fascination, for the moment when he'd be caught. It seemed inevitable as he made no attempt at caution. 'Once an actor always an actor,' I thought. 'Even their sins have to be public.'

But, somehow, he seemed to bear a charmed life (or he was better at his trade than I supposed); he continued his thieving with a truly dazzling impudence, even bowing to his victims with an old-world courtesy, as if what he was doing was the most charming thing imaginable.

I wondered if I ought to interfere. In common decency I

149

ought to have done something; but I was a stranger in the town, still dazed from travel and with lost time beating inside me like a dinosaur's heart . . . lumbering towards a glazed extinction. I'd already tried reviving myself with strong spirits; but, although they were willing, the flesh proved weak, and the town and the sky were apt to sway . . .

Sick and bemused, I watched the aged villain sidle up beside a woman who stood, like a gaudy tooth, in the mouth of a bright arcade. Her handbag was hanging open – like another arcade and in went that wicked old man's hand. I was going to call out – to warn her, when she shut her bag with such a crocodile snap that she must have had those trespassing fingers off at the knuckles. I winced at the violence of it, and then reflected thankfully that he'd been punished enough. I sighed and sat back, as it were, inside my head again . . .

Suddenly he saw me watching him. He looked briefly alarmed and then, to my horrible embarrassment, he stretched out both his wrists and came straight at me, as if imploring me to arrest him for his crimes!

I tried to escape, to wave him away, but it was no use; he kept coming after me, nodding his head in the meekest and most abject fashion. I felt stupid and helpless, and, at the same time, furiously angry with the theatrical old thief. He was deliberately making a fool of me; he knew quite well that I could never have stood up in court and given evidence against him. He knew I'd have been ashamed to accuse so old and pitiful a vagrant. Oh yes, he could see right through me.

And – I could see right through him! It happened in an instant. It was as he crossed a patch of uninterrupted sun. The light went clean through him! He was a tissue-paper man, of overlapping greys and blues and yellows, with sturdy legs, sandalled feet and pavement moving, it seemed, inside of him!

What I'd taken for a charmed life had been a charmed death. He was a phantom! An apparition! A ghost!

'D'ye see me? D'ye see me?' he whispered, coming close. His voice was thin and sharp, like a toothache in the mind; and his breath reeked of worms.

'No – no! Go away!'

'Then who are ye talking to?' demanded the cunning spectre. 'Who are ye bidding begone?'

'Myself. I'm talking to myself. I'm ill . . . from travel and too much wine.'

'*In vino veritas*!' said he, with a triumphant snigger. 'There's truth in wine, didn't ye know?'

'If you're the truth,' said I, 'then please heaven send me a lie!'

'Holy Mother of God!' said he, with the broadest of Irish brogues. 'Niver say sich a thing to a ghost, sir!'

All this in blazing Rundle Street, where crowds sauntered, children fought and shrieked and a white-faced traveller swayed and argued, it seemed, with himself.

'A hair of the dog that bit ye,' advised the hateful thing that floated by my side. 'That's what'll set ye up, sir!'

I shuddered at the thought.

'Pluck a hair from that savage beast,' said I, 'and you'll drive it mad with rage!'

He chuckled – that is, if you can imagine a toothache chuckling – and indulged himself in a passing pocket. I hated him worse than ever. Although I knew that no one but myself could see him, I felt an acute sense of shame to be in his company; it was as if, at any moment, he *would* be seen, and I would be taken for his accomplice. He was, in all respects, repulsive. He was a disgrace to the dead and a perpetual misery to the living.

Picking pockets was by no means the worst of his offences. He had an unwholesome passion for pretty girls, of which Rundle Street was always full.

He'd wisp up behind them, slip his vague arms round their waists and caress them shamelessly, so that they'd seem to be enveloped in a dirty mist, with the merest sketches of hands stroking them, and the notion of an elderly Irish face, floating and blurring their unsuspecting cheeks.

He was a vulgar and horrible old ghost; and he was made ten times worse by having about him the relics of Gaelic charm. He'd smile most engagingly . . . and his lips would writhe back helplessly almost to his ears, revealing quantities of damaged bone. It was impossible to look at him without feeling sick. He was so transparent that the whole world seemed to be his moving, steaming guts; and all bright eyes, smiling lips and flowing hair made ulcers in his liver and lungs.

'In Dublin's fair city,' he began to sing screechingly, as he flitted from female to female, 'where girls are so pretty,

I first set me eyes on sweet Molly Malone!

She wheeled her wheelbarrow through the streets broad and narrow,

Crying, Cockles and Mussels, alive, alive oh!'

He danced on in front of me and, floating backwards and waving his arms, encouraged me to join in the chorus:

'Alive, alive oh!' I responded unthinkingly; and a party of Japanese ladies turned on me with porcelain smiles.

'Alive, alive oh! Crying, Cockles and Mussels, alive, alive, oh!'

'Why that's a fine thing,' said he, 'to sing to a man long dead, sir!'

He winked, and three rows of oriental pearls glimmered through him, turning him into a trinket box of blisters, cysts and boils.

Then he screeched on with the ballad of the fishmonger's pretty daughter:

'She died of a faver, and no one could save her,

And that was the end of sweet Molly Malone.

Her ghost wheels her barrow through streets broad and narrow,

Crying, Cockles and Mussels, alive, alive, oh!'

'Alive, alive oh!' I began, when he halted me with a look that might have been tragic, had I not been able to see a child all over ice-cream and a laughing mother right through it.

'That's enough sir. They're all dead now. Cockles and Mussels and Molly Malone. D'ye know Dublin, sir?'

'No.'

'God save us! A traveller like yourself and not to know

Dublin? Then ye'll not know Drogheda nor the green, green banks of the Boyne, neither?'

'No. Not them, either.'

'Then will ye do me a favour, sir? An old ghost asks ye. When ye return across the ocean, go to Ireland and take a stroll by the lovely banks of the Boyne. And as ye walk, sing soft and sweet to the ghost of – Molly Malone.'

'And what shall I say to her if she appears?' I asked ironically. 'Shall I inquire after her business affairs?'

He winked; and his eye seemed to come out, leaving a smudge in the air.

'Just you say to her, sir, that you've seen the ghost of Gentleman George when ye was at the other side of the world.'

'And what shall I tell her of Gentleman George?'

'Have ye no imagination, sir? Say he'll come back to her one of these fine days! Say that ye saw him sinning in Rundle Street in the fond hopes of being taken up by the ghost of a magistrate and being transported straight back from whence he'd come!'

'Did she promise to wait for you, then?'

'We kissed and dallied, sir. We exchanged our vows.'

'How long ago?'

'Two hundred years, sir.'

'A long time for a pretty girl to wait.'

'Alas, sir! She never grew old. She was drownded when she was scarce eighteen. The cursed ferryman tipped her into the Boyne!'

He laid his hands across his heart, in which a window of cameras winked expensively, like open sores.

Then, linking his touchless arms through mine, he drew me on and confided his history, with that curious mixture of pain and pride with which a sufferer tells you of his weeks in hospital and of the operation that saved his life. But somehow, whatever he said, however earnestly he expressed himself, it was impossible to believe him. He was so transparent that there was always some mocking contradiction oozing and blistering inside his heart or head.

He was, he said, the ghost of a convict who'd been transported to Botany Bay some hundred and eighty years before. He'd been born in the town of Maynooth, in County Kildare, in the year 1753. He'd been born in lawful wedlock, he assured me; but from what he told me after, it would seem that that was his only lawful act.

He stole as easily as he breathed. His father had been a silversmith and his mother had been a sempstress; so it was in his blood.

'How so?' I asked him

'Why, sir – a knowledge of pockets and a passion for what goes into 'em!'

I smiled involuntarily; and this pleased him inordinately, as it seemed to convince him that he'd not lost his Irish charm. He told me that, when he'd been a tiny infant, he'd been taken to kiss the Blarney Stone, which had given him the gift of the honied tongue. I wondered, privately, that he'd not stolen that stone while he was at it. Certainly, he seemed to have stolen everything else.

He'd stolen in churches, he'd stolen in streets; he'd stolen in pleasure gardens and he'd even nicked a diamond coronet and star at the court of St James's on the Queen's own birthday. He'd pilfered in Dublin, he'd thieved in Cork; he'd stolen in Newcastle, he'd stolen in York; also in fair Edinburgh, although, he admitted with a frown, Scottish pockets seemed to be sewn on the tight side. He'd been in prison and had stolen there. He had worn the whole world, it seemed, like a suit of old clothes, with every pocket his own. Had his arm been long enough, he'd have picked God's pocket and stolen the sun.

All this he confessed to me, as if expecting admiration for his impudence; but once again his transparency undid him. Whenever I glanced at him (and I tried not to), I saw, not a charming rogue, but a hideous sketch of an old man, with all the freshness of life moving about inside him like a wormy, cancerous growth.

'And do you think,' said I, interrupting him, 'that the ghost of sweet Molly Malone will want you back again, Gentleman

George? She was a fishmonger. That's an honest trade. What would she want with a thief?'

'Poetical licence,' said he. 'Her name was Mary. Mary Egerton. And she was an actress . . . the finest that ever trod the boards! Nonetheless, sir, I take yer point. So ye may tell her, if ye'll be so good, that Gentlemen George died an honest man. That'll please her, sir. Tell her that I had me moment of glory when I saw the light!'

I also saw the light; and a great muddy mess it made inside of him. It boiled and bubbled like a filthy drain.

'I was condemned, sir, for the pilfering of a paltry silver watch. 'Twas a sort of justice, I suppose. I'd hoped for time, in a manner o' speaking, to serve me, and I ended up serving time. In a word, sir, I was sentenced to be transported to Botany Bay for the term of me natural life.'

'And your moment of glory?'

'On the way over, sir. It happened at sea. There was a great storm and I came face to face with me Maker and saw the error of me ways.'

'Is that all?'

'Not a bit of it! That was the beginning. There was, d'ye see, a mutiny in the air. A great deal of talk of Freedom and Revolution and taking the ship. They asked me to join 'em . . . but, as I told ye, I'd seen the error of me ways. George Barrington, I said to meself (Barrington's me name, sir!), mutiny is a sin. And sins never prosper. So I went to the captain and quietly put him on his guard.

'Now this good man turned out to be a gentleman. "George Barrington," said he. "By coming to me like that you have saved this vessel and, maybe, two hundred human lives."

'"'Tis nothing, sir," said I. "I only did me duty."

'"George Barrington," said he. "Duty must be rewarded."

'"Captain," said I. "Duty is its own reward. I ask no more than that."

'"George Barrington," said he. "You are an honest man. I think that maybe England has misjudged you."

155

' "Captain," said I. "That may very well be. But anyone can make a mistake. I forgive them."

' "George Barrington," said he. "You show a fine nature. But New South Wales shall make no such mistake. You shall be free."

' "Captain," said I. "We are all under the hand of the Almighty. Whatever is in that hand, I will take."

'When we landed at Port Jackson, I was awarded a cash prize by the ship's owner and, soon after, on account of me tact and skill and general popularity, I was made superintendent of all the convicts; a situation, sir, which I filled with honour and distinction till the end of me days.

'Had the same trust been shown me in England, sir, I might say that, saving me Catholic faith, I'd have become Prime Minister of that fair land. When I died, sir, there were tears washing the streets of Sydney.'

'Then why,' I asked him, as he snivelled slightly, 'are you up to your old tricks again? What are you doing picking pockets in Adelaide when you might be with the ghosts of your Sydney friends? What became of your moment of glory, Gentelman George?'

'Well might you ask,' said he, drying his eyes on a lady's blouse. 'There's none more unforgiving than the dead, sir. That's what became of it.'

He paused and crucified himself across the front of a hamburger stand, where strings of wrinkled onions made more tears down his cheeks.

'They cast me out. No sooner was I buried than they took their revenge. Even my wife and daughters have turned their backs on me.'

'Why so, Gentleman George?'

'Because I am a ghost. Because they can see through me. When we were all solid flesh and blood and quick with life, they were glad enough to shake me by the hand and thank me from the bottoms of their hears for saving them from the dreadful consequences of the mutiny. "George Barrington," they said. "You saviour of us all!" But now, when all me life and charm is gone, they look right through me and see what ought never to be seen. They see that, maybe, I was thinking chiefly of meself. They see horrible things and a creeping, mean betrayal.'

'But you did save them!'

'Yes indeed, sir. But, maybe, my motives were a trifle mixed. Now you, sir, can understand that a soul may have mixed motives and yet be more good than bad. Not so the dead. They're a virtuous lot, sir. Virtuous to excess. They cannot say, as you might, "He's only human!" Oh no! Not to a ghost. There's no compassion in the grave. I tell you sir, if you've an enemy, forgive him while there's time. Once dead, there's no forgiving any more. There's not a dead man from here to Dublin who'd shake me by the hand!'

'Nor a woman, neither, Gentleman George?'

He shook his head.

'I've tried to sin, sir. That's partly why you see me at it now. I need punishment, sir. I need it badly. But it's no use. I've not the substance to be wicked. Even a five dollar bill goes through me fingers like a pint of air; and all I feel is an itch too deep for scratching.'

'And would you have me say all this to – to sweet Molly Malone?'

'And she not yet eighteen?' sighed the old ghost. 'Ah! Ye're a hard man, sir! Just you tell her, when ye stroll by the banks of the Boyne, that Gentleman George still loves her even as he did when they parted, which was before ever he darkened his heart. Tell her that, when the trade winds blow long and fair, I'll be coming back . . . back . . . back . . . back.'

I stared at him, expecting to see some poisonous eruption within, some ulcerous sight, some malignant contradiction of his words.

But I could no longer see through him. Either I was recovering – or he was. He was translucent, not transparent. He stood before me like a marvellous tear in the air. He was shining, shining. . . .

'I love her,' he whispered; and dwindled away. . . .

Man-Size In Marble

EVELYN NESBIT

Although every word of this story is as true as despair, I do not expect people to believe it. Nowadays a 'rational explanation' is required before belief is possible. Let me then, at once, offer the 'rational explanation' which finds most favour among those who have heard the tale of my life's tragedy. It is held that we were 'under a delusion', Laura and I, on that 31st October; and that this supposition places the whole matter on a satisfactory and believable basis. The reader can judge, when he, too, has heard my story, how far this is an 'explanation', and in what sense it is 'rational'. There were three who took part in this: Laura and I and another man. The other man still lives, and can speak to the truth of the least credible part of my story.

I never in my life knew what it was to have as much money as I required to supply the most ordinary needs – good colours, books, and cab-fares – and when we were married we knew quite well that we should only be able to live at all by 'strict punctuality and attention to business'. I used to paint in those days, and Laura used to write, and we felt sure we could keep the pot at least simmering. Living in town was out of the question, so we went to look for a cottage in the country, which should be

158

at once sanitary and picturesque. So rarely do these two qualities meet in one cottage that our search was for some time quite fruitless. We tried advertisements, but most of the desirable rural residences which we did look at proved to be lacking in both essentials, and when a cottage chanced to have drains it always had stucco as well and was shaped like a tea-caddy. And if we found a vine or rose-covered porch, corruption invariably lurked within. Our minds got so befogged by the eloquence of house-agents and the rival disadvantages of the fever-traps and outrages to beauty which we had seen and scorned, that I very much doubt whether either of us, on our wedding morning, knew the difference between a house and a haystack. But when we got away from friends and house-agents, on our honeymoon, our wits grew clear again, and we knew a pretty cottage when at least we saw one. It was at Brenzett – a little village set on a hill over against the southern marshes. We had gone there, from the seaside village where we were staying, to see the church, and two fields from the church we found this cottage. It stood quite by itself, about two miles from the village. It was a long, low building, with rooms sticking out in unexpected places. There was a bit of stone-work – ivy-covered and moss-grown, just two old rooms, all that was left of a big house that had once stood there – and round this stone-work the house had grown up. Stripped of its roses and jasmine it would have been hideous. As it stood it was charming, and after a brief examination we took it. It was absurdly cheap. The rest of our honeymoon we spent in grubbing about in secondhand shops in the county town, picking up bits of old oak and Chippendale chairs for our furnishing. We wound up with a run up to town and a visit to Liberty's, and soon the low oak-beamed lattice-windowed rooms began to be home. There was a jolly old-fashioned garden, with grass paths, and no end of hollyhocks and sunflowers, and big lilies. From the window you could see the marsh-pastures, and beyond them the blue, thin line of the sea. We were as happy as the summer was glorious, and settled down into work sooner than we ourselves expected. I was never tired of sketching the view and the wonderful cloud effects from the open lattice, and Laura would sit at the table and write verses about them, in which I mostly played the part of foreground.

We got a tall old peasant woman to do for us. Her face and figure were good, though her cooking was of the homeliest; but she understood all about gardening, and told us all the old names of the coppices and cornfields, and the stories of the smugglers and highwaymen, and, better still, of the 'things that walked,' and of the 'sights' which met one in lonely glens of a starlight night. She was a great comfort to us, because Laura hated houskeeping as much as I loved folklore, and we soon came to leave all the domestic business to Mrs Dorman, and to use her legends in little magazine stories which brought in the jingling guineas.

We had three months of married happiness, and did not have a single quarrel. One October evening I had been down to smoke a pipe with the doctor – our only neighbour – a pleasant young Irishman. Laura had stayed at home to finish a comic sketch of a village episode for the *Monthly Marplot*. I left her laughing over her own jokes, and came in to find her a crumpled heap of pale muslin weeping on the window seat.

'Good heavens, my darling, what's the matter?' I cried, taking her in my arm. She leaned her little dark head against my shoulder and went on crying. I had never seen her cry before – we had always been so happy, you see – and I felt sure some frightful misfortune had happened.

'What *is* the matter? Do speak.'

'It's Mrs Dorman,' she sobbed.

'What has she done?' I inquired, immensely relieved.

'She says she must go before the end of the month, and she says her niece is ill; she's gone down to see her now, but I don't believe that's the reason, because her niece is always ill. I believe someone has been setting her against us. Her manner was so queer—'

'Never mind, Pussy,' I said; 'whatever you do, don't cry, or I shall have to cry too, to keep you in countenance, and then you'll never respect your man again!'

She dried her eyes obediently on my handkerchief, and even smiled faintly.

'But you see,' she went on, 'it is really serious, because these village people are so sheepy, and if one won't do a thing you may be quite sure none of the others will. And I shall have to cook the dinners, and wash up the hateful greasy plates: and you'll have to carry cans of water about, and clean the boots and knives – and we shall never have any time for work, or earn any money, or anything. We shall have to work all day, and only be able to rest when we are waiting for the kettle to boil!'

I represented to her that even if we had to perform these duties, the day would still present some margin for other toils and recreations. But she refused to see the matter in any but the greyest light. She was very unreasonable, my Laura, but I could not have loved her any more if she had been as reasonable as Whately.

'I'll speak to Mrs Dorman when she comes back, and see if I can't come to terms with her,' I said. 'Perhaps she wants a rise in her screw. It will be all right. Let's walk up to the church.'

The church was a large and lonely one, and we loved to go there, especially upon bright nights. The path skirted a wood, cut through it once, and ran along the crest of the hill through two meadows, and round the churchyard wall, over which the old yews loomed in black masses of shadow. This path, which was partly-paved, was called 'the bier-balk,' for it had long been the way by which the corpses had been carried to burial. The churchyard was richly treed, and was shaded by great elms which stood just outside and stretched their majestic arms in benediction over the happy dead. A large, low porch let one into the building by a Norman doorway and a heavy oak door studded with iron. Inside, the arches rose into darkness, and between them the reticulated windows, which stood out white in the moonlight. In the chancel, the windows were of rich glass, which showed in faint light their noble colouring, and made the black oak of the choir pews hardly more solid than the shadows. But on each side of the altar lay a grey marble figure of a knight in full plate armour lying upon a low slab, with hands held up in everlasting prayer, and these figures, oddly enough, were always to be seen if there was any glimmer of light in the church. Their names were lost, but the peasants told of them that they had been fierce and wicked men, marauders by land and sea, who had been the scourge of their time, and had been guilty of deeds so foul that the house they had lived in – the big house, by the way, that had stood on the site of our cottage – had been stricken by lightning and the vengeance of Heaven. But for all that, the gold of their heirs had bought them a place in the church. Looking at the bad hard faces reproduced in the marble, this story was easily believed.

The church looked at its best and weirdest on that night, for the shadows of the yew trees fell through the windows upon the floor of the nave and touched the pillars with tattered shade. We sat down together without speaking, and watched the solemn beauty of the old church, with some of that awe which inspired its early builders. We walked to the chancel and looked at the sleeping warriors. Then we rested some time on the stone seat in the porch, looking out over the stretch of quiet moonlit meadows, feeling in every fibre of our being the peace of the night and of our happy love; and came away at last with a sense that even scrubbing and blackleading were but small troubles at their worst.

Mrs Dorman had come back from the village, and I at once invited her to a *tête-à-tête*.

'Now, Mrs Dorman,' I said, when I had got her into my painting-room, 'what's all this about your not staying with us?'

'I should be glad to get away, sir, before the end of the month,' she answered, with her usual placid dignity.

'Have you any fault to find, Mrs Dorman?'

'None at all sir; you and your lady have always been most kind, I'm sure –'

'Well, what is it? Are your wages not high enough?'

'No sir, I gets quite enough.'

'Then why not stay?'

'I'd rather not' – with some hesitation – 'my niece is ill.'

'But your niece has been ill ever since we came.'

No answer. There was a long and awkward silence. I broke it.

'Can't you stay for another month?' I asked.

'No, sir. I'm bound to go by Thursday.'

And this was Monday!

'Well, I must say, I think you might have let us know before. There's no time now to get any one else, and your mistress is not fit to do heavy housework. Can't you stay till next week?'

I was convinced that all she wanted was a brief holiday, which we should have been willing enough to let her have, as soon as we could get a substitute.

'But why must you go this week?' I persisted. 'Come, out with it.'

Mrs Dorman drew the little shawl, which she always wore, tightly across her bosom, as though she were cold. Then she said, with a sort of effort –

'They say, sir, as this was a big house in Catholic times, and there was a many deeds done here.'

The nature of the 'deeds' might be vaguely inferred from the inflection of Mrs Dorman's voice – which was enough to make one's blood run cold. I was glad that Laura was not in the room. She was always nervous, as highly-strung natures are, and I felt that these tales about our house, told by this old peasant woman, with her impressive manner and contagious credulity, might have made our home less dear to my wife.

'Tell me all about it, Mrs Dorman,' I said; 'you needn't mind about telling me. I'm not like the young people who make fun of such things.'

Which was partly true.

'Well, sir' – she sank her voice – 'you may have seen in the church, beside the altar, two shapes.'

'You mean the effigies of the knights in armour,' I said cheerfully.

'I mean them two bodies, drawed out man-size in marble,' she returned, and I had to admit that her description was a thousand times more graphic than mine, to say nothing of a certain weird force and uncanniness about the phrase 'drawed out man-size in marble.'

'They do say, as on All Saints' Eve them two bodies sits up on their slabs, and gets off of them, and then walks down the aisle, *in their marble*' – (another good phrase, Mrs Dorman) – 'and as the church clock strikes eleven they walks out of the church door, and over the graves, and along the bier-balk, and if it's a wet night there's the wet marks of their feet in the morning.'

'And where do they go?' I asked, rather fascinated.

'They comes back here to their home, sir, and if any one meets them –'

'Well, what then?' I asked.

But no – not another word could I get from her, save that her niece was ill and she must go. After what I had heard I scorned to discuss the niece, and tried to get from Mrs Dorman more details of the legend. I could get nothing but warnings.

'Whatever you do, sir, lock the door early on All Saints' Eve, and make the cross-sign over the doorstep and on the windows.'

'But has any one ever seen these things?' I persisted.

'That's not for me to say. I know what I know, sir.'

'Well, who was here last year?'

'No one, sir; the lady as owned the house only stayed here in summer, and she always went to London a full month afore *the* night. And I'm sorry to inconvenience you and your lady, but my niece is ill and I must go on Thursday.'

I could have shaken her for her absurd reiteration of that obvious fiction, after she had told me her real reasons.

She was determined to go, nor could our united entreaties move her in the least.

I did not tell Laura the legend of the shapes that 'walked in their marble', partly because a legend concerning our house might perhaps trouble my wife, and partly, I think, from some more occult reason. This was not quite the same to me as any other story, and I did not want to talk about it till the day was over. I had very soon ceased to think of the legend, however. I was painting a portrait of Laura, against the lattice window, and

I could not think of much else. I had got a splendid background of yellow and grey sunset, and was working away with enthusiasm at her face. On Thursday, Mrs Dorman went. She relented, at parting, so far as to say –

'Don't you put yourself about too much, ma'am, and if there's any little thing I can do next week, I'm sure I shan't mind.'

From which I inferred that she wished to come back to us after Hallowe'en. Up to the last she adhered to the fiction of the niece with touching fidelity.

Thursday passed off pretty well. Laura showed marked ability in the matter of steak and potatoes, and I confess that my knives, and the plates, which I insisted upon washing, were better done than I had dared to expect.

Friday came. It is about what happened on that Friday that this is written. I wonder if I should have believed it, if any one had told it to me. I will write the story of it as quickly and plainly as I can. Everything that happened on that day burnt into my brain. I shall not forget anything, nor leave anything out.

I got up early, I remember, and lighted the kitchen fire, and had just achieved a smoky success, when my little wife came running down, as sunny and sweet as the clear October morning itself. We prepared breakfast together, and found it very good fun. The housework was soon done, and when brushes and brooms and pails were quiet again, the house was still indeed. It is wonderful what a difference one makes in a house. We really missed Mrs Dorman, quite apart from considerations concerning pots and pans. We spent the day in dusting our books and putting them straight, and dined gaily on cold steak and coffee. Laura was, if possible, brighter and gayer and sweeter than usual, and I began to think that a little domestic toil was really good for her. We had never been so merry since we were married, and the walk we had that afternoon was, I think, the happiest time of my life. When we had watched the deep scarlet clouds slowly pale into leaden grey against a pale-green sky, and saw the white mists curl up along the hedgerows in the distant marsh, we came back to the house, silently, hand in hand.

'You are sad, my darling,' I said, half-jestingly, as we sat down together in our little parlour. I expected a disclaimer, for my own silence had been the silence of complete happiness. To my surprise she said –

'Yes, I think I am sad, or rather I am uneasy. I don't think I'm very well. I have shivered three or four times since we came in and it is not cold, is it?'

'No,' I said, and hoped it was not a chill caught from the treacherous mists that roll up from the marshes in the dying light. No – she said, she did not think so. Then, after a silence she spoke suddenly –

'Do you ever have presentiments of evil?'

'No,' I said, smiling, 'and I shouldn't believe in them if I had.'

'I do,' she went on; 'the night my father died I knew it, though he was right away in the north of Scotland.' I did not answer in words.

She sat looking at the fire for some time in silence, gently stroking my hand. At last she sprang up, came behind me, and, drawing my head back, kissed me.

'There, it's over now,' she said. 'What a baby I am! Come, light the candles, and we'll have some of these new Rubinstein duets.'

And we spent a happy hour or two at the piano.

At about half-past ten I began to long for the good-night pipe, but Laura looked so white that I felt it would be brutal of me to fill our sitting-room with the fumes of strong cavendish.

'I'll take my pipe outside,' I said.

'Let me come, too.'

'No, sweetheart, not tonight; you're much too tired. I shan't be long. Get to bed, or I shall have an invalid to nurse tomorrow as well as the boots to clean.'

I kissed her and was turning to go, when she flung her arms round my neck, and held me as if she would never let me go again. I stroked her hair.

'Come, Pussy, you're over-tired. The housework has been too much for you.'

166

She loosened her clasp a little and drew a deep breath.

'No. We've been very happy today, Jack, haven't we? Don't stay out too long.'

'I won't, my dearie.'

I strolled out of the front door, leaving it unlatched. What a night it was! The jagged masses of heavy dark cloud were rolling at intervals from horizon to horizon, and thin white wreaths covered the stars. Through all the rush of the cloud river, the moon swam, breasting the waves and disappearing again in the darkness. When now and again her light reached the woodlands they seemed to be slowly and noiselessly waving in time to the swing of the clouds above them. There was a strange grey light over all the earth; the fields had that shadowy bloom over them which only comes from the marriage of dew and moonshine, or frost and starlight.

I walked up and down, drinking in the beauty of the quiet earth and changing sky. The night was absolutely silent. Nothing seemed to be abroad. There was no skurrying of rabbits, or twitter of the half-asleep birds. And though the clouds went sailing across the sky, the wind that drove them never came low enough to rustle the dead leaves in the woodland paths. Across the meadows I could see the church tower standing out black and grey against the sky. I walked there thinking over our three months of happiness – and of my wife, her dear eyes, her loving ways. Oh, my little girl! my own little girl; what a vision came then of a long, glad life for you and me together!

I heard a bell-beat from the church. Eleven already! I turned to go in, but the night held me. I could not go back into our little warm rooms yet. I would go up to the church. I felt vaguely that it would be good to carry my love and thankfulness to the sanctuary whither so many loads of sorrow and gladness had been borne by the men and women of the dead years.

I looked in at the low window as I went by. Laura was half lying on her chair in front of the fire. I could not see her face, only her little head showed dark against the pale blue wall. She was quite still. Asleep, no doubt. My heart reached out to her, as I went on. There must be a God, I thought, and a God who was good. How otherwise could anything so sweet and dear as she have ever been imagined?

I walked slowly along the edge of the wood. A sound broke the stillness of the night, it was a rustling in the wood. I stopped and listened. The sound stopped too. I went on, and now distinctly heard another step than mine answer mine like an echo. It was a poacher or a wood-stealer, most likely, for these were not unknown in our Arcadian neighbourhood. But whoever it was, he was a fool not to step more lightly. I turned into the wood, and now the footstep seemed to come from the path I had just left. It must be an echo, I thought. The wood looked perfect in the moonlight. The large dying ferns and the brushwood showed where through thinning foliage the pale light came down. The tree trunks stood up like Gothic columns all around me. They reminded me of the church, and I turned into the bier-balk, and passed through the corpse-gate between the graves to the low porch. I paused for a moment on the stone seat where Laura and I had watched the fading-landscape. Then I noticed that the door of the church was open, and I blamed myself for having left it unlatched the other night. We were the only people who ever cared to come to the church except on Sundays, and I was vexed to think that through our carelessness the damp autumn airs had had a chance of getting in and injuring the old fabric. I went in. It will seem strange, perhaps, that I should have gone half-way up the aisle before I remembered – with a sudden chill, followed by a sudden rush of self-contempt – that this was the very day and hour when, according to tradition, the 'shapes drawed out man-size in marble' began to walk.

Having thus remembered the legend, and remembered it with a shiver, of which I was ashamed, I could not do otherwise than walk up towards the altar, just to look at the figures – as I said to myself; really what I wanted was to assure myself, first, that I did not believe the legend, and, secondly, that it was not true. I was rather glad that I had come. I thought now I could tell Mrs

There, in the recess of the window, I saw her

Dorman how vain her fancies were, and how peacefully the marble figures slept on through the ghastly hour. With my hands in my pockets I passed up the aisle. In the grey dim light the eastern end of the church looked larger than usual, and the arches above the two tombs looked larger too. The moon came out and showed me the reason. I stopped short, my heart gave a leap that nearly choked me, and then sank sickeningly.

The 'bodies drawed out man-size' *were gone*, and their marble slabs lay wide and bare in the vague moonlight that slanted through the east window.

Were they really gone? or was I mad? Clenching my nerves, I stooped and passed my hand over the smooth slabs, and felt their flat unbroken surface. Had some one taken the things away? Was it some vile practical joke? I would make sure, anyway. In an instant I had made a torch of a newspaper, which happened to be in my pocket, and lighting it held it high above my head. Its yellow glare illumined the dark arches and those slabs. The figures *were* gone. And I was alone in the church; or was I alone?

And then a horror seized me, a horror indefinable and indescribable – an overwhelming certainty of supreme and accomplished calamity. I flung down the torch and tore along the aisle and out through the porch, biting my lips as I ran to keep myself from shrieking aloud. Oh, was I mad – or what was this that possessed me? I leaped the churchyard wall and took the straight cut across the fields, led by the light from our windows. Just as I got over the first stile, a dark figure seemed to spring out of the ground. Mad still with that certainty of misfortune, I made for the thing that stood in my path, shouting, 'Get out of the way, can't you!'

But my push met with a more vigorous resistance than I had expected. My arms were caught just above the elbow and held as in a vice, and the raw-boned Irish doctor actually shook me.

'Would ye?' he cried, in his own unmistakable accents – 'would ye, then?'

'Let me go, you fool,' I gasped. 'The marble figures have gone from the church; I tell you they've gone.'

He broke into a ringing laugh. 'I'll have to give ye a draught tomorrow, I see. Ye've bin smoking too much and listening to old wives' tales.

'I tell you, I've seen the bare slabs.'

'Well, come back with me. I'm going up to old Palmer's – his daughter's ill; we'll look in at the churchyard and let me see the bare slabs.'

'You go if you like,' I said, a little less frantic for his laughter; 'I'm going home to my wife.'

'Rubbish, man,' said he; 'd'ye think I'll permit of that? Are ye to go saying all yer life that ye've seen solid marble endowed with vitality, and me to go all me life saying ye were a coward? No, sir – ye shan't do ut.'

The night air – a human voice – and I think also the physical contact with this six feet of solid common sense, brought me back a little to my ordinary self, and the word 'coward' was a mental shower-bath.

'Come on, then,' I said sullenly; 'perhaps you're right.'

He still held my arm tightly. We got over the stile and back to the church. All was still as death. The place smelt very damp and earthy. We walked up the aisle. I am not ashamed to confess that I shut my eyes: I knew the figures would not be there. I heard Kelly strike a match.

'Here they are, ye see, right enough; ye've been dreaming or drinking, asking yer pardon for the imputation.'

I opened my eyes. By Kelly's expiring vesta I saw two shapes lying 'in their marble' on their slabs. I drew a deep breath, and caught his hand.

'I'm awfully indebted to you,' I said. 'It must have been some trick of light, or I have been working rather hard, perhaps that's it. Do you know, I was quite convinced they were gone.'

'I'm aware of that,' he answered rather grimly; 'ye'll have to be careful of that brain of yours, my friend, I assure ye.'

He was leaning over and looking at the right-hand figure, whose stony face was the most villainous and deadly in expression.

'By Jove,' he said, 'something has been afoot here – this hand is broken.'

And so it was. I was certain that it had been perfect the last time Laura and I had been there.

'Perhaps some one has *tried* to remove them,' said the young doctor.

'That won't account for my impression,' I objected.

'Too much painting and tobacco will account for that, well enough.'

'Come along,' I said, 'or my wife will be getting anxious. You'll come and have a drop of whisky and drink confusion to ghosts and better sense to me.'

'I ought to go up to Palmer's, but it's so late now I'd best leave it till the morning,' he replied. 'I was kept late at the Union, and I've had to see a lot of people since. All right, I'll come back with ye.'

I think he fancied I needed him more than did Palmer's girl, so, discussing how such an illusion could have been possible, and deducing from his experience large generalities concerning ghostly apparitions, we walked up to our cottage. We saw, as we walked up the garden-path, that bright light streamed out of the front door, and presently saw that the parlour door was open too. Had she gone out?

'Come in,' I said, and Dr Kelly followed me into the parlour. It was all ablaze with candles, not only the wax ones, but at least a dozen guttering, glaring tallow dips, stuck in vases and ornaments in unlikely places. Light, I knew, was Laura's remedy for nervousness. Poor child! Why had I left her? Brute that I was.

We glanced round the room, and at first we did not see her. The window was open, and the draught set all the candles flaring one way. Her chair was empty and her handkerchief and book lay on the floor. I turned to the window. There, in the recess of the window, I saw her. Oh, my child, my love, had she gone to that window to watch for me? And what had come into the room behind her? To what had she turned with that look of frantic fear and horror? Oh, my little one, had she thought that it was I whose step she heard, and turned to meet – what?

She had fallen back across the table in the window, and her body lay half on it and half on the window-seat, and her head hung down over the table, the brown hair loosened and fallen to the carpet. Her lips were drawn back, and her eyes wide, wide open. They saw nothing now. What had they seen last?

The doctor moved towards her, but I pushed him aside and sprang to her; caught her in my arms and cried –

'It's all right, Laura! I've got you safe, wifie.'

She fell into my arms in a heap. I clasped her and kissed her, and called her by all her pet names, but I think I knew all the time that she was dead. Her hands were tightly clenched. In one of them she held something fast. When I was quite sure that she was dead, and that nothing mattered at all any more, I let him open her hand to see what she held.

It was a grey marble finger.

A Little Ghost

HUGH WALPOLE

Ghosts? I looked across the table at Truscott and had a sudden desire to impress him. Truscott has, before now, invited confidences in just the same way, with his flat impassivity, his air of not caring whether you say anything to him or not, his determined indifference to your drama and your pathos. On this particular evening he had been less impassive. He had himself turned the conversation towards Spiritualism, séances, and all that world of humbug, as he believed it to be, and suddenly I saw, or fancied that I saw, a real invitation in his eyes, something that made me say to myself: 'Well, hang it all, I've known Truscott for nearly twenty years; I've never shown him the least little bit of my real self; he thinks me a writing money-machine, with no thought in the world beside my brazen serial stories and the yacht that I purchased out of them.'

So I told him the story, and I will do him the justice to say that he listened to every word of it most attentively although it was far into the evening before I had finished. He didn't seem impatient with all the little details that I gave. Of course, in a ghost story, details are more important than anything else. But was it a ghost story? Was it a story at all? Was it true even in its material background? Now, as I try to tell it again, I can't be sure. Truscott is the only other person who has ever heard it, and at the end of it he made no comment whatever.

It happened long ago, long before the War, when I had been married for about five years, and was an exceedingly prosperous journalist, with a nice little house and two children in Wimbledon.

I lost suddenly my greatest friend. That may mean little or much as friendship is commonly held, but I believe that most Britishers, most Americans, most Scandinavians, know before they die one friendship at least that changes their whole life experience by its depth and colour. Very few Frenchmen, Italians or Spaniards, very few Southern people at all, understand these things.

The curious part of it in my particular case was that I had known this friend only four or five years before his death, that I had made many friendships both before and since that have endured over much longer periods, and yet this particular friendship had a quality of intensity and happiness that I have never found elsewhere.

Another curious thing was that I met Bond only a few months before my marriage, when I was deeply in love with my wife, and so intensely preoccupied with my engagement that I could think of nothing else. I met Bond quite casually at someone's house. He was a large-boned, broad-shouldered, slow-smiling man with closs-cropped hair turning slightly grey, and our meeting was casual; the ripening of our friendship was casual; indeed, the whole affair may be said to have been casual to the very last. It was, in fact, my wife who said to me one day, when we had been married about a year or so: 'Why, I believe you care more for Charlie Bond than for anyone else in the world.' She said it in that sudden, disconcerting, perceptive way that some women have. I was entirely astonished. Of course I laughed at the idea. I saw Bond frequently. He came often to the house. My wife, wiser than many wives, encouraged all my friendships, and she herself liked Charlie immensely. I don't suppose that anyone disliked him. Some men were jealous of him; some men,

175

the merest acquaintances, called him conceited; women were sometimes irritated by him because so clearly he could get on very easily without them; but he had, I think no real enemy.

How could he have had? His good nature, his freedom from all jealousy, his naturalness, his sense of fun, the absence of all pettiness, his common sense, his manliness, and at the same time his broad-minded intelligence, all these things made him a most charming personality. I don't know that he shone very much in ordinary society. He was very quiet and his wit and humour came out best with his intimates.

I was the showy one, and he always played up to me, and I think I patronized him a little and thought deep down in my subconscious self that it was lucky for him to have such a brilliant friend, but he never gave a sign of resentment. I believe now that he knew me, with all my faults and vanities and absurdities, far better than anyone else, even my wife, did, and that is one of the reasons, to the day of my death, why I shall always miss him so desperately.

However, it was not until his death that I realized how close we had been. One November day he came back to his flat, wet and chilled, didn't change his clothes, caught a cold, which developed into pneumonia, and after three days was dead. It happened that that week I was in Paris, and I returned to be told on my doorstep by my wife of what had occurred. At first I refused to believe it. When I had seen him a week before he had been in splendid health; with his tanned, rather rough and clumsy face, his clear eyes, no fat about him anywhere, he had looked as though he would live to a thousand, and then, when I realized that it was indeed true, I did not during the first week or two grasp my loss.

I missed him, of course; was vaguely unhappy and discontented; railed against life, wondering why it was always the best people who were taken and the others left; but I was not actually aware that for the rest of my days things would be different, and that that day of my return from Paris was a crisis in my human experience. Suddenly one morning, walking down Fleet Street, I had a flashing, almost blinding need of Bond that was like a revelation. From that moment I knew no peace. Everyone seemed to me dull, profitless and empty. Even my wife was a long way away from me, and my children, whom I dearly loved, counted nothing to me at all. I didn't, after that, know what was the matter with me. I lost my appetite, I couldn't sleep, I was grumpy and nervous. I didn't myself connect it with Bond at all. I thought that I was overworked, and when my wife suggested a holiday, I agreed, got a fortnight's leave from my newspaper, and went down to Glebeshire.

Early December is not a bad time for Glebeshire, it is just then the best spot in the British Isles. I knew a little village beyond St Mary's Moor, that I had not seen for ten years, but always remembered with romantic gratitude, and I felt that that was the place for me now.

I changed trains at Polchester and found myself at last in a little jingle driving out to sea. The air, the wide open moor, the smell of the sea delighted me, and when I reached my little village, with its sandy cove and the boats drawn up in two rows in front of a high rocky cave, and when I ate my eggs and bacon in the little parlour of the inn overlooking the sea, I felt happier than I had done for weeks past; but my happiness did not last long. Night after night I could not sleep. I began to feel acute loneliness and knew at last in full truth that it was my friend whom I was missing, and that it was not solitude I needed, but his company. Easy enough to talk about having his company, but I only truly knew, down here in this little village, sitting on the edge of the green cliff, looking over into limitless sea, that I was indeed never to have his company again. There followed after that a wild, impatient regret that I had not made more of my time with him. I saw myself, in a sudden vision, as I had really been with him, patronizing, indulgent, a little contemptuous of his good-natured ideas. Had I only a week with him now, how eagerly I would show him that I was the fool and not he, that I was the lucky one every time!

One connects with one's own grief the place where one feels it, and before many days had passed I had grown to loathe the little village, to dread, beyond words, the long, soughing groan of the sea as it drew back down the slanting beach, the melancholy wail of the seagull, the chattering women under my little window. I couldn't stand it. I ought to go back to London, and yet from that too, I shrank. Memories of Bond lingered there as they did in no other place, and it was hardly fair to my wife and family to give them the company of the dreary, discontented man that I just then was.

And then, just in the way that such things always happen, I found on my breakfast-table one fine morning a forwarded letter. It was from a certain Mrs Baldwin, and, to my surprise, I saw that it came from Glebeshire, but from the top of the county and not its southern end.

John Baldwin was a Stock Exchange friend of my brother's, a rough diamond, but kindly and generous, and not, I believed very well off. Mrs Baldwin I had always liked, and I think she always liked me. We had not met for some little time and I had no idea what had happened to them. Now in her letter she told me that they had taken an old eighteenth-century house on the north coast of Glebeshire, not very far from Drymouth, that they were enjoying it very much indeed, that Jack was fitter than he had been for years, and that they would be delighted, were I ever in that part of the country, to have me as their guest. This suddenly seemed to me the very thing. The Baldwins had never known Charlie Bond, and they would have, therefore, for me no association with his memory. They were jolly, noisy people, with a jolly, noisy family, and Jack Baldwin's personality was so robust that it would surely shake me out of my gloomy mood. I sent a telegram at once to Mrs Baldwin, asking her whether she could have me for a week, and before the day was over I received the warmest of invitations.

Next day I left my little fishing village and experienced one of those strange, crooked, in-and-out little journeys that you must undergo if you are to find your way from one obscure Glebeshire village to another.

A Little Ghost

About midday, a lovely, cold blue December midday, I discovered myself in Polchester with an hour to wait for my next train. I went down into the town, climbed the High Street to the magnificent cathedral, stood beneath the famous Arden Gate, looked at the still more famous tomb of the Black Bishop, and it was there, as the sunlight, slanting through the great east window, danced and sparkled about the wonderful blue stone of which that tomb was made, that I had a sudden sense of having been through all this before, of having stood just there in some earlier time, weighed down by some earlier grief, and that nothing that I was experiencing was unexpected. I had a curious sense, too, of comfort and condolence, that horrible grey loneliness that I had felt in the fishing village suddenly fell from me, and for the first time since Bond's death I was happy. I walked away from the cathedral, down the busy street, and through the dear old market-place, expecting I know not what. All that I knew was that I was intending to go to the Baldwin's and that I would be happy there.

The December afternoon fell quickly, and during the last part of my journey I was travelling in a ridiculous little train, through dusk, and the little train went so slowly and so casually that one was always hearing the murmurs of streams beyond one's window, and lakes of grey water suddenly stretched like plates of glass to thick woods, black as ink, against a faint sky. I got out at my little wayside station, shaped like a rabbit-hutch, and found a motor waiting for me. The drive was not long, and suddenly I was outside the old eighteenth-century house, and Baldwin's stout butler was conveying me into the hall with that careful, kindly patronage, rather as though I were a box of eggs that might very easily be broken.

It was a spacious hall, with a large open fireplace, in front of which they were all having tea. I say 'all' advisedly, because the place seemed to be full of people, grown-ups and children, but mostly children. There were so many of these last that I was not, to the end of my stay, to be able to name most of them individually.

Mrs Baldwin came forward to greet me, introduced me to one

or two people, sat me down and gave me my tea, told me that I
wasn't looking at all well, and needed feeding up, and explained
that Jack was out shooting something, but would soon be back.

My entrance had made a brief lull, but immediately everyone
recovered and the noise was terrific. There is a lot to be said for
the freedom of the modern child. There is a lot to be said against
it, too. I soon found that in this party, at any rate, the elders were
completely disregarded and of no account. Children rushed
about the hall, knocked one another down, shouted and
screamed, fell over grown-ups as though they were pieces of
furniture, and paid no attention at all to the mild 'Now,
children' of a plain, elderly lady who was, I supposed, a
governess. I fancy that I was tired with my criss-cross journey,
and I soon found a chance to ask Mrs Baldwin if I could go up to
my room. She said: 'I expect you find these children noisy. Poor
little things. They must have their fun. Jack always says that one
can only be young once, and I do so agree with him.'

I wasn't myself feeling very young that evening (I was really
about nine hundred years old), so that I agreed with her and
eagerly left youth to its own appropriate pleasures. Mrs Baldwin
took me up the fine broad staircase. She was a stout woman,
dressed in bright colours, with what is know, I believe, as an
infectious laugh. Tonight, although I was fond of her, and knew
very well her good, generous heart, she irritated me, and for
some reason that I could not quite define. Perhaps I felt at once
that she was out of place there and that the house resented her,
but in all this account, I am puzzled by the question as to
whether I imagine now, on looking back, all sorts of feelings that
were not really there at all, but come to me now because I know
of what happened afterwards. But I am so anxious to tell the
truth, the whole truth, and nothing but the truth, and there is
nothing in the world so difficult to do as that.

We went through a number of dark passages, up and down
little pieces of staircase that seemed to have no beginning, no
end, and no reason for their existence, and she left me at last in
my bedroom, said that she hoped I would be comfortable, and

that Jack would come and see me when he came in, and then paused for a moment, looking at me. 'You really don't look well,' she said. 'You've been overdoing it. You're too conscientious. I always said so. You shall have a real rest here. And the children will see that you're not dull.'

Her last two sentences seemed scarcely to go together. I could not tell her about my loss. I realized suddenly, as I had never realized in our older acquaintance, that I should never be able to speak to her about anything that really mattered.

She smiled, laughed and left me. I looked at my room and loved it at once. Broad and low-ceilinged, it contained very little furniture, an old four-poster, charming hangings, some old rose-coloured damask, an old-gold mirror, an oak cabinet, some high-backed chairs, and then for comfort, a large arm-chair with high elbows, a little quaintly shaped sofa dressed in the same rose colour as the bed, a bright crackling fire, and a grandfather clock. The walls, faded primrose, had no pictures, but on one of them, opposite my bed, was a gay sampler worked in bright colours of crimson and yellow and framed in oak.

I liked it, I loved it, and drew the arm-chair in front of the fire, nestled down into it, and before I knew, I was fast asleep.

How long I slept I don't know, but I suddenly woke with a sense of comfort and well-being which was nothing less than exquisite. I belonged to it, that room, as though I had been in it all my days. I had a curious sense of companionship that was exactly what I had been needing during these last weeks. The house was very still, no voices of children came to me, no sound anywhere, save the sharp crackle of the fire and the friendly ticking of the old clock. Suddenly I thought that there was someone in the room with me, a rustle of something that might have been the fire and yet was not.

I got up and looked about me, half smiling, as though I expected to see a familiar face. There was no one there, of course, and yet I had just that consciousness of companionship that one has when someone whom one loves very dearly and knows very intimately is sitting with one in the same room. I even went to the other side of the four-poster and looked around me, pulled for a moment at the silver-coloured curtains, and of course saw no one. Then the door suddenly opened, and Jack Baldwin came in, and I remembered having a curious feeling of irritation as though I had been interrupted. His large, breezy, knickerbockered figure filled the room. 'Hallo!' he said. 'Delighted to see you. Bit of luck your being down this way. Have you got everything you want?'

That was a wonderful old house. I am not going to attempt to describe it, although I have stayed there quite recently. Yes, I stayed there on many occasions since that first of which I am now speaking. It has never been quite the same to me since that first time. You may say, if you like, that the Baldwins fought a battle with it and defeated it. It is certainly now more Baldwin than – well, whatever it was before they rented it. They are not the kind of people to be defeated by atmosphere. Their chief duty in this world, I gather, is to make things Baldwin, and very good for the world too; but when I first went down to them the house was still challenging them. 'A wee bit creepy,' Mrs Baldwin confided to me on the second day of my visit.

'What exactly do you mean by that?' I asked her. 'Ghosts?'

'Oh, there are those, of course,' she answered. 'There's an underground passage, you know, that runs from here to the sea, and one of the wickedest of the smugglers was killed in it, and his ghost still haunts the cellar. At least, that's what we were told by our first butler here; and then, of course, we found that it was the butler, not the smuggler, who was haunting the cellar, and since his departure the smuggler hasn't been visible.' She laughed. 'All the same, it isn't a comfortable place. I'm going to wake up some of those old rooms. We're going to put in some more windows. And then there are the children,' she added.

Yes, there were the children. Surely the noisiest in all the world. They had reverence for nothing. They were the wildest savages, and especially those from nine to thirteen, the cruellest and most uncivilized age for children. There were two little boys, twins I should think, who were nothing less than devils, and regarded their elders with cold, watching eyes, said nothing in protest when scolded, but evolved plots afterwards that fitted precisely the chastiser. To do my host and hostess justice, all the children were not Baldwins, and I fancy the Baldwin contingent was the quietest.

Nevertheless, from early morning until ten at night, the noise was terrific and you were never sure how early in the morning it would recommence. I don't know that I personally minded the noise very greatly. It took me out of myself and gave me something better to think of, but, in some obscure and unanalysed way, I felt that the house minded it. One knows how the poets have written about old walls and rafters rejoicing in the happy, careless laughter of children. I do not think this house rejoiced at all, and it was queer how consistently I, who am not supposed to be an imaginative person, thought about the house.

But it was not until my third evening that something really happened. I say 'happened', but did anything really happen? You shall judge for yourself.

I was sitting in my comfortable arm-chair in my bedroom, enjoying that delightful half-hour before one dresses for dinner. There was a terrible racket up and down the passages, the children being persuaded, I gathered, to go into the schoolroom and have their supper, when the noise died down and there was nothing but the feathery whisper of the snow – snow had been falling all day – against my window-pane. My thoughts suddenly turned to Bond, directed to him as actually and precipitately as though he had suddenly sprung before me. I did not want to talk of him. I had been fighting his memory these last days, because I had thought that the wisest thing to do, but now he was too much for me.

I luxuriated in my memories of him, turning over and over all sorts of times that we had had together, seeing his smile, watching his mouth that turned up at the corners when he was amused, and wondering finally why he should obsess me the way

183

that he did, when I had lost so many other friends for whom I had thought I cared much more, who, nevertheless, never bothered my memory at all. I sighed, and it seemed to me that my sigh was very gently repeated behind me. I turned sharply round. The curtains had not been drawn. You know the strange, milky pallor that reflected snow throws over objects, and although three lighted candles shone in the room, moon-white shadows seemed to hang over the bed and across the floor. Of course there was no one there, and yet I stared and stared about me as though I were convinced that I was not alone. And then I looked especially at one part of the room, a distant corner beyond the four-poster, and it seemed to me that someone was there. And yet no one was there. But whether it was that my mind had been distracted, or that the beauty of the old snow-lit room enchanted me, I don't know, but my thoughts of my friend were happy and reassured. I had not lost him, I seemed to say to myself. Indeed, at that special moment, he seemed to be closer to me than he had been while he was alive.

From that evening a curious thing occurred. I only seemed to be close to my friend when I was in my own room – and I felt more than that. When my door was closed and I was sitting in my arm-chair, I fancied that our new companionship was not only Bond's, but was something more as well. I would wake in the middle of the night or in the early morning and feel quite sure that I was not alone; so sure that I did not even want to investigate it further, but just took the companionship for granted and was happy.

Outside that room, however, I felt increasing discomfort. I hated the way in which the house was treated. A quite unreasonable anger rose within me as I heard the Baldwins discussing the improvements that they were going to make, and yet they were so kind to me, and so patently unaware of doing anything that would not generally be commended, that it was quite impossible for me to show my anger. Nevertheless, Mrs Baldwin noticed something. 'I am afraid the children are worrying you,' she said one morning, half interrogatively. 'In a way it will be a rest when they go back to school, but the Christmas holidays is their time, isn't it? I do like to see them happy, poor little dears.'

The poor little dears were at that moment being Red Indians all over the hall.

'No, of course, I like children,' I answered her. 'The only thing is that they don't – I hope you won't think me foolish – somehow quite fit in with the house.'

'Oh, I think it's so good for old places like this,' said Mrs Baldwin briskly, 'to be woken up a little. I'm sure if the old people who used to live here came back they'd love to hear all the noise and laughter.'

I wasn't so sure myself, but I wouldn't disturb Mrs Baldwin's contentment for anything.

That evening in my room I was so convinced of companion-ship that I spoke.

'If there's anyone here,' I said aloud, 'I'd like them to know that I'm aware of it and am glad of it.'

Then, when I caught myself speaking aloud, I was suddenly terrified. Was I really going crazy? Wasn't that the first step towards insanity when you talked to yourself? Nevertheless, a moment later I was reassured. There *was* someone there.

That night I woke, looked at my luminous watch and saw that it was a quarter past three. The room was so dark that I could not even distinguish the posters of my bed, but – there was a faint glow from the fire, now nearly dead. Opposite my bed there seemed to me to be something white. Not white in the accepted senses of a tall, ghostly figure; but, sitting up and staring, it seemed to me that the shadow was very small, hardly reaching above the edge of the bed.

'Is there anyone there?' I asked. 'Because, if there is, do speak to me. I'm not frightened. I know that someone has been here all this last week, and I am glad of it.'

Very faintly then, so faintly that I cannot to this day be sure that I saw anything at all, the figure of a child seemed to me to be visible.

We all know we have at one time and another fancied that we have seen visions and figures, and then have discovered that it was something in the room, the chance hanging of a coat, the reflection of a glass, a trick of moonlight that has fired our imagination. I was quite prepared for that in this case, but it seemed to me then that as I watched the shadow moved directly in front of the dying fire, and delicate as the leaf of a silver birch, like the trailing rim of some evening cloud, the figure of a child hovered in front of me.

Curiously enough the dress, which seemed to be of some silver tissue, was clearer than anything else. I did not, in fact, see the face at all, and yet I could swear in the morning that I had seen it, that I knew large, black, wide-open eyes, a little mouth very faintly parted in a timid smile, and that beyond anything else I had realized in the expression of that face fear and bewilderment and a longing for some comfort.

After that night the affair moved very quickly to its little climax.

I am not a very imaginative man, nor have I any sympathy with the modern craze for spooks and spectres. I have never seen, nor fancied that I had seen, anything of a supernatural kind since that visit, but then I have never known since that time such a desperate need of companionship and comfort, and is it not perhaps because we do not want things badly enough in this life that we do not get more of them? However that may be, I was sure on this occasion that I had some companionship that was born of a need greater than mine. I suddenly took the most frantic and unreasonable dislike of the children in that house. It was exactly as though I had discovered somewhere in a deserted part of the building some child who had been left behind by mistake by the last occupants and was terrified by the noisy exuberance and ruthless selfishness of the new family.

For a week I had no more definite manifestations of my little friend, but I was as sure of her presence there in my room as I was of my own clothes and the arm-chair in which I used to sit.

It was time for me to go back to London, but I could not go. I asked everyone I met as to legends and stories connected with the old house, but I never found anything to do with a little child. I looked forward all day to my hour in my room before dinner, the time when I felt the companionship closest. I sometimes woke in the night and was conscious of its presence, but, as I have said, I never saw anything.

One evening the older children obtained leave to stay up later. It was somebody's birthday. The house seemed to be full of people, and the presence of the children led after dinner to a perfect riot of noise and confusion. We were to play hide-and-seek all over the house. Everybody was to dress up. There was, for that night at least, to be no privacy anywhere. We were all, as Mrs Baldwin said, to be ten years old again. I hadn't the least desire to be ten years old, but I found myself caught into the game, and had, in sheer self-defence, to run up and down the passages and hide behind doors. The noise was terrific. It grew and grew in volume. People got hysterical. The smaller children jumped out of bed and ran about the passages. Somebody kept blowing a motor-horn. Somebody else turned on the gramophone.

Suddenly I was sick of the whole thing, retreated into my room, lit one candle and locked the door. I had scarcely sat down in my chair when I was aware that my little friend had come. She was standing near to the bed, staring at me, terror in her eyes. I have never seen anyone so frightened – her little breasts panting beneath her silver gown, her very fair hair falling about her shoulders, her little hands clenched. Just as I saw her there were loud knocks on the door, many voices shouting to be admitted, a perfect babel of noise and laughter. The little figure moved, and then – how can I give any idea of it? – I was conscious of having something to protect and comfort. I saw nothing, physically I felt nothing, and yet I was murmuring. 'There, there, don't mind. They shan't come in. I'll see that no one touches you. I understand. I understand.' For how long I sat like that I don't

187

know. The noises died away, voices murmured at intervals, and then were silent. The house slept. All night I think I stayed there comforting and being comforted.

I fancy now – but how much of it may not be fancy? – that I knew that the child loved the house, had stayed so long as was possible, at last was driven away, and that that was her farewell, not only to me, but to all that she most loved in this world and the next.

I do not know – I could swear to nothing. Of what I am sure is that my sense of loss in my friend was removed from that night and never returned. Did I argue with myself that that child companionship included also my friend? Again, I do not know. But of one thing I am now sure, that if love is strong enough, physical death cannot destroy it, and however platitudinous that may sound to others, it is platitudinous no longer when you have discovered it by actual experience for yourself.

That moment in that fire-lit room, when I felt that spiritual heart beating with mine, is and always will be enough for me.

One thing more. Next day I left for London, and my wife was delighted to find me so completely recovered – happier, she said, than I had ever been before.

Two days afterwards, I received a parcel from Mrs Baldwin. In the note that accompanied it, she said:

I think that you must have left this by mistake behind you. It was found in the small drawer in your dressing-table.

I opened the parcel and discovered an old blue silk hand-kerchief, wrapped round a long, thin wooden box. The cover of the box lifted very easily, and I saw inside it an old painted wooden doll, dressed in the period, I should think, of Queen Anne. The dress was very complete, even down to the little shoes, and the little grey mittens on the hands. Inside the silk skirt there was sewn a little tape, and on the tape, in very faded letters, 'Ann Trelawney, 1710.'

The Mistress in Black

ROSEMARY TIMPERLEY

The school was deathly quiet and seemed to be deserted. Nervously I approached it from the road, followed a path round the side of the building and came to the main entrance. I tried the door but it was locked, so I rang the bell.

Footsteps approached. The door opened. A tall, pleasant-faced man with a grey moustache stood there.

'Good morning,' I said. 'I'm Miss Anderson. I have an appointment with the Headmistress at ten o'clock.'

'Oh, yes. Come in, Miss. I'm the caretaker.' He stood aside for me to pass and closed the door again. 'If you'll wait here, I'll see if Miss Leonard is ready for you.'

He went along the corridor in front of me, turned to the right and vanished.

With my back to the front door, I looked round the hall. On the wall to my left was a green baize notice-board with a few notices neatly arranged and secured with drawing-pins. I wondered whether that board would still be so tidy when the vacation was over and the children were back. Past the notice-board were swing doors opening on to an empty gymnasium, its equipment idle, its floor shining with polish. The paintwork was fresh and the place looked as if it had just been redecorated. To

189

my right were a number of other doors, closed and mysterious –
for everything in an unfamiliar building seems mysterious. And
ahead of me, to the left of the corridor and alongside it, was a
flight of stairs leading upwards.

My nervousness increased. Interviews always panic me and I
really neeeded this job. Trembling a little, I waited. The silence
itself seemed to make a noise in my ears. I listened for the
caretaker's returning footsteps.

Suddenly a woman appeared at the top of the stairs and began
to descend. She startled me as she had made no sound in her
approach, and I was reminded of one of my previous headmist-
resses whose habit of wearing soft-soled shoes had given her an
uncanny ability to turn up silently when she was least expected.
This woman on the stairs was pale, dark, very thin, and wearing
a black dress unrelieved by any sort of ornament. Unsmiling,
she looked at me with beautiful but very unhappy dark eyes.

'Miss Leonard?' I said.

She didn't reply or even pause, merely moved towards the
doors of the gymnasium. At the same moment I heard the
caretaker's returning footsteps and turned to see him re-enter
the corridor.

'This way, dear,' he called. 'Miss Leonard will see you now.'

As I went towards him, I thought I smelt something burning,
so hesitated. Again I looked through the glass at the top half of
the gymnasium doors. The woman in black was out of sight.

'What's the matter?' The caretaker came up to me. 'Feeling
nervous?'

'Yes, I am – but it's not that – I thought I smelt burning.'

He looked at me sharply. 'No, not now,' he said. 'That's all
over, and I should know. But I've got a bonfire going in the
grounds. Maybe the smoke is blowing this way.'

'That'll be it. Anyway, I can't smell it any more. Was that
Miss Leonard I saw a second ago?'

'Where?' he asked.

'On the stairs, then she went into the gymnasium –'

'You're in a proper state of nerves, you are,' he said, as I followed him along the corridor. 'There's no one in the building today except you, me and Miss Leonard, and she's in her office waiting for you. Coming on the staff, are you?'

'I hope so. I've applied for the job of English teacher.'

'Good luck, then,' he said.

We stopped outside a door.

'This is Miss Leonard's room, Miss.' He knocked on the door. A voice called: 'Come in!'

And I went into the Headmistress's room.

Miss Leonard was at her desk, the window behind her. She rose immediately, a plump yet dignified figure with neat white hair and a pink suit which heightened the colour in her cheeks. She was utterly unlike the woman in black.

She smiled. 'Do come right in and sit down, Miss Anderson. I'm glad to see you. It's not easy to find staff at a moment's notice at the end of the autumn term.'

'It's not easy to find a job at this time either,' I said. 'Most schools are fixed up for the whole of the school year.'

'We were too – then suddenly there was a vacancy. Now, you're twenty-five, you have a B.A. degree in English, and two years' teaching experience.' She was looking at my letter of application which lay on her desk.

'That's right, Miss Leonard.'

'You haven't been teaching for the past twelve months. May I ask why?'

'My mother and I went to live in Rome with my sister and her husband, who is Italian. Mother was ill and she wanted to see my sister again before – well, Mother's dead now so I decided to come back to England.'

'And do you know anything about this school?'

'No. I simply answered your advertisement.'

'I'm glad you did.' She picked up a folder of papers and handed it to me. 'In here I've enclosed your timetable for next term and details of syllabus and set books. So you can 'do your homework' before you arrive.'

'You mean I've got the job?'

'Yes. Why not?'

'That's marvellous. Thank you.'

We talked for a while then, as she took me back to the main door, she said: 'You'll find the rest of the staff very nice and friendly.'

'I think I've seen one of them already,' I said.

'Really? Which one?'

'I don't know. It was just that she came down the stairs while I was waiting in the hall. She was wearing a black dress.'

Miss Leonard said casually: 'Staff do come back during the vacation sometimes, to collect forgotten property or whatever. Good-bye for the present, Miss Anderson. When you arrive on the first day of term, come to my office and I'll show you the staff room, then take you to your first class.'

And the interview was over.

Christmas passed, January began, diligently I studied my folder of information and then, on the night before first day of term, snow fell. My lodgings were a train journey away from the school and on the very morning when I wanted to be punctual, my train stuck. Ice on the points. By the time I reached the school, I was late, and distraught.

Added to this, the school itself looked different under snow. I couldn't even find the path to the main door. I took a wrong path, lost myself wandering round the building, then peered through a classroom window.

Lights were on inside. About thirty-five little girls in white blouses and dark tunics were sitting at their desks and listening to the teacher. That teacher was the dark, thin woman in the black dress whom I had seen before. Fascinated, I stood and gazed. It was like watching a silent play, myself in the outside dark, the actors in the light, playing their parts.

In the front row of the class was a little girl with golden hair falling like bright rain over her shoulders. Next to her was a dark child, her black hair cropped close as a boy's. And next to this one was a child with a mop of red curls.

The Mistress in Black

All the pupils were attentive, but this red-haired child was gazing at the teacher with an expression of adoration. It was touching, yet a little alarming. No human being deserves that much young worship. . . .

I retraced my steps along the wrong path in the snow, found the right one and finally reached the entrance door. It was not locked this time. I let myself in and hurried to Miss Leonard's room.

'Come in!' she called in answer to my knock.

As I went in I blurted out: 'I'm so sorry I'm late. It was my train – the snow –'

'Never mind, Miss Anderson. I guessed as much. I'll take you to the staff room.'

She led me up the stairs from the hall, along a first floor corridor, into a room. It was an ordinary staff room – notice-board, lockers, tables, hard chairs, easy chairs, electric fire. The light was on but the room was empty – at least, I thought it was empty at first, then realized that someone was sitting in one of the chairs. I saw her only out of the corner of my eye, and she was in a chair in the far corner of the room, away from the fire; so although I recognized her as the woman in black, I didn't turn to look at her. If I thought anything, it was just that she had a bit of a nerve to leave her class, which I'd seen her teaching a few minutes ago, and come to sit in the staff room – and now she's been caught out by the entrance of the Headmistress.

Miss Leonard, however, took no notice of her. She said: 'This will be your locker, Miss Anderson. The bell will ring any minute now for the end of first period, then I'll take you to your first class. It's a double-period of English – you'll have seen that from your timetable. Mrs Gage is looking after them at the moment – she's our biology teacher – and she'll be glad to see you as by rights these first two periods should be her free ones. That's why the staff room is empty.'

But the staff room was not empty. There was the woman in black, looking at me seriously, with those beautiful sad dark eyes. . . .

Miss Leonard led the way to my first class. The teacher there looked quickly round as we entered. She was a lively, dark, fairly young woman with eagerly bent shoulders and black-rimmed spectacles. She wore a red sweater and brown skirt.

'Here we are, Mrs Gage,' said Miss Leonard. 'Now you'll get your second free period all right.' She faced the class. 'Now, girls, this is Miss Anderson, your new English teacher. Help her as much as you can, won't you?'

And I too stood facing the class. It was the same class which I had seen through the window only fifteen minutes earlier. There was the child with fair hair in the front row, and the dark one next to her – and. . . .

No. It was different. The child with curly red hair was not there. Her desk empty. And, of course, the teacher was different. . . .

Miss Leonard and Mrs Gage left the room. I was on my own with this familiar, unfamiliar class. I spent the next forty minutes or so in trying to get to know them, checking on their set books, and so on, then the bell rang for morning break and I returned to the staff room.

The chair where the woman in black had been sitting was empty now but other chairs were occupied. The staff had gathered for elevenses. I heard someone say, above the noise of the many voices: 'How does that damned chair get over into the corner like that? Who puts it there?'

'Night cleaners have strange ways,' said another voice.

'Extraordinary about night cleaners,' said the first. 'They work here for years, and so do we – and which of us are the ghosts? We co-exist, but never meet.'

A woman in an overall came in with a tray bearing a pot of coffee and cups and saucers. Mrs Gage came over to me.

'Coffee, Miss Anderson?'

'Oh – thank you.'

'How do you like it?'

'Black. No sugar.'

'Same here.' She collected coffee for us both.

'Sorry you missed a free period because of me,' I said. 'My train got held up in the snow.'

'That's all right.'

Sipping my coffee, I studied the other women around me.

'Doesn't everyone come here for coffee at break?' I asked Mrs Gage.

'Everyone! It's only our elevenses that keep us going.'

'Then where is – well – one of the teachers? She was taking your class – my class – this morning – I saw her through the window –'

'Not that class,' said Mrs Gage. 'I started with them immediately after morning assembly.'

'But it *was* that class. I recognized some of the girls. And the one with red hair wasn't there.'

Mrs Gage looked at me sympathetically. 'You're all upset over being late, aren't you? And maybe you're upset for other reasons too. I don't blame you. It's not easy to be taking Miss Carey's place.'

'Miss Carey? Who –' But as I tried to ask more, the woman in the overall came to collect our dirty cups and the bell rang for third period. We all went off to our classes.

I still had one more period with the same class I'd taken before – or so I thought, until I reached the room. Then I saw that the teacher's chair was already occupied.

The woman in black sat there.

And the child with red hair was in the third desk in the front row.

'Sorry,' I murmured, withdrew again, and stood in the corridor to re-examine my timetable. Surely I hadn't made a mistake – no – I was right – this was my class. So I went back. And the teacher's chair was empty now. So was the third desk in the front row. . . .

That was when I began to be afraid. So afraid that a sick shiver travelled down my spine, sweat sprang out on my skin, and I needed all my self-control to face the class and give a lesson.

At the end of the lesson, when the bell rang for next period, I asked the class in general: 'Where's the girl who sits there?' I indicated the third desk in the front row.

No one answered. The children became unnaturally quiet and stared at me.

'Well?' I said.

Then the fair-haired child said: 'No one sits there, Miss.' And the dark child next to her added: 'That was Joan's desk.'

'But where is Joan?'

Silence again.

Then Mrs Gage walked in. 'Hello, Miss Anderson. We seem to be playing Box and Cox this morning. Do you know which class to go to for last period?'

'Yes, thank you. I've got my timetable.' I hurried away.

Busyness is the best panacea for fear, and I was very busy getting to know a different class until the bell rang for lunch. Back to the staff room again – and it was full again – and there was Mrs Gage, kindly taking me under her wing.

'Miss Leonard asked me to look after you until you can find your way around,' she said. 'The staff dining-room is on the second floor. Would you like to come up with me?'

I was glad of the offer.

The staff, all female, sat at three long tables in the dining-room, and the place was as noisy as a classroom before the teacher arrives! Two overalled women, one of whom I had seen at break, served our meal. Conversation was mostly 'shop' – the besetting sin of female teachers. As the newcomer, I kept quiet, but I looked at those women one by one, trying to identify the woman in black.

She wasn't there.

Unhungry, I did my best with the meat pie and carrots, then when rice pudding and prunes arrived (for teachers have children's diet) I murmured to Mrs Gage: 'Who is the member of staff who wears a black dress?'

She looked around. 'No one, as far as I can see.'

'No – she's not here – but I've seen her.'

'Really? But I think everyone's here today. We do go out for lunch sometimes, but when the weather is like this it's easier to have it on the premises. What was she like?'

'Dark, pale, thin, not very young – with lovely eyes –'

'And wearing a black dress, you said?'

'Yes.'

Mrs Gage gave a small, unamused laugh. 'Sounds like Miss Carey, but you can't possibly have seen her.'

'The one who's left – whose place I've taken –'

'No-one could take Joanna's place.'

'Oh – I didn't mean –'

'Miss Anderson, I'm sorry. I didn't mean anything either.' She didn't look at me, but she had stopped eating her prunes.

'Did something bad happen to her?' I asked.

'She tried to burn down the school.'

The words were whispered and the noise of the voices around us was so loud that I thought I must have misheard, so I said: 'What?'

'She tried to burn down the school,' Mrs Gage repeated. Others at our table heard her this time. Conversation faded, ceased. Heads turned towards Mrs Gage.

'Don't all look at me like that,' said Mrs Gage. 'I'm only telling Miss Anderson what happened last term. She has a right to know.' Leaving her sweet unfinished, she pushed back her chair with a scraping noise and left the room. I sat petrified. Murmurs of conversation began again, but no one spoke to me, so I pretended to eat a little more, then rose and left.

I found my way back to the staff room.

Mrs Gage, cigarette in hand, was sitting by the electric fire. 'Sorry about that,' she said. 'Until you asked, I presumed you knew. It was in the newspapers.'

'I've been living in Italy. I only came back just before Christmas. Could you tell me what happened, before the others return from lunch?'

'Sure. Have a fag. Rotten first day for you.' She passed me a cigarette and lit it for me.

'This smell of burning,' I said. 'I've noticed it before.'

'It's only our cigarettes, Miss Anderson. And we'd better get them smoked before the rest of the staff come back. Some of them abhor cigarette smoke. These spinsters!'

'I'm one too.'

'Not really. You're still young. So you want to know about Joanna Carey?'

'Of course I do. After all, I've seen her. Did she get the sack, and now she comes back uninvited – or what?'

'Mr dear child, you can't have seen her. She's dead.'

'Then whom did I see?'

Mrs Gage ignored this question. She said: 'Miss Carey, Joanna, had been a teacher here for twenty years. She was excellent at her job and the kids adored her. Then, about a year ago, she changed.'

'In what way?'

'Not in the way she taught. Her teaching was always brilliant. But in her attitude. After being most understanding and sympathetic with the young, she gradually became more and more cynical, to the point of cruelty. She made it clear to all of us, staff and pupils, that she now hated her job and only went on doing it because she had to earn a living somehow.'

'But why did this happen?'

'Why? Who knows why anything? But in fact I do know more about her than most of the staff. Joanna and I were friends, before she changed. She often visited my husband and me, in the old days. She and I had occasional heart-to-hearts over the washing-up. So I learned something of her private life. She loved a married man, for about ten years. That *was* her private life. Then he ditched her – decided to 'be a good boy' again. When it happened, she told me, and she laughed, and didn't seem to care very much. But it was from that moment that she began to change, grow bitter, disillusioned. The world went stale to her. The salt had lost its savour. She began to take revenge, not against the man, but against everyone else with whom she came into contact. That meant us – staff and kids. She was filled with hate, and hate breeds hate. Even I, who had been

198

her friend, began to avoid her. She was left alone.'

'You said she tried to burn down the school.'

'She did. She failed in that. But while she was trying, she burned herself to death. And one of the children.'

'One of the children? Oh, no!'

'It's true, Miss Anderson. I wouldn't say it if it weren't. I, of all people, once so friendly with Joanna – I'd be the last person to admit it, if it weren't true. But it happened.'

'What exactly did happen?'

'One Friday evening, towards the end of last term, she came back to school. This is what the police found out when they investigated afterwards. Everyone except Mr Brown, the care-taker, had gone. She soaked the base of the long curtains in the gymnasium with paraffin and set fire to them. Imagine the flare-up that would make – all those curtains in that big room. Why she didn't get away afterwards, no one knows. Maybe she fainted. Maybe she deliberately *let* herself be burned – like that Czech student – you know. People do these things. When they're desperate. Mr Brown saw the flames, sent for the fire service, and after they'd come and put out the fire, her body was found among the ashes of the curtains.'

'And the child? You said—'

'Yes. Little Joan Hanley. A deaf little girl with red curly hair. She adored Joanna. She was found there too, burned to death, among the ashes of the curtains.'

'But how did she come to be there in the first place?'

'Once again, no-one knows. She was one of Joanna's worship-pers. There were several in the school. Girls' schools are diabolical in this respect. Rather like all-female wards in hospitals. Joan Hanley would have done anything in the world for Joanna Carey. So did Joanna invite the child to the "party?" I don't know. But it looks like it.'

'Didn't the police find out anything about why Joan Hanley was there?'

'They tried. She had told her parents that she was going to the cinema, which she often did on Friday nights. When she didn't come home at her usual time, her parents wondered – and the next thing they knew, the police were on their doorstep, telling them that their daughter had been burned to death at the school. That's all I know, Miss Anderson – all any of us knows. Since it happened, workmen have put the gymnasium to rights, hence all the fresh paint and the pretty new curtains. These tragedies are happening all the time, all over the world – I know that – but when I think of Joanna, in her hatred and bitterness, drawing a child into such a burning – Oh, God!' She put her hands over her face.

The staff room became deathly quiet. Only the two of us there, Mrs Gage and me, crouching over the electric fire, our cigarettes burning down, the silent snow covering the world outside – and God knows why I suddenly looked behind me.

I looked at that chair in the far corner of the room. It was no longer empty. The woman in black sat there. She looked straight at me, with those tragic eyes.

Then the staff room door burst open and the other women poured in, filling the quietness with noise, filling the empty chairs with bodies, talking 'shop' – and I thought: No wonder Joanna Carey took a hate against all this. And yet – to burn a child – along with oneself – No!

'I didn't!' The sound came over, clearly, loudly, as if it filled the world. Yet no one seemed to hear it. I had spoken into my head only.

'I'll prove it,' said the loud voice in my head. 'Come!'

Mrs Gage was leaning back in the chair by the fire. She had lit another cigarette and closed her eyes. She looked tired out, and no wonder. I got up and left the room, that room full of talking women.

I walked, blindly, yet guided, along the unfamiliar corridors. Outside, in the snow, the children were having snowball battles. They were having a lovely lunch-hour! Heaven was outside. Hell was within.

I walked, without knowing why, into the classroom which I had seen through the window, the classroom where I had taught during the second and third periods of the school morning.

I walked up to the third desk in the front row.

I sat down at that desk, as if I were the little girl, Joan Hanley, who had, day after day, sat down at that desk. . . .

I opened the desk lid. There was nothing inside.

I looked at the scratching and carved initials on the top of the desk lid.

I found: 'J. H. LOVES J. C.' And, over it, an unsymmetrical heart pierced by a rather wonky arrow.

But I knew already that J. H. had loved J. C. I had seen the child's face through the window, only this morning – I had seen what did not exist – yet which did exist –

What to do now?

My hand, guided, by God knows whom or what, put its fingers into the empty inkwell-socket. The fingers found a closely folded piece of paper.

I unfolded it, carefully, and read:

'Dear Mum and Dad, I do not love you. I love Miss Carey. Where she goes, I go. I follow her everywhere. Tonight I have followed her to the school. She has gone to the gymnasium. I shall follow her there. Something is going to happen. That is why I am writing. Whatever she does, I shall do too. Because I love her. I must hurry now, to be with her. Funny really – as she does not even know I follow her! I'll put this under my inkwell. I don't expect you'll ever read it, but you never know. Yours sincerely – Your daughter, Joan.'"

'I didn't know she was there!' cried that voice in my head, loud with its silence. 'I didn't know she was there!'

'Of course you didn't!' I answered aloud, loudly. 'It's all right! I'll tell them!'

The classroom door opened and Miss Leonard walked in.

'Miss Anderson, what on earth are you doing?'

What on earth was I doing? I was sitting at a dead child's desk, a scrap of paper in my hand, and 'talking to myself.'

'I've found something, Miss Leonard.' I passed her the letter.

She read it. 'So *that's* what happened,' she said. 'Miss Carey

201

didn't take the child there with her at all. The little girl secretly imitated her goddess, even to the point of suicide. Where did you find the letter?'

'In the inkwell-socket. I'm surprised it hasn't been found before, maybe by one of the children.'

'No. I cleared that desk myself, removed the inkwell and didn't think to look underneath it. And the children never touch this desk. I did think of removing it, but that's too much like giving in to superstition. What made *you* look there, Miss Anderson?'

'She – she led me here – she spoke in my head – I don't understand it – but it happened –'

'You're psychic, aren't you? Did you know that already?'

'Not until I came to this school.'

'You saw her on the day of your interview, didn't you?'

'Yes. On the stairs.'

'I remember. And I fobbed you off with a practical explanation.'

'Did you ever see her, Miss Leonard.'

'No. But Mr Brown did, more than once. And one of the children, last term, after the fire, insisted that Miss Carey wasn't dead as she'd seen her in the corridor. Neither of them was lying. Some individuals see and hear more than others. Have you been very frightened?'

'At first I wasn't, because I thought she was real. Later, I did feel frightened.'

'And now?'

'Now I just feel desperately sorry for her. Her eyes, Miss Leonard. If you could have seen the sadness in her eyes!'

'Mr Brown mentioned that. You may talk to him if you like, but please no talk of ghosts to anyone else.'

'Of course not. Anyway, I think she'll go away now. She'll be free of the place. She's been punished so dreadfully. Maybe ghosts are people in purgatory and we see them around us all the time without realizing that they are ghosts.'

'Maybe *you* do,' said Miss Leonard, smiling a little.

The two retreating figures cast no shadows on the snow

The bell rang for the beginning of afternoon school. A wail of disappointment rose from outside. I looked out of the window, saw the children cease their snowballing and move obediently towards the building.

Only one figure moved away from the building, moved through the oncoming crowd of girls, who took no notice of her at all. She walked farther away, on and on, past the playground, across the snow-covered playing-field. A pale sun was shining and the snow dazzled, accentuating the thin, dark outline of the woman in black. She looked so utterly alone. Then a small figure began to follow her, running quickly and eagerly, and the sun turned the little figure's mop of red curls into a flame shaped like a rose.

The child overtook the woman in black and walked beside her, lightly, dancingly. And the two retreating figures cast no shadows on the snow, and left no footprints.

An Apparition

GUY DE MAUPASSANT

We had been talking about sequestration in connection with a recent lawsuit. It was towards the end of an evening spent among friends, at an old house in the Rue de Grenelle, and every one of us had told a story – a story supposed to be true. Eventually, the aged Marquis de la Tour Samuel, who was eighty-two, got to his feet and, leaning against the mantelpiece, said, in a rather tremulous voice:

I too have experienced something strange, so strange in fact that I have been haunted by it all my life. It is more than half a century since the incident happened, but not a month has passed without my seeing it all again in a dream. The impression, the imprint of terror, if you can follow me, has stayed with me ever since that day. For ten minutes I underwent such a ghastly fright that ever since a kind of perpetual fear has remained in my soul. Unexpected noises make me tremble to the bottom of my heart and things obscurely seen in the darkness almost impel me irresistibly to flee. In brief, at night I am afraid.

I wouldn't have confessed to that when I was younger! But now I can say anything. At eighty-two I don't feel obliged to be courageous in the presence of imaginary dangers. I have never given way before any real danger.

But the affair disturbed me so utterly and caused me such profound, mysterious and awful distress, that I never mentioned it to anyone. I have suppressed it in the depths of my being, those depths in which tormented secrets are hidden, the secrets and frailties we are ashamed of. I shall tell it to you precisely as it happened, without any attempt at explanation. Undoubtedly it can be explained – unless I were mad at the time. But I wasn't mad and I will prove it. You are at liberty to think what you choose. But these are the plain facts.

It was in the year 1827, in July. I was stationed at Rouen. One day, as I was strolling along the quay, I came across a man whom I thought I knew – without being able to remember exactly who he was. Impulsively, I made as if to stop; the stranger noticed this, glanced at me . . . and embraced me.

He was a friend of my youth whom I had liked immensely. It was five years since I had set eyes on him and he seemed to be fifty years older. His hair was completely white and he moved with a stoop as if utterly worn out. He saw my astonishment and told me what had happened to shatter his life.

He had fallen desperately in love with a young girl and had married her. But, after a single year of supreme love and happiness, she had died suddenly – of heart trouble – perhaps of love. On the day she was buried, he abandoned his château and went to live in his house in Rouen. There he existed, desperate and lonely, eaten up by grief, and so unhappy that he contemplated suicide.

'Now I have met you again,' he said, 'I shall ask you to do me an important favour: to go to my former home and obtain for me, from the bureau in my bedroom – our bedroom – certain documents which I urgently require. I can't send a servant or even a lawyer, as utter discretion and complete secrecy are needed. For my own part, nothing on earth would persuade me to go into that house again. I will give you the key of the room – which I myself locked on departing – and the key of the bureau and also a note to my gardener, instructing him to open up the château for you. But come and have breakfast with me tomorrow morning and we will arrange everything.'

An Apparition

I agreed to do him this small favour. It wouldn't be much of a trip, for his property was only a few miles out of Rouen, and could easily be reached in an hour by horse. So at ten o'clock next day I went round to his house and we had breakfast together . . . yet he hardly spoke a word.

He asked me to forgive him, but the idea of the visit I was going to make to the bedroom in the château, the scene of his past happiness, overwhelmed him. Certainly he was strangely disturbed and preoccupied, as if some unknown conflict were going on in his soul.

Eventually he told me in detail what I must do. It was quite simple. I was to obtain two bundles of letters and a roll of documents from the first drawer on the right-hand side of the bureau to which I had the key. He added, 'I do not need to request you not to look at them.'

I was offended by that and told him so in no uncertain manner. 'Do forgive me, I am suffering so much,' he said brokenly and began to weep.

At about one o'clock I left him and set off on my mission.

The weather was splendid and I rode across the fields listening to the larks singing and to the rhythmical tapping of my sword against my boot. Presently I came to the forest and walked my horse. Branches of trees brushed my face as I rode and, every now and then, I caught a leaf in my teeth and chewed it eagerly, for the sheer joy of being alive that sometimes fills one with intense happiness.

As I drew near the château, I took the letter for the gardener out of my pocket to have a look at it and was surprised to find it was sealed. I was so astonished and vexed by this that I was on the point of returning without having carried out my promise; but decided this would show too much sensitiveness. Quite possibly my friend had sealed the envelope unthinkingly, he had been so upset.

The château had the appearance of having been neglected for a score of years. The gate was open wide and so derelict it was a wonder it was still hanging; the paths were smothered in weeds and the flowerbeds and the lawn were all one.

My loud knocking aroused the old man who emerged from a side-door. He seemed bewildered with astonishment at my visit. He read the letter I gave him, examined it again and again, surveyed me suspiciously, put the letter in a pocket and eventually demanded: 'Well, then, what do you want?'

'As you have only just read your master's instructions, you should know what I want. I wish to enter the château.'

He was flabbergasted. 'You mean . . . you propose to go into . . . her room?'

I was beginning to lose patience. 'Look here! Are you going to stand there cross-questioning me?'

'No, monsieur,' he said in confusion; 'it's only . . . well, it's only because the room hasn't been open since . . . since she died. If you don't mind waiting for a few minutes I'll go myself to see . . . if . . .'

I interrupted him angrily: 'Look, what are you talking about? You can't get into the room, as I have the key!'

'All right, monsieur, I will show you the way,' was all he could say at that.

'Just show me the staircase and then leave me. I will find the way without you.'

'But, monsieur . . .'

I was really angry by now. 'Shut up or I'll give you something to think about.' I brushed past him and entered the château.

I made my way first through the kitchen; then a couple of rooms occupied by the caretaker and his wife; next, through a spacious hall by which I came to the staircase. I went up the stairs . . . and soon recognized the door described by my friend.

I opened it without difficulty and went in. The room was so dark that to begin with I couldn't make out a thing. I came to a halt, my nostrils assailed by the unpleasant, mouldering smell of untenanted rooms, of dead rooms. Presently, as my eyes grew used to the darkness, I could see quite clearly a large untidy bedroom, the bed covered only by mattress and pillows – on one of which was the obvious impression of an arm or a head, as if somebody had been resting there recently.

An Apparition

The chairs were all out of place. I noticed that a door, probably leading to an ante-room, had been left half open.

I went straight to the window, which I opened to let in the daylight. But the clasps of the shutters had become so rusty I couldn't make them budge. I even attempted to break them with my sword, but couldn't. As I was becoming vexed by my unavailing efforts and anyhow could see quite well in the gloom, I gave up the idea of obtaining more light and went across to the bureau.

I sat down in a chair, undid the lid of the bureau and opened the drawer in question. It was crammed full. I required only three bundles of papers, which I knew how to identify, and started to look for them.

I was peering closely in an attempt to make out the writing on them, when I seemed to hear – feel, rather – something rustling behind me. I took no notice, thinking that a draught from the window was causing the movement. But, the next moment, a similar movement, barely perceptible, made me shiver unaccountably and disturbingly. I felt so stupid at this, that pride prevented my turning round. By now I had located the second bundle of documents and was on the point of picking up the third when a long, poignant sigh, coming from near my shoulder, made me leap like a madman from my chair and land several feet away. As I leapt, I turned round, my hand on the hilt of my sword, and, in truth, if I hadn't felt it at my side, I would have fled like a coward.

A tall woman, clad in white, stood looking at me from behind the chair where I had been sitting a moment ago. I almost collapsed with the tremor that passed through me. No one could appreciate that fearful terror unless he had experienced it! The mind grows blank; the heart stands still; the whole body becomes limp as a sponge, as if life itself were ebbing.

I don't believe in ghosts, yet I surrendered utterly to a dreadful fear of the dead; and I endured more in those few moments than in the rest of my life, simply from that overwhelming terror of the supernatural. If she hadn't spoken, I think I would have died! But she spoke, she spoke in a gentle, sad voice, that set my nerves tingling. I daren't say I had regained control of myself and come to my senses. No! I was so scared I hardly knew what I was doing; but a certain innate pride, a shred of soldierly instinct, caused me, in spite of myself, to maintain some kind of bold front. I was keeping up appearances to myself, I suppose, and to her, whoever she might be, woman or ghost. It was only afterwards I realized all this, for I can tell you, when the apparition appeared, I thought of nothing. I was afraid.

She said: 'Oh, monsieur! You can do me a great service.'

I endeavoured to reply, but I couldn't utter a word. Nothing but a vague sound issued from my throat.

She went on: 'Will you? You can save me, cure me. I am suffering fearfully. I am suffering, oh, how I suffer!' and she sat down slowly in the chair.

'Will you?' she asked, regarding me.

I signified assent by nodding, for I was still voiceless.

Thereupon she held out to me a tortoiseshell comb and murmured: 'Comb my hair, please comb my hair! That will cure me. It must be combed. Look at my head – how I suffer. My hair burns me so!'

Her hair, unplaited, was very long and very black. It hung over the back of the chair and reached to the floor. Why did I take that comb with a shudder, why did I take that long, black hair that made my skin creep as if I were handling snakes? I don't know.

That feeling has stayed in my fingers to this day and I still shiver when I think of it.

I combed her hair. I handled – I don't know how – those ice-cold tresses. I untangled them, loosened them. She sighed and bowed her head, appearing to be content. All at once she exclaimed 'Thank you!' and snatched the comb from my hand and fled through the half-open door.

Left to myself, I went through the terrified agitation of a person who wakes up from a nightmare. At last I came to my senses; I hastened to the window and with a great effort broke open the shutters, letting in a flood of light. At once I ran to the door through which she had gone. I found it closed and immovable!

Then a frantic wish to flee overcame me in the kind of panic soldiers experience in battle. I clutched the three bundles of letters on the open bureau; ran from the room, rushed down the stairs four at a time, found myself outside, I don't know how, and seeing my horse a few paces away leaped into the saddle and galloped off.

I only halted on reaching Rouen and my own house. Flinging the bridle to my groom, I hurried to my room, where I locked myself in to think. For an hour I speculated anxiously whether I had been the victim of an hallucination. Surely I must have had one of those mysterious nervous shocks, one of those mental disturbances that give rise to miracles, to which the supernatural owes its influence.

I was almost convinced I had seen a vision, experienced an hallucination, when I went to the window. I happened to glance at my chest. My military cape was covered with hairs; the long hair of a woman, which had got caught in the buttons! One by one, with trembling fingers, I plucked them off and flung them away.

Then I summoned my groom. I was too distressed to go and see my friend that day; moreover, I wanted to consider more fully what I ought to tell him. I sent him his letters, for which he gave the groom a receipt. He inquired after me very particularly. He was told I was unwell, that I had had sunstroke or some such thing. He appeared to be exceedingly anxious. At daybreak next morning I visited him, determined to tell him the truth. He had gone out on the previous evening and had not yet returned. I called again during the course of the day. My friend was still absent. I waited a whole week. He did not appear. At length I informed the authorities. A search was started, but not the least trace of his whereabouts or the manner of his disappearance was discovered.

A thorough examination was made of the derelict château.

Nothing of a suspicious nature came to light. There was no sign that a woman had been concealed there.

The inquiries led to nothing and the search was abandoned. For more than half a century I have heard nothing. I know no more than before.

The Ghost of Thomas Kempe

PENELOPE LIVELY

Young James Harrison's life has been made a misery since the arrival on the scene of the poltergeist, Thomas Kempe, a sorcerer whose mischievous exploits are all blamed on the innocent boy who refuses to become his apprentice.

Mr and Mrs Harrison were unusually irritable the next morning. They had had a very disturbed night, it seemed. The alarm clock, apparently, had kept going off at irregular intervals from midnight onwards.

'Why did it do that, dad?' said James. He, too, had suffered: his bedcover had been twitched off three times, but there was no point in mentioning that.

'It's gone wrong, I presume,' said Mr Harrison, snappishly.

James said nothing: if the people had to be so unswerving in their beliefs the only thing you could do was to let them go their own way.

The day passed uneventfully at school except for one or two

more jokes about sorcery and sorcerer's apprentices from Mr Hollings, which James endured with resignation.

On the way home Simon said, 'Do they?'

'Do they what?'

'Believe in poltergeists.'

'No, they jolly well don't,' said James morosely.

'Oh,' said Simon. He picked up a stick from the gutter and began to run it along the wall of the row of cottages they were passing. The cottages were old: they must have stood square and solid in the middle of Ledsham for a very long time, maybe even since Thomas Kempe himself had stumped down this street, his head full of schemes and machinations about his neighbours and recipes for curing gout and palsy and the pox. People had been going about their business past those walls year after year, different people in different times with different thoughts in their heads. Now, one small window displayed a notice saying that Walls Ice-cream was sold here, and on one of the front doors someone had chalked 'Arsenal for the Cup'. The chimney stacks bristled with television aerials.

'Nobody believes in him except me,' said James. 'And I wouldn't if I didn't have to.'

'Perhaps,' said Simon thoughtfully, 'he's only there for you.'

'What do you mean?'

'Perhaps he's a kind of personal ghost. I mean, maybe he's real all right but only for you.'

James considered this. It was possible.

'Well even if he is, the things he does are real for other people. Or he wouldn't be causing all this trouble, would he?'

'Maybe you should try talking to him again.'

'And have more encyclopaedias chucked at me?' said James. 'Thanks very much.'

They walked on in silence for a minute or two. There was a workman on the church tower, doing something to the stone-work and carrying on a shouted conversation with a friend at the bottom about the seven-a-side match on Saturday afternoon.

'Trouble is,' said James, 'he's not in our time, is he? He's in his time, whenever that was, and he thinks like people thought in his time, and so you can't explain things to him in the same way we explain things to each other.'

'I should think he must be a bit bothered,' said Simon. 'It must be like waking up and discovering everyone except you has gone mad. Like a bad dream.'

'I'm not sure he cares,' said James gloomily. 'I think he's just having a good time. I mean, nobody here can do anything to him, can they? Since he's not even here properly. He can get away with anything,' Possibilities unfurled themselves, each more alarming than the last. The sorcerer could rampage unchecked, while he, James, would be trapped in the ferment he left behind, held answerable for things he could not explain because no one would listen . . .

'We've got to *do* something,' he said.

But Simon's attention had been distracted by the sight of unauthorized persons in the form of some boys from the other end of Ledsham throwing stones at the chestnut tree in *their* road. He vanished, leaving James with feelings of resentment: there was no doubt about it, Simon was only half-involved in the problem of Thomas Kempe. Interested, prepared to help up to a point, but not, like James, plunged into it day and night, like it or not.

He was still facing this fact, which made him feel isolated but, at the same time, challenged, like heroes of old confronted with impossibly difficult tasks, when he reached Mrs Verity's cottage. Mrs Verity was sitting on a chair in the doorway, enjoying the afternoon sunshine and keeping an eye on the various activities of East End Lane.

'Who'd like a mint humbug?'

'Yes, please,' said James.

'Let's see now, there were in my pinny pocket . . . Here we are, dear. I've just seen your mother go past with her shopping so she'll be back now. There was one of those Bakery bags in her basket so I expect she's got something nice for your tea. There's nurse's car – I wonder where she's going?' Mrs Verity shifted her chair slightly to improve her view of the street. 'The telly repair van's still outside the Bradley's, I see. That's the best part of an hour he's been there.'

James stared up at Mrs Verity's thatched roof, admiring the patterned bit at the top and thinking that it must be very dull just being interested in what other people were up to. Starlings sat on the ridge of the roof, whistling and chattering. They gave the impression of doing much the same as Mrs Verity.

Mrs Verity was talking about school. She asked James how he liked it and James said it was all right thanks and told her a bit about the project they were doing and Mrs Verity said 'Fancy!' and 'Dear me, it wasn't like that in my day.' And then rather surprisingly, she began to tell James a long story about a Sunday School when she was a small girl that began most unpromisingly and suddenly got very funny and unexpected. The Sunday School, it seemed, was a weekly session of torment during which all the Ledsham children of the time were made to sit in the cold and dusty silence of the church hall for two hours on end listening to the Scriptures read aloud, neither moving nor speaking on pain of instant and dreadful punishment. And on one never-to-be-forgotten occasion the children had slowly and delightedly become aware that the Vicar's dour sister who was responsible for inflicting this torture upon them was herself falling inexorably asleep . . .

'We all looked at each other and nobody hardly dared breathe and we waited till she dozed right off, sitting there in her chair with the Bible in her hand, and then my brother Robert – he was ever such a wicked boy, my brother, always in hot water, but he did well for himself later, manager of the Co-op. in Rugby he was till he retired – Robert signed to us all and we all got up, quiet as mice – not a sound, and we crept out and left her there and we turned the key in the lock behind us. And then we rushed out into the sunshine whooping and screeching like a lot of little savages and we played a wild game in the churchyard, in and out the gravestones. I can remember it now. Though it seems funny to think back – you hardly feel it could be the same person as you

are now. But they say the child is father to the man, don't they?'
She looked anxiously at James as though wondering whose
father he might be and James stared back at her with a new
interest. Somewhere, deep within stout, elderly Mrs Verity,
with her rheumaticky hands that swelled up around her
wedding ring, and her bad back that bothered her in damp
weather, there sheltered the memory of a little girl who had
behaved outrageously in Sunday School. And that, when you
stopped to think about it, was a very weird thing indeed.

He was just about to ask what happened when the Vicar's
sister woke up when a tremendous gust of wind sent the starlings
tumbling off the roofs – Mrs Verity's dress ballooned around
her.

'Gracious! What a gale! I'll have to go inside.'

Air formed itself into a solid pressure on James' right arm,
tugging him away from Mrs Verity's door. Another bank of it
hustled him down the lane towards East End Cottage. Mrs
Verity was controlling her skirts with one hand and pulling her
chair into the house with the other.

'Goodbye for now, dear.'

James shouted 'Goodbye' as the wind gave him a final shove
on to the opposite pavement and instantly subsided. Seething
with indignation he ran the rest of the way home.

Bully. Busybody. Who does he think he is? I can talk to Mrs
Verity if I want to, can't I?

Does he think he owns me, or something?

Mrs Verity had been right about the Bakery bag. There were
cream splits for tea, which James found very heartening. After a
while he felt sufficiently restored to tease Helen about her new
dress.

'What's it s'posed to be? I never saw such a weird object. Oh, *I*
know – it's a football jersey that someone left out in the rain so it
got all soggy and stretched so it wasn't any use any more . . .'

'It's a striped shift. Julia's got one too.'

'It's shifted all right. Shifted in all the wrong directions.

Why's it such a peculiar shape – oh, *sorry*, that's you. I thought it was the dress . . .'

'Mum!' wailed Helen.

'Enough!' said Mrs Harrison. 'And finish your tea, please. I want to clear up before the Vicar comes.'

'The *Vicar*?'

'About the choir.'

The Vicar, however, arrived before Mrs Harrison had had time to establish order in the kitchen. Moreover, he was one of those people who like to make it instantly clear that they are unusually accommodating and easygoing, and refused to be steered into the sitting-room.

'Please – I do hate people to put themselves out – just carry on as though I weren't here.'

That, thought James, would be a bit difficult. The Vicar was six feet tall and stout into the bargain. He had already clipped his head on a beam as he came in and was trying desperately to suppress a grimace of pain.

'Oh dear,' said Mrs Harrison, sweeping crockery into the sink. 'These blessed ceilings. I'm so sorry. Will you have a cup of tea? I'll just make some fresh.'

The front door slammed with a loud bang, making the Vicar jump. 'I never refuse a cup of tea – but please – I don't want to be a nuisance.'

'No trouble,' said Mrs Harrison. 'James, do something about that dog. It seems to have gone mad.'

Tim had gone into the now familiar routine that indicated, James realized with a sinking heart, that Thomas Kempe was not far away. He grabbed him. The Vicar, too, was looking at him, though apparently for different reasons.

'Dear me, how like the stray who got in and took the joint from our larder last week. Curious to see two mongrels so much alike, eh? Well, well. And how's school, young man?'

'Fine,' said James, 'thanks.' Tim was struggling violently, and lunging with bared teeth at a point somewhere behind the Vicar. The windows rattled. 'These autumn winds,' said the Vicar. 'I always think of those at sea.'

'What? said Mrs Harrison. 'Oh, yes, yes, quite.' She slammed the lid on the teapot irritably.

The electric fire flickered. Upstairs, distantly, came the sound of an alarm clock going off. A cup jinked in its saucer on the dresser.

'Do sit down,' said Mrs Harrison. 'James, pull up a chair for the Vicar.'

James fetched the windsor chair from the corner and placed it by the table. He still had one hand on its arm as the Vicar began to lower himself into it, and so felt the whole thing twitch, stagger, and jerk suddenly sidweways, so that the Vicar, prodded violently in the hip, lurched against the table and almost fell.

'James!' said Mrs Harrison angrily. 'Look what you're doing!'

'Sorry,' said James in confusion, straightening the chair. The Vicar sat down, rubbing his hip and also apologizing. Tim began to bark hysterically.

'Put that dog out!' shouted Mrs Harrison.

With Tim outside, things were quieter, except for another bang as the back door, this time, slammed. The Vicar passed a hand across his forehead and rubbed his head, furtively.

'Family life, eh! There's always something going on, what?'

'Never a dull moment,' said Mrs Harrison grimly. 'Milk?'

'Oh – please – yes, if I may . . . So kind of you. I do hope I'm not interrupting. I'm sure you're very busy, like we all are in these days, eh?'

'Not at all,' said Mrs Harrison. 'James, pass the Vicar his tea, will you?'

James, with extreme caution, carried cup and saucer across the room. He was standing in front of the Vicar, and the Vicar's fingers were just closing on the edge of the saucer, when the cup jolted, tipped, hung at an angle of forty-five degrees, and turned over. Tea flowed into the saucer, and thence in a cascade on to the Vicar's trousers.

'James!' said Mrs Harrison in a strangled voice.

There was a great deal of mopping and exclaiming. The Vicar apologized, and then apologized again. James apologized. Mrs

Harrison's face had taken on that pinched, gathered look that foretold an outburst as soon as circumstances permitted. Finally, the Vicar, dried off and supplied with a new cup of tea, stopped saying how sorry he was and began to talk about choir practices. Mrs Harrison liked to sing sometimes: she said it allowed her to let off steam. Furthermore, she thought it would be a good idea if James sang. James, knowing this, had been hoping to beat a retreat. He sidled towards the door. 'My son,' said Mrs Harrison, glaring at him, 'sings too. After a fashion.'

'My dear boy,' the Vicar said, 'you must come along. We've got some other chaps about your age.'

James mumbled that he'd love to, or words to that effect. He was pinned to the spot now, by a steely look from his mother.

'Splendid, eh?' said the Vicar. 'Tell you what, I'll just jot down the times of our practices, shall I?' He patted his pockets.

Mrs Harrison said, 'James. Fetch the telephone pad, please, and a pencil.'

James opened the kitchen door, which swung shut again behind him, and crossed the hall. The telephone pad had a shopping list on it which said 'Onions, cereals, elastic bands, disinfectant.' Underneath that was a message about an electrician who would call back later, and a picture of a spaceman (drawn by James), and underneath that was a message from Thomas Kempe in large letters, which said 'I am watchynge ye.'

'Go on and watch then,' shouted James, in a fury. 'See if I care!'

There was crash. The barometer had leapt off the wall and lay on the floor, the glass cracked. And a series of loud bangs, apparently made by some kind of blunt instrument such as a hammer, reverberated through the house.

The kitchen door flew open. The banging ceased instantly. Mrs Harrison was standing there saying the kind of things that were to be expected, only slightly toned down in deference to the Vicar, who was standing behind her, with a dazed expression on his face. He had hit his head on the beam again, James realized.

'. . . must apologize for my son's appalling behaviour,' concluded Mrs Harrison.

'Boys will be boys,' said the Vicar, without conviction. 'Eh? And now I really must be on my way. So kind . . . So glad we can look forward to having you with us . . .' He edged sideways through the front door, stooping, with the air of a man who wanted only to be unobtrusive and had always wished himself several sizes smaller.

James picked up the barometer and waited for the wrath to come.

Upstairs, later, James catalogued the extent of his mother's displeasure in the Personal Notebook. 'No pudding, obviously. Maybe I'll die of sarvation, and *then* they'll be sorry. Bed straight after supper. Which is why I'm here. No Simon to play for two days.' He turned over the page, and a new message confronted him, written with surly disregard across a whole clean page of the notebook.

I lyke not Priestes.

James tore it out, screwed it into a ball, and hurled it across the room.

For the rest of that evening, and the next day, James was plagued by something which was lurking in the back of his mind, but which he could not quite pin down. In that book in the library, 'A Clergyman' had talked at great length not only about ghosts he had know, but also the disposing of ghosts. There had been a word which kept cropping up. Exercising them, or something like that. But how had it been done? And who by? He asked Simon. Simon could not remember either. Indeed it was difficult to involve him very deeply in the problem. He was, James realized, a little bitterly, an interested spectator. Sympathetic, helpful to a point, but sceptical and a spectator only.

There was no point in raising the matter with his parents again. They did not believe in ghosts: therefore there were no such things.

It occurred to him that this was a subject on which Mrs Verity might well have something to say. Naturally, he would not mention Thomas Kempe. That would be madness. It would be all over Ledsham in five minutes. And straight back to his parents, who would say he had made the whole thing up. No, the thing would be to raise the subject in a general sort of way, and see what happened . . .

'Ghosts?' said Mrs Verity. 'Why, good gracious, I could tell you a thing or two about ghosts. Believe in them? Well, what I always say is, we don't know the answers to everything, do we? I mean, there's some things in this world you can't explain and maybe we're not meant to.'

It became clear that not only did Mrs Verity believe firmly in ghosts but she relished a good haunting, and knew about plenty. Ghost story followed ghost story in bewildering succession: what Mrs Verity's sister had seen in the churchyard after the Christmas Carol Service, what old Charlie at the Bull had heard in the yard one night, the story they used to tell about the Manor, in the old days. Ledsham apparently crawled with ghosts. In such abundance they rather lost their impact: James began to grow restless. At last he managed to stem the flow and ask how you got rid of them.

'You have them exorcised, don't you, dear?' said Mrs Verity. 'By an exorcist. Excuse me just a moment – I can see Mrs Simpson just down the road and I've been wanting a word with her . . .'

So he had, in a way, been right. Ghosts were a domestic problem, if not a particularly common one. And ordinary, ghost-believing people simply got someone in to deal with them like they'd get a plumber or a window-cleaner. But he, of course, had to have parents who insisted on denying their existence even when living cheek by jowl, so to speak, with a particularly active one.

If you need a plumber, or anything in that line, you look in the Yellow Pages of the Telephone Directory, don't you? Right, then. James looked, not entirely hopefully. As he had expected, there were no exorcists. Nothing between Exhibition Stand Contractors and Export Agents. There was nothing for it but to consult Mrs Verity again. Cautiously, though, in case her interest was aroused.

'Do I know any exorcists? Well, let me see now . . . There's Mrs Nash, but she's really more in the fortune-telling and teacup line. I don't think she's ever done much in the spiritual way. Of course sometimes you find the Vicar'll turn his hand to that kind of thing, but not this one, I'm told. Now, when they had that trouble at Church Hanborough, years ago, at that old place there, they called in Bert Ellison. Mind, he's a wart-charmer really. And water-divining he does, too, they say. Why do you ask, dear?'

James did not dare pursue the matter too far. He returned to the Yellow Pages, and found that Wart-charmers and Water-Diviners are not included either. There was, however, a Bert Ellison, Builder, who lived in one of the cottages behind the church.

The thought of confronting this person all on his own, and stating his business, threw James into confusion. He imagined what might happen: 'Will I come and get rid of a ghost for you? I'm a builder, aren't I? Says so, doesn't it? Bert Ellison, builder. I wouldn't like to think you might be trying to make a fool of me . . .'

A particularly restless evening, however, during which Thomas Kempe fused the television set and broke a milk jug, stiffened his resolve. The next day, after school, he walked round to the lane behind the church.

There was a small blue notice-board attached to the wall of Bert Ellison's cottage. It said only that he was a Builder and Decorator, and gave Free Estimates, without mentioning his other activities, which was discouraging but perhaps only to be expected. James knocked at the door.

The man who opened it wore a dusty boiler-suit and had a mug of tea in one hand. He was heavily-built, and slightly balding. 'Yes?' he said.

James said, 'Mr. Ellison?'

'That's me.'

'I've come about a – well, a job that needs doing.'

'Decorating, is it?' said Bert Ellison, taking a gulp of tea.

'No, no, it isn't, actually.'

'Building, then?'

'No,' said James. 'Not that either.'

Bert Ellison looked at him reflectively. 'I don't know you, do I? Come from your mum, have you? What's her name, then?'

'I'm James Harrison. We live at East End Cottage. Actually it's for me, the job, not for my mum.'

'Is it, now? Well, I'm blowed. Bit young, aren't you, to be handing out jobs?'

'It's just a small job,' said James unhappily. 'At least I hope it is.'

'I think you'd better come in,' said Bert Ellison, 'and tell me about this job of yours. Mind, I'm not saying as I can fix you up. We'll have to see.'

'Thank you very much, Mr Ellison,' said James.

'You'd better call me Bert, if we're going to do business together.'

Bert was clearly not married. The kitchen was full of empty milk bottles and socks drying on a line over the stove. Tins of paint and brushes littered the table, along with the remains of some fish and chips in newspaper and a large brown teapot.

'Now then?'

James decided to plunge straight in. 'There's a ghost in our house,' he said, 'and I thought – at least somebody told me – maybe you could do something about it.'

Bert poured himself another cup of tea, and began to roll a cigarette. He stuck it in the corner of his mouth, lit it, and said. 'Just the one?'

'Yes,' said James, taken aback.

'It's as well to ask. I've known them come in pairs. Or more. Been there long, has it?'

'About a week or so. Or at least I've only known about it that long.'

'Could have been dormant,' said Bert, 'and something sparked it off, like. Why've you come about it, and not your mum?'

'She doesn't believe in them. Nor does my dad.'

'Ah. You find people like that from time to time. No point in arguing with 'em. It's best just to get on with the job, I always say. They'll thank you for it in the long run. Now, what's he been up to, this bloke?'

James described the sorcerer's activities in detail. Bert Ellison listened intently, drinking tea and smoking. When James had finished he passed a large hand across his chin once or twice, and stared out of the window.

'You've got a problem there, all right,' he said. 'I never come across one quite like that before. The knocking, yes, and the breaking things, and all that. It's the notes is unusual. I never came across one as could write up to now.'

'He must've lived there,' said James, 'hundreds of years ago.'

'That's right. They're often the worst to get rid of, too. They feel at home. Stands to reason, doesn't it?'

'Can't you do anything, then?'

'I'll have a go, but I can't promise too much, mind. Still, I daresay I can fix you up. There's a charge, of course.'

'I've only got forty pence at the moment,' said James. 'I've been having a bit of trouble about pocket money lately.'

'We'll say five bob, shall we,' said Bert. 'I do a reduced rate for pensioners, too.'

'Thank you very much.'

'How about I look in tomorrow evening?'

'The thing is,' said James, 'I don't know what to say to my mum about you.'

'Ah. Now you've got a point there. Being as how she's a non-believer, as you might say. She's not seen these notes, then?'

'No. And if I showed her she'd just say I'd written them.'

'Ah. Fair enough. What's she done about this clock, then, and the telly packing up?'

'She took the clock to the shop in the High Street and the electrician's coming tomorrow.'

Bert snorted contemptuously. 'If you've got dry rot in the floorboards, you don't just slap new lino down on top, do you? That won't do her much good. Still, if that's the way she feels about it there's not much use you going home and saying "Look mum, I got a bloke coming in tomorrow to see about the ghost", is there?'

'No,' said James.

Bert tapped blunt, competent-looking fingers on the table-top for a moment. Then he said, 'Got any building jobs need doing?'

'Well . . .' said James. 'It was all done before we moved in, really. The catch on my window's broken, though. She did say she'd get that done some time. Oh, and they did say I needed some shelves, too.'

'There you are, then. Now what you've go to do is, go home and start in on them about that and when they say "Well, yes, but who's going to do it?" you chip in smart and say you've heard about this Bert Ellison as everyone speaks so highly of and how you'll nip along and ask him yourself . . .'

'Yes!' said James excitedly. 'Yes, I could do that.'

'. . . and then I come round and fix your shelves and see to the window and while I'm there I'll have a think about the other business as well. How about that?'

'Great!' said James. 'Thanks very much.'

'So you look in on your way home from school, eh? And if everything's in order I'll be round later in the evening.'

'Bert Ellison?' said Mrs Harrison. 'I've never heard of him.'

'He's really a very well-known builder,' said James earnestly. 'Quite famous, actually. I'm surprised you don't know about him. I'm sure he'd do the shelves much better than anyone else.'

Mr Harrison, who had listened without saying anything, got up and began to put his coat on.

'At this point,' he said, 'one's bound to ask oneself certain questions. One: why, all of a sudden, does James want something urgently done in the way of mending a window and

putting up some shelves that he's shown little or no interest in
hitherto? And two: given all this, why does he go still further and
produce a particular builder that he wants to do the job? One is
tempted even to suspect some sort of conspiracy between the
two of them . . .'

'Dad!' said James, in the most shocked and offended voice he
could manage.

'. . . if it weren't quite beyond belief that a perfectly sane,
adult chap such as Bert Ellison should associate himself in any
way with some lunatic scheme of James'.'

'Why? Do you know him?' said Mrs Harrison.

'Slightly. Or at least I know of him. He's been doing some
work in the church. He seems quite all right. I should think we
might entrust the shelves to him. James' sudden involvement
will no doubt be one of those things that we shall never get to the
bottom of. Like many others. Eh, James?'

'It's no good looking as though you don't know what he
means,' said Helen. 'What about my dressing-gown cord being
found tied to the big apple tree? And the empty ink-bottles in
the vegetable patch . . . ?'

James sighed: there is nothing more boring than trying to
explain things to people who aren't going to appreciate what it is
you are up to. You've got to use something to haul provisions up
a rock-face with, haven't you? And if you do scientific experiments, you're bound to leave a few bits and pieces around, aren't
you? (No point in telling Helen lettuces do not grow blue if
watered with diluted ink: she wouldn't even care).

'So can I say it's all right if he comes tonight?' he said,
ignoring Helen.

'I suppose so.'

Bert Ellison arrived on a bicycle shortly after tea, whistling.
He looked so ordinary, so, in fact, like a builder on his way to put
up some shelves that for a moment James' faith was shaken.
Only ten minutes before he had enjoyed saying to Simon. 'Well,
I'm afraid I'll have to go now because I've got this exorcist
coming to see to the poltergeist.' Simon had been satisfactorily

astonished. But now here was Bert, in white overalls, with a cigarette tucked behind his ear, and a black bag of tools, not looking in the least like an exorcist.

'Oh,' said Mrs Harrison. 'Yes, of course, the window, and the shelves . . . I'd better take you up.'

James, lurking behind her in the hall, fidgeted anxiously, and saw Bert's gaze come up over her shoulder and fall on him. The man pushed his cap back from his forehead, unhitched the cigarette from his ear and said. 'Maybe your young lad could do that. Not to bother you, see?' James was filled with relief.

Mrs Harrison said, 'Well, yes, you could, couldn't you, James?' and went back into the kitchen. James looked at Bert Ellison, and Bert Ellison nodded, and they went upstairs, James leading and Bert following, his heavy tread making the whole staircase sway slightly.

James opened the door to his room and they went in. Tim, asleep on the bed, woke up with a start and growled.

Bert look at him thoughtfully. 'I seen him before,' he said. 'Let's think now . . . At the butcher's before Christmas, and The Red Lion before that, and the corner shop the year before that. He knows when he's on to a good thing, that one.' Tim, with an evil look, slunk past him and out of the door. Bert set his tools down with a clatter and surveyed the room. 'Right, then, where are we putting these shelves?'

'But,' began James anxiously, 'the other thing . . .'

'Look,' said Bert, 'we've got to be doing something, haven't we? If your mum decides to come up. Not larking about looking for ghosts. These shelves has got to go up, and be heard to go up.'

James understood. 'Here,' he said. 'Under the window.'

Bert began to measure, and cut pieces of wood. 'So he played up when the Vicar was here, this bloke?'

'I'll say,' said James. 'It was one of the worst times. Knocked things over, and banged.'

'Then it's not worth trying bell, book and candle,' said Bert, 'if he's got no respect for the Church. I'd just be wasting my time. Nor's it worth getting twelve of them.'

'Twelve what?'

'Vicars,' said Bert briefly.

James had a delightful, momentary vision of twelve enormous Vicars following one another up the stairs, hitting their heads on the beams and apologizing in chorus. But Bert was not just being fanciful. He was not a man given to fancy. Apparently ghosts were normally exorcised by twelve priests in the old days. Or seven, sometimes. Or just one, if skilled in such matters.

'But that won't do with this blighter,' said Bert. He lit the cigarette from behind his ear, made some token noises with hammer and nails, and looked round the room reflectively. James waited for him to come to a decision, anxious, but at the same time deeply thankful to be thus sharing the burden of responsibility for Thomas Kempe. He felt relieved of a heavy weight, or at least partly relieved.

'No,' said Bert. 'We won't try anything like that. Nor talking to him, neither, since you saw you've already had a go. You know what I think? I think we'll try bottling him.' He put a plank of wood across a chair, and knelt on it, and began to saw it in half, whistling through his teeth.

'Bottling him?' said James, wondering if he could have heard correctly.

'That's right. I'll be wanting a bottle with a good firm stopper. Cork 'ud be best. And seven candles.'

'Now?'

'Might as well get on with it, mightn't we?'

James raced downstairs. On the landing he slowed up, remembering the need for discretion. He crept down the next flight, and tiptoed into the larder. He could hear his mother and Helen talking in the kitchen, and from overhead came reassuringly ordinary sawing and hammering noises made by Bert. He felt nervous on several counts: there was the problem of someone asking him what he wanted, and also he kept expecting the sorcerer to manifest himself in some way. What was he doing? Could he be scared of Bert Ellison? Or was he biding his time, before launching some furious attack? From what Thomas Kempe had revealed of his character hitherto he didn't seem the

229

kind of person to be all that easily routed, even by as phlegmatic an opponent as Bert Ellison.

There were various empty medicine bottles on the larder shelf. He selected the one with the tightest-fitting cork and began to look for candles. There was a box of gaily coloured birthday-cake ones, complete with rose-shaped holders, but they seemed inappropriate. He hunted round and unearthed a packet of uncompromisingly plain white ones – an emergency supply for electricity cuts. They were just right: serviceable and not frivolous. He was just putting them under his arm when the door opened.

'Mum says if you're picking at the plum tart you're not to,' said Helen. 'What *are* you doing with those candles?'

'The builder needs them,' said James. 'He's got to solder the shelves with something, hasn't he? He can't solder the rivets without a candle, can he? Or the sprockets,' He stared at her icily: Helen's ignorance of carpentry was total, he knew.

She looked at the candles suspiciously. 'I don't see . . .' she began.

'You wouldn't, said James, wriggling past her. 'I should go and ask Mum to explain. Very slowly and carefully so you'll be able to follow her all right. Or if you like I will later on,' He shot up the stairs without waiting to hear what she had to say.

Bert had cleared the table and moved it to the centre of the room.

'Ah,' he said, 'that'll do fine. We'll have it in the middle, the bottle, and the candles in a circle round, like. He seems to be keeping himself to himself, your chap. I thought we'd have heard something from him by now.'

'So did I,' said James.

'Maybe he's lying low to see what we've got in mind. Is that his pipe on the shelf there?'

'Yes.'

Bert walked over and picked it up. As he did so the window slammed shut.

'There. He don't like having his property interfered with. Well, that signifies.'

A draught whisked round the table

'Can we get on,' said James uneasily, 'with whatever we're going to do.'

'No good rushing a thing like this,' said Bert. 'You've got to take your time. Make a good job of it.' He fiddled around with the bottle and candles, arranging them to his liking. Then he struck a match and lit the candles. The flames staggered and twitched for a moment, then settled down into steady, oval points of light.

'We'd best draw the curtains,' said Bert. 'We don't want people looking in from outside. Then pull up a chair and sit down.'

With the curtains drawn, the room was half dark, the corners lost in gloom, everything concentrated on the circle of yellow lights on the table. Bert and James sat opposite one another. The candles made craggy black shadows on Bert's face, so that it seemed different: older, less ordinary. Downstairs, a long way away, the wireless was playing and someone was running a tap.

Bert took out a handkerchief and wiped his forehead. 'Right, then:' He cleared his throat and said ponderously, 'Rest, thou unquiet spirit!'

There was dead silence. —Bert, catching James' eye, looked away in embarrassment and said, 'I don't hold with thee-ing and thou-ing, as a rule, but when you're dealing with a bloke like this – well, I daresay he'd expect it.'

James nodded. They sat quite still. Nothing happened.

'Return from whence thou come – came,' said Bert. 'Begone!'

Two of the candles on James' side of the table guttered wildly, and went out.

'Ah!' said Bert. 'Now he's paying us a bit of attention.'

They waited. James could hear his mother's voice, distantly, saying something about potatoes from the sack in the shed. Uneasy, he leaned across towards Bert and whispered, 'Will it take long?'

'Depends,' said Bert. 'It's no good chivvying these characters. You've got to let them take their time.'

A draught whisked round the table. Three more candles went out.

'Cheeky so-and-so, isn't he?' said Bert.

'Does he know what he's supposed to do?' whispered James.

'He knows all right.'

But how would *they* realize it if when Thomas Kempe did decide to conform and get into the bottle, James wondered? He wanted to ask, but felt that perhaps too much talk was unsuitable. Presumably Bert, as an experienced exorcist, would know in some mysterious way.

'Come on, now,' said Bert. 'Let's be 'aving you.'

The last two candle-flames reached up, long and thin, then contracted into tiny points, went intensely blue, and vanished.

'That's it!' said Bert. He got up and drew the curtains.

James looked round anxiously. 'Didn't it work?'

'No. He wasn't having any. When the candles go out, that's it.'

'Couldn't we try again?'

'There wouldn't be any point to it. If he don't fancy it, then he don't fancy it, and that's that. He's an awkward cuss, no doubt about it.'

The stairs creaked. James whipped the candles off the table and into his drawer. Bert hastily began to saw up a piece of wood.

Mrs Harrison came in. 'Everything all right?' she said. 'You mustn't let James get in your way, Mr Ellison. I'm afraid he hangs around rather, sometimes.'

'That's all right,' said Bert, 'I'm not fussed. I can send him packing when I've had enough.'

'Good. What a funny smell. Wax, or something.'

'That'll be my matches,' said Bert, 'I daresay.'

Mrs Harrison said, 'Candles, I'd have thought.' She looked round, sniffing.

'Not to my way of thinking,' said Bert. 'That's a match smell, that is.'

'Oh. Well, maybe.' She gave Bert a look tinged with misgiving and looked at the pile of half-sawn wood: the thought seemed to be passing through her mind that not much had been achieved so far.

'I got behind,' said Bert amiably. 'We've been having a bit of a chat, me and your lad here. Found we had one or two interests in common, as you might say.'

'Oh?' said Mrs Harrison.

'History. People that aren't around any more. We've both got a fancy for that kind of thing.' Bert's right eyelid dropped in a conspicuous wink, aimed towards James.

'That's nice,' said Mrs Harrison. 'We hadn't realized James was particularly interested in history, I must say.'

'It's often their own parents as knows children least, isn't it?' said Bert.

'I'm not entirely sure about that,' said Mrs Harrison drily. James, avoiding her eye, busied himself with a pile of nails.

'So, one way and another I think I'll have to come back another time and finish off,' said Bert, stowing hammer and saw into his black bag. 'I like to make a proper job of anything I take on. See it through to the end.'

Mrs Harrison said, 'Right you are, then,' and went downstairs. James and Bert Ellison, left alone, looked at each other.

'No,' said Bert. 'I can see she wouldn't have much time for ghosts, your mum. A bit set in her ways, maybe. Got opinions.'

'Yes,' said James with feeling. 'She has.'

'Not that I've got anything against that. I like a woman to know her own mind. But it's no good setting yourself up against it. You'd just be wasting your breath.' He pushed his ruler and pencil into the pocket of his white overalls, closed the tool-bag, and stood up.

James said anxiously. 'What about tomorrow? Is there something else you can try?'

'To be honest with you,' said Bert, 'there's not a lot. Vicars is out. He don't fancy the bottle.' His large stubby fingers came down on his palm, ticking off possibilities. 'We could try fixing him with a job as would keep him busy, but I'd guess he's too fly to be taken in with that one. Or we could try circle and rowan stick. Is your father an Oxford man, by any chance?'

'An Oxford man?'

'Did he go to Oxford University?'

'No,' said James. 'Why?'

'In the old days you used an Oxford man for laying a ghost. But I daresay there's not many would take it on nowadays. They've got fancy ideas in education now, I hear.'

'Isn't there anything then?' said James disconsolately.

It's a tricky job, this one, no doubt about that.'

'You see I'm getting blamed for everything he does. It's no pocket money, and no pudding, and worse, I should think, when they run out of punishments.'

'That's a bit thick,' said Bert.

'I'll say.'

'The trouble is, them being non-believers. In the normal way of things it'd be them as would have called me in, in the first place. Things would have been a lot more straightforward.'

They were going down the stairs now. James glanced anxiously at the closed kitchen door. Bert nodded and lowered his voice. 'Tell you what, I got those shelves to finish off, so I'll be back.'

'Thank you very much,' said James. 'Oh, I nearly forgot . . .' He reached into his jeans pocket for his money.

'No charge,' said Bert. 'Not till the job's done satisfactory.' He climbed on to his bike and rode away down the lane, the black bag bumping against the mudguard.

James had been right in thinking that the sorcerer might be biding his time. That evening, as though in compensation for the restraint he had shown during Bert Ellison's visit (if it had been restraint, and not, perhaps, a temporary retreat in face of a professional enemy) he let rip. Doors slammed, and the house echoed with thumps and bumps, almost invariably coming from whatever area James was currently occupying, so that cries of 'James! Stop that appalling noise!' rang up and down the stairs. The television set, just repaired, developed a new fault: a high-pitched buzzing that coincided oddly with all weather-forecasts and any programme involving policemen or doctors (which seemed to be most of them). The teapot parted from its handle when Mrs Harrison lifted it up, with catastrophic results. Something caused Tim, sleeping peacefully under the kitchen table, to shoot out yelping as though propelled by someone's foot, colliding with, and tripping up, Mr Harrison, who fell against the dustbin which overturned, shooting tea-leaves and eggshells across the floor . . . You could put whatever interpretation you liked on all this: coincidence, carelessness, the weather, the malevolence of fate. James knew quite well to what he would attribute it, and so, apprently did Tim, who abandoned his usual evening sleeping-places and went to sulk in the long grass at the end of the orchard.

After a couple of hours Mr and Mrs Harrison, both remarkably even-tempered people in the normal way of things, were reduced to a state of simmering irritation, which eventually resulted in both James and Helen being sent to bed early and, they felt, unloved. They shared their resentment on the stairs.

'It's not fair,' said Helen.

'It's not *our* fault.'

'Everything keeps going wrong these days. I think it's something to do with this house.'

James stared. Such perception was unlike Helen: she seemed usually to notice only the obvious. Perhaps she was changing. Since they seemed to have established a temporary truce, he decided to investigate further.

'Helen?'

'Do you believe in ghosts?'

Helen said cautiously. 'Do you?'

'Well. I s'pose so. Yes, actually I do.'

'So do I, really.'

They looked at each other.

'*They* don't,' said Helen. 'Mum and Dad.'

'I know. But lots of people do.'

'Why do you want to know anyway? I say, you don't think there's one in this house, do you?'

James hesitated, tempted to confide. But you never knew with Helen . . . She might well laugh, tell everyone, never let him hear the end of it. And he'd have to share Bert Ellison.

'Shouldn't think so,' he said, turning away. 'Good night.'

'Good night.'

He climbed the last few stairs to his room slowly, thinking of what he might have said to her. 'Yes, as a matter fact there is. He's called Thomas Kempe, Esq., and he lived here a few hundred years ago and was a kind of sorcerer and crazy doctor and village policeman and general busybody and he thinks he's come back to start all over again with me helping and he keeps writing me messages and as a matter of fact I've been sharing my bedroom with him for over a week now.' Ha ha!

He opened the door. The bottle he and Bert Ellison had used in the exorcism attempt was in the middle of the floor, smashed. Beside it was Thomas Kempe's latest message, written in felt pen on the back of an envelope.

Doe not thinke that I am so dull of witte that I may be thus trycked twyce.

The Occupant of the Room

ALGERNON BLACKWOOD

He arrived late at night by the yellow *diligence*, stiff and cramped after the toilsome ascent of three slow hours. The village, a single mass of shadow, was already asleep. Only in front of the little hotel was there noise and light and bustle – for a moment. The horses, with tired, slouching gait, crossed the road and disappeared into the stable of their own accord, their harness trailing in the dust; and the lumbering *diligence* stood for the night where they had dragged it – the body of a great yellow-sided beetle with broken legs.

In spite of his physical weariness, the schoolmaster, revelling in the first hours of his ten-guinea holiday, felt exhilarated. For the high Alpine valley was marvellously still; stars twinkled over the torn ridges of the Dent du Midi where spectral snows gleamed against rocks that looked like ebony; and the keen air smelt of pine forests, dew-soaked pastures, and freshly sawn wood. He took it all in with a kind of bewildered delight for a few minutes, while the other three passengers gave directions about their luggage and went to their rooms. Then he turned and walked over the coarse matting into the glare of the hall, only

just able to resist stopping to examine the big mountain map that
hung upon the wall by the door.

And, with a sudden disagreeable shock, he came down from
the ideal to the actual. For at the inn – the only inn – there was no
vacant room. Even the available sofas were occupied . . .

How stupid he had been not to write! Yet it had been
impossible, he remembered, for he had come to the decision
suddenly that morning in Geneva, enticed by the brilliance of
the weather after a week of rain.

They talked endlessly, this gold-braided porter and the
hardfaced old woman – her face was hard, he noticed –
gesticulating all the time, and pointing all about the village with
suggestions that he ill understood, for his French was limited
and their *patois* was fearful.

'*There!*' – he might find a room, 'or *there!* But we are, *hélas*,
full – more full than we care about. To-morrow, perhaps – if So-
and-So give up their rooms –!' And then, with much shrugging
of shoulders, the hard-faced old woman stared at the gold-
braided porter, and the porter stared sleepily at the
schoolmaster.

At length, however, by some process of hope he did not
himself understand, and following directions given by the old
woman that were utterly unintelligible, he went out into the
street and walked towards a dark group of houses she had
pointed out to him. He only knew that he meant to thunder at a
door and ask for a room. He was too weary to think out details.
The porter half made to go with him, but turned back at the last
moment to speak with the old woman. The houses sketched
themselves dimly in the general blackness. The air was cold.
The whole valley was filled with the rush and thunder of falling
water. He was thinking vaguely that the dawn could not be very
far away, and that he might even spend the night wandering in
the woods, when there was a sharp noise behind him and he
turned to see a figure hurrying after him. It was the porter –
running.

And in the little hall of the inn there began a confused three-cornered conversation, with frequent muttered colloquy and whispered asides in *patois* between the woman and the porter – the net result of which was that, 'If Monsieur did not object – there *was* a room, after all, on the first floor – only it was in a sense 'engaged'. That is to say –'

But the schoolmaster took the room without inquiring too closely into the puzzle that had somehow provided so suddenly. The ethics of hotel-keeping had nothing to do with him. If the woman offered him quarters it was not for him to argue with her whether the said quarters were legitimately hers to offer.

But the porter, evidently a little thrilled, accompanied the guest up to the room and supplied in a mixture of French and English details omitted by the landlady – and Minturn, the schoolmaster, soon shared the thrill with him, and found himself in the atmosphere of a possible tragedy.

All who know the peculiar excitement that belongs to lofty mountain valleys where dangerous climbing is a chief feature of the attractions, will understand a certain faint element of high alarm that goes with the picture. One looks up at the desolate, soaring ridges and thinks involuntarily of the men who find their pleasure for days and nights together scaling perilous summits among the clouds, and conquering inch by inch the icy peaks that for ever shake their dark terror in the sky. The atmosphere of adventure, spiced with the possible horror of a very grim order of tragedy, is inseparable from any imaginative contemplation of the scene: and the idea Minturn gleaned from the half-frightened porter lost nothing by his ignorance of the language. This Englishwoman, the real occupant of the room, had insisted on going without a guide. She had left just before daybreak two days before – the porter had seen her start – and . . . she had not returned! The route was difficult and dangerous, yet not impossible for a skilled climber, even a solitary one. And the Englishwoman was an experienced mountaineer. Also, she was self-willed, careless of advice, bored by warning, self-confident to a degree. Queer, moreover; for she kept entirely to herself, and sometimes remained in her room with locked doors, admitting no one, for days together; a 'crank', evidently, of the first water.

This much Minturn gathered clearly enough from the porter's talk while his luggage was brought in and the room set to rights; further, too, that the search party had gone out and *might*, of course, return at any moment. In which case—. Thus the room was empty, yet still hers. 'If Monsieur did not object – if the risk he ran of having to turn out suddenly in the night –' It was the loquacious porter who furnished the details that made the transaction questionable; and Minturn dismissed the loquacious porter as soon as possible, and prepared to get into the hastily arranged bed and snatch all the hours of sleep he could before he was turned out.

At first, it must be admitted, he felt uncomfortable – distinctly uncomfortable. He was in some one else's room. He had really no right to be there. It was in the nature of an unwarrantable intrusion; and while he unpacked he kept looking over his shoulder as though some one were watching him from the corners. Any moment, it seemed, he would hear a step in the passage, a knock would come at the door, the door would open, and there he would see this vigorous Englishwoman looking him up and down with anger. Worse still – he would hear her voice asking him what he was doing in her room – her bedroom. Of course, he had an adequate explanation, but still – !

Then, reflecting that he was already half undressed, the humour of it flashed for a second across his mind, and he laughed – *quietly*. And at once, after that laughter, under his breath, came the sudden sense of tragedy he had felt before. Perhaps, even while he smiled, her body lay broken and cold upon those awful heights, the wind of snow playing over her hair, her glazed eyes staring sightless up to the stars . . . It made him shudder. The sense of this woman whom he had never seen, whose name even he did not know, became extraordinarily real. Almost he could imagine that she was somewhere in the room with him, hidden, observing all he did.

He opened the door softly to put his boots outside, and when he closed it again he turned the key. Then he finished unpacking and distributed his few things about the room. It was soon done; for, in the first place, he had only a small Gladstone and a knapsack, and secondly, the only place where he could spread his clothes was the sofa. There was no chest of drawers, and the cupboard, an unusually large and solid one, was locked. The Englishwoman's things had evidently been hastily put away in it. The only sign of her recent presence was a bunch of faded *Alpenrosen* standing in a glass jar upon the washhand stand. This, and a certain faint perfume, were all that remained. In spite, however, of these very slight evidences, the whole room was pervaded with a curious sense of occupancy that he found exceedingly distasteful. One moment the atmosphere seemed subtly charged with a 'just left' feeling; the next it was a queer awareness of 'still here' that made him turn and look hurriedly behind him.

Altogether, the room inspired him with a singular aversion, and the strength of this aversion seemed the only excuse for his tossing the faded flowers out of the window, and then hanging his mackintosh upon the cupboard door in such a way as to screen it as much as possible from view. For the sight of that big, ugly cupboard, filled with the clothing of a woman who might then be beyond any further need of covering – thus his imagination insisted on picturing it – touched in him a startled sense of the incongruous that did not stop there, but crept through his mind gradually till it merged somehow into a sense of a rather grotesque horror. At any rate, the sight of that cupboard was offensive, and he covered it almost instinctively. Then, turning out the electric light, he got into bed.

But the instant the room was dark he realised that it was more than he could stand; for, with the blackness, there came a sudden rush of cold that he found it hard to explain. And the odd thing was that, when he lit the candle beside his bed, he noticed that his hand trembled.

This, of course, was too much. His imagination was taking liberties and must be called to heel. Yet the way he called it to order was significant, and its very deliberateness betrayed a mind that has already admitted fear. And fear, once in, is difficult to dislodge. He lay there upon his elbow in bed and carefully took note of all the objects in the room – with the intention, as it were, of taking an inventory of everything his senses perceived, then drawing a line, adding them up finally, and saying with decision, 'That's all the room contains! I've counted every single thing. There is nothing more. *Now* – I may sleep in peace!'

And it was during this absurd process of enumerating the furniture of the room that the dreadful sense of distressing lassitude came over him that made it difficult even to finish counting. It came swiftly, yet with an amazing kind of violence that overwhelmed him softly and easily with a sensation of enervating weariness hard to describe. And its first effect was to banish fear. He no longer possessed enough energy to feel really afraid or nervous. The cold remained, but the alarm vanished. And into every corner of his usually vigorous personality crept the insidious poison of a *muscular* fatigue – at first – that in a few seconds, it seemed, translated itself into *spiritual* inertia. A sudden consciousness of the foolishness, the crass futility of life, of effort, of fighting – of all that makes life worth living, oozed into every fibre of his being, and left him utterly weak. A spirit of black pessimism, that was not even vigorous enough to assert itself, invaded the secret chambers of his heart . . .

Every picture that presented itself to his mind came dressed in grey shadows; those bored and sweating horses toiling up the ascent to – nothing! That hard-faced landlady taking so much trouble to let her desire for gain conquer her sense of morality – for a few francs! That gold-braided porter, so talkative, fussy, energetic, and so anxious to tell all he knew! What was the use of them all? And for himself, what in the world was the good of all the labour and drudgery he went through in that preparatory school where he was junior master? What could it lead to? Wherein lay the value of so much uncertain toil, when the ultimate secrets of life were hidden and no one knew the final goal? How foolish was effort, discipline, work! How vain was pleasure! How trivial the noblest life! . . .

With a jump that nearly upset the candle Minturn challenged this weak mood. Such vicious thoughts were usually so remote from his normal character that the sudden vile invasion produced a swift reaction. Yet, only for a moment. Instantly, again, the depression descended upon him like a wave. His work – it could lead to nothing but the dreary labour of a small headmastership after all – seemed as vain and foolish as his holiday in the Alps. What an idiot he had been, to be sure, to come out with a knapsack merely to work himself into a state of exhaustion climbing over toilsome mountains that led to nowhere – resulted in nothing. A dreariness of the grave possessed him. Life was a ghastly fraud! Religion a childish humbug. Everything was merely a trap – a trap of death; a coloured toy that Nature used as a decoy! But a decoy for what? For nothing! There was no meaning in anything. The only *real* thing was – DEATH. And the happiest people were those who found it soonest.

Then why wait for it to come?

He sprang out of bed, thoroughly frightened. This was horrible. Surely mere physical fatigue could not produce a world so black, an outlook so dismal, a cowardice that struck with such sudden hopelessness at the very roots of life? For, normally, he was cheerful and strong, full of the tides of healthy living; and this appalling lassitude swept the very basis of his personality into nothingness and the desire for death. It was like the development of a Secondary Personality. He had read, of course, how certain persons who suffered shocks developed thereafter entirely different characteristics, memory, tastes, and so forth. It had all rather frightened him. Though scientific men vouched for it, it was hardly to be believed. Yet here was a similar thing taking place in his own consciousness. He was, beyond question, experiencing all the mental variations of – *someone else!* It was un-moral. It was awful. It was – well, after all, at the same time, it was uncommonly interesting.

244

And this interest he began to feel was the first sign of his returned normal Self. For to feel interest is to live, and to love life.

He sprang into the middle of the room – then switched on the electric light. And the first thing that struck his eye was – the big cupboard.

'Hallo! There's that – beastly cupboard!' he exclaimed to himself, involuntarily, yet aloud. It held all the clothes, the swinging skirts and coats and summer blouses of the dead woman. For he knew now – somehow or other – that she *was* dead . . .

At that moment, through the open window, rushed the sound of falling water, bringing with it a vivid realisation of the desolate, snow-swept heights. He saw her – positively *saw* her! – lying where she had fallen, the frost upon her cheeks, the snowdust eddying about her hair and eyes, her broken limbs pushing against the lumps of ice. For a moment the sense of spiritual lassitude – of the emptiness of life – vanished before this picture of broken effort – of a small human force battling pluckily, yet in vain, against the impersonal and pitiless potencies of inanimate nature – and he found himself again his normal self. Then instantly, returned again that terrible sense of cold, nothingness, emptiness . .

And he found himself standing opposite the big cupboard where her clothes were. He suddenly wanted to see those clothes – things she had used and worn. Quite close he stood, almost touching it. The next second he had touched it. His knuckles struck upon the wood.

Why he knocked is hard to say. It was an instinctive movement probably. Something in his deepest self dictated it – ordered it. He knocked at the door. And the dull sound upon the wood into the stillness of that room brought – horror. Why it should have done so he found it as hard to explain to himself as why he should have felt impelled to knock. The fact remains that when he heard the faint reverberation inside the cupboard, it brought with it so vivid a realisation of the woman's presence that he stood there shivering upon the floor with a dreadful sense of anticipation; he almost expected to hear an answering knock from within – the rustling of the hanging skirts perhaps – or, worse still, to see the locked door slowly open towards him.

And from that moment, he declares that in some way or other he must have partially lost control of himself, or at least of his better judgment; for he became possessed by such an over-mastering desire to tear open the cupboard door and see the clothes within, that he tried every key in the room in the vain effort to unlock it, and then, finally, before he quite realised what he was doing – rang the bell!

But, having rung the bell for no obvious or intelligent reason at two o'clock in the morning, he then stood waiting in the middle of the floor for the servant to come, conscious for the first time that something outside his ordinary self had pushed him towards the act. It was almost like an internal voice that directed him . . . and thus, when at last steps came down the passage and he faced the cross and sleepy chambermaid, amazed at being summoned at such an hour, he found no difficulty in the matter of what he should say. For the same power that insisted he should open the cupboard door also impelled him to utter words over which he apparently had no control.

'It's not *you* I rang for!' he said with decision and impatience. 'I want a man. Wake the porter and send him up to me at once – hurry! I tell you, hurry—!'

And when the girl had gone, frightened at his earnestness, Minturn realised that the words surprised himself as much as they surprised her. Until they were out of his mouth he had not known what exactly he was saying. But now he undesrstood that some force, foreign to his own personality, was using his mind and organs. The black depression that had possessed him a few moments before was also part of it. The powerful mood of this vanished woman had somehow momentarily taken possession of him – communicated, possibly, by the atmosphere of things in the room still belonging to her. But even now, when the porter, without coat or collar, stood beside him in the room, he did not understand why he insisted, with a positive fury admitting no denial, that the key of that cupboard must be found and the door instantly opened.

The scene was a curious one. After some perplexed whispering with the chambermaid at the end of the passage, the porter managed to find and produce the key in question. Neither he nor the girl knew clearly what this excited Englishman was up to, or why he was so passionately intent upon opening the cupboard at two o'clock in the morning. They watched him with an air of wondering what was going to happen next. But something of his curious earnestness, even of his late fear, communicated itself to them, and the sound of the key grating in the lock made them both jump.

They held their breath as the creaking door swung slowly open. All heard the clatter of that other key as it fell against the wooden floor – within. The cupboard had been locked *from the inside*. But it was the scared housemaid, from her position in the corridor, who first saw – and with a wild scream fell crashing against the banisters.

The porter made no attempt to save her. The schoolmaster and himself made a simultaneous rush towards the door, now wide open. They too, had seen.

There were no clothes, skirts or blouses on the pegs, but they saw the body of the Englishwoman suspended in mid-air, the head bent forward. Jarred by the movement of unlocking, the body swung slowly round to face them . . . Pinned upon the inside of the door was a hotel envelope with the following words pencilled in straggling writing:

'Tired – unhappy – hopelessly depressed . . . I cannot face life any longer . . . All is black. I must put an end to it . . . I meant to do it on the mountains, but was afraid. I slipped back to my room unobserved. This way is easiest and best. . . .'

The Haunted Mill

JEROME K. JEROME

Well, you all know my brother-in-law, Mr Parkins (began Mr Coombes, taking the long clay pipe from his mouth, and putting it behind his ear; we did not know his brother-in-law, but we said we did, so as to save time), and you know of course that he once took a lease of an old mill in Surrey, and went to live there.

Now you must know that, years ago, this very mill had been occupied by a wicked old miser, who died there, leaving – so it was rumoured – all his money hidden somewhere about the place. Naturally enough, everyone who had since come to live at the mill had tried to find the treasure; but none had ever succeeded, and the local wiseacres said that nobody every would, unless the ghost of the miserly miller should, one day, take a fancy to one of the tenants, and disclose to him the secret of the hiding-place.

My brother-in-law did not attach much importance to the story, regarding it as an old woman's tale, and, unlike his predecessors, made no attempt whatever to discover the hidden gold.

'Unless business was very different then from what it is now,' said my brother-in-law, 'I don't see how a miller could very well have saved anything, however much a miser he might have been: at all events, not enough to make it worth the trouble of looking for it.'

Still, he could not altogether get rid of the idea of that treasure.

One night he went to bed. There was nothing very extraordinary about that, I admit. He often did go to bed of a night. What *was* remarkable, however was that exactly as the clock of the village church chimed the last stroke of twelve, my brother-in-law woke up with a start, and felt himself quite unable to go to sleep again.

Joe (his Christian name was Joe) sat up in bed, and looked around.

At the foot of the bed something stood very still, wrapped in shadow.

It moved into the moonlight, and then my brother-in-law saw that it was a figure of a wizened little old man, in knee-breeches and a pig-tail.

In an instant the story of the hidden treasure and the old miser flashed across his mind.

'He's come to show me where it's hid,' thought my brother-in-law; and he resolved that he would not spend all this money on himself, but would devote a small percentage of it towards doing good to others.

The apparition moved towards the door: my brother-in-law put on his trousers and followed it. The ghost went downstairs into the kitchen, glided over and stood in front of the hearth, sighed and disappeared.

Next morning, Joe had a couple of bricklayers in, and made them haul out the stove and pull down the chimney, while he stood behind with a potato-sack in which to put the gold.

They knocked down half the wall, and never found so much as a four-penny bit. My brother-in-law did not know what to think.

The next night the old man appeared again, and again led the way into the kitchen. This time, however, instead of going to the

The boots passed through the body,
and broke a looking-glass

fireplace, it stood more in the middle of the room, and sighed there.

'Oh, I see what he means now,' said my brother-in-law to himself; 'it's under the floor. Why did the old idiot go and stand up against the stove, so as to make me think it was up the chimney?'

They spent the next day in taking up the kitchen floor; but the only thing they found was a three-pronged fork, and the handle of that was broken.

On the third night, the ghost reappeared, quite unabashed, and for a third time made for the kitchen. Arrived there, it looked up at the ceiling and vanished.

'Umph! he don't seem to have learned much sense where he's been to,' muttered Joe, as he trotted back to bed; 'I should have thought he might have done that first.'

Still, there seemed no doubt now where the treasure lay, and the first thing after breakfast they started pulling down the ceiling. They got every inch of the ceiling down, and they took up the boards of the room above.

They discovered about as much treasure as you would expect to find in an empty quart-pot.

On the fourth night, when the ghost appeared, as usual, my brother-in-law was so wild that he threw his boots at it; and the boots passed through the body, and broke a looking-glass.

On the fifth night, when Joe awoke, as he always did now at twelve, the ghost was standing in a dejected attitude, looking very miserable. There was an appealing look in its large sad eyes that quite touched my brother-in-law.

'After all,' he thought, 'perhaps the silly chap's doing his best. Maybe he has forgotten where he really did put it, and is trying to remember. I'll give him another chance.'

The ghost appeared grateful and delighted at seeing Joe prepare to follow him, and led the way into the attic, pointed to the ceiling, and vanished.

'Well, he's hit it this time, I do hope,' said my brother-in-law; and next day they set to work to take the roof off the place.

It took them three days to get the roof thoroughly off, and all they found was a bird's nest; after securing which they covered up the house with tarpaulins, to keep it dry.

You might have thought that would have cured the poor fellow of looking for treasure. But it didn't.

He said there must be something in it all, or the ghost would never keep on coming as it did; and that, having gone so far, he would go on to the end, and solve the mystery, cost what it might.

Night after night, he would get out of his bed and follow that spectral old fraud about the house. Each night, the old man would indicate a different place; and, on each following day, my brother-in-law would proceed to break up the mill at the point indicated, and look for the treasure. At the end of three weeks, there was not a room in the mill fit to live in. Every wall had been pulled down, every floor had been taken up, every ceiling had had a hole knocked in it. And then, as suddenly as they had begun, the ghost's visits ceased; and my brother-in-law was left in peace, to rebuild the place at his leisure.

'What induced the old image to play such a silly trick upon a family man and a ratepayer?' Ah! that's just what I cannot tell you.'

Some said that the ghost of the wicked old man had done it to punish my brother-in-law for not believing in him at first; while others held that the apparition was probably that of some deceased local plumber and glazier, who would naturally take an interest in seeing a house knocked about and spoilt. But nobody knew anything for certain.

The Harpsichord

ELIZABETH LE FANU

It was a shattering blow. These were to have been the best summer holidays they had every had. Alicia had arrived yesterday after her first term away from home and Giles was due tomorrow. Now here was Mother with a troubled face and a telegram in her hand, to say that Giles had been in contact with scarlet fever. That meant he must stay on at school for ten long days, 'Or else,' began Mother, and stopped.

'Or else what?'

'I could fetch him home by car and keep him in quarantine here for ten days, but that would mean packing you off somewhere.'

'Oh, couldn't we be in different parts of the house, and shout through the doors, and keep ten yards apart in the garden – or five yards—'

But Mother shook her head. 'No, it would be impossible.' and as she clearly would not give way on this point Alicia did not waste time in argument.

'Of course Giles must come home,' she decided. 'Now, where shall I go?'

'I'm sure Cousin Bee would have you. She's kindness itself and always says she doesn't notice one more among so many.'

Alicia considered it for a moment.

'Too much like school,' she said, 'without a minute to yourself,' After another pause for reflection she asked. 'Would Aunt Sophie have me?'

Mother looked surprised. 'Wouldn't it be a little dull, darling? They are both rather old and fragile.'

Alicia said 'I know – but they are very nice and reasonable, and they have a heavenly piano. I haven't had a chance to enjoy myself in peace with a piano for three months and that's what I want to do.'

There had been an allotted half-hour's practice daily at school, but with 'The Merry Peasant' prattling in the imperfectly sound-proofed cell to the right, and 'The Death of Ase' dragging on painfully to the left, Alicia could only struggle with the notes and do her best to drown them.

Mother arranged it all on the telephone, and she and Alicia drove off through the warm, still afternoon. Aunt Sophie was waiting for them in the coolness of her dark panelled hall, and Uncle Frederic emerged from his own room and blinked at Alicia in a very friendly way. They had a lady-like tea under the trees, not like their picnics at home, and Alicia felt it was all rather like a dream. Then Mother drove away, as she was going straight on to collect Giles, saying, 'We shall be over to fetch you in ten days from now, and I'll ring up and we can talk sometimes.'

Aunt Sophie, wearing a large shady hat, took Alicia round the garden, and told her she could come and pick the peaches and plums whenever she wanted to, and then she showed her her room and said it was such a pleasure to them both to have her there, and they hoped she would not be too dull.

Alicia unpacked her suitcase and came downstairs with all the music she had brought with her. She met Uncle Frederic in the hall and said, 'May I please play the piano? I haven't been able to play properly – I mean to wander about on the piano like I do at home – for months and months. And yours is such a heavenly piano.'

Uncle Frederic said, 'Oh dear, dear! Tut-tut, my dear child, this is most unlucky – how very unfortunate – Sophie, this is indeed a calamity. Here is Alicia with her music wanting to play – and the piano, dear child, had been found to have moth in it and has had just at this moment of all others to go to Mr Bagenal to have the felts renewed. A charming man and a most excellent craftsman and a thorough musician – we could not wish for a better man. But it is most unlucky happening just now.'

Here was another bolt from the blue – two in one day. Poor Alicia was stricken. When she saw Uncle Frederic's face, quite pink with distress, she managed to say, 'Never mind, Uncle Frederic, it can't be helped.' But she felt the acutest disappointment and a sense of emptiness and frustration she could hardly bear. She escaped upstairs again, wondering how she was going to get through the next ten days, and almost regretted Cousin Bee's noisy party.

Without any particular motive she wandered up to the top of the house and looked into several unfamiliar rooms: they had a severe and withdrawn appearance and she felt rather shy of entering. A boxroom, with some old-fashioned pieces of furniture shrouded in dust-sheets, two cane trunks and a doll's house, was more inviting. Alicia thought this would be worth exploring later on – she did not feel the heart for it now, and in the hope of finding some books she went on down a short passage and a half-staircase and opened the door of a small white-panelled room.

The other rooms had seemed to repel her, but this room invited her in. There was a low window seat with bookshelves on either side, and she sat down and looked into the garden, with straight box-bordered paths and ripe peaches and plums on the walls. Beyond that were rolling fields and far away the faint contour of Salisbury Plain against the evening sky.

Alicia looked out of the window for a long time, then she began to look at the books in the shelves. There were some illustrated natural-history books that she liked very much, written in a polite and stilted manner but with beautiful, accurate pictures of flowers and birds. She pored over them until the fading light made it hard to see the small print – then she sat up and looked all around the little room. It was faded but very pretty, and Alicia felt at home there. She sat in the chairs in turn, looked in the mirror and then crossed the room to examine – what was it? It was made of light polished wood, inlaid with patterns of flowers and it looked almost like – but it couldn't be – a piano?

Alicia tremblingly raised a polished lid – and saw two keyboards, one slightly above the other, with faded yellowish ivory keys, and one or two stops, like an organ, at the side. She struck a few notes and they sounded quite different from the notes of a piano – they had a bright glittering sound that was most exciting.

What can it be? thought Alicia. It's the most thrilling thing – you can play it like a piano, but it's quite different – more exciting – and lovely, too, though it's horribly out of tune. But why two keyboards and what on earth are these stops for? And the pedal – not like a piano pedal.

She pulled up a chair and tried playing bits of everything she could think of. Some went better than others. A Haydn minuet sounded more alive and sparkling than it ever had before – 'It might have been written for the thing, whatever it is,' cried Alicia: but when she tried 'The Death of Ase' on it, it made her burst out laughing. She was puzzled to notice a great black scar running across the polished wood, and the intricate inlay had been damaged, too – how and when she could not guess.

At last she heard sounds from the garden – she looked out of the window and in the dim light she could see Aunt Sophie and Uncle Frederic moving about the garden and calling her. 'Gracious, I've been here for ages! They must think I'm lost – perhaps they think I've run away.' Alicia felt her way up the little staircase and along the passages and raced downstairs, forgetting that she had felt very like running away when she climbed up them an hour or two ago.

'Aunt Sophie, Uncle Frederic, here I am! I've found the most extraordinary thing upstairs, in a dear little white room over the garden – I saw you out of the window – I'm sorry I've been so long, but I've been staying up there with my discovery. What is it? Like a piano – but not – with a lovely sound like gold wires.'

They looked relieved and bewildered: and now Uncle Frederic's face cleared and he said. 'My dear child, it's your great-great-grandmother's harpsichord. She played it very beautifully, I believe. It has always been kept in her own room, where she used to play it, and where you found it. Mr Bagenal did it up for us many years ago and he comes sometimes to look after it. But a harpsichord goes out of tune very quickly and I fear it must be sadly out of tune now?'

'Yes it is,' agreed Alicia, 'but may I play it while I'm here, all the same? Oh please say yes!'

'Yes, indeed you may. How glad I am you discovered it. But we will go tomorrow into Salisbury and try to persuade Mr Bagenal to come back with us and put it into order, and he will I am sure tell you something about the instrument and how it should be played.'

After supper Uncle Frederic pointed to a picture on the drawing-room wall and said, 'This is your great-great-grandmother – she was Alicia, too, you know, and you were named after her.'

Alicia looked with interest and gave a cry of delight – 'Why she is playing the harpsichord – my harpsichord – in that very room.'

Aunt Sophie was looking from Alicia to the girl in the picture. 'My dear, you are very like her – look, Frederic, it's most curious. It has never stuck me before – she is paler than you, of course, but the line of the forehead and cheek – and her hair – it's most striking.'

Uncle Frederic was looking too and nodding his head. 'And you are both musicians,' he said. 'I want to hear you play the harpsichord, Alicia, and bring it to life again.'

Alicia was intent on the picture. 'Who is this?' she asked, 'this man in black, with white hair, with his hand over his eyes, listening to the music?'

'We don't know his name,' replied Uncle Frederic, 'nothing seems to be known of him. He may have been her music-master. Rather a severe one, I should suppose. He looks a crotchety old gentleman, don't you think?'

Alicia looked closely at him. 'No, I don't think so, but he has a very sad face, and there's something about him I can't quite understand. I should like to find out.'

The next morning they set out to visit Mr Bagenal, as Uncle Frederic had promised. He had not driven to Salisbury for some time and Aunt Sophie was plainly nervous of his doing so. She sat beside him, stiff and upright in her seat, and said, 'Slowly here, dear,' or 'Carefully please, Frederic,' at road-junctions and blind corners – although he was in fact driving both slowly and carefully, Alicia thought.

In the main street Aunt Sophie shut her eyes convulsively and opened them only when they reached Mr Bagenal's shop. He proved to be as charming as Uncle Frederic had reported, and he showed Alicia a little clavichord, a virginals, which was like an oblong painted box placed on a table, and a fine harpsichord which he was doing up, and explained something of the differences between them. He allowed her to play on them and to compare the gentle tender tone of the clavichord and the pretty tinkling virginals (this might, he said, have been Queen Elizabeth's own instrument) with the more brilliant harpsichord. She was enthralled, and blushed with pleasure when she head Mr Bagenal tell Uncle Frederic that she played with real intelligence and musical feeling.

Mr Bagenal shook his head when Aunt Sophie said she hoped they might have the Blüthner piano back in a few days for Alicia to play, and said it would be a matter of weeks; but he consented to come there and then to attend to the harpsichord.

So he drove back to lunch with them and answered Alicia's many questions with interest and good humour. Then she took him to the little white-panelled room, and while she watched him open the harpsichord and adjust the jacks he told her a great deal about it, and spoke lovingly of the instrument for which Bach and Scarlatti and Couperin and Haydn wrote – 'Then

Haydn *did* mean that minuet to be played on a harpsichord!'
cried Alicia. He gave her a lesson in the use of the stops and the
double keyboard and much else. He was as puzzled as she was by
the great black scar across the instrument.

'It was the first thing I noticed when your uncle asked me to
restore it, years ago now, and I've never been able to account for
it,' he said. 'It looks almost as if the wood had been burnt –
something has seared right into it, one can't imagine how. And
look here – the ivory must have been broken off two of the keys at
the same time. You can see that it has been replaced – oh!
probably as much as a hundred years ago – look, the ivory on
these A and B keys is not quite so old and yellow.'

When Mr Bagenal had gone (in a taxi – Aunt Sophie would
not hear of Uncle Frederic driving into Salisbury again) Alicia
remembered the picture in the drawing-room and looked closely
at it to see if the harpsichord already bore the black scar at the
time when it was painted: but time had darkened the picture and
obscured the details and it was impossible to tell. She mused
over it for a time, wondering what her namesake had been
playing so long ago.

She longed to know more about the dark figure in the
background: was he perhaps a notable performer on the
harpsichord? And what was it about him that so interested and
baffled her?

She spent the rest of that day in the little panelled room,
playing all the Mozart and Haydn sonatas she knew, and trying
to put into practice what Mr Bagenal had told her. She was
entranced by the crisp, clear tone of the harpsichord, and the
brilliant, sparkling sounds she was able to produce. It was all
new and exciting to her, and yet somehow she had the feeling
that she was coming back to an old friend, and that she and the
harpsichord understood each other very well.

Uncle Frederic's voice broke the spell. 'This is delightful,
Alicia – I had no idea you could play so well. You have indeed
brought the old harpsichord to life again, and it is the greatest
pleasure to hear it.'

When they came downstairs to Aunt Sophie in the drawing-room she said, 'Alicia dear, aren't you lonely up there? You have been playing for hours.'

'Lonely?' echoed Alicia. 'No, I feel at home in that little room, as if I had known it always, and not lonely in the least. I don't know why,' she added after a moment, looking a little puzzled, and her eyes strayed back to the picture as if seeking an explanation there.

The next morning was so glorious that Alicia went straight into the garden and stayed there till lunch-time, only wishing that Giles was there too, to enjoy the warm peaches off the wall and look with her at the natural history books she had found – he knew more about birds and butterflies than she did.

By the afternoon she could stay away from her little white room no longer. She knelt at the window for a time and looked at the garden from there; then for some reason she picked up the loose cushion on the window-seat and found that underneath was a hinged lid. This she lifted up and discovered a cupboard below it. Inside, a layer of fine dust covered piles of faded sheets of music.

They must have lain there undisturbed for a long time. Alicia held them close to the window and blew off the dust. 'I don't believe anyone has touched this music since the other Alicia put it away,' she said. 'This is the music she used to play. What funny old fashioned titles. '*Nouvelles Suites de Pièces de Clavecin*,' by Jean Philippe Rameau. 'The famous "Méthode" for the Clavecin or Harpsichord by François Couperin' – that looks rather heavy going. 'Six Sonatas for the Harpsichord by Domenico Scarlatti' – Oh! I don't know where to begin!'

She propped the yellowish sheets of music before her and began to play, one piece after another – on and on she went. It was like a new world opening before her. She felt a mastery over the music which she had never had before. Her fingers were stronger and surer and she was filled by a sense of encouragement and sympathy.

Once or twice she had the strange feeling that she was doing again something she had done before, long, long ago. But it was only a fleeting impression, and was gone before she could pin it

down. The interest of the music absorbed her beyond everything else.

What she could not account for was the comfortable sensation
of having close by her a sympathetic listener, a friendly presence
radiating encouragement and somehow imbuing her with
powers she did not know she possessed.

But it was only puzzling when she thought about it afterwards
– nothing could be more natural than this feeling of happy
companionship and mutual understanding which possessed her
again as soon as she sat at the harpsichord in her little white
room the next afternoon.

Time slipped by and the shadows moved along the wall as she
played on – dipping into all Alicia's music and rejoicing at her
own unexpected prowess.

As the room grew darker she became increasingly aware of a
figure which seemed strangely familiar listening intently in the
shadowy corner. She was working away at a Pastorale of
Scarlatti's now, playing it with enjoyment and feeling, though
still imperfectly.

'You stumble at the old place, Alicia,' said a gentle half-
humorous voice, which she felt she had always known.

'Yes – the old place,' she replied, 'but have patience with me
and I will get it right.'

She tried again. 'Gently, child, don't hurry it – like this,' and
he hummed the lovely phrase . . .

The lesson went on for a long time, till at last Uncle Frederic
appeared at the door. 'Alicia, it is late and almost dark – Aunt
Sophie sent me to fetch you. So odd – I thought I heard voices as
I came along the passage. My imagination is leading me astray.'

Alicia looked wonderingly at him, rather as if she had been
startled out of a dream. She was silent and preoccupied that
evening, and sat gazing at the picture in the drawing-room as if
trying to read there the answer to a riddle. Then she shook her
head and laughed, kissed Aunt Sophie goodnight, and cried,
'I've never been so happy! The days go too fast.'

Indeed, the days slipped by almost unnoticed, and when
Alicia's mother rang up at breakfast-time one morning to say

that Giles was as well as possible and they hoped to come and fetch her home the following day, she felt a pang of regret she could hardly conceal. With a face full of dismay she turned to Aunt Sophie. 'I'll be going home tomorrow! Giles hasn't got it – scarlet fever, I mean. Of course that's splendid – but I wish it didn't mean today is my last day.'

Aunt Sophie flushed with pleasure. 'That is very nice of you Alicia, and we shall miss you dreadfully. I only wish on your last day Uncle Frederic and I did not have to go out together – but it is such a long-standing promise . . .'

'Of course you must go. No, indeed I won't be lonely. I want a long last lesson on the harpsichord. I still have heaps to learn.'

It was a heavy, close afternoon with a hint of thunder, and the stillness was almost oppressive.

'It feels as if it's waiting for something to happen, it's so quiet,' said Alicia, and she waved to Aunt Sophie and Uncle Frederic from the steps as they drove away.

The garden was full of warm smells, but the birds were hushed and not a leaf was stirring. Alicia chose a ripe peach – 'My last.' She looked up at the house leaning above her, and waved towards the window of her little white room, then she turned and slowly climbed the familiar stairs.

'Here I am,' she said, and sat down as usual.

All through the long, still afternoon she played on and he listened. She did not see the darkening sky, nor hear the foreboding mutter of thunder – she was too intent to notice the sudden swirl of wind which rattled the open window and then died as suddenly.

As she turned the pages of her music she came on one she had not opened before – 'His Meditation,' by Giles Farnaby. 'I've not played this for – how long?' whispered Alicia. But there was a great black scar right across the page. 'Just like the scar on the harpsichord: surely this was never here before? I can scarcely see the notes.' She bent close to make them out, and then clearly and sweetly the delicate phrases followed each other in ordered succession.

She played with the ease and surrender of long acquaintance, in the absolute stillness of an ominous hush. Then the mood of the music changed, and she faltered. 'Come, let me show you – I will play this for you,' he said, and he seated himself at the harpsichord in her place.

Alicia listened to the enchanted sounds, and marvelled at the magic of his playing.

Gradually as she listened she became possessed by the sensation which she had begun to feel once before, the realization that this had happened to her before, in some far-away half remembered existence, and that she was powerless to prevent the catastrophe she knew was coming.

'Oh, come away,' she cried. 'Stop – stop playing! It's coming—'

There was a blinding flash and deafening roar of thunder.

Alicia lay still on the floor until Uncle Frederic and Aunt Sophie found her there and carried her downstairs.

She opened her eyes at last, and looked wonderingly at them for a moment, before she found her voice to ask what had happened.

'Oh dear Alicia – don't try to talk yet, for a little while. We found you upstairs, unconscious, on the floor – the lightning must have come right in at the window. Drink a little water, now, and then smell this sal volatile, if you can. The music you had been playing was lying on the floor – it is a miracle you escaped as you did. We found you lying at a little distance away, not sitting at the harpsichord. But how do you feel, Alicia?'

'All right now, thank you, only I've a headache all over,' said Alicia, and then she was silent and thoughtful for a long time.

Suddenly Aunt Sophie, who was watching her face, said 'Frederic – the likeness to your grandmother's picture, it's quite uncanny – look!' Alicia was very pale, and it was partly this no doubt that made the resemblance between the two so startling.

'It might be you,' said Uncle Frederic in an almost scared voice. 'Sitting at your harpsichord.' Then he added, half playfully, 'But what about the crotchety old gentleman in the corner, Alicia? Is he as severe as he looks?'

Alicia sprang up and stood before the picture. 'Oh! you don't

263

understand,' she cried. 'He plays wonderfully – you can't believe how beautifully he plays. And he isn't severe, he's – don't you see – he's *blind*! It was the lightning. That's why he looks so sad – that's what I could not make out about him. The lightning struck him as he was playing – it struck him instead of me.'

She broke off. Aunt Sophie looked very much alarmed – she put her hand to Alicia's forehead and said, 'Hush, dear, don't excite yourself. Don't talk any more now, just come quietly to bed – she must be quite delirious, Frederic.'

'Oh, you'll never understand,' cried Alicia, and with a sudden impulse she stretched up to the picture and kissed the pale hand at his side, and then the hand covering his eyes. 'No, they'll never understand,' she cried in despair. Then she allowed Aunt Sophie to lead her away to bed.

She was glad enough to lie between the cool sheets and lay her head on the pillow. Just before she fell sleep she sat up and said aloud, 'I know what I'll do – I'll tell the whole thing to Mr Bagenal. He will understand.'

The next morning she slept on and on and was only awakened by a vigorous fanfare on a motor-horn under her window.

'It's Giles – they've come to fetch me home,' she cried. She jumped out of bed and ran downstairs to find Aunt Sophie looking agitated in the midst of explanations to her mother. 'I've crept in several times this morning, and she's breathing quite regularly and has much more colour – but she's still asleep . . .'

'Hullo,' cried Giles, 'what's all this about you being struck by lightning? You lucky pig – nothing whatever has happened to me, and I've wasted ten days without you. Come on, pack up your bag, there's no time to be lost – the holidays are going to begin in earnest now.'

Giles swept her off – there was no time for a farewell visit to the harpsichord or the little white room, and she could barely glance at the picture on the drawing-room wall amid the flurry of thankyous and goodbyes before she was whirled away on the road for home.

The White Cat of Drumgunniol

J. SHERIDAN LE FANU

There is a famous story of a white cat, with which we all become acquainted in the nursery. I am going to tell a story of a white cat very different from the amiable and enchanted princess who took that disguise for a reason. The white cat of which I speak was a more sinister animal.

The traveller from Limerick towards Dublin, after passing the hills of Killaloe upon the left, as Keeper Mountain raises high in view, finds himself gradually hemmed in, up the right, by a range of lower hills. An undulating plain that dips gradually to a lower level than that of the road interposes, and some scattered hedgerows relieve its somewhat wild and melancholy character.

One of the few human habitations that send up their films of turf-smoke from that lonely plain, is the loosely-thatched, earth-built dwelling of a 'strong farmer,' as the more prosperous of the tenant-farming classes are termed in Munster. It stands in a clump of trees near the edge of a wandering stream, about half-way between the mountains and the Dublin road, and had been for generations tenanted by people named Donovan.

In a distant place, desirous of studying some Irish records which had fallen into my hands, and inquiring for a teacher capable of instructing me in the Irish language, a Mr Donovan, dreamy, harmless and learned, was recommended to me for the purpose.

I found that he had been educated as a Sizar in Trinity College, Dublin. He now supported himself by teaching, and the special direction of my studies, I suppose, flattered his national partialities, for he unbosomed himself of much of his long-reserved thoughts, and recollections about his country and his early days. It was he who told me this story, and I mean to repeat it, as nearly as I can, in his own words.

I have myself seen the old farm-house, with its orchard of huge mossgrown apple trees. I have looked round on the peculiar landscape; the roofless, ivied tower, that two hundred years before had afforded a refuge from raid and rapparee, and which still occupies its old place in the angle of the haggard; the bush-grown 'liss', that scarcely a hundred and fifty steps away records the labours of a bygone race; the dark and towering outline of old Keeper in the background; and the lonely range of furze and heath-clad hills that form a nearer barrier, with many a line of grey rock and clump of dwarf oak or birch. The pervading sense of loneliness made it a scene not unsuited for a wild and unearthly story. And I could quite fancy how, seen in the grey of a wintry morning, shrouded far and wide in snow, or in the melancholy glory of an autumnal sunset, or in the chill splendour of a moonlight night, it might have helped to tone a dreamy mind like honest Dan Donovan's to superstition and a proneness to the illusions of fancy. It is certain, however, that I never anywhere met with a more simple-minded creature, or one on whose good faith I could more entirely rely.

When I was a boy, said he, living at home at Drumgunniol, I used to take my Goldsmith's *Roman History* in my hand and go down to my favourite seat, the flat stone, sheltered by a hawthorn tree beside the little lough, a large and deep pool, such as I have heard called a tarn in England. It lay in the gentle hollow of a field that is overhung toward the north by the old orchard, and being a deserted place was favourable to my studious quietude.

One day reading here, as usual, I wearied at last, and began to look about me, thinking of the heroic scenes I had just been reading of. I was wide awake as I am at this moment, and I saw a woman appear at the corner of the orchard and walk down the slope. She wore a long, light grey dress, so long that it seemed to sweep the grass behind her, and so singular was her appearance in a part of the world where female attire is so inflexibly fixed by custom, that I could not take my eyes off her. Her course lay diagonally from corner to corner of the field, which was a large one, and she pursued it without swerving.

When she came near I could see that her feet were bare, and that she seemed to be looking steadfastly upon some remote object for guidance. Her route would have crossed me – had the tarn not interposed – about ten or twelve yards below the point at which I was sitting. But instead of arresting her course at the margin of the lough, as I had expected, she went on without seeming conscious of its existence, and I saw her, as plainly as I see you, sir, walk across the surface of the water, and pass, without seeming to see me, at about the distance I had calculated.

I was ready to faint from sheer terror. I was only thirteen years old then, and I remember every particular as if it had happened this hour.

The figure passed through the gap at the far corner of the field, and there I lost sight of it. I had hardly strength to walk home, and was so nervous, and ultimately so ill, that for three weeks I was confined to the house, and could not bear to be alone for a moment. I never entered that field again, such was the horror with which from that moment every object in it was clothed. Even at this distance of time I should not like to pass through it.

This apparition I connected with a mysterious event; and, also, with a singular liability, that has for nearly eight years distinguished, or rather afflicted, our family. It is no fancy. Everybody in that part of the country knows all about it. Everybody connected what I had seen with it.

I will tell it all to you as well as I can.

When I was about fourteen years old – that is about a year after the sight I had seen in the lough field – we were one night expecting my father home from the fair of Killaloe. My mother sat up to welcome him home and I with her, for I liked nothing better than such a vigil. My brothers and sisters, and the farm servants, except the men who were driving home the cattle from the fair, were asleep in their beds. My mother and I were sitting in the chimney corner chatting together, and watching my father's supper, which was kept hot over the fire. We knew that he would return before the men who were driving home the cattle, for he was riding, and told us that he would only wait to see them fairly on the road, and then push homeward.

At length we heard his voice and the knocking of his loaded whip at the door, and my mother let him in. I don't think I ever saw my father drunk, which is more than most men of my age, from the same part of the country, could say of theirs. But he could drink his glass of whisky as well as another, and he usually came home from fair or market a little merry and mellow, and with a jolly flush in his cheeks.

Tonights he looked sunken, pale and sad. He entered with the saddle and bridle in his hand, and he dropped them against the wall, near the door, and put his arms round his wife's neck, and kissed her kindly.

'Welcome home, Meehal,' said she, kissing him heartily.

'God bless you, mavourneen,' he answered.

And hugging her again, he turned to me, who was plucking him by the hand, jealous of his notice. I was little, and light of my age, and he lifted me up in his arms and kissed me, and my arms being about his neck, he said to my mother:

'Draw the bolt, acuishla.'

She did so, and setting me down very dejectedly, he walked to the fire and sat down on a stool, and stretched his feet toward the

I was ready to faint from sheer terror

glowing turf, leaning with his hands on his knees.

'Rouse up, Mick, darlin',' said my mother, who was growing anxious, 'and tell me how did the cattle sell, and did everything go lucky at the fair, or is there anything wrong with the landlord, or what in the world is it that ails you, Mick, jewel?'

'Nothin,' Molly. The cows sould well, thank God, and there's nothin' fell out between me an' the landlord, an' everything's the same way. There's no fault to find anywhere.'

'Well, then, Mickey, since so it is, turn round to your hot supper, and ate it, and tell us is there anything new.'

'I got my supper, Molly, on the way, and I can't ate a bit,' he answered.

'Got your supper on the way, an' you knowin' 'twas waiting for you at home, an' your wife sitting up an' all!' cried my mother reproachfully.

'You're takin' a wrong meanin' out of what I say,' said my father. 'There's something happened that leaves me that I can't ate a mouthful, and I'll not be dark with you, Molly, for, maybe it ain't very long I have to be here, an' I'll tell you what it was. It's what I've seen, the white cat.'

'The Lord between us and harm!' exclaimed my mother, in a moment as pale and as chap-fallen as my father; and then, trying to rally, with a laugh, she said: 'Ha! 'tis only funnin' me you are. Sure a white rabbit was snared a Sunday last, in Grady's wood; an' Teigue seen a big white rat in the haggard yesterday.'

' 'Twas neither rat nor rabbit was in it. Don't ye think but I'd know a rat or a rabbit from a big white cat, with green eyes as big as halfpennies, and its back riz up like a bridge, trottin' on and across me, and ready, if I dar' stop, to rub its sides against my shins, and maybe to make a jump and seize my throat, if that it's a cat, at all, an' not something worse?'

As he ended his description in a low tone, looking straight at the fire, my father drew his big hand across his forehead once or twice, his face being damp and shining with the moisture of fear, and he sighed, or rather groaned, heavily.

My mother had relapsed into panic, and was praying again in

her fear. I, too, was terribly frightened, and on the point of crying, for I knew all about the white cat.

Clapping my father on the shoulder, by way of encouragement, my mother leaned over him, kissing him, and at last began to cry. He was wringing her hands in his, and seemed in great trouble.

'There was nothin' came into the house with me?' he asked, in a very low tone, turning to me.

'There was nothin,' father,' I said, 'but the saddle and bridle that was in your hand.'

'Nothin' white kem in at the doore wid me?' he repeated.

'Nothin' at all,' I answered.

'So be it,' said my father, and making the sign of the cross, he began mumbling to himself, and I knew he was saying his prayers.

Waiting for a while, to give him time for this exercise, my mother asked him where he first saw it.

'When I was riding up the bohereen,' – the Irish term meaning a little road, such as leads up to a farm-house – 'I bethought myself that the men was on the road with the cattle, and no one to look to the horse barrin' myself, so I thought I might as well leave him in the crooked field below, an' I tuck him there, he bein' cool, and not a hair turned, for I rode him aisy all the way. It was when I turned, after lettin' him go – the saddle and bridle bein' in my hand – that I saw it, pushin' out o' the long grass at the side o' the path, an' it walked across it, in front of me, an' then back again, before me, the same way, an' sometimes at one side, an' then at the other, lookin' at me wid them shinin' eyes; and I consayted I heard it growlin' as it kep' beside me – as close as ever you see – till I kem up to the doore, here, an' knocked an' called, as ye heerd me.'

Now, what was it, in so simple an incident, that agitated my father, my mother, myself, and finally, every member of this rustic household, with a terrible foreboding? It was this that we, one and all, believed that my father had received, in thus encountering the white cat, a warning of his approaching death.

The omen had never failed hitherto. It did not fail now. In a week after my father took the fever that was going, and before a month he was dead.

My honest friend, Dan Donovan, paused here; I could perceive that he was praying, for his lips were busy, and I concluded that it was for the repose of that departed soul.

In a little while he resumed.

It is eighty years now since that omen first attached to my family. Eighty years? Ay, is it? Ninety is nearer the mark. And I have spoken to many old people, in those earlier times, who had a distinct recollection of everything connected with it.

It happened in this way.

My grand-uncle, Connor Donovan, had the old farm of Drumgunniol in his day. He was richer than ever my father was, or my father's father either, for he took a short lease of Balraghan, and made money of it. But money won't soften a hard heart, and I'm afraid my grand-uncle was a cruel man – a profligate man he was, surely, and this is mostly a cruel man at heart. He drank his share, too, and cursed and swore, when he was vexed, more than was good for his soul, I'm afraid.

At that time there was a beautiful girl of the Colemans, up in the mountains, not far from Capper Cullen. I'm told that there are no Colemans there now at all, and that family has passed away. The famine years made great changes.

Ellen Coleman was her name. The Colemans were not rich. But, being such a beauty, she might have made a good match. Worse than she did for herself, poor thing, she could not.

Con Donovan – my grand-uncle, God forgive him! – sometimes in his rambles saw her at fairs or patterns, and he fell in love with her, as who might not?

He used her ill. He promised her marriage, and persuaded her to come away with him; and, after all, he broke his word. It was just the old story. He tired of her, and he wanted to push himself in the world; and he married a girl of the Collopys, that had a great fortune – twenty-four cows, seventy sheep, and a hundred and twenty goats.

He married this Mary Collopy, and grew richer than before; and Ellen Coleman died broken-hearted. But that did not trouble the strong farmer much.

He would have liked to have children, but he had none, and this way the only cross he had to bear, for everything else went much as he wished.

One night he was returning from the fair of Nenagh. A shallow stream at that time crossed the road – they have thrown a bridge over it, I am told, some time since – and its channel was often dry in summer weather. When it was so, as it passes close by the old farm-house of Drumgunniol, without a great deal of winding, it makes a sort of road, which people then used as a short cut to reach the house by. Into this dry channel, as there was plenty of light from the moon, my grand-uncle turned his horse, and when he had reached the two ash-trees at the meeting of the farm he turned his horse short into the river-field, intending to ride through the gap at the other end, under the oak-tree, and so he would have been within a few hundred yards of his door.

As he approached the 'gap' he saw, or thought he saw, with a slow motion, gliding along the ground towards the same point, and now and then with a soft bound, a white object, which he described as being no bigger than his hat, but what it was he could not see, as it moved along the hedge and disappeared at the point to which he himself was tending.

When he reached the gap the horse stopped short. He urged and coaxed it in vain. He got down to lead it through, but it recoiled, snorted and fell into a wild trembling fit. He mounted it again. But its terror continued, and it obstinately resisted his caresses and his whip. It was bright moonlight, and my grand-uncle was chafed by the horse's resistance and, seeing nothing to account for it, and being so near home, what little patience he possessed forsook him, and, plying his whip and spur in earnest, he broke into oaths, and curses.

All of a sudden the horse sprang through, and Con Donovan, as he passed under the broad branch of the oak, saw clearly a woman standing on the bank beside him, her arm extended, with the hand of which, as he flew by, she struck him a blow upon the shoulders. It threw him forward upon the neck of the horse, which, in wild terror, reached the door at a gallop, and stood there quivering and steaming all over.

Less alive than dead, my grand-uncle got in. He told his story, at least, so much as he chose. His wife did not quite know what to think. But that something very bad had happened she could not doubt. He was very faint and ill, and begged the priest should be sent for forthwith. When they were getting him to his bed they saw distinctly the marks of five fingerpoints on the flesh of his shoulder, where the spectral blow had fallen. These singular marks – which they said resembled in tint the hue of a body struck by lightning – remained imprinted on his flesh, and were buried with him.

When he had recovered sufficiently to talk with the people about him – speaking, like a man at his last hour, from a burdened heart, and troubled conscience – he repeated his story, but said he did not see, or, at all events, know, the face of the figure that stood in the gap. No one believed him. He told more about it to the priest than to others. He certainly had a secret to tell. He might as well have divulged it frankly, for the neighbours all knew well enough that it was the face of dead Ellen Coleman that he had seen.

From that moment my grand-uncle never raised his head. He was a scared, silent, broken-spirited man. It was early summer then, and at the fall of the leaf in the same year he died.

Of course there was a wake, such as beseemed a strong farmer so rich as he. For some reason the arrangements of this ceremonial were a little different from the usual routine.

The usual practice is to place the body in the great room, or kitchen, as it is called, of the house. In this particular case there was, as I told you, for some reason, an unusual arrangement. The body was placed in a small room that opened upon the greater one. The door of this, during the wake, stood open. There were candles about the bed, and pipes and tobacco on the

table, and stools for such guests as chose to enter, the door
standing open for their reception.

The body, having been laid out, was left alone, in this smaller
room, during the preparation for the wake. After nightfall one of
the women, approaching the bed to get a chair which she had left
near it, rushed from the room with a scream, and, having
recovered her speech at the further end of the 'kitchen,' and
surrounded by a gaping audience, she said, at last:

'May I never sin, if his face bain't riz up again the back o' the
bed, and he starin' down to the doore, wid eyes as big as pewter
plates, that id be shinin' in the moon!'

'Arra, woman! Is it cracked you are?' said one of the farm boys
as they are termed, being men of any age you please.

'Agh, Molly, don't be talkin', woman! 'Tis what ye consayted
it, goin' into the dark room, out o' the light. Why didn't ye take a
candle in your fingers, ye aumadhaun?' said one of her female
companions.

'Candle, or no candle, I seen it.' insisted Molly. 'An' what's
more, I could a'most tak' my oath I seen his arum, too, stretchin'
out o' the bed along the flure, three times as long as it should be,
to take hould o' me by the fut.'

'Nansinse, ye fool, what id he want o' yer fut?' exclaimed one
scornfully.

'Gi' me the candle, some o' yez – in the name o' God,' said old
Sal Doolan, that was straight and lean, and a woman that could
pray like a priest almost.

'Give her a candle,' agreed all.

But whatever they might say, there wasn't one among them
that did not look pale and stern enough as they followed Mrs
Doolan, who was praying as fast as her lips could patter, and
leading the van with a tallow candle, held like a taper, in her
fingers.

The door was half open, as the panic-stricken girl had left it;
and holding the candle on high the better to examine the room,
she made a step or so into it.

If my grand-uncle's hand had been stretched along the floor, in the unnatural way described, he had drawn it back again under the sheet that covered him. And tall Mrs Doolan was in no danger of tripping over his arm as she entered. But she had not gone more than a step or two with her candle aloft, when, with a drowning face, she suddenly stopped short, staring at the bed which was now fully in view.

'Lord, bless us, Mrs Doolan, ma'am, come back,' said the woman next to her, who had fast hold of her dress, or her 'coat' as they call it, and drawing her backwards with a frightened pluck, while a general recoil among her followers betokened the alarm which her hesitation had inspired.

'Whist, will yez?' said the leader, peremptorily, 'I can't hear my own ears wid the noise ye're making, an' which iv yez let the cat in here, an' whose cat is it?' she asked peering suspiciously at a white cat that was sitting on the breast of the corpse.

'Put it away, will yez?' she resumed, with horror at the profanation. 'Many a corpse as I sthretched and crossed in the bed the likes o' that I never seen yet. The man o' the house, wid a brute baste like that mounted on him, like a phooka, Lord forgi' me for namin' the like in this room. Dhrive it away, some o' yez! Out o' that, this minute, I tell ye.'

Each repeated the order, but no one seemed inclined to execute it. They were crossing themselves, and whispering their conjectures and misgivings as to the nature of the beast, which was no cat of that house, nor one that they had ever seen before. On a sudden, the white cat placed itself on the pillow over the head of the body, and having from that place glared for a time at them over the features of the corpse, it crept softly along the body towards them, growling low and fiercely as it drew near.

Out of the room they bounced, in dreadful confusion, shutting the door fast after them, and not for a good while did the hardiest venture to peep in again.

The white cat was sitting in its old place, on the dead man's breast, but this time it crept quietly down the side of the bed, and disappeared under it, the sheet which was spread like a coverlet, and hung down nearly to the floor, concealing it from view.

Praying, crossing themselves, and not forgetting a sprinkling of holy water, they peeped, and finally searched, poking spades, 'wattles,' pitchforks and such implements under the bed. But the cat was not to be found, and they concluded that it had made its escape among their feet as they stood near the threshold. So they secured the door carefully, with hasp and padlock.

But when the door was opened next morning they found the white cat sitting, as if it had never been disturbed, upon the breast of the dead man.

Again occurred very nearly the same scene with a like result, only that some said they saw the cat afterwards lurking under a big box in the corner of the outer-room, where my grand-uncle kept his leases and papers, and his prayer-book and beads.

Mrs Doolan heard it growling at her heels wherever she went; and although she could not see it, she could hear it spring on the back of her chair when she sat down, and growl in her ear, so that she would bounce up with a scream and a prayer, fancying that it was on the point of taking her by the throat.

And the priest's boy, looking round the corner, under the branches of the old orchard, saw a white cat sitting under the little window of the room where my grand-uncle was laid out and looking up at the four small panes of glass as a cat will watch a bird.

The end of it was that the cat was found on the corpse again, when the room was visited, and do what they might, whenever the body was left alone, the cat was found again in the same ill-omened contiguity with the dead man. And this continued, to the scandal and fear of the neighbourhood, until the door was opened finally for the wake.

My grand-uncle being dead, and, with all due solemnities, buried, I have done with him. But not quite yet with the white cat. No banshee every yet was more inalienably attached to a family than this ominous apparition is to mine. But there is this difference. The banshee seems to be animated with an affectionate sympathy with the bereaved family to whom it is hereditarily attached, whereas this thing has about it a suspicion of malice. It is the messenger simply of death. And its taking the shape of a cat – the coldest, and they say, the most vindictive of brutes – is indicative of the spirit of its visit.

When my grandfather's death was near, although he seemed quite well at the time, it appeared not exactly, but very nearly in the same way in which I told you it showed itself to my father.

The day before my Uncle Teigue was killed by the bursting of his gun, it appeared to him in the evening, at twilight, by the lough, in the field where I saw the woman who walked across the water, as I told you. My uncle was washing the barrel of his gun in the lough. The grass is short there, and there is no cover near it. He did not know how it approached but the first he saw of it, the white cat was walking close round his feet, in the twilight, with an angry twist of its tail, and a green glare in its eyes, and do what he would, it continued walking round and round him, in larger or smaller cirlces, till he reached the orchard, and there he lost it.

My poor Aunt Peg – she married one of the O'Brians, near Oolah – came to Drumgunniol to go to the funeral of a cousin who died about a mile away. She died herself, poor woman, only a month after.

Coming from the wake, at two or three o'clock in the morning, as she got over the stile into the farm of Drumgunniol, she saw the white cat at her side, and it kept close beside her, she ready to faint all the time, till she reached the door of the house, where it made a spring up into the whitethorn tree that grows close by, and so it parted from her. And my little brother Jim saw it also, just three weeks before he died. Every member of our family who dies, or takes his death-sickness at Drumgunniol, is sure to see the white cat, and no one of us who sees it need hope for long life after.

The Three Sisters

W. W. JACOBS

Thirty years ago on a wet autumn evening the household of Mallett's Lodge was gathered round the death-bed of Ursula Mallow, the eldest of the three sisters who inhabited it. The dingy moth-eaten curtains of the old wooden bedstead were drawn apart, the light of a smoking oil-lamp falling upon the hopeless countenance of the dying woman as she turned her dull eyes upon her sisters. The room was in silence except for an occasional sob from the youngest sister, Eunice. Outside the rain fell steadily over the streaming marshes.

'Nothing is to be changed, Tabitha,' gasped Ursula to the other sister, who bore a striking likeness to her, although her expression was harder and colder; 'this room is to be locked up and never opened.'

'Very well,' said Tabitha brusquely; 'though I don't see how it can matter to you then.'

'It does matter,' said her sister with startling energy. 'How do you know, how do I know that I may not sometimes visit it? I have lived in this house so long I ,am certain that I shall see it again. I *will* come back. Come back to watch over you both and see that no harm befalls you.'

'You are talking wildly,' said Tabitha, by no means moved at her sister's solicitude for her welfare. 'Your mind is wandering; you know that I have no faith in such things.'

Ursula sighed, and beckoning to Eunice, who was weeping silently at the bedside, placed her feeble arms around her neck and kissed her.

'Do not weep, dear,' she said feebly. 'Perhaps it is best so. A lonely woman's life is scarce worth living. We have no hopes, no aspirations; other women have had happy husbands and children, but we in this forgotten place have grown old together. I go first, but you must soon follow.'

Tabitha, comfortably conscious of only forty years and an iron frame, shrugged her shoulders and smiled grimly.

'I go first,' repeated Ursula in a new and strange voice as her heavy eyes slowly closed, 'but I will come for each of you in turn, when your lease of life runs out. At that moment I will be with you to lead your steps whither I now go.'

As she spoke the flickering lamp went out suddenly as though extinguished by a rapid hand, and the room was left in utter darkness. A strange suffocating noise issued from the bed, and when the trembling women had relighted the lamp, all that was left of Ursula Mallow was ready for the grave.

That night the survivors passed together. The dead woman had been a firm believer in the existence of that shadowy borderland which is said to form an unhallowed link between the living and the dead, and even stolid Tabitha, slightly unnerved by the events of the night, was not free from certain apprehensions that she might have been right.

With the bright morning their fears disappeared. The sun stole in at the window, and seeing the poor earthworn face on the pillow so touched it and glorified it that only its goodness and weakness were seen, and the beholders came to wonder how they could ever have felt any dread of aught so calm and peaceful. A day or two passed, and the body was transferred to a massive coffin long regarded as the finest piece of work of its kind ever turned out of the village carpenter's workshop. Then a slow and melancholy cortège headed by four bearers wound its solemn way across the marshes to the family vault in the grey old church, and all that was left of Ursula was placed by the father and mother who had taken that self-same journey some thirty years before.

To Eunice as they toiled slowly home the day seemed strange and Sabbath-like, the flat prospect of marsh wilder and more forlorn than usual, the roar of the sea more depressing. Tabitha had no such fancies. The bulk of the dead woman's property had been left to Eunice, and her avaricious soul was sorely troubled and her proper sisterly feelings of regret for the deceased sadly interfered with in consequence.

'What are you going to do with all that money, Eunice?'' she asked as they sat at their quiet tea.

'I shall leave it as it stands,' said Eunice slowly. 'We have both got sufficient to live upon, and I shall devote the income from it to supporting some beds in the children's hospital.'

'If Ursula had wished it to go to a hospital,' said Tabitha in her deep tones, 'she would have left the money to it herself. I wonder you do not respect her wishes more.'

'What else can I do with it then?' inquired Eunice.

'Save it,' said the other with gleaming eyes, 'save it.'

Eunice shook her head.

'No,' said she, 'it shall go to the sick children, but the principal I will not touch, and if I die before you it shall become yours and you can do what you like with it.'

'Very well,' said Tabitha, smothering her anger by a strong effort; 'I don't believe that was what Ursula meant you to do with it, and I don't believe she will rest quietly in the grave while you squander the money she stored so carefully.'

'What do you mean?' asked Eunice with pale lips. 'You are trying to frighten me; I thought that you did not believe in such things.'

Tabitha made no answer, and to avoid the anxious inquiring gaze of her sister, drew her chair to the fire, and folding her gaunt arms, composed herself for a nap.

For some time life went on quietly in the old house. The room of the dead woman, in accordance with her last desire, was kept firmly locked, its dirty windows forming a strange contrast to the prim cleanliness of the others. Tabitha, never very talkative, became more taciturn than ever, and stalked about the house and the neglected garden like an unquiet spirit, her brow roughened into the deep wrinkles suggestive of much thought. As the winter came on, bringing with it the long dark evenings, the old house became more lonely than ever, and an air of mystery and dread seemed to hang over it and brood in its empty rooms and dark corridors. The deep silence of night was broken by strange noises for which neither the wind nor the rats could be held accountable. Old Martha, seated in her distant kitchen, heard strange sounds upon the stairs, and once, upon hurrying to them, fancied that she saw a dark figure squatting upon the landing, though a subsequent search with candle and spectacles failed to discover anything. Eunice was disturbed by several vague incidents, and, as she suffered from a complaint of the heart, rendered very ill by them. Even Tabitha admitted a strangeness about the house, but, confident in her piety and virtue, took no heed of it, her mind being fully employed in another direction.

Since the death of her sister all restraint upon her was removed, and she yielded herself up entirely to the stern and hard rules enforced by avarice upon its devotees. Her housekeeping expenses were kept rigidly separate from those of Eunice and her food limited to the coarsest dishes, while in the matter of clothes the old servant was by far the better dressed. Seated alone in her bedroom this uncouth, hard-featured creature revelled in her possessions, grudging even the expense of the candle-end which enabled her to behold them. So completely did this passion change her that both Eunice and Martha became afraid of her, and lay awake in their beds night after night trembling at the chinking of the coins at her unholy vigils.

One day Eunice ventured to remonstrate. 'Why don't you bank your money, Tabitha?' she said; 'it is surely not safe to keep such large sums in such a lonely house.'

'Large sums!' repeated the exasperated Tabitha, 'large sums; what nonsense is this? You know well that I have barely sufficient to keep me.'

'It's a great temptation to housebreakers,' said her sister, not pressing the point. 'I made sure last night that I heard somebody in the house.'

'Did you?' said Tabitha, grasping her arm, a horrible look on her face. 'So did I. I thought they went to Ursula's room, and I got out of bed and went on the stairs to listen.'

'Well?' said Eunice faintly, fascinated by the look on her sister's face.

'There was *something* there,' said Tabitha slowly. 'I'll swear it, for I stood on the landing by her door and listened; something scuffling on the floor round and round the room. At first I thought it was the cat, but when I went up there this morning the door was still locked, and the cat was in the kitchen.'

'Oh, let us leave this dreadful house,' moaned Eunice.

'What!' said her sister grimly; 'afraid of poor Ursula? Why should you be? Your own sister who nursed you when you were a babe, and who perhaps even now comes and watches over your slumbers.'

'Oh!' said Eunice, pressing her hand to her side, 'if I saw her I should die. I should think that she had come for me as she said she would. O God! have mercy on me, I am dying.'

She reeled as she spoke, and before Tabitha could save her, sank senseless to the floor.

'Get some water,' cried Tabitha, as old Martha came hurrying up the stairs, 'Eunice has fainted.'

The old woman, with a timid glance at her, retired, reappearing shortly afterwards with the water, with which she proceeded to restore her much-loved mistress to her senses. Tabitha, as soon as this was accomplished, stalked off to her room, leaving her sister and Martha sitting drearily enough in the small parlour, watching the fire and conversing in whispers.

It was clear to the old servant that this state of things could not last much longer, and she repeatedly urged her mistress to leave a house so lonely and so mysterious. To her great delight Eunice

283

at length consented, despite the fierce opposition of her sister, and at the mere idea of leaving gained greatly in health and spirits. A small but comfortable house was hired in Morville, and arrangements made for a speedy change.

It was the last night in the old house, and all the wild spirits of the marshes, the wind and the sea seemed to have joined forces for one supreme effort. When the wind dropped, as it did at brief intervals, the sea was heard moaning on the distant beach, strangely mingled with the desolate warning of the bell-buoy as it rocked to the waves. Then the wind rose again, and the noise of the sea was lost in the fierce gusts which, finding no obstacle on the open marshes, swept with their full fury upon the house by the creek. The strange voices of the air shrieked in its chimneys, windows rattled, doors slammed, and even the very curtains seemed to live and move.

Eunice was in bed, awake. A small night-light in a saucer of oil shed a sickly glare upon the worm-eaten old furniture, distorting the most innocent articles into ghastly shapes. A wilder gust than usual almost deprived her of the protection afforded by that poor light, and she lay listening fearfully to the creakings and other noises on the stairs, bitterly regretting that she had not asked Martha to sleep with her. But it was not too late even now. She slipped hastily to the floor, crossed to the huge wardrobe, and was in the very act of taking her dressing-gown from its peg when an unmistakable footfall was heard on the stairs. The robe dropped from her shaking fingers, and with a quickly beating heart she regained her bed.

The sounds ceased and a deep silence followed, which she herself was unable to break although she strove hard to do so. A wild gust of wind shook the windows and nearly extinguished the light, and when its flame had regained its accustomed steadiness she saw that the door was slowly opening, while the huge shadow of a hand blotted the papered wall. Still her tongue refused its office. The door flew open with a crash, a cloaked figure entered and, throwing aside its coverings she saw with a horror past all expressing the napkin-bound face of the dead

Ursula smiling terribly at her. In her last extremity she raised her faded eyes above for succour, and then as the figure noiselessly advanced and laid its cold hand upon her brow, the soul of Eunice Mallow left its body with a wild shriek and made its way to the Eternal.

Martha, roused by the cry, and shivering with dread, rushed to the door and gazed in terror at the figure which stood leaning over the bedside. As she watched, it slowly removed the cowl and the napkin and exposed the fell face of Tabitha, so strangely contorted between fear and triumph that she hardly recognised it.

'Who's there?' cried Tabitha in a terrible voice as she saw the old woman's shadow on the wall.

'I thought I heard a cry,' said Martha, entering. 'Did anybody call?'

'Yes, Eunice,' said the other, regarding her closely. 'I, too, heard the cry, and hurried to her. What makes her so strange? Is she in a trance?'

'Aye,' said the old woman, falling on her knes by the bed and sobbing bitterly, 'the trance of death. Ah, my dear, my poor lonely girl, that this should be the end of it! She has died of fright,' said the old woman, pointing to the eyes, which even yet retained their horror. 'She has seen something *devilish*.'

Tabitha's gaze fell. 'She has always suffered with her heart,' she muttered; 'the night has frightened her; it frightened me.'

She stood upright by the foot of the bed as Martha drew the sheet over the face of the dead woman.

'First Ursula, then Eunice,' said Tabitha, drawing a deep breath. 'I can't stay here. I'll dress and wait for the morning.'

She left the room as she spoke, and with bent head proceeded to her own. Martha remained by the bedside, and gently closing the staring eyes, fell on her knees and prayed long and earnestly for the departed soul. Overcome with grief and fear, she remained with bowed head until a sudden sharp cry from Tabitha brought her to her feet.

'Well,' said the old woman, going to the door.

'Where are you?' cried Tabitha, somewhat reassured by her voice.

'In Miss Eunice's bedroom. Do you want anything?'

Her voice rose suddenly to a scream 'Quick! For God's sake! Quick, or I shall go mad. *There is some strange woman in the house.*'

The old woman stumbled hastily down the dark stairs. 'What is the matter?' she cried, entering the room. 'Who is it? What do you mean?'

'I saw it,' said Tabitha, grasping her convulsively by the shoulder. 'I was coming to you when I saw the figure of a woman in front of me going up the stairs. It is – can it be Ursula come for the soul of Eunice, as she said she would?'

'Or for yours? said Martha, the words coming from her in some odd fashion, despite herself.

Tabitha, with a ghastly look, fell cowering by her side, clutching tremulously at her clothes. 'Light the lamps,' she cried hysterically. 'Light a fire, make a noise; oh, this dreadful darkness! Will it never be day!'

'Soon, soon,' said Martha, overcoming her repugnance and trying to pacify her. 'When the day comes you will laugh at these fears.'

'I murdered her,' screamed the miserable woman, 'I killed her with fright. Why did she not give me the money? 'Twas no use to her. Ah! *Look there!*'

Martha, with a horrible fear, followed her glance to the door, but saw nothing.

'It's Ursula,' said Tabitha, from between her teeth. 'Keep her off! Keep her off!'

The old woman, who by some unknown sense seemed to feel the presence of a third person in the room, moved a step forward and stood before her. As she did so Tabitha waved her arms as though to free herself from the touch of a detaining hand, half-rose to her feet, and without a word fell dead before her.

At this the old woman's courage forsook her, and with a great cry she rushed from the room, eager to escape from this house of death and mystery. The bolts of the great door were stiff with age, and strange voices seemed to ring in her ears as she strove wildly to unfasten them. Her brain whirled. She thought that the dead in their distant rooms called to her, and that a devil stood on the step outside laughing and holding the door against her. Then with a supreme effort she flung it open, and heedless of her night-clothes passed into the bitter night. The path across the marshes was lost in the darkness, but she found it; the planks over the ditches slippery and narrow, but she crossed them in safety, until at last, her feet bleeding and her breath coming in great gasps, she entered the village and sank down more dead than alive on a cottage doorstep.

Sonata For Harp and Bicycle

JOAN AIKEN

'No one is allowed to remain in the building after five p.m.,' Mr Manaby told his new assistant, showing him into the little room that was like the inside of an egg carton.

'Why not?'

'Directorial policy,' said Mr Manaby. But that was not the real reason.

Gaunt and sooty, Grimes Buildings lurched up the side of a hill towards Clerkenwell. Every little office within its dim and crumbling exterior owned one tiny crumb of light – such was the proud boast of the architect – but towards evening the crumbs were collected, absorbed and demolished as by an immense vacuum cleaner, and yielded to an uncontrollable mass of dark that came tumbling in through windows and doors to take their place. Darkness infested the building like a flight of bats returning willingly to roost.

'Wash hands, please. Wash hands, please,' the intercom began to bawl in the passage at four-forty-five. Without much need of prompting the staff hustled like lemmings along the corridors to the green and blue-tiled washrooms that mocked the encroaching dusk with an illusion of cheerfulness.

'All papers into cases, please,' the Tannoy warned, five

minutes later. 'Look at your desks, ladies and gentlemen. Any documents left lying about? Kindly put them away. Desks must be left clear and tidy. Drawers must be shut.'

A multitudinous shuffling, a rustling as of innumerable bluebottles might have been heard by the attentive ear after this injunction, as the employees of Moreton Wold and Company thrust their papers into briefcases, clipped statistical abstracts together and slammed them into filing cabinets; dropped discarded copy into wastepaper baskets. Two minutes later, and not a desk throughout Grimes Buildings bore more than its customary coating of dust.

'Hats and coats on, please. Hats and coats on, please. Did you bring an umbrella? Have you left any shopping on the floor?'

At three minutes to five the home-going throng was in the lifts and on the stairs; a clattering staccato-voiced flood momentarily darkened the great double doors of the building, and then as the first faint notes of St Paul's came echoing faintly on the frosty air, to be picked up near at hand by the louder chime of St Biddulph's on the Wall, the entire premises of Moreton Wold stood empty.

'But why is it?' Jason Ashgrove, the new copywriter, asked his secretary. 'Why are the staff herded out so fast in the evenings? Not that I'm against it, mind you, I think it's an admirable idea in many ways, but there is the liberty of the individual to be considered, don't you think?'

'Hush!' Miss Golden, casting a glance towards the door, held up her felt-tip in warning or reproof. 'You mustn't ask that sort of question. When you are taken on to the Established Staff you'll be told. Not before.'

'But I want to know now,' said Jason in discontent. 'Do you know?'

'Yes I do,' Miss Golden answered tantalisingly. 'Come on, or we shan't have done the Oat Crisp layout by a quarter to.' And she stared firmly down at the copy in front of her, lips folded, candyfloss hair falling over her face, lashes hiding eyes like peridots, a girl with a secret.

Jason was annoyed. He rapped out a couple of rude and witty

rhymes which Miss Golden let pass in a withering silence.

'What do you want for Christmas, Miss Golden? Sherry? Fudge? Bath cubes?'

'I want to go away with a clear conscience about Oat Crisps,' Miss Golden retorted. It was not true; what she chiefly wanted was Mr Jason Ashgrove, but he had not realised this yet.

'Come on, don't be a tease! I'm sure you haven't been on the Established Staff all that long,' he coaxed her. 'What happens when one is taken on, anyway? Does the Managing Director have us up for a confidential chat? Or are we given a little book called The Awful Secret of Grimes Buildings?'

Miss Golden wasn't telling. She opened her desk drawer and took out a white towel and a cake of rosy soap.

'Wash hands, please! Wash hands, please!'

Jason was frustrated. 'You'll be sorry,' he said. 'I shall do something desperate.'

'Oh no, you mustn't!' Her eyes were large with fright. She ran from the room and was back within a couple of minutes, still drying her hands.

'If I took you out to dinner, wouldn't you give me just a tiny hint?'

Side by side Miss Golden and Mr Ashgrove ran along the green-floored corridors, battled down the white marble stairs, among the hundred other employees from the tenth floor, and the nine hundred from the floors below.

He saw her lips move as she said something, but in the clatter of two thousand feet the words were lost.

'. . . f-f-fire-escape,' he heard, as they came into the momentary hush of the coir-carpeted entrance hall. And '. . . it's to do with a bicycle. A bicycle and a harp.'

'I don't understand.'

Now they were in the street, chilly with the winter-dusk smells of celery on barrows, of swept-up leaves heaped in faraway parks, and cold layers of dew sinking among the withered evening primroses in the building sites. London lay about them wreathed in twilit mystery and fading against the barred and smoky sky. Like a ninth wave the sound of traffic overtook and swallowed them.

'Please tell me!'

But, shaking her head, she stepped on to a scarlet home-bound bus and was borne away from him.

Jason stood undecided on the pavement, with the crowds dividing round him as round the pier of a bridge. He scratched his head and looked about him for guidance.

An ambulance clanged, a taxi screeched, a drill stuttered, a siren wailed on the river, a door slammed, a van hooted, and close beside his ear a bicycle bell tinkled its tiny warning.

A bicycle, she had said. A bicycle and a harp.

Jason turned and stared at Grimes Buildings.

Somewhere, he knew, there was a back way in, a service entrance. He walked slowly past the main doors, with their tubs of snowy chrysanthemums, and on up Glass Street. A tiny furtive wedge of darkness beckoned him, a snicket, a hacket, an alley carved into the thickness of the building. It was so narrow that at any moment, it seemed, the over-topping walls would come together and squeeze it out of existence.

Walking as softly as an Indian, Jason passed through it, slid by a file of dustbins, and found the foot of the fire-escape. Iron treads rose into the mist, like an illustration to a Gothic fairytale.

He began to climb.

When he had mounted to the ninth storey he paused for breath. It was a lonely place. The lighting consisted of a dim bulb at the foot of every flight. A well of gloom sank beneath him. The cold fingers of the wind nagged and fluttered at the edges of his jacket, and he pulled the string of the fire-door and edged inside.

Grimes Buildings were triangular, with the street forming the base of the triangle, and the fire-escape the point. Jason could see two long passages coming towards him, meeting at an acute angle where he stood. He started down the left-hand one, tiptoeing in the cave-like silence. Nowhere was there any sound, except for the faraway drip of a tap. No nightwatchman would stay in the building; none was needed. No precautions were taken. Burglars gave the place a wide berth.

Jason opened a door at random; then another. Offices lay everywhere about him, empty and forbidding. Some held lipstick-stained tissues, spilt powder, and orange-peel; others were still foggy with cigarette smoke. Here was a director's suite of rooms – a desk like half an acre of frozen lake, inch-thick carpet, roses, and the smell of cigars. Here was a conference room with scattered squares of doodled blotting-paper. All equally empty.

He was not sure when he first began to notice the bell. Telephone, he thought at first, and then he remembered that all the outside lines were disconnected at five. And this bell, anyway, had not the regularity of a telephone's double ring: there was a tinkle, and then silence: a long ring, and then silence: a whole volley of rings together, and the silence.

Jason stood listening, and fear knocked against his ribs and shortened his breath. He knew that he must move or be paralysed by it. He ran up a flight of stairs and found himself with two more endless green corridors beckoning him like a pair of dividers.

Another sound now: a waft of ice-thin notes, riffling up an arpeggio like a flurry of sleet. Far away down the passage it echoed. Jason ran in pursuit, but as he ran the music receded. He circled the building, but it always outdistanced him, and when he came back to the stairs he heard it fading away on to the storey below.

He hesitated, and as he did so, heard once more the bell: the bicycle bell. It was approaching him fast, bearing down on him, urgent, menacing. He could hear the pedals, almost see the shimmer of an invisible wheel. Absurdly, he was reminded of the insistent clamour of an ice-cream vendor, summoning children on a sultry Sunday afternoon.

There was a little fireman's alcove beside him, with buckets and pumps. He hurled himself into it. The bell stopped beside him, and then there was a moment while his heart tried to shake itself loose in his chest. He was looking into two eyes carved out of expressionless air; he was held by two hands knotted together out of the width of dark.

'Daisy? Daisy?' came the whisper. 'Is that you, Daisy? Have you come to give me your answer?'

Jason tried to speak, but no words came.

'It's *not* Daisy! Who are you?' The sibilants were full of threat. 'You can't stay here! This is private property.'

He was thrust along the corridor. It was like being pushed by a whirlwind – the fire door opened ahead of him without a touch, and he was on the openwork platform, clutching the slender rail. Still the hands would not let him go.

'How about it?' the whisper mocked him. 'How about jumping? It's an easy death compared with some.'

Jason looked down into the smoky void. The darkness nodded to him like a familiar.

'You wouldn't be much loss, would you? What have you got to live for?'

Miss Golden, Jason thought. She would miss me. And the syllables Berenice Golden lingered in the air like a chime. Drawing on some unknown deposit of courage he shook himself loose from the holding hands, and ran down the fire escape without looking back.

Next morning when Miss Golden, crisp, fragrant and punctual, shut the door of Room 92 behind her, she stopped short by the hat-pegs with a horrified gasp.

'Mr *Ashgrove*! Your *hair*!'

'It makes me look very distinguished, don't you think?' he said.

It did indeed have this effect, for his Byronic dark cut had changed to a stippled silver.

'How did it happen? You've not –' her voice sank to a whisper – '*You've not been in Grimes Buildings after dark?*'

'What if I have?'

'Have you?'

'Miss Golden – Berenice,' he said earnestly. 'Who was Daisy? I can see that you know. Tell me her story.'

'Did you see him?' she asked faintly.

'Him?'

'William Heron – the Wailing Watchman. Oh,' she exclaimed in terror. 'I can see that you must have. Then you are doomed – doomed!'

'If I'm doomed,' said Jason, 'let's have coffee and you tell me all about it.'

'It all happened over fifty years ago,' said Berenice, as she spooned out coffee powder with distracted extravagance. 'Heron was the night watchman in this building, patrolling the corridors from dusk to dawn every night on his bicycle. He fell in love with a Miss Bell who taught the harp. She rented a room – this room – and gave lessons in it. She began to reciprocate his love, and they used to share a picnic supper every night at eleven, and she'd stay on a while to keep him company. It was an idyll, among the fire-buckets and the furnace-pipes.

'On Christmas Eve he had summoned up the courage to propose to her. The day before he had told her that he was going to ask her a very important question. Next night he came to the Buildings with a huge bunch of roses and a bottle of wine. But Miss Bell never turned up.

'The explanation was simple. Miss Bell, of course, had been losing a lot of sleep through her nocturnal romance, as she gave lessons all day, and so she used to take a nap in her music-room between seven and ten every evening, to save going home. In order to make sure that she would wake up, she persuaded her father, a distant relation of Graham Bell who shared some of the more famous Bell's mechanical ingenuity, to install an alarm device, a kind of telephone, in her room, which called her every evening at ten. She was far too modest and shy to let Heron know that she spent those hours actually in the building, and to give him the chance of waking her himself.

'Alas! On this important evening the gadget failed and she never woke up. Telephones were in their infancy at that time, you must remember.

'Heron waited and waited. At last, mad with grief and jealousy, having rung up her home and discovered that she was not there, he concluded that she had rejected him, ran to the fire-escape, and cast himself off it, holding the roses and the bottle of wine. He jumped from the tenth floor.

'Daisy did not long survive him, but pined away soon after; since that day their ghosts have haunted Grimes Buildings, he vainly patrolling the corridors on his bicycle in search of her, she playing her harp in the small room she rented. *But they never meet.* And anyone who meets the ghost of William Heron will himself within five days leap down from the same fatal fire-escape.'

She gazed at him with tragic eyes.

'In that case we mustn't lose a minute,' said Jason and he enveloped her in an embrace as prolonged as it was ardent. Looking down at the gossamer hair sprayed across his shoulder, he added, 'Just the same, it is a preposterous situation. Firstly, I have no intention of jumping off the fire-escape—' here, however, he repressed a shudder as he remembered the cold, clutching hands of the evening before – 'And secondly, I find it quite nonsensical that those two inefficient ghosts have spent fifty years in this building without coming across each other. We must remedy the matter, Berenice. We must not begrudge our new-found happiness to others.'

He gave her another kiss so impassioned that the electric typewriter against which they were leaning began chattering to itself in a frenzy of enthusiasm.

'This very evening,' he went on, looking at his watch, 'we will put matters right for that unhappy couple, and then, if I really have only five more days to live, which I don't for one moment believe, we will proceed to spend them together, my bewitching Berenice, in the most advantageous manner possible.'

She nodded, spellbound.

'Can you work a switchboard?' She nodded again. 'My love, you are perfection itself. Meet me in the switchboard room, then, at ten this evening. I would say, have dinner with me, but I shall need to make one or two purchases and see an old R.A.F.

Suddenly the door flew open again

friend. You will be safe from Heron's curse in the switchboard room if he always keeps to the corridors.'

'I would rather meet him and die with you,' she murmured.

'My angel, I hope that won't be necessary. Now,' he said sighing, 'I suppose we should get down to our day's work.' Strangely enough, the copy they wrote that day, although engendered from such agitated minds, sold more packets of Oat Crisps than any other advertising matter before or since.

That evening when Jason entered Grimes Buildings he was carrying two bottles of wine, two bunches of red roses, and a large canvas-covered bundle. Miss Golden, who had concealed herself in the telephone exchange before the offices closed for the night, gazed at these things with interest.

'Now,' said Jason after he had greeted her, 'I want you first of all to ring our own extension.'

'No one will reply, surely?'

'I think *she* will reply.'

Sure enough, when Berenice rang extension 170 a faint, sleepy voice, distant and yet clear, whispered, 'Hullo?'

'Is that Miss Bell?'

'. . . Yes.'

Berenice went a little pale. Her eyes sought Jason's and, prompted by him, she said formally, 'Switchboard here, Miss Bell, your ten o'clock call.'

'Thank you,' whispered the telephone.

'Excellent,' Jason remarked, as Miss Golden replaced the receiver with a trembling hand. He unfastened his package and slipped its straps over his shoulders. 'Now, plug in the intercom.'

Berenice did so, and then announced, loudly and clearly, 'Attention. Night watchman on duty, please. Night watchman on duty. You have an urgent summons to Room 92. You have an urgent summons to Room 92.'

Her voice echoed and reverberated through the empty corridors, then the Tannoy coughed itself to silence.

'Now we must run. You take the roses, sweetheart, and I'll carry the bottles.'

Together they raced up eight flights of stairs and along the green corridor to Room 92. As they neared the door a burst of music met them – harp music swelling out, sweet and triumphant. Jason took one of the bunches of roses from Berenice, opened the door a little way, and gently deposited the flowers, with the bottle, inside the door. As he closed it again Berenice said breathlessly, 'Did you see anything?'

'No,' he said. 'The room was too full of music.'

His eyes were shining.

They stood hand in hand, reluctant to move away, waiting for they hardly knew what. Suddenly the door flew open again. Neither Berenice nor Jason, afterwards, cared to speak of what they saw then, but each was left with a memory, bright as the picture on a Salvador Dali calendar, of a bicycle bearing on its saddle a harp, a bottle of wine, and a bouquet of red roses, sweeping improbably down the corridor and far, far away.

'We can go now,' said Jason. He led Berenice to the fire door, tucking the other bottle of Mâcon into his jacket pocket. A black wind from the north whistled beneath, as they stood on the openwork iron platform, looking down.

'We don't want our evening to be spoilt by the thought of that curse hanging over us,' he said, 'so this is the practical thing to do. Hang on to the roses. And holding his love firmly, Jason pulled the ripcord of his R.A.F. friend's parachute and leapt off the fire-escape.

A bridal shower of rose petals adorned the descent of Miss Golden, who was possibly the only girl to be kissed in mid-air in the district of Clerkenwell at ten minutes to midnight on Christmas Eve.

Acknowledgements

The publishers would like to extend their grateful thanks to the following authors, publishers and others for kindly granting permission to reproduce the extracts and stories included in this anthology.

THE MUSIC OF ERICH ZANN by H. P. Lovecraft. Reprinted by permission of the author and the author's agents, Scott Meredith Literary Agency, Inc., 845 Third Avenue, New York, New York 10022.

A SCHOOL STORY by M. R. James from *The Ghost Stories of M. R. James.* Reprinted by permission of Edward Arnold (Publishers) Ltd.

THE CAT ROOM by R. Chetwynd-Hayes. Reprinted by permission of the author.

LAURA by Saki from *The Complete Short Stories of Saki (H. H. Munro)*, copyright 1930 by the Viking Press Inc.; copyright renewed 1958 by the Viking Press, Inc. Used by permission.

SMOKE GHOST by Fritz Leiber. © 1941 by Street & Smith Publishing Company and © 1947 by Fritz Leiber Jr. and reprinted by permission of the author and E. J. Carnell Literary Agency.

AN ADELAIDE GHOST by Leon Garfield from *A Swag of Stories* edited by Leon Garfield and published by Ward Lock Ltd. Reprinted by permission of the author.

A LITTLE GHOST by Hugh Walpole. Reprinted by permission of Sir Rupert Hart-Davis.

THE MISTRESS IN BLACK by Rosemary Timperley from *The Fifth Ghost Book* edited by Rosemary Timperley. Reprinted by permission of the author and Hutchinson Books Ltd.

THE GHOST OF THOMAS KEMPE from the book of the same name by Penelope Lively. Reprinted by permission of the author, William Heinemann Ltd. and E. P. Dutton Inc. Copyright © 1973 by Penelope Lively.

THE OCCUPANT OF THE ROOM by Algernon Blackwood. Reprinted by permission of the Estate of Algernon Blackwood.

THE HARPSICHORD by Elizabeth Le Fanu from *The Times Anthology of Ghost Stories*. Reprinted by permission of the publishers, Jonathan Cape Ltd.